# THE DEMON UPRISING

## DEMON HUNTER BOOK ONE

### KERRY ADCOCK

**The Demon Uprising**
Paperback Edition
Copyright © 2022 (as revised) Kerry Adcock

Published in the United States by Wolfpack Publishing, Las Vegas

CKN Christian Publishing
An Imprint of Wolfpack Publishing
5130 S. Fort Apache Road 215-380
Las Vegas, NV 89148

cknchristianpublishing.com

Paperback ISBN - 978-1-63977-939-0

# THE DEMON UPRISING

# CHAPTER ONE

**Solomon's Temple**
**City of Jerusalem**
**Judah**
**609 BC**

IN THE EARLY MORNING HOURS, the night seemed to shroud the city in an uncommon darkness. The high priest, Hilkiah, stood in the Holy of Holies in the temple in Jerusalem. His aged and wrinkled face showed the worry on his mind. Torches lit the carved gold covered interior of the most sacred location in Judah.

"Are you sure we must do this?" asked one Levite named Aviram.

The elderly man felt like the weight of his world rested on his shoulders. He nodded sadly, "Yes, I feel it must be done."

"But you found the books of the law and the other writings in the scrolls that you brought to King Josiah," replied Aviram. "He's done so much. He removed the prostitutes of Baal from the temple and began celebrating the Passover again. He removed all the idols and put the sacred ark back in its place. Surely it can't be moved again?"

Hilkiah looked up at the two giant golden cherubim that stood guard on both sides of the sarcophagus that held the Ark of the

Covenant. Tears began to flow. "I know, but the king lies on his death bed, wounded by Egyptian arrows. I fear the king's

enemies will use it as an excuse to destroy the ark once and for all, then bring back the pagan rituals. We must preserve it at all costs."

"But what about the prophesy?" asked another priest. "It said a seer of spirits and slayer of evil will defeat a horrible demon in battle and save the sacred ark?"

"Yes, I believe it to be true and the prophecy will come true no matter where the ark is located. We must trust God."

He turned and walked to a side wall and slid a golden panel aside. Inside was a handle which he pulled and then walked back to the center of the room with the other priests. A moment later, they heard the sound of stone grinding on stone, and then the floor holding the men and the sarcophagus began to slowly descend. They were lowered down well below the floor and finally came to a stop. One of the priests stepped off the platform, lit a torch, and glanced down a tunnel that led off into the distance. Hilkiah was thankful that King Solomon had wisely constructed this secret escape route in the temple. The sarcophagus was moved carefully from the platform by the other priests. It was opened and they carefully removed the Ark of the Covenant using sturdy poles. The men lifted the golden chest and began a slow walk down the tunnel. Hilkiah pulled the lever again and the platform began to rise back to its original location in the Holy of Holies. With a heavy heart he followed the others down the tunnel but stopped suddenly. Did he hear something? Was it the sound of scratching on rock? Hilkiah shook his head and continued down the tunnel and out of sight. In the darkness a set yellow eyes blinked and watched the procession.

———

**Sutton County, Texas**
**Present Day**

THE SUN SHONE brightly over the vast west Texas landscape as a lone rider on horseback rode to the top of a small mesa. He tilted his black low crowned Stetson hat back on his head, sat tall in the saddle and he gazed out across the land. "Beautiful, isn't it, Buck?" asked Jake to his roan-colored horse. Buck, head down, nibbled at some grass while off in the distance as a small group of cattle grazed, ignoring the man on the hill.

After sitting for a while, the rider turned his horse and rode back toward a group of buildings in the distance when out of the corner of his eye he caught the sight of vultures circling off to the south. He spurred Buck down through a dry wash and up the other side to investigate and as he approached the clearing saw the carcass of what once was one of his cows. He thought it odd that the scavengers were lurking around, but none had approached the carcass. As he rode closer Buck abruptly shied away, spooked by something unseen so Jake dismounted. The horse had been around dead animals before and it never bothered him. If something scared Buck then Jake wanted to be prepared so he removed his Winchester model 94, 30-30 rifle from the scabbard attached to his saddle and approached the area carefully.

The small clearing had been the scene of a bloody massacre. The bovine's carcass had been ripped to shreds and strewn around. Scavengers can sometimes scatter bones and flesh, but this was different. This was violent and brutal. Either a pack of animals or something very large did this, thought Jake.

The smell of rotting flesh was overpowering so he removed a handkerchief from his pocket and covered his mouth as he approached a large piece of the dead animal. He shook his head in confusion. This just doesn't look right, he thought. Normally there'd be thousands of flies buzzing but even they stayed away from the carcass. He squatted down and carefully examined a section of exposed ribs. A large bite had been taken out of the side which had sliced easily through the ribs. He also noticed large claw marks too large for a wolf or cougar. Something else was out there and it was big.

Jake stood up slowly, looked around, but saw nothing unusual.

He scouted around and saw plenty of hoof prints mixed with large tracks that didn't look familiar. Upon closer observation he noticed they appeared reptilian but too large for anything from this area. The print in the dirt was deep meaning it was heavy and it had four clawed toes. Jake had the odd feeling that he'd seen these wounds and tracks before, and there was a particular smell in the air around the carcass he'd smelled before. It smelled like ashes and rotten eggs, or like sulfur. He walked slowly back to Buck who looked off to the north and pawed the ground with his hoof. Jake gazed in that direction but didn't see anything, and then he remembered.

It was years ago when Jake was in the military during a covert mission in Iraq. He'd found a carcass of a cow near a remote village with the same type of bite and claw marks. It also had that same stench. He knew back then it was strange, but the other members of his unit dismissed it as an animal attack. They teased the "West Texas Boy" about imagining monsters in the desert, but Jake felt it was different.

He stepped into the saddle and kept his rifle ready. They started towards the house and Buck picked up the pace, more than happy to head home.

Jake rode into the yard of his modest ranch house. A dog was asleep on the porch and raised his head at Jake's approach. Roscoe was part wolf-part dog. As a pup he'd wandered up to the ranch one morning and decided that he liked it, so he stayed. He turned out to be a good cow dog and could herd cattle as well as any rider and last longer. Roscoe was loyal and a great help when he wasn't asleep on the porch.

Jake led Buck into the barn where he stripped the saddle off, brushed him down, and fed him.

After a quick shower he climbed into his old red Ford pickup to drive into town. Roscoe jumped into the passenger seat where he usually rode as Jake headed in for some groceries, gasoline, and feed. He drove down the dirt road away from the house towards the highway that covered his truck with another coat of west Texas dust which turned it a shade of brown. Turning left onto the small highway, he drove the remaining ten miles into town while whistling to the latest country song on his truck radio. Roscoe hung his head out of the passenger window enjoying the wind in his face.

Driving into town, the first thing Jake saw was the old, rusted water tower with the faded words "Welcome to Shady Oak" painted on it. The town consisted of the usual small-town businesses -a grocery store, feed store, Dairy Queen fast food restaurant, a "home cooking" type restaurant, churches, elementary, junior and senior high school. Jake stopped at one of the two gas stations in town and filled up with gas. A thin, middle-aged attendant named Ed wearing jeans, a faded green shirt, and a worn-out John Deere Tractor baseball cap came out and leaned against the pump.

"Mornin', Jake. How's the ranch comin' along?"

"Good morning, Ed. It's slow going but I'm in no hurry."

"How about the stock pond? You gonna need some help cleaning it out before it gets too hot?"

"I'll be sure and get it cleaned out, but I'll give you a yell if I need anything."

Jake couldn't afford to hire full time help yet, but some of the hands from the Circle R ranch nearby would pitch in and help during round up. During the summer he'd hire one of the high school teen's part time to help him.

"Have you lost any stock lately? Several of the ranches have lost some cattle."

Jake raised an eyebrow in surprise. He thought about mentioning the mutilated cow then decided not to until he knew more about the missing stock. "Is something going on?"

Ed shuffled his feet and spat on the ground. "Ranches all over the area are losing stock. At first cows just up and vanished, but the other day someone found a carcass. It had been ripped to pieces. They found some strange animal tracks. Some folks say it's an alligator left in the wild, and others say its aliens."

Jake just shrugged. He hadn't noticed any major losses in his small herd of fifty or so cattle except for the occasional older cow or stray calf that had fallen victim to a pack of coyotes or a lone cougar looking for an easy meal. That was until he found the mutilated cow.

They continued the usual small talk while Jake paid for his gas and turned to leave.

"Hey Jake, you seen that pastor gal down at that new church?" asked Ed with a smirk.

"Nope," snapped Jake.

"She sure is purdy, even for a preacher woman."

"I haven't seen her, but thanks for the info on the missing stock. I'll keep an eye out for aliens or wild alligators." He climbed into the truck and drove over to the small grocery store up the street. Jake chuckled to himself. Alligators or aliens loose in west Texas.

He then thought about the woman Ed had mentioned. The woman had arrived six months ago. He'd heard that some of the town folks hadn't readily accepted her as many small towns still felt the pulpit was strictly for men.

At the store he loaded his cart with bread, coffee, sugar, flour, meat, and microwavable meals for those quick meals. Mrs. Creet, the owner's wife, and cashier was a kind, elderly woman who seemed to know everything about everyone. They chatted about the weather, grass conditions, and the strange missing cattle while she rang up his groceries. Jake thought he'd make it out without her sticking her nose into his business, but he was wrong. As he was gathering his bags of groceries Mrs. Creet smiled and asked, "Have you seen Miss Thompson today?"

Jake frowned. Here we go again. "No, Ma'am."

"I saw her just this morning. She is such a lovely woman, and bright too. I don't attend her services, but I hear tell that she has a voice of an angel. It's a shame that you don't come in and visit more often."

"Yes ma'am, I mean, no ma'am." He could feel himself blush. I'm too busy for this nonsense, he thought. "I have a lot of work to do out at the ranch that keeps me busy."

"No man should ever be too busy to visit a lovely woman, even if she is a preacher woman," said Mrs. Creet with a smile.

"No, ma'am...I mean...yes, ma'am." Jake was getting frustrated and started out the door. "I... I need to get back to the ranch. Nice seeing you, Mrs. Creet."

Little miss busybody!

Jake drove back home with a frown. "Can't a man simply do some shopping without being harassed about women?"

Roscoe barked.

"A lot you know."

He'd met the woman once, while in town. He remembered her dark hair and brown eyes, but a preacher? A small west Texas town was not the normal place for a woman to start a church. He drove back home in silence while Roscoe hung his head out of the truck window, tongue out, ears flapping in the wind, and barked at anything and everything.

———

**Jerusalem**
**Judah**
**587 BC**

THE BABYLONIAN KING Nebuchadnezzar stood outside his royal tent and watched Jerusalem burn. After a thirty-month siege of the city the walls were breached, and the killing had begun. Zedekiah, the king he had set up in Judah, had revolted against him and then allied himself with Pharaoh. He brought this on himself, thought Nebuchadnezzar. His thoughts were interrupted by one of his staff who approached him. "Your majesty, we have word of the Jew king. He has fled towards Jericho with his family. We will capture him soon enough."

"Good," said the Babylonian ruler. "And then I'll deal with him." He turned and walked back inside his spacious and elaborately furnished tent. Across the tent he noticed a large demon slouching casually in a chair. He had short dark red fur with brown swirls along his skin. His large head had large yellow eyes set in front and large teeth. Huge leathery wings were folded behind him. His arms were muscular, and hands had curved sharp claws.

"Make yourself at home my friend," said Nebuchadnezzar.

"I already have," answered the demon.

Nebuchadnezzar smiled. "They've located my runaway king. I'll deal with him later."

"And what will you do with him?"

"I haven't decided yet. Killing him would be too easy. He must be made an example."

The demon picked up a chalice of wine and drank. "What about the golden chest?"

"The Ark of Covenant?"

The demon nodded.

"The priests must have taken it and hid it somewhere. It was gone from their little temple. The spot where it sat was empty." He shrugged. "We'll find it."

The demon squeezed and crushed the metal goblet. "I want that chest."

Nebuchadnezzar walked over and sat in a huge overstuffed wooden chair inlaid with different colored gems. He glanced over at the demon. "Ghazi, my friend, why do you want that chest so badly? We have taken all off their treasures, gold, silver, and jewels. I can build cities for you, or monuments for you, why a small golden box?"

"Because it's special to them," replied the demon named Ghazi with a sneer.

Nebuchadnezzar picked up a bowl of fruit and began eating. "We'll find one of the temple priests and extract the hiding place."

"Make sure your horde doesn't kill all of them."

Before the Babylonian ruler could respond a voice outside of the tent spoke. "Lord Ghazi, I have news of the chest you seek."

Ghazi tilted his ugly head towards the voice. "Come inside and explain."

"I live in the darkness your lordship, the light will blind me," whined the voice.

"If you don't show yourself, being blinded by light will not be the only thing you will have to worry about," grumbled Ghazi.

The tent flap moved, and a short, thin demonic form hesitantly inched inside the tent. His skin was white, and he had small leathery wings. He held his clawed arm across his eyes to block the light from the firelight and candles.

"Who are you?" demanded Ghazi.

"I am known as Pararim."

"So where is the chest?"

The albino demon hesitated for only three seconds when Ghazi backhanded him across the room. "Talk now if you want to live," growled Ghazi.

"Yes, my lord. I live in the tunnels under the city. I live in the darkness. Many years ago, I watched the humans take their golden chest through a tunnel under their temple and hide it."

Ghazi grinned, showing razor sharp teeth. "Of course, a secret tunnel." He turned to Nebuchadnezzar, "Have your men check under the floor in that temple and find that chest."

Days later a long caravan proceeded east towards Babylon. With the weak or disabled left behind, the surviving Israelites were forced into captivity and began the long-forced march east. King Zedekiah who had been forced to watch his family killed, then blinded, led the procession followed by the newly obtained Ark of the Covenant.

No spirit seer or demon killer came to save them.

---

**Three Miles West of Shady Oak**
**Sutton County, Texas**
**Present Day**

FRED LONGETTE TOOK a last swallow of his beer and threw the empty can at the trash pile in the corner of his ramshackle single wide trailer home. He'd finished his six pack of beer for the evening. He turned the window air conditioner in the trailer down a notch and sat back in his recliner to watch a few minutes of the news before going to bed. Fred was a widower of ten years who lived off his small social security payments and the chickens he raised. Recently something kept invading his hen house and eating his profits, so he kept a double-barreled shotgun next to the recliner just in case.

Fred awoke two hours later to the sound of his chickens squawking. He grabbed his shotgun, stumbled to his feet, and jerked open the flimsy door of the trailer. "Whoever you are, you better git. I got a shotgun full of buckshot waitin' for you."

He grabbed his flashlight off of the small table by the door and clicked it on, but the batteries were dead. In the minute or so that it took him to change batteries the sound of the chickens quieted down. These batteries were almost drained too. Beer was more important than batteries. The dim flashlight beam only lit up a few feet in front of Fred as he stepped out of the trailer and walked toward the henhouse, cursing to himself the whole way.

When he reached the henhouse, he saw that the fence had been ripped down and the door to the henhouse had been torn away. He'd only taken a few steps forward when he stepped on something soft. He bent down and shined the dim light on the vague shape of one of the chickens that had been ripped to shreds. Fred cursed and cocked both hammers back on his shotgun. He shined the light into the henhouse and was shocked at what he saw. The inside of the henhouse was a bloody mess. Feathers drifted in the air, blood covered the walls, and his chickens were gone.

Fred shined his light around the area. He'd lost his main meal ticket and he was going to make someone pay. "Alright, I know you're out there. I'm going to call the sheriff and have you arrested for this. You better come out now and save me the trouble of huntin' you down."

Suddenly a quick movement caught his eye, he swung around, shined his quickly dimming flashlight, but nothing was there. He heard shuffling behind him so his spun around to see nothing. His head ached and his flashlight was almost dead. "This ain't funny anymore. You better come out now or I'll unload this here buckshot." He saw movement to his right, spun, and fired one of the shotgun barrels. He thought he'd hit something, but nothing was there. Fred felt a cold chill down his spine. *What could move that fast?* Another movement to his left drew a blast from his other shotgun barrel. He shined his flashlight in that direction, but nothing was there, and then the flashlight went out.

In the darkness Fred glanced around and saw off to his right a set of yellow glowing eyes. He backed toward the trailer when he heard a sound behind him and turned to see another set of yellow glowing eyes. He then smelled an odd smell like rotten eggs.

"You're funny, whoever you are. You can't scare me with those fake yellow lights. I'll turn you in to the sheriff." But Fred was scared. He quickly turned and ran towards the trailer but was knocked down from behind. His shotgun was knocked away and when he tried to get up something heavy pinned him down. His head was held down, but he saw, out of the corner of his eye, a huge head bend down and stare at him with one of the glowing yellow eyes.

"Don't kill me," pleaded Fred. "I don't have any money. Take whatever you want."

The thing with the yellow eyes stared at him for a moment and then smiled. Fred saw in a brief instant a set of large, razor-sharp teeth. He panicked and screamed, but no one heard him.

------

**50 miles northeast of the Red Sea**
**Kingdom of Saudi Arabia**

A LONG WHITE limo drove across the hot, arid desert north of the holy city of Makkah. The highway was bumpy and worn from wind and sand. The limo approached a large compound that seemed to have sprung up in the middle of the desert. High walls circled the area with razor wire encircling the top. The limo stopped at a small guard shack at the entrance. A guard dressed in khaki fatigues exited the air-conditioned building and approached the car. After a brief conversation with the limo driver, the guard opened the gate and allowed them to continue into the compound. What was dry and cracked outside the compound was just the opposite on the inside. Well-manicured lawns, trees and bushes were the norm. The limo drove past a small golf course, an Olympic size swimming pool, and tennis courts. A white stone building stood in the middle of the compound. The building resembled a two-story mosque-like palace with almost gothic architecture intertwined with the repetitive artwork quite common in Muslim countries. Eastern-styled domed roofs adorned each end. The limo stopped under the front, covered portico.

Two men dressed in traditional Arabic robes exited the limo and entered a much cooler interior. They walked down the long, color-fully tiled floor to an ornate carved walnut door. Inside the room was a modest but expensive office reception area with a young Middle Eastern man sitting behind a desk. The assistant picked up the phone and pushed one of the buttons. "Your guests have arrived," he said.

"Thank you, Kateb. Wait ten minutes and send them in," answered the voice on the other line.

Moments later the two men were ushered into a door from the hallway opened, and two men entered a room where the floors and walls were covered with expensive Persian carpets and draperies. In the middle of the room was a small round table surrounded by large pillows and cushions.

A tall, dark-haired man dressed in traditional clothing waited inside. The two men embraced.

"Peace be upon you and your family, Akram Fawwaz," said the man to the elder of the two men.

"Peace be upon you, Hassan Ghazi," replied Akram.

The second man was much younger and greeted Ghazi with a nod. The older man, Akram Fawwaz, was one of the wealthy elites who owned a vast corporation that controlled a large percentage of the oil and minerals being exported. The younger man was his son, Azim Fawwaz. They all reclined at the table and began discussing minor interests while Kateb brought in a tray with coffee. The thick eastern coffee was poured, and each sipped in silence while inhaling the strong aroma.

"Have you considered my request, Akram?" asked Ghazi, breaking the silence.

"My dear friend, I've considered what you've proposed. I am old and have learned much. I can't condone violence in the name of Allah. Our great religion doesn't come from violence or hatred, but peace. The way to true Islam is through mutual respect and under-standing. I am truly sorry."

The room was deathly quiet for a few moments. Ghazi sat and sipped his tea before speaking. He set the cup down and smiled. "I understand your situation, Akram, and I know that you have thought a great deal about it. I am sorry that you have chosen not to enter in this venture. I harbor no ill feelings about your decision, and I hope that we can continue to work as partners in other dealings."

"Of course, we can," said Akram with a wide smile. They finished their coffee and prepared to leave. Ghazi walked them to the door of the small room where they embraced. As Ghazi stepped back, Akram's eyes became wide with shock. A knife protruded from Akram's sternum. He opened his mouth to speak, tried to step forward, but slowly sank to the floor. He looked over at his son, Azim, as if to ask why while Azim simply stood and watched. The old man's eyes rolled up in his head and he died.

"A foolish, old man," said Ghazi.

"Yes," answered Azim. "He'd grown soft from love of comforts and lost sight of the true way."

Ghazi used his cell phone to make a call and moments later several men entered and carried away Akram's body. "Make sure it looks like an American assassination. It will help to cement our other relationships with the extremists," instructed Ghazi.

"We must make the infidels pay for their unbelief and bring them to their knees," Azim fumed.

"Yes, and with your aid our plan cannot fail. I will contact you later with more details."

Azim bowed and left the room, following the men who carried his dead father.

After the group left, Ghazi reentered his office which was lavishly decorated. The floor was covered by expensive Persian rugs and a large wooden desk sat in the middle of the room. Beautiful paintings depicting the world of Islam hung on the walls.

The man Ghazi however no longer looked like the tall man they had seen earlier, instead he was in his true identity, a demon. With the help of that moron, Azim, everything was going as planned and he would soon become king. He thought back to his previous plans with Nebuchadnezzar but how he converted because of that Jew,

Daniel. Eventually his plans completely failed when King Darius of Babylon listened to Daniel who even survived his attempts to have him killed. So many plans were ruined back then but now he could see his goal in sight, and nothing was going to stop him.

No one knew Hassan Ghazi's real identity except for his fellow demons. The rest of the world only knew he was rumored to be the son of a rich Arab, but he seemed to have appeared out of nowhere and amassed a huge fortune. His business dealings appeared legitimate, but his methods had often been questionable. His plan was to pretend to be a Muslim to use Azim and his fanatical ways to achieve Ghazi's goals. He'd first thought was to use fanatical extremists in America by pretending to be a member of the Arian nation or the Klu Klux Klan but it was easier to obtain information and supplies outside of the United States.

So, on the outside he seemed a devoted Muslim, but on the inside, something much more malignant.

# CHAPTER TWO

**J Double T Ranch**
**Sutton County, Texas**

THE WESTERN PART of Texas was beautiful in the spring. The air is clean, the grass is green, and the summer's scorching hot temperatures have not cooked the earth.

Jake finished riding part of the fence line on the eastern boundary checking for breaks. He'd need to stretch a new section of fence after the news about the missing cattle. He wanted to move his small herd into a new section since Jake needed every head for his growing ranch.

On a good day one could see for miles across the low brush, mesquite, and pecan tree-covered region. He rode Buck in a trot into view of the ranch house and immediately noticed a blue Ford Explorer parked under the pecan tree that shaded the west side of the house.

*Pam!*

Pamela Martin was the owner of the local newspaper, bookstore, coffee shop, and the primary force behind the church led by the new pastor, Ellie Thompson. *What's Pam stirring up now*, thought Jake as he rode into the yard.

Pam sat in the shade on the porch in a rocking chair while Roscoe slept on the floor next to her. Pam was a feisty blonde woman who wore the latest fashion jeans, a starched white shirt, and pink boots. Ellie Thompson occupied another rocking chair and was Pam's opposite. She had long dark black hair in a bun and wore a conservative dark blue polo shirt, khaki dress pants, and black dress shoes.

*Oh great! Double team!*

Jake stopped at the corral next to the barn and tied Buck up next to the water trough so he could drink. He stripped off the saddle and blanket and tossed it on the top fence railing. He'd have to put it away and brush Buck down later. He removed his model 94 Winchester rifle from the saddle's scabbard and walked as slowly as possible to the house, dreading what these two females might have in store for him. *I hope she didn't come to preach a sermon*, thought Jake.

Dressed in his old Stetson hat, work shirt, jeans, worn leather chaps, and boots with spurs jingling; Jake looked like he had just stepped off the pages of some western novel.

"Morning, ladies," he said as he stepped on the porch.

"Morning, Jake," said Pam with a bright smile.

"Good morning, Mr. Taft," said Ellie in a more business-like voice.

"Are you going to shoot us for trespassing," asked Pam jokingly.

Jake set the rifle down against one of the front porch posts. "You never know when you need it to keep away unwanted varmints." He hoped the comment would give them the idea they shouldn't have come without being invited.

"I had to talk to Mr. Hernandez up the road about his missing stock, and crazy Fred Longette's missing," said Pam. "It's an article for the newspaper. We thought we'd drop in and visit. Fortunately, we've only been waiting here a few minutes."

Not wanting to be rude, Jake invited them inside for refreshments. As they entered the kitchen, Jake looked down at Roscoe. "Some guard dog you are."

Roscoe wagged his tail.

Soon they sat in the living room drinking iced tea. "What did Mr. Hernandez say about his missing stock?" asked Jake.

Pam sat her tea glass on the coffee table, pulled out a notepad, and flipped through the pages. "According to Mr. Hernandez, he's lost fifteen head of cattle in the last two months."

Jake shrugged his shoulders. "He has over five hundred head of cattle, but that's still a lot of missing stock even for a large herd."

Pam sat and flipped through her notepad, making a mental count. "According to my latest calculations, the total amount of lost cattle in the last two months for the entire county is almost two hundred," she said somberly.

*200 head of cattle!*

Jake was no expert, but he couldn't imagine that a pack of coyotes or a single cougar could eat that much beef in just two months. He thought about the carcass he found. *Could it be rustlers or something else?* Even in modern times, there were still people who stole cattle and sold them in other states at auctions, or to tanning companies who don't ask questions.

"I might've lost one or two in the last couple of months, but nothing like that," explained Jake.

Pam nodded and wrote something in her notepad. "Maybe because your herd is smaller," thought Pam out loud. "They didn't risk taking a lot of cattle that would immediately be noticed. Maybe they think the larger ranches won't notice the loss."

"What about Longette?" asked Jake.

"Now this is odd, even for him," explained Pam. "One of his neighbor's dogs dragged up a couple of his dead chickens so they went to check on him. They found more dead chickens, but the rest were gone along with Fred. Something strange is going on."

Jake nodded. "I'll keep an eye out for him."

They sat quietly for a few minutes. Jake could see Ellie out of the corner of his eye. She looked around the room as she reached up and pushed a loose strand of hair behind her ear.

"Your ranch is very nice," said Ellie. "Is it the original building?"

Jake nodded. "The ranch house has stood for over a hundred

years but was run down when I bought it. I restored as much as I could to its original state but added plumbing, air conditioning, and heating. The house's spilt into two buildings connected by the porch. This side is the kitchen and formal area, and the other side is the sleeping quarters."

"Sleeping quarters?" asked Ellie. "Sounds like military jargon?"

"Jake was a highly decorated soldier," added Pam. "He was a Major."

Jake frowned at Pam. She knew his background and didn't hesitate to blab about it.

At the age of 35, after being honorably discharged from the military, he purchased the small ranch and planned to live out the rest of his life in the peace and solitude of west Texas.

When they finished their tea Ellie walked over to a sideboard cabinet and looked at some of Jake's photos and awards. "What part were you in?"

"I was in the Army, ma'am."

"Jake was in some kind of special secret stuff," added Pam.

Jake frowned at her which made Ellie smile. "Please call me Ellie," she said. "It sounds exciting. I imagine you've been to some wonderful places and done exciting things."

Jake noticed that he liked the sound of her voice. It seemed to fill the emptiness of the house. "Well, I've seen lots of places, but some I'd just soon forget."

Ellie blushed. "I'm sorry. I didn't mean to bring up any bad memories."

"You didn't. The good times outweigh the bad." Jake noticed how her brown eyes seemed warm and bright. *Was it getting hot in here?*

"Are these pictures of you in the military?" she asked.

Jake nodded. He didn't like talking about himself but with her it seemed different, so he explained about the various group photos taken in the desert, mountains, jungles, and other odd-looking places.

Ellie couldn't help but notice how broad his shoulders were while he stood next to her, and how his gray eyes seemed to offset his tanned skin. *I thought he said it was air conditioned in here, it sure is getting warm,* she thought.

"You're obviously very brave and our country owes you a great debt of thanks. I'm sure your family is very proud of you."

"Thank you. My parents were killed a few years back by a drunk driver while I was in the military."

"Oh, I'm so sorry, Mr. Taft."

"You can call me Jake and it was a long time ago. Now it's just me and Roscoe."

They stood and looked at the photos. They both seemed uncomfortable about what to say next. Roscoe seemed to sense it, padded over to Ellie, and sat. She reached down and began scratching him behind his ear.

Pam stood up and stretched. "Well, we'd better go." They walked outside without further discussion. "It was a lovely visit. You have a beautiful ranch," said Ellie as she got into the SUV.

Jake smiled, nodded, and said, "Thanks". He walked over to Pam as she was getting into the driver's side. "I'll get you for this, Pamela Martin." His frown didn't discourage her big smile. "I don't know what you're talking about Jake."

As the vehicle disappeared in a cloud of dust, Jake returned to the house to clean up. *Why did the house seem too quiet now?* "Women! Who needs em'?" said Jake out loud.

Roscoe whined in response.

"Who asked you? Traitor!"

———

**Port City of Al Jubayl,**
**Kingdom of Saudi Arabia**

AZIM TRAVELED QUICKLY EAST to the coastal port of Al Jubayl on the Persian Gulf. After receiving his marching orders from Ghazi, he called his contacts in Iran to launch their plan. Azim waited outside a small coffee shop near the docks. After waiting nearly forty-five minutes, a small, nondescript boat pulled into a slot. A young man exited the boat and casually walked to the coffee shop.

"Peace be upon you, Azim," said the man.

"Peace be upon you, Levent," answered Azim in the typical Muslim greeting. "Did you have an easy trip?"

The other man nodded. "Allah has been kind to us. It was smooth sailing across the gulf. No one suspected we carried the answer to all our prayers."

Azim smiled. "Allah surely has smiled on us." He'd worked with Levent many times on other operations against the United States and its allies. They both had traveled to Iraq many times when the Americans occupied the country. Azim was responsible for a multitude of car bombs, assassinations, and road-side ambushes. He and Levent felt they were great heroes in the fight against the Western world. Even though democracy had come to Iraq, they were still determined to do everything they could to bring it down and begin a rule under Islamic law. This meeting was the beginning of the end of the United States and eventually the world.

They sat and drank coffee while a wooden box approximately ten feet by ten feet was unloaded from the boat and onto a rented truck. On the side were stenciled the words "Fragile Antiquity." Azim gathered the forged shipping papers and thanked Levent. The typical clearances were signed along with a customary payment to the customs clerk, and they were soon on their way back to Ghazi's compound. Azim sat back in a seat and relaxed.

———

**Hassan Ghazi's Compound**
**Kingdom of Saudi Arabia**

GHAZI SAT in his overstuffed chair, picked up the phone, and dialed Azim who answered on the first ring.

"I see that you've safely brought the golden chest," said Ghazi.

"Yes, all is as you wished."

"Do you have your people set up to take the U.S. President's daughter?"

"Yes, all we need is your final approval."

"Then you will have it," said Ghazi.

"And may Allah guide our steps," answered Azim.

"Of course," replied Ghazi. "Let me know when it's completed". He hung up without waiting for a reply. He sat for a minute, and then broke into a wide sinister grin.

# CHAPTER THREE

**J Double T Ranch**
**Sutton County, Texas**

IT HAD BEEN a long hard day of work. After working for days putting up a line of fence posts, Jake strung barbed wire to each. It was easier and less dangerous than it was 100 years ago, but it was still backbreaking work. If the barbed wire broke loose and a man became tangled in it, he could be a prisoner of it for days, or die from blood loss and exposure if no help came.

Finishing up, Jake drove his pickup back to the ranch and began unloading supplies into the barn. It was getting late, and he thought how good a hot shower and dinner would be. He'd stacked some of the unused barbed wire spools in the corner of the barn when he felt the presence of someone else. He didn't hear anything, but rather felt a presence. Jake glanced over his shoulder and froze.

Under the barn lights stood a man at least seven feet tall with skin the color of golden brass. He was dressed in white clothing with a golden belt, and on the belt was a scabbard covered in jewels and etched with strange symbols that contained the largest golden sword

Jake had ever seen. Jake thought he was seeing things, so he shook his head, but the figure remained.

"Greetings, Jacob Travis Taft, from the Most High God," said the man in a deep voice but with a reassuring smile. After the initial shock of seeing such a strange man in his barn, Jake quickly recovered and stared at him suspiciously. He didn't look like a rustler, but Jake wasn't sure what he was.

"Very funny," said Jake slightly irritated. "Who sent you? Pam? Or did the boys from the Circle R send you? What are you, a wrestling reject or a wanna be comic book convention hero?"

The man cocked his head to the side and stared at Jake. He then seemed to understand and chuckled. "You think some of your friends sent me as a joke? No, Jacob, this is no joke. I have been sent from heaven."

The hairs on the back of Jake's neck stood up. *Am I hallucinating? Did I get too much sun today?* He'd left his rifle in the truck outside but always kept an old 410 single shot shotgun in the barn to keep mice and other creatures out of the feed. He glanced to his right at the corner of a horse stall where Jake had left it against the post. "Look, buddy, I don't know who sent you, but I don't need anything," explained Jake casually as he took a step near the shotgun. "I just need a hot bath and something to eat." The man didn't speak, but simply waited. Jake grabbed the shotgun, spun it around, and pointed it directly at the man. "Okay, funny guy, who are you?" demanded Jake.

"My name is Malachy. I was sent from God," answered the man calmly.

Jake was beginning to lose his patience. "Look, Malachy or whatever your real name is I'm tired and hungry so get out."

The man didn't move.

That only made Jake more irritated. He cocked the hammer back on the shotgun. "I'll only give you one more chance before I blow a hole in you big enough to drive my truck through."

The man named Malachy raised one eyebrow and with blinding quickness stepped forward and knocked the shotgun out of Jake's hand. The shotgun skidded against the barn floor to a stop near a bale of hay.

The man stepped back and spoke. "Jacob, I wish you no harm."

Jake stood and stared in amazement. He'd never seen anyone move so quickly and so calmly. Jake was an expert in deadly hand to hand combat but had been disarmed as easily as if he was a child. He looked up into the man's eyes and was even more amazed to see flames flickering in his pupils. Tiny streaks of lightning ran across the whites of his eyes. *Maybe there was more to this guy than a joke,* thought Jake. "Since I can't convince you to leave, who sent you and what do you want?"

Malachy smiled. "I've been sent to fulfill an ancient prophecy. Jacob, as you're aware the world is changing and not always for the best. Wars and famine are at an all-time high. Terrorism is at the doorstep of every country. In your country morals are being replaced by total freedom of the individual. Satan has twisted the idea of freedom into doing whatever you want by saying it's a personal right. It's family versus family. Fathers kill families and mothers kill their children. Violence floods the streets of every city and invades today's music. Children go to schools, afraid of being shot, or attacked by gangs.

"Religions of all types and ways are growing everywhere. Satan and his demons are taking advantage of this. Satanism and the occult are now a protected religion. The 'Deceiver' is no longer satisfied with being subtle to try to gain ground; he's beginning to be more obvious. There will be a time soon when demons will rise up and not be afraid to be seen. These demons will not try to hide but come out and show their evil so it's time for someone to step forward and stop him."

Jake took in everything Malachy said. "So, what has that got to do with me?"

"You've been prophesized to stop their plans."

"What?" Jake chuckled. "Me? I'm just a cowboy trying to build a life here for myself. You came to the wrong place."

"You've been chosen, Jacob."

"No way," growled Jake. "First of all, I'm not even sure who you really are. Second, even if you are who you say you are, I did my service to God and country. I'm not concerned with some old prophecy. I'm staying right here. You can choose someone else. I've done my time."

"Very well," said Malachy patiently. "It's your choice. I will, however, return in a few days after you've had time to think about it."

"Don't waste your time. The answer is still no." Jake turned and pointed toward the stack of barbed wire. "Now if you wanted to be helpful you could lend a hand with this barbed wire. Something's killing or stealing our cattle and we've got to protect them." He glanced back and Malachy was gone.

Jake instantly darted over and snatched up the shotgun from the ground. He quickly searched the barn but found no one. He checked the ground where Malachy had been, but there were no footprints. *How could someone that large not make any footprints?* He went outside and thoroughly searched the area around the corral and up beside the barn but couldn't find any sign of the man.

Jake tipped his Stetson back on his head. "Well, I'll be." *Did I imagine it all?* Jake strolled across the yard to the house and found Roscoe asleep on the porch. "You didn't see a seven-foot giant with golden skin and a huge sword, did you?" asked Jake.

Roscoe opened one eye and looked at Jake.

"Guess not," said Jake.

———

**Twenty-Two miles south of Shady Oak**
**Sutton County, Texas**

IT WAS JUST AFTER MIDNIGHT, and they were hungry again. The two shadowy forms suddenly appeared out of the darkness. The smell of sulfur and ash filled the air.

Several head of cattle lay nearby on the ground sleeping while a few nibbled on short grass. The creatures were slightly smaller than the average cow but more muscular. They blended with the dark almost perfectly, and slowly, carefully crept toward the resting cattle. One of the bovines caught a whiff of sulfur and rotted meat. Looking to the left, the animal could only see two sets of glowing yellow eyes. Sensing that these creatures were even more dangerous than coyotes or other normal predators the cow immediately leapt to its feet. The remaining cattle also caught the putrid smell and bounded to their feet.

The two dark forms split and stalked the group on either side. The cattle bolted away from the two but with amazing speed the two were among the cattle in an instance. The herd scattered into different directions in a vain attempt to escape. One creature leapt atop the back of one the cows, dragging it to the ground immediately. It opened its mouth showing razor sharp teeth and clamped down on the back of the bovine, severing the spinal cord, and in an instant the struggle was over. Another member of the small herd met the same fate. The remaining cattle stampeded in terror.

The two creatures sat next to their kills, calmly devouring flesh and crushing bone with evil delight.

---

**J Double T Ranch**
**Sutton County, Texas**

JAKE CONTINUED PUTTING up the remaining barbed wire fence but the visit from the strange giant kept nagging at him. If it had been a practical joke, no one had claimed responsibility, and that bothered Jake. *Was it for real?* He hated to go back into town again, but he needed his questions answered.

He and Roscoe were soon on Highway 8 just outside of town. Roscoe had his head out of the passenger window, enjoying the wind in his face. Jake contemplated what he was going to say once he got to town. He needed to talk to someone about what he'd seen and there was only one person he could think of.

The church was located on a side street where Jake had never been before. He parked alongside several cars and trucks outside the portable church building. A small sign stood out front advertised the church, Shady Oak Community Church, Ellie Thompson, Pastor.

He and Roscoe entered through the main doors but didn't see anyone inside. Most of the building was an open area where they probably held the worship service. Chairs were stacked neatly against one wall allowing the room to be used for many purposes. One part was sectioned off by rooms. He found a door marked 'Office' and entered. No one was at the secretary's desk, but Jake could hear voices coming from an adjoining room. After a few minutes of waiting, he knocked quietly on the door.

Mr. Tillon, a middle-aged man, and part owner in the nearby feed store, answered the door. "Jake, it's great to see you. How are you?" he said with a big smile. "We were just finishing up some church business. Please come in."

Jake hesitated but stepped in. Besides Mr. Tillon, there was Pam, a younger man, and another woman he didn't know. They were all helping Ellie clean up coffee cups and pick up papers. Ellie was surprised at seeing him and broke out in a wide smile. "Jake, I'm so glad to see you. Can we help you with something?" She then kept cleaning up in hopes that he wouldn't notice she'd blushed.

"I need to talk to you about something. It's important. If you have time," explained Jake with his hat in his hand.

"Of course, just give us a minute to clean up and we can talk."

Pam came over carrying a trash bag and wearing a huge grin. "Why, Jake, I'm so glad to see you here," she said. "Can I get you some coffee?"

"Afternoon, Pam," answered Jake flatly. "No, thank you." He then thought about his strange visitor. "By the way, did you send someone to see me the other day?"

Pam looked at him, confused.

"Never mind."

Pam reached down to pet Roscoe. "Hi, Roscoe, is he treating you good?"

Roscoe wagged his tail as if he was starved for attention while she stroked his fur. The two men finished, said their goodbyes, and left.

"I'm gone now, Ellie," said Pam. "I have work backlogged at the newspaper waiting for me. If you need anything, call me." She turned and winked at Jake as she went out the door.

Jake rolled his eyes.

The other woman in the group was Janet Pearston. She was the part time secretary who went to her desk and started working.

Ellie invited him into her office. It was small with a desk and high-back chair. The desk was tidy with a computer on one side and a picture of an elderly couple presumably her parents on the other side. There were two chairs set in front of the desk with a very small bookshelf against one wall. Roscoe found himself a spot next to one of the chairs.

"Nice office," said Jake trying to be courteous.

"Thank you. I know it's small, but the elders wanted me to have a place to myself. I wanted more room for worship and teaching, so we compromised."

"And you got the broom closet?"

Ellie laughed.

He had never heard her laugh before, and it sounded wonderful.

She propped the door open, sat in the chair next to Roscoe, and scratched him behind one ear. Jake glanced out the open door and saw Janet at her desk typing on her computer. "I need to talk to you about something," he said, then indicated the open door, "Confidentially."

Ellie nodded. "I understand, but its common practice in today's world to leave the door open when people of the opposite gender are meeting. It's for our protection."

Jake frowned, reached over, and abruptly closed the door. Ellie's eyes widened slightly.

"I need this to be between the two of us," explained Jake. "Roscoe can protect you."

Ellie looked down at Roscoe who was enjoying the attention. "Very well," she said in her business-like voice. "So how can I help you?"

Jake sat for a moment and shuffled his feet. Ellie noticed how out of place the big man seemed to be, sitting in a small chair, in a cramped office. Her business-like manner started to fade.

"Is everything ok?" she asked.

Jake didn't say anything for a second.

"Jake, what's wrong? What is it?"

He made a weak smile. "I'm not sure how to begin, but I beg you to keep an open mind about what I'm going to tell you."

Ellie nodded.

"I had a visitor the other night," he said.

Ellie raised an eyebrow. "A visitor? A rustler?"

Jake shook his head. "No, not a rustler, this was no ordinary visitor. Please don't say anything until after I've explained everything."

Ellie nodded and kept silent. Jake then went on to explain the strange visitor named Malachy. He described his physical features, what he said, and the quickness Malachy possessed in disarming Jake when he pointed the shotgun at the giant. He explained how he seemed to have disappeared and the lack of footprints. Jake felt he might've embarrassed himself with such a wild story, but he felt he wanted her to know everything. He finished after what seemed like an eternity of explaining. "Well, that's it," he said and took a final deep breath. "What do you think?"

Ellie sat in her chair deep in thought then got up and went to her bookcase. She retrieved a large reference Bible off the shelf and put it on her desk. She sat down behind her desk and began to thumb through it until she found what she was looking for. She read for a moment and then looked up at Jake.

Jake was bent over the desk trying to see what she was reading when she looked up. He looked into her brown eyes and saw not only sincerity, but also apprehension. Ellie reached out and touched his hand which was warm and soft. "I wanted to check something before I said anything. Have you ever read the book of Daniel?"

Jake thought for a minute. "I remember being taught the story of Daniel and the lion's den when I was a child. I also remember something about three men being saved while in a fiery oven. That's about it. Why?"

Ellie pointed to a spot in the Bible. "In the last chapter of the book of Daniel, an angel appeared to Daniel. This angel is described in detail. The amazing thing is he looks exactly like the man you described."

Jake looked as if he'd been kicked by a mule. "Are you telling me that guy is supposed to be some sort of angel?"

Ellie closed the Bible and replaced it on the bookshelf. "I'm not saying that it was an angel. I'm saying that the man you described looked just like the one in the Bible. Could it be you read it as a child and don't remember? Could your subconscious have brought it out?"

Jake began to pace the little office. "I'm not sure about anything. I don't remember reading anything like that as a child. Could it have been a joke played on me by someone? What about this prophecy?"

Ellie heard the sadness in his voice. "I know you saw something," she said firmly. "And I don't think it was a joke. I don't know of anyone around here who would've enough biblical knowledge to pull off a scam in such detail."

Jake nodded his head. "I agree. I asked Pam about it in case she was the culprit, but she didn't seem to know what I was talking about. If not, then who was it and what's going on?"

Ellie rested her elbows on the desk and massaged her temples with her slender fingers. "I don't know anything about an ancient prophecy or what you saw except for what you told me. The only thing I can say right now is to wait and see if he returns."

Jake stopped pacing and sat down in the chair. Roscoe began licking his hand. Jake sat and thought for a minute. "Well, I know more now than I did before," he said with a sigh. "Thank you for your time. I agree. At this point all I can do is to wait and see what happens."

Ellie smiled and picked up a business card. She wrote something on it and handed it to Jake. "Here's my church business card. On the back is my personal cell phone number. As soon as you know something, please let me know."

Jake placed the card in his shirt pocket and got up to leave. "Thanks for listening. If he shows up again, at least I might have a handle on what to expect and ask, if he does show up." They both walked to the front door of the church. Jake felt awkward. He didn't know what to say.

Ellie reached out, took his hand, and placed her other hand on top. "Jake, I'm glad you came to see me. I'm sure it was difficult to tell me, but I'm so pleased you did. We'll get to the bottom of this," she said. "We'll figure it out, together," she added. She watched Jake climb into the truck and drove away with Roscoe barking out of the window. Ellie sighed and walked slowly back inside. They didn't teach this in seminary.

# CHAPTER FOUR

**FR 86**
**3 miles east of NE 231st Street**
**Ocala National Forest**
**Florida**

THE EVENING WAS WARM, and a young couple sat on the tailgate of the teenager's green Chevy pickup. He parked inside the beautiful Ocala National Forest on a side road. The young man had gotten a couple of bottles of beer from his older brother, and they sipped it from paper cups as his truck radio played the latest pop rock music. They enjoyed being alone while taking in the beautiful sights and smells of the forest.

But they weren't alone. Something was watching.

Jimmy and Paula were both high school seniors who looked forward to going to college after graduation next month. They sat and talked about the future while sipping the bitter-tasting beer.

A huge form slowly crept out of the trees toward the front of the truck, allowing the music to mask its approach. The couple giggled and occasionally kissed until they felt a bump against the truck.

"What was that?" asked Paula.

Jimmy giggled and took another sip of his beer. "Maybe it's the boogey man come to get you."

"That's not funny, Jimmy."

"Don't' worry, baby. It's probably nothing. It's just a big possum or maybe a gator."

"A gator?"

"Yeah, and it's here to nip your toes off," teased Jimmy. Both sat with their legs dangling off the tailgate. Paula jerked her legs up and sat crossed legged.

"Jimmy Buchanan, that's not nice," she said with a giggle.

They both sipped more beer when a horrible putrid, rotting smell drifted over the couple.

"What is that terrible smell?" asked Paula. As one they both turned toward the odor when a huge creature leapt into the bed of the pickup. Frozen in shock, they both stared into the eyes of something not of this world.

The creature moved to within inches of their terrified faces. The creature had a large snout and small yellow eyes that glowed. Its skin seemed to be alive as insects and other slimy, living things covered its body. When it moved closer, clumps of maggots and bugs fell off its shoulders onto the bed of pickup. It grinned, showing jagged teeth.

After the initial shock Jimmy shoved Paula off the tailgate and yelled for her to run.

The monster looked down at them, threw back its head slinging hundreds of maggots into the night air, and laughed. The smell from its mouth was that of rotting flesh and sulfur.

Paula grabbed Jimmy by the arm and pulled him off the truck's tailgate when the heinous thing grabbed Jimmy by the front of the shirt. Jimmy struggled to break the creature's grip, but the revolting thing lifted him into the air, knocking Paula backward onto the ground.

The devil continued to laugh as it held Jimmy over its head. Jimmy screamed for Paula to run. The thing rammed its clawed hand into Jimmy's chest and pulled out his heart. Paula leapt to her feet and fled down the dirt road in total terror.

**Ghazi's Compound**
**Kingdom of Saudi Arabia**

AZIM ARRIVED WITH THE BOX. He'd been debriefed by Ghazi and told to begin another part of their plan.

After years of negotiations with Iran and millions poured into certain bank accounts, the time was finally here. He walked down the hall of his palace to a small elevator. After entering, he quietly rode several levels down and exited into a small hallway lit by a string of single light bulbs strung along bare concrete walls. Ghazi walked a small distance to the end of the corridor where a steel door stood. A keypad was embedded in the wall and he entered a set of numbers and placed his hand over the palm pad which scanned his palm and fingerprints.

With a quiet hiss, the two-foot-thick door opened as easily as a door on a child's doll house. As he stepped across the threshold, lights came on automatically.

The room was the size of a single car garage. The walls, ceiling, and floor were polished steel. In the center of the room on a large pedestal sat the unopened wooden box. As per his instructions, a crowbar was left next to the box. Ghazi picked up the pry bar and began carefully prying the top off the box. He then pried the sides loose and let them fall to the floor. The item inside was wrapped in several layers of bubble wrap and foam. He carefully removed the wrap until the final piece fell. Covered in sweat, he stepped back and gazed upon the item in sheer hatred.

The Ark of the Covenant.

**Shaley's Pub**
**4951 North Broadway**
**Chicago, Illinois**

THE EVENING CROWD already filled up Shaley's Pub located in the uptown part of Chicago. The bar was filled with the usual patrons. It had become an informal meeting place for men and women from various corporations, financial businesses, research labs, and companies.

By city fire code the main doors were always left unlocked and open. While the crowd talked, laughed, and drank, the doors suddenly closed. No one noticed until a young man tried to leave, but the door was locked. He yelled for the bartender to open the door so one of the bartenders tried to unlock the door but found that a chain had been wrapped around the outside door handles. The bartender stood and scratched his head when a commotion at the rear of the bar brought everyone's attention. Two strange-looking figures entered wearing hoods and long coats.

"It's a robbery," screamed one of the young executives. Several of the patrons grabbed cell phones to call for help. The potential robbers had their faces hidden in the shadows of their hoods, but no one missed their eyes. They glowed yellow.

One of the men stepped forward and pointed his arm at the crowd. Most thought it was a semiautomatic weapon, but on second glance was unsure what it was. Several squid-like tentacles slithered out from the end of the sleeve. They all stared in surprise at seeing the strange tentacles and thinking it must be some sort of joke, the room soon filled with laughter.

The laughter suddenly turned to terror as the ends of the small fingerlike apertures glowed and flames erupt, spraying the crowd.

The crowd turned into a stampede of people as they fled to the front door, knocking over tables, trampling over several patrons in a vain attempt to escape. The ones closest to the entrance pounded on the door. One young research lab worker grabbed a chair and lifted it over his head to heave through the glass window. A tentacle seemed to know what he was about to do and spat a stream of fire that engulfed the man. He dropped the chair and ran screaming through the pub, bumping into others, setting them ablaze.

The two figures cackled as they sprayed the remaining occupants of the bar with the burning, liquid-like hell.

# CHAPTER FIVE

**University of Colorado**
**Boulder, Colorado**

THE SUN ROSE over the beautiful University of Colorado at Boulder, considered one of the most beautiful campuses in the United States. Most of the 29,000 students were already awake and active on campus.

Ann Campbell was already making her way across campus to the math building located on the main campus which sat at the base of the Rocky Mountains. Ann was in her third year studying architecture. She was a bright and beautiful twenty-year old blonde who hoped to graduate ahead of schedule and get a position with a prominent architectural firm on the East Coast.

The one thing that helped assure Ann's success was being the daughter of the current President of the United States, William Campbell.

The sun was just rising, illuminating the red tile roofs and sandstone buildings as she walked across a grassy area called the engineering quadrangle. Ann was conversing with another young woman, Beth Sills. Sills was Ann's good friend and companion as well as a United States Secret Service agent assigned to protect her. Ann didn't want a guard following her everywhere she went, but in the post 9-11 world, her father insisted someone protect his only child.

Agent Sills had reluctantly taken the assignment after working in the counterfeit section of the Secret Service. The twenty-nine-year-old agent had hoped to be assigned to protect the President himself but instead she was sent to accompany Ann. At first, Agent Sills felt it was a waste of time to follow a college student everywhere, but soon the two had become friends.

It started like any other day. The morning would be spent in class, lunch, and then off to the library where Ann did most of her research and studying. Agent Sills had become very adept at being her research assistant as well as her bodyguard. The late afternoon and evening would be spent at the gym followed by more studying.

After lunch they strolled toward the Norlin Library at the heart of the campus for an afternoon of studying. "That was the most boring class I've ever been in," said Agent Sills as they walked up the steps to the building.

"Oh Beth, you're just bored because you didn't understand it," answered Ann with a giggle.

Agent Sills smiled back. "Hey, math was never my strong subject. That's why I went into the Secret Service."

Ann turned then looked at her friend and protector. She was slightly taller than Ann and had medium length blonde hair which she usually kept up in a ponytail.

"So how did someone bad at math get into the treasury department?" asked Ann.

With a wicked grin, Agent Sills answered. "Would you believe I cheated on the entrance exam?" They both laughed as they entered the library.

The Norlin Library was named after University of Colorado President George Norlin and contained over 15 million books, some dated back to the 15th century. As they entered the main library, they passed one of the campus police officers.

"Afternoon, Bill," said Agent Sills.

Bill Owens, a retired Denver police officer smiled back. "Good afternoon, ladies. I see you're back for another round of studying?" Owens knew who Ann was and that Sills was her assigned bodyguard.

The two women smiled. "Of course, we are, I love studying," answered Ann.

Agent Sills rolled her eyes.

"So, how's your daughter doing?" asked Ann. "I saw her in biology class this morning?"

Owens smiled even bigger at the mention of his daughter. After retiring from the police force, he moved to Boulder and took a job at the campus police department to help pay for his daughter's tuition.

"Oh, she's just fine. She wants more money for things, the usual." They smiled, nodded, and continued into the main area of the library.

They saw students reading, studying, and napping. They walked past a large set of bay windows that had been an outer wall at one time but converted into a study area to enlarge the library. They found an empty table where Ann deposited her backpack and started removing her papers. Agent Sills sat and scanned the interior of the room as a habit, but only noticed students studying. Ann noticed a young man two tables over.

"Beth, isn't that guy over there hot?"

Agent Sills glanced at a young man reading. "Uh huh," she answered. "But we came here to study, not ogle the men."

Ann sighed, "Yes, ma'am." She gave a mock salute. "All work and no play. That's me. Now if I can't look, neither can you." She gave Agent Sills a small piece of paper. "Go pull these books so I can make good grades and make you proud."

Agent Sills gave her a friendly frown. "Don't run off," she said as she left to go retrieve the books.

A young female student watched the two from an upstairs area. The dark-haired coed wearing a traditional Muslim hijab quietly walked down the stairs and over toward Ann. As she passed, she stumbled, bumped into Ann, and dropped her books to the floor.

"Oh, I'm so sorry," said the woman with a slight Middle Eastern accent as she bent down to pick up the books.

"Here, let me help you." Ann bent over to help.

While they were both bent down collecting books and papers, the woman quickly pulled a syringe from her jacket pocket and jabbed it into Ann's thigh. Ann looked up in surprise before collapsing into the woman's arms. As if on cue, two male students quickly came over and half carried, half dragged Ann toward the door. As they neared the exit, Officer Owens approached them.

"Is everything ok?" he asked.

The young female student spoke up. "She just fainted. We're taking her over to the campus health clinic to get her checked out."

Owens looked at the unconscious woman and realized it was Ann.

"Where's her friend?" he asked hurriedly.

"Oh, she's gathering her backpack. She'll follow in a minute," answered the woman.

Owens turned and looked over at the table where they'd been sitting. He saw Ann's books and backpack, but Agent Sills was nowhere to be seen.

"Wait a minute," he ordered. "Let me see your ID."

"Of course, officer," said the woman and reached into her purse.

"You need to wait until I can find her friend to go with her." He looked around for her bodyguard, but as he turned back, one of the young men leveled a small caliber semi-automatic handgun at him.

"We're leaving now," he said in a Middle Eastern accent.

"What the...." said Officer Owens as he jumped back and grabbed for his service weapon.

The young man calmly shot him twice in the head. The woman appeared shocked at the gunfire and froze temporarily until the man said something angrily to her in Arabic. The group turned and fled out the door with Ann's unconscious body in tow.

Agent Sills was in an aisle collecting books when she heard the two shots. Dropping the books, she dashed down the aisle just in time to see Officer Owens on the floor and a small group of people going out the door. Agent Sills glanced over to the table where Ann had been.

"Oh no, Ann."

Most of the students ducked under tables or ran towards other exits. Agent Sills ran towards the door and hurdled over a student who was hunkered on the floor. She withdrew her weapon from the waist pack she always wore.

"Secret Service, everyone you need to stay down," she yelled as she ran toward the door. "Call 911," she snapped at the librarian at the front desk who was peeking over the edge of the desk. Agent Sills sprinted out the west side doors of the library in time to see the three kidnappers carrying Ann down the sidewalk north toward a van parked on Pleasant Street.

"Secret Service, freeze," yelled Agent Sills towards the group. One of the young men looked back and could see that the agent would be able to overtake them before they got to the van. He said something to the other man in Arabic. The man released Ann and pulled a weapon from under his jacket while the other man continued carrying Ann toward the van. The kidnapper pointed his weapon at Agent Sills and fired.

Agent Sills stopped at the bottom of the steps and pointed her semi-automatic at them and returned fire. For a few seconds the air was filled with the sound of gun fire. The man was struck in the throat and went down immediately.

After hitting the man, Agent Sills suddenly felt a burning sensation in her upper chest. She felt weak and couldn't hold onto her weapon any longer. Her knees went weak, and she fell to the sidewalk.

From where she lay, she could see the words inscribed on the building at the entrance to the library, "Enter Here the Timeless Fellowship of the Human Spirit". Agent Sills heard the screeching of tires and then everything went black.

———

**The White House**

**1600 Pennsylvania Avenue Northwest**
**Washington D.C.**

THE PRESIDENT of the United States, William Campbell, sat in a Queen Ann chair by a large coffee table in the oval office, discussing trade relations with Vice President, George Dayton and the Secretary of State, Phil Jennings.

The Senator from Utah was two and a half years into his first term as President. He was fifty years old, but his salt and pepper hair and blue eyes made him look younger than he was. His presidency had been routine, handling homeland security, inflation, social security problems, and terrorism, but that was all about to change.

President Campbell's chief of staff, John Wohlman, stepped into the room quietly. He approached the President. "I'm sorry to interrupt Mr. President, but there has been an emergency."

"Go ahead, John," said the President.

Wohman hesitated a minute as President Campbell got up and walked over to his desk. He looked at Wohlman and frowned. "What is it?"

"Mr. President, it saddens me to inform you that your daughter, Ann, has been kidnapped."

President Campbell stopped, stunned. "What?"

Wohlman looked down at the papers in his hands. "I'm sorry, Mr. President. According to preliminary reports she was abducted from her campus library. Witnesses say two or three suspects were seen carrying her out of the library when gun fire erupted. A campus police officer was reported killed, and Agent Sills has been critically injured."

The President placed his hands on the desk and leaned over heavily as his knees felt weak. *Ann?* "Why were they carrying her? What did they do to her? Do we have any leads?"

Wohlman felt sick. He wasn't just the President's chief of staff but also a close friend. He had known Ann all her life. His hands trembled as he looked at the early report. "We have several FBI agents from the Denver office on the way now, sir. I can only guess she was rendered unconscious somehow. Agent Sills fatally wounded one of the suspects as they were escaping. His body is being held at the local morgue and will be transferred to Denver as soon as possible. No group has claimed responsibility yet. Everything is still preliminary, sir".

The President sat in his chair slowly and rested his head in his hands for several minutes. Dayton, Wohlman and Jennings stood quietly.

Wohlman finally spoke. "Mr. President, I've taken the liberty of calling the Directors of Homeland Security, FBI, CIA, and the Joint Chiefs of Staff for a meeting in an hour."

"Thank you, John," President Campbell said and looked up, his face pale. "Now, comes the hard part. I have to tell her mother."

———

**J Double T Ranch**
**Sutton County, Texas**

JAKE CONTINUED the constant work of a single rancher to build a life for himself. He tried to keep busy to distract himself from thinking about his strange visitor and Ellie. He wasn't sure how he felt about either one as both were a mystery to him.

He'd been hurt emotionally during a relationship as a young man, so he had no desire to start a new one and certainly not with a female pastor. But no matter how hard he tried, he couldn't forget the sound of Ellie's voice and the way she smiled. It gave him both a feeling of warmth and dread. *What did she expect from him? Was she just showing kindness and concern because of her job?*

Then there was the matter of his strange visitor. It was a puzzle Jake couldn't put together. Part of him wanted Malachy to never show again, but another part wanted to know for sure.

———

**Industrial Complex**
**1521 6ᵗʰ Ave**

## Denver, Colorado

ANN CAMPBELL OPENED her eyes to a dark room. Her head throbbed and her mouth felt dry, like a mouth full of cotton. She looked around in the dimly lit room. There was a small window with dirty panes ten feet up and was the only light filtering in. There was a chair and an old, used mattress. Her right wrist was handcuffed to a water pipe protruding from the wall. The place smelled of grease, oil, and gasoline. *What happened?* All she could recall was helping a young woman with her books then everything went black. *What about Beth? Where was she? Was she all right?* Her head hurt and the world seemed to spin when she tried to sit up. She lay back down and tried to ease her headache. She knew she had been kidnapped, but by whom and for what reason?

# CHAPTER SIX

**J Double T Ranch**
**Sutton County, Texas**

JAKE HAD FINISHED a long day moving his small herd around to ensure that they didn't overgraze the land. With cattle mysteriously missing or being eaten, he was trying to keep his investment safe.

After a shower and a quick meal, he settled down for a quiet evening before going to bed. His cell phone chirped, and he answered. It was Ellie. "Hi, Jake, I hope I haven't interrupted anything important?"

"Evening, Ellie. No, you haven't. Roscoe and I were just sitting on the porch enjoying the sunset."

"I bet it's beautiful."

"Why yes, it is. Maybe you could come out and see for yourself sometime...I mean when you get the time...if you're not too busy." Jake felt stupid. Ellie was the pastor of a church and had many more things to do than to come out and see a sunset.

"Is that an invitation?"

Jake blushed. *Why did this woman make me act different than I had with other women? Why did she make me talk like an ignorant baboon?*

"My door's always open...I mean you're always welcome to come and visit," Jake shook his head. *I'm doing it again.*

"I'd be glad to come for a visit," said Ellie. "But the reason I called is to check if you'd heard from your so-called heavenly visitor?"

Jake let out a heavy sigh. "Not yet. I'm beginning to wonder if I imagined the whole thing."

"You didn't imagine it, Jake. Sometimes we must be patient and see. Based on what your visitor told you about these demons, creatures, or monsters coming out of the dark so to speak, I asked Pam to do some checking for me. Don't worry, I didn't tell her why. I just asked her to see if there have been any unusual things in the news."

Jake was afraid to ask. "What did you find out?" he asked quietly.

Ellie took a deep breath. "Well, it's very interesting if that's the right word for it. Pam found some articles about some unusual occurrences that could be what we're looking for. One article was about two teenagers attacked in Florida and the boy is still missing. The girl said it was some sort of monster. The report said the teens had been drinking so her account is questionable. The news believes it to be a serial kidnapper or pedophile of some sort. Several other people have disappeared recently in that area."

Jake sat and listened as Ellie rustle some papers.

"Let's see," she continued. "On this report a disco dance club was attacked by an unknown group. It happened in the outskirts of Frankfurt, Germany. Several people were killed, and numerous people were injured. Some of the injured said the attackers were described as looking like monsters from some fantasy or science fiction movie. They said they had large teeth; some were winged and had glowing yellow eyes. The authorities dismiss the account as mass hysteria or an attack by the Bader-Meinhof gang in disguise."

"Sounds like the authorities have an answer for everything," commented Jake sarcastically.

"It seems so. This last one was in a Chicago bar. It was a fire with the patrons still inside. The front doors were chained and locked, believed to have been done by the arsonists before the fire was set. The fatality rate was horrible, but there were a couple of badly burned survivors. They said the arsonists were two men in disguise. They wore hoods, long coats, and masks. The patrons were all young executives, bankers, or laboratory techs, but the fire marshal and arson investigators have not ruled out some sort of gang activity."

Jake thought for a minute. All these incidents were so far apart and seemed unrelated. *Could it still be the work of some demonic force?* Ellie interrupted his thoughts.

"Have you heard the news about the President's daughter?"

"I heard it on the radio," answered Jake. "They didn't mention anything about monsters, just three Middle Eastern people believed to be the kidnappers."

"Do you think it could be these monsters doing?"

"I doubt it, but you can never tell. I don't know anything about monsters and demons."

"What do you think we should do?" asked Ellie. Her voice sounded weak, almost vulnerable.

Jake felt it too. "There's nothing we can do right now but wait. If this self-proclaimed angel shows back up, maybe he can shed some light on it, if he ever does show up."

"He will, I just know he will. Call me as soon as you find out something," said Ellie. "I have a feeling it will be soon."

Jake said he would and hung up. He sat and watched the remaining sunset fade away to darkness. He just wished he was as positive about it all as Ellie was.

———

**Twenty Miles West of Shady Oaks**
**Highway 8**
**Sutton County, Texas**

TWO CAMPERS SET up a tent next to Highway 8. Paul and Susan Whitton were hitchhiking across America. Life in Los Angeles was too expensive, and they'd decided to go east. They were well on their way to Tennessee where Susan had relatives just outside of Knoxville.

Paul had put up their small two-person tent while Susan fixed them a small meal of sandwiches and drinks. They sat and watched the sun set in the west. Soon they crawled into their sleeping bags and fell asleep.

Susan suddenly came awake. She didn't know what she heard that had awakened her, but she knew it was late at night. She nudged Paul. "Wake up, something's outside," she whispered.

Paul grunted and rolled over.

"Wake up. I'm telling you there's something out there," she whispered again.

Paul raised his head and listened. "I don't hear anything. Maybe you dreamed it."

They both came wide awake when they heard a high-pitched screech that pierced the tranquil night air.

"What was that?" she whispered.

"I don't know but stay in here. I'll go check."

Susan grabbed him by the arm. "No, stay here, maybe it'll go away."

"Don't be silly. It's some kind of animal. I'll throw a few rocks around and scare it off." Paul then unzipped the tent and climbed out while Susan pulled the edge of the sleeping bag up to her chin.

She heard Paul stomping around when another sound intruded. It sounded like something was shuffling around outside.

"Paul?"

She heard the shuffling sound again and Paul stomped around to the back of the tent.

"Whatever you are, you better high tail it," yelled Paul.

Susan heard a rock hit the ground where Paul had thrown it. She heard the shuffling sound from the other side of the tent. "Paul, it's on the other side of the tent." She listened as Paul stomped around to the other side of their small tent and stopped. There was a sound of shuffling.

"Get away from me," screamed Paul suddenly.

Susan's eyes widened in fright as she listened to the sound of a struggle. Paul screamed again and then everything went quiet. Susan stared at the door to the tent as she listened to what sounded like something being shredded. Her body refused to move but her eyes caught movement in front of the tent, and she came face to face with a set of yellow eyes. They moved closer and a tongue slithered into the tent. Her body began to shake and tremble as a huge head seemed to engulf the small opening to the tent accompanied by a large set of teeth. Susan's eyes refused to close when everything went black.

————

## J Double T Ranch
## Sutton County, Texas

JAKE LEFT the house early the next morning to work on the stock pond before it became too hot. After several hours of backbreaking work, he returned to cool off and fix himself something to eat before going to work on the corral next to the barn. Some of the railings were getting old and needed to be replaced. Jake was warming up some soup on the kitchen stove when he heard cloth moving and glanced over his shoulder to see Malachy standing by the kitchen table.

"Greetings from the Most High God," said Malachy with a smile.

Jake wasn't as shaken about seeing him as he was the first time. "Thanks, do you want some lunch?" It was the only thing he could think to say. *Way to go Taft. That sounded stupid. Angels don't eat.* He expected Malachy to decline but was surprised when he accepted so Jake poured two cups of coffee and set them down on the table. He also made two bowls of soup, sat, and motioned for Malachy to join him. Malachy's huge body dwarfed the kitchen chair as he sat down. They both sipped their hot brew. Out of the corner of his eye Jake watched the giant man while they both tasted their soup in silence.

Feeling awkward, Jake sought to break the silence. "I didn't know your kind...well I mean...I didn't know your type of... people...ate or drank?"

Malachy smiled. "We don't need food or drink to sustain us. We do enjoy eating and drinking as a show of hospitality. It also gives us a chance to enjoy the tastes and smells of creation. In your ancient times it was an insult not to accept or offer someone food and drink. Sitting at a meal with someone and breaking bread so to speak was very important."

"I'll try and remember that," said Jake. He put down his coffee cup and sat back in his chair. Jake had the chance to appraise the man once more. He was dressed in the same white clothes with the golden belt and huge sword. His skin was still the color of golden brass. The pupils of Malachy's eyes had the same flame flickering in the center and when he spoke tiny lightning flashes danced across the whites of his eyes.

"Soooo…why are you here again?" asked Jake.

Malachy had finished his soup and sat his coffee cup on the table. "I know my prior appearance was somewhat of a shock and puzzle to you. No one expects to have a visitor like me. You needed time to adjust and think about what was asked."

"But why me, I'm not the best or the greatest. I'm just an ex-G.I. trying to make a simple cowboy living for myself."

Malachy looked at Jake and smiled. "Jacob, throughout man's history God has chosen the most unlikely people. He chose a shepherd boy over his older brothers to be a king, and a man plowing a field became a prophet. A young boy sold into slavery in Egypt became second to a pharaoh and saved a nation. God chose a fisherman, a crooked tax collector, and even a Jew who hated Christians to do his work. He chose everyday people, not kings, rulers, or politicians.

"From the day you were born until now everything you've done has brought you to this point in time. You were wild and hard to live with at times."

"I was a little rambunctious, wasn't I?" Jake said with a chuckle and then his eyes widen. "Wait a minute. How do you know that?"

Malachy looked Jake in the eye. "I was there when you tried to ride that bull and broke your arm. I was there when you hit your first homerun."

"So, you're my guardian angel?" asked Jake.

Malachy shrugged and simply said, "I also was there the night of the senior prom."

Jake rolled his eyes. "I got stinkin' drunk that night."

"And you threw up in your father's car too," said Malachy with a frown.

"I was grounded for a month after that," said Jake.

They both chuckled.

Malachy then looked at him with a more somber gaze. "And I was also there the night before you left to go into the military. I was on the beach after your going away party."

Jake frowned at the mention of that.

Malachy continued, "You and the young lady, Diane, had made so many plans for the future, but she told you she didn't want to be the wife of a military man. She returned the diamond ring you gave her."

Jake felt his stomach turn. "Why bring that up?"

"When she left you walked the beach for hours. I walked along side. You finally threw the ring into the gulf," explained Malachy.

"Yeah, I remember."

Malachy reached out toward Jake with a closed hand. He opened his hand slowly, and in the palm was a diamond ring. Jake sat stunned.

"Take it," said Malachy with a smile.

Jake took the ring, turned it over and over in his hand. It sparkled as if he'd just purchased it. He looked up at Malachy. "How did you find it?"

Malachy continued to smile, reached over, and touched Jake on the shoulder. "I retrieved it for you. I thought that you might want it someday."

Jake nodded as he stared at the ring.

# CHAPTER SEVEN

**Airborne Somewhere
over the Mediterranean Sea**

GHAZI SAT in his comfortable chair in the luxurious cabin of his personal leer jet. He was flying toward the United States. In the storage compartment was the Ark of the Covenant in a crate marked "antiquities". Everything was going smoothly. His personal phone rang.

"Peace be upon you, Hassan," said the familiar voice of Azim.

"Peace be upon you and your family, Azim," answered Ghazi. "I hope you have great news for me?"

"All has gone according to plan. The operation in Colorado was successful and the American President's daughter is now in our hands."

Hassan broke into a broad smile. "Excellent news."

Azim knew that Ghazi did not tolerate failure and was reluctant to tell the complete details about the kidnapping. He hesitated a moment before continuing. "There was a small complication, however."

"What?" growled Ghazi.

"There was a policeman who tried to interfere, and they had to use force. The policeman was killed, and the secret service agent was critically wounded," explained Azim.

"I care not for their losses, just that the operation was a success."

"One of our beloveds was killed by the agent and had to be left behind," said Azim reluctantly.

"It is unfortunate that one of our own has been killed. I feel the loss," lied Ghazi. "We must ensure that he cannot be traced back to us. You must retrieve his body or if not, do what must be done. I trust you will make the arrangements, Azim. You have never let me down before."

The phone was silent for a few seconds before Azim answered. "All will be taken care of. Allah has blessed us so far. We cannot fail."

"Then make it happen." Ghazi hung up the phone. He sat for a few minutes contemplating what effect this error had in his plans. He surmised that ultimately it would not make a difference.

He walked to his private bar and poured himself a drink. Soon his plans will come together, the world would be under his control, and he could then do as he pleased.

―――――

**J Double T Ranch**
**Sutton County, Texas**

MALACHY GAVE Jake a few moments to gather his thoughts. He knew it was a lot for Jake to take in so quickly.

"Jacob, it's time," he said softly but firmly.

Jake looked up at Malachy and nodded. "What do we do now?"

Malachy smiled. "Nothing, it's been done. You've been given the ability to see demons and others when no one else can. Even when these creatures change their appearance to be humanlike you will be able to detect them, and that will give you an advantage. It will take some getting used to seeing these hellions everywhere all the time. You also have been given the ability to kill them, and whatever weapon you have at hand will kill any demon."

Jake nodded. "So where do I start?"

"Florida."

---

**Situation Room**

**The White House**

**1600 Pennsylvania Ave**

**Washington D.C.**

THE PRESIDENT SAT at the head of a huge oval table in the famed situation room where many life and death decisions had been made over the years. The 5,000 square foot White House situation and crisis room was actually more of a small complex with offices, a small kitchen, and room for thirty personnel who monitor world events twenty-four hours a day. The room was covered in wood panels that held numerous flat panel televisions.

After giving the disturbing news to the first lady, he'd waited with her until he was notified that all his advisors had arrived.

He felt he had aged ten years in the last few hours. His daughter was missing, presumed kidnapped, and he had no idea by whom or why. He looked around the room at his staff. "John, any news yet?" he asked his chief of staff.

Wohlman cleared his throat and spoke slowly. "Nothing yet from the kidnappers, Mr. President, and no one has claimed responsibility yet. We have a list of possible terrorists' groups that it could be."

The President nodded and looked over at his FBI director, Bill Chisom, "Anything from Colorado?"

Bill Chisom was a fifty-year old career FBI agent who had worked his way up from the bottom. He still wore a traditional crew cut and kept in good physical condition even though he was no longer a field agent. "Mr. President, our agents are on the scene. The body of the dead kidnapper is on a helicopter headed back to Denver for a full autopsy and ID."

"What about Agent Sills?"

"Agent Sills came out of surgery. She's listed in critical but stable condition. I have an agent standing by when she wakes. Several agents are working with the local police interviewing witnesses. The crime scene is currently being processed for evidence.

"As of right now we know two men and one woman took Miss Campbell out of the building and carried her to a van nearby. It was described briefly as a blue panel van, probably stolen."

"Thank you, Bill," said the President sadly. "Bob, do you have any idea who these people might be?"

Robert Heppell, the Director of the CIA, was in his late forties, short and rotund. He smoked too much, and his face had a pale sickly color of someone who needed exercise badly. "Mr. President," Heppell began. "I have put all our agents on high alert. I instructed them to start pushing their informants for information on which scum did this. I sent a request to our analysts to try to put together some sort of profile to help us identify the terrorists. I've got everyone available working on it."

"Thank you," said the President. He breathed heavily.

"I also spoke with the director of homeland security as she's currently in California," added Chisom. "We've put the nation at the highest level of security. All border agents and agencies have been notified and are on the look-out. All the airports and ports are being covered as much as we can. Sadly, we don't have enough officers to cover everywhere."

"How's the first lady?" asked Vice President Dayton.

The President looked around the room. "She's holding up as well as can be expected. I know each of you will do everything you can to bring Ann home. It's frustrating to sit and wait until we know something. I want this to be made perfectly clear. I want my daughter back alive. Any other means or conditions are unacceptable."

They all nodded. The meeting adjourned and each went their own way. The President and Wohlman remained.

"We'll find her, Mr. President," Wohlman said as confidently as he could.

"I want her back alive and well, or God help the souls of the terrorists if they don't," said the President with clinched fists.

# CHAPTER EIGHT

**Boulder Community Hospital**
**1100 Balsam**
**Boulder, Colorado**

FBI AGENT OSCAR RUIZ stood outside room 18 of the twenty-two room Intensive Care Unit. He arrived hours ago from Denver.

Oscar was a twenty-year veteran of the FBI and was looking forward to his retirement in a few years. He was short and a little stocky. His full head of hair had streaks of gray, but his mustache was still dark black. He shook his head. *The president's daughter kidnapped.* He was the senior agent on the scene.

The crime scene technicians had completed processing the library without any luck. There were thousands of fingerprints and too many eyewitnesses. The majority said they heard shooting and saw several people going out the door but were too busy running or hiding to be sure of anything. The campus security tapes were being examined.

The body was the only real evidence they had. The corpse was at the county morgue in Denver waiting for an autopsy and identification. Agent Ruiz was hoping that Agent Sills could give him something else to go on, but she was too heavily medicated earlier to talk when she came out of surgery. The doctors said she was lucky and should recover barring any major infection. Agent Ruiz nodded to the FBI agent guarding the door and glanced inside the room. He could see her in the bed hooked up to several monitors and I.V. bags.

The nurse attending to her looked up when he walked in. "Agent, you can see her, but just for a moment," she explained in a firm voice. "She's under heavy sedation, so she may not be able to give you much information, but don't take long. She needs rest."

"I understand. I'll just be a moment." Agent Ruiz quietly stepped over to the bed. Agent Sills looked very pale. "Agent Sills?" he said quietly. Agent Sills' eyes blinked open and slowly looked over at him glassy eyed.

"Agent Sills, I'm Special Agent Ruiz from the FBI in Denver. Do you remember me?"

Sills looked at him for a minute before she recognized him. She'd met him at a terrorist seminar in Denver a year ago. She smiled a weak smile. "Oscar," she answered in slurred speech.

"Yes, you remember. That's good. The doctors say you're going to be fine. You need rest. I'm here to find out about Miss Campbell."

Agent Sills' eyes widened. "Ann," she said, and her heart-rate monitor began to accelerate.

Agent Ruiz put his hand on her shoulder to calm her. "You need to rest. I'll find her for you. I need to know what happened."

Agent Sills relaxed. She lay still for a moment or two trying to remember through the fog of medication. "Getting books and I heard shots…Three people… I went out after them…shots… shot one," she explained.

"Yes, you did, Beth. You just rest now. I'll talk to you later when you've rested more," he said soothingly.

"My fault…wasn't there," said Agent Sills. A tear ran down her cheek. "Failed."

Agent Ruiz patted her arm. "No, you didn't," he said. "You did everything you could to save her. You rest now. I've got work to do. I'll check on you later." Agent Ruiz slipped out into the hallway, glanced back through the window, and she was already asleep.

**Office of the Medical Examiner**
**660 Bannock Street**
**Denver, Colorado**

ONE OF THE employees was busy examining a body that had recently been brought to them from Boulder. Normally they didn't conduct other counties' autopsies but apparently this one was special. His first clue was the FBI agent stationed outside the door to the exam room.

The body had been fingerprinted, washed, and he'd just finished photographing it with 35mm film which is a sharper and clearer print than digital. The examiner put down the camera and took an overview of the body. The obvious cause of death was a single gunshot wound to the throat. He was of possible Middle Eastern descent and appeared to be in his early twenties. Before beginning the gruesome task of preparing the corpse for the subsequent autopsy investigation, he decided to walk down to the break room and get a soda. He told the FBI agent at the door that he'd be right back and walked to the end of the hall to the break room. The examiner picked out which soda he wanted and put coins in the machine then decided to get a quick candy bar too. He'd long ago lost any queasiness about eating around dead bodies.

He strolled back down the hall and noticed the FBI agent was not sitting outside. The chair was empty. *Maybe he needed a smoke break*, thought the examiner. He pushed open the door to the exam room, but the door jammed halfway. He looked down and saw blood seeping under the door.

*What the...*

He looked around the door to see what was blocking the door and on the floor was the body of the FBI agent. An ice pick protruded from the base of his skull and his throat had been cut. The camera lay on the floor next to the agent's body with the film cartridge cover open. The examiner looked up at the exam table... the corpse was gone.

**Industrial Complex**
**1521 6<sup>th</sup> Ave**
**Denver, Colorado**

ANN WAS AWAKENED by a noise from outside. It sounded like an overhead door being raised. Still handcuffed to a drainpipe, she lay on the mattress and listened. She could hear muted voices coming from the other side of the door. She was able to hear snippets of the conversation. Most of it was in English, but some was in another language.

"Did you...the body?" asked a female voice.

"Yes," answered a male.

"Did you...documents?" she asked.

"Yes...exposed...removed the body," said the male.

*A body? Whose body? Beth's?* thought Ann

———

**Interstate 25**
**Denver, Colorado**

LATER THAT NIGHT Agent Ruiz drove back from Boulder when his cell phone rang, it was Agent Kimbell.

"Oscar, we have a problem," said Agent Kimbell. He sounded stressed.

"What?"

"There was an incident at the medical examiner's office," he explained. "Someone entered and removed the corpse brought in from Boulder. Some of the evidence collected was ruined also."

"What?" Agent Ruiz yelled. "Where was Owens? He was stationed outside until we got the county guys to relieve him."

There was silence on the other end.

"I'm sorry, Oscar, but Owens is dead."

Agent Ruiz's knuckles turned white as he gripped the steering wheel harder. "Get the crime scene people over there now and see if they can get something. Keep me updated. I'll call Washington."

"Acknowledged, and Oscar, sorry about Owens."

"Yeah, me too."

*How do I tell Washington someone snatched the main lead in this kidnapping right out from under our noses and lost a valuable agent too? What else could go wrong?*

———

**Industrial Complex**
**1521 6th Ave**
**Denver, Colorado**

ANN COULD TELL it was getting dark as the light from the dim window darkened. She heard the occasional sounds of Arabic and English conversation and movement when suddenly she heard the door latch being thrown back. The door opened, and a female stepped into the room. Ann looked up at the woman and recognized her as the student she had spoken to right before everything went dark.

"How are you feeling?" asked the young Middle Eastern woman.

"Like you care," answered Ann sarcastically. "The accommodations stink."

The woman made a slight smile. "I'm glad you've kept your sense of humor. I have brought you something to eat." The woman turned to a man standing just out of view and retrieved a tray with two sandwiches and a soda can. She set it down on the floor next to the mattress. Ann thought about picking it up and throwing it at them, but she remembered that Beth had told her always to eat to keep strong. Denying oneself nourishment makes a weak victim and lessens the chances for escape. Ann picked up the prepackaged sandwich, opened it, and began eating. The woman smiled and turned to leave.

"Why are you doing this?" asked Ann.

The woman turned and looked down at Ann. "I'm sorry that

you've been brought into this, but you're a valuable pawn in a very big game. Follow our instructions, and you will not be harmed."

Ann frowned but kept eating her sandwich. "You know my father will never give into your demands."

The young woman raised an eyebrow and looked Ann up and down. "We will see. We will see." She walked out, closed the door, and bolted it.

# CHAPTER NINE

**J Double T Ranch**
**Sutton County, Texas**

AT SUNUP JAKE drove out to check on his stock. It didn't appear that he was losing a large number of stock, but he did notice one or two missing. He hadn't found any more carcasses. He decided to call Ellie. It was late when Malachy left last night, and he didn't want to wake her.

He drove back to the ranch house and as he approached, he noticed someone sitting in one of the rocking chairs. He didn't see a vehicle and wondered why someone would walk all the way up to his ranch. He parked the truck in front of the house and parked. He looked through the windshield at the man who just sat in the rocking chair and waited. Jake climbed out of the truck but stood next to it with the door open so he could reach his shotgun which he kept in the truck.

"Howdy, can I help you?"

The man didn't say anything and just rocked in the chair. He was an older man with a bushy mustache and lambchop sideburns. His clothes were out of style about a hundred years ago. He wore a broad cloth shirt, brown pants stuffed down inside old worn-out boots. Something about him seemed out of place but yet like he belonged.

Roscoe climbed out of the truck and trotted over to man, sat, and wagged his tail. He didn't appear armed with a weapon and Roscoe didn't seem concerned, so Jake stepped up on the porch.

"Is there something I can do for you?" asked Jake.

The man smiled. "No boy, I don't need anything. I'm just enjoying the view on my front porch."

*Your front porch* thought Jake. "This is my ranch," explained Jake.

The man chuckled. "It is now, but I built this ranch sonny boy."

"Who are you?" asked Jake.

"My name is Ned Parker."

Jake raised an eyebrow. "I bought the ranch after a Jonathon Parker died."

Ned Parker nodded. "Yep, he was one of my descendants."

It then dawned on Jake what he was seeing. "You're a ghost?"

Parker laughed again. "After your little pow pow with your angel friend, Malachy, I wondered how long it would be before you would see me."

Jake was surprised at the mention of the big angel's name. "You saw Malachy?"

"Of course I did. I watched him take that shotgun away from you in the barn the other night. The look on your face was priceless," said Parker. He laughed again and slapped his knee.

Malachy said he'd be able to see things beyond the norm, so Jake looked carefully at Parker and realized that even though he was solid there was a slight transparency to him. "How long have you been here?"

"Why all the life and since then so I've watched my son and his sons live here. I was concerned when the ranch was sold but you've done a fine job son, a fine job."

Jake took off his hat and scratched his head. "So why are you here and not up there…in heaven or somewhere else?"

"I love it here," replied Ned. "This is my home. When I get tired of being here, I'll make the next step but for now you have me here to look after you and that pretty preacher gal that came around the other day."

At the mention of her name, he remembered that he'd planned to call her. He didn't carry his cell phone with him when he was out on the range even though he knew he should in case something happened, and he needed to call for help. Jake was old fashion in that aspect. He didn't have a computer, fax, or television and only used the cell phone as needed. Jake stepped inside and retrieved his cell phone then dialed the number to Ellie's church. He wasn't sure how to explain it, but he wanted to hear her voice again. He realized that he missed the sound of it. The phone rang a couple of times before someone picked up.

"Good morning, Shady Oaks Community Church," said a female voice.

Jake remembered the bubbly part-time secretary from his last visit. "This is Jake Taft. Is Ellie there?"

"Hi, Mr. Taft, I'm sorry but Pastor Thompson and Mr. Tillon went to Pecos. They found a used piano there to use for our church services. They should be back tonight though. Can I leave her a message?'

Jake was obviously disappointed. He really wanted to talk to her. He told Janet that he would call back and hung up. Feeling somewhat let down, he leaned on one of the fence rails and looked across the beautiful view of west Texas. *Where was all this taking me? All I ever wanted was to work this ranch and live in peace, but obviously things have changed.* Ellie had mentioned something about attacks in Florida when Malachy told him to start there. Jake thought about the giant's calm, patient, peaceful demeanor. He was both amazing and a puzzle. *If they knew all this, why don't they stop it themselves?* Jake liked plans, time schedules, and goals completed. He wanted everything quickly, concisely and to the point, but he was quickly learning that doesn't always work. *It would be nice if Malachy had a cell phone so I could just call him.* Jake chuckled out loud, getting a huff from Roscoe who had been sleeping on the front porch. *Wait a minute. Cell phone! Ellie has a cell phone.* Jake walked inside to his desk where he found the church card that she'd given him, and on the back was her cell phone number. He dialed the number and after a few rings, she answered.

"Ellie here," she said in her normal cheerful voice.

It was music to his ears. "Ellie, this is Jake."

"Jake, I'm so glad to hear from you. How are you? I've missed you...I mean...I've missed not hearing from you. Did you get a visit from you know who?"

Jake could tell that she was not alone, probably with Mr. Tillon. "Is Mr. Tillon there with you?" he asked.

"Why yes, Mr. Tillon says hello," replied Ellie. "We're in Pecos picking up a piano. We can have more music now. Is there something you need to tell me?"

Jake thought for a moment. *What should he tell her? Should I tell her everything?* "Ellie, I had a visit from Malachy again. You're not going to believe this, but he convinced me to look into some recent demonic activity."

The line went quiet for a few seconds, and then Ellie whispered, "Demonic activity?"

"Yes, but I'll have to explain it in person," replied Jake.

"We'll be back tomorrow. We're staying the night here in Pecos. I really want to see you...I mean talk to you in person about it. I'll call you as soon as I get back in town."

"All right, call me as soon as you get back. I really need to see you...I want to talk to you...you know...about this." *I'm babbling again.*

"I promise I'll call you as soon as I get in," she said and hung up.

Jake sat back in the rocking chair and stared out at the sky. *Where was all this leading?*

————

**FBI Office**
**8000 East 36th Avenue**
**Denver, Colorado**

AGENT RUIZ ARRIVED EARLY to his office to read over some of the preliminary reports on the abduction. He'd made his call to the deputy director in Washington about the incident at the medical examiner's office, and obviously he was not happy about the turn of events. The deputy director would take care of the details of the Owens' family notifications and brief the director.

Jim Kimbell came into the office. He was an ex-marine who'd been assigned to the Denver office for five years. "Morning, Oscar."

Agent Ruiz grunted at him as he drank his coffee. Agent Kimbell sat in a chair next to the desk and began going through some of his notes. Agent Ruiz looked up from his papers. "It says here that they were able to get a partial latent print off the door plate at the morgue?"

Agent Kimbell nodded and passed over a sheet of paper containing a preliminary crime scene report. "Yep, we got lucky on that account. We also got lucky in the fact that they failed to get the fingerprint card of the suspect. The examiner had slipped it into his lab coat before he went to get a snack. We're running the prints through IAFIS. Did we get any luck on the van?"

Agent Ruiz shook his head. "No. Boulder PD found the vehicle abandoned in a parking lot three miles away. It had been reported stolen the day before. The van had been wiped clean so it's a dead end. I do have the tape from the security camera from the library."

He picked up a remote and turned on a television sitting on a stand in the corner. He pushed the start button and they both watched the tape as the incident unfolded in ten second intervals as the recorder rotated between the different cameras.

"Most of it can't help us," explained Agent Ruiz. "I've been over it, dozens of times. There are a few side angle shots of the kidnappers but nothing we can get a positive ID on. Let's just hope we get something back on the prints."

---

**Industrial Complex**
**1521 6th Ave**

## Denver, Colorado

ANN HAD SLEPT FITFULLY. It was chilly and damp. She'd shivered most of the night and being handcuffed to a drainpipe made it hard for her to turn over or get comfortable. She had been lying awake for a while thinking of a possible way of escape when she heard footsteps approach. The door latch was thrown back and the same young woman came in. She looked down at Ann and noticed she was shivering. "He didn't give you a blanket?" she asked.

Ann waved her arm around. "I'm sorry, but I couldn't get room service last night."

The woman frowned, turned, and said something in Arabic to someone out of view. A moment later she was given a wool blanket which she passed to Ann. Without saying anything, Ann wrapped the blanket around herself.

The woman stared at her for a moment. "We'll be moving to a new location soon. It'll be more comfortable where you're going."

Ann looked up at the strange kidnapper. "Why are you doing this? What do you hope to gain from all of this?"

The young woman leaned against the doorframe. "What I do is not for myself, but for my cause. We hope to save the world from itself."

"By kidnapping me?"

"As I said before, you're just a pawn, a means to an end."

"And what is that end?"

"To change the world."

Ann sadly shook her head. She knew then she was dealing with a group of fanatical kidnappers and not money-hungry opportunists, but despite herself she was curious about this young woman. "What's your name?"

The young woman hesitated and then shrugged. "My name is Amira. There is much to get ready. We'll be leaving soon. If you cooperate, there will be no reason to drug you, but if you resist, we will." With that Amira closed the door and threw the door bolt.

Ann wrapped her blanket around her tighter and thought about one thing…escape.

---

**FBI Office**
**8000 East 36th Avenue**
**Denver, Colorado**

AGENT RUIZ RETURNED from lunch to find nothing new on the dead kidnapper. He sat at his desk and went back over the reports, printouts, and photos hoping to see something that he missed. He desperately needed a break.

Like an answer to a prayer his office door flew open and in came Agent Kimbell with a computer printout. He was grinning from ear to ear as he handed the computer print out to him. "IAFIS came through for us. The guy's name was Abdul-Samad Tariq. He's on a student visa."

Ruiz looked over the sheet. He noticed the kidnapper had an address in an apartment complex and a work address in an industrial complex over 6th Ave. "Let's get Denver P.D. over to his apartment and see if we can get luckier. We'll go check his last known work address."

---

**Industrial Complex**
**1521 6th Ave**
**Denver, Colorado**

THE DOOR BOLT was thrown back and Amira entered Ann's cell. "It's time for us to go."

Ann nodded and got to her feet. The man unlocked her handcuff and she followed Amira out of the room into what appeared to be a warehouse of some sort. A four-door sedan was waiting for them in the empty warehouse. Ann and Amira walked toward the car when Ann appeared to trip on the hem of the blanket. Amira grabbed the blanket to catch her, but Ann released the blanket and sprinted away.

"Stop her," yelled Amira.

The man reached into his waist band, removed a gun, and pointed it at Ann.

"No, don't shoot her," she yelled in Arabic. "Ghazi wants her alive. Catch her."

The man grunted in frustration and sprinted after the fleeing hostage.

Ann ran faster than she thought she could. She saw a door she hoped led to the outside. She ran straight to the door and shoved.

Locked!

She glanced over her shoulder to see the man running toward her. She turned and ran down the length of the warehouse desperately looking for a way out. She came to another door and found it unlocked. She threw it open, slammed the door and locked it. She found herself in an inner office.

She searched frantically for a phone, but the office held only desks and chairs. She saw a small window on the far wall. The man began banging on the door. Ann grabbed a chair and smashed out the window. She climbed upon a desk to reach the window when the man kicked the door open.

Agents Ruiz and Kimbell drove toward the industrial complex when Ruiz's cell phone chirped. He answered, listened for a few minutes, and then hung up.

"The apartment was empty."

Ruiz pushed on the accelerator, pushing the government vehicle far past the speed limit. In a matter of minutes, they pulled into the industrial complex.

"I hate these complexes. It's like a maze," commented Agent Kimbell. They began looking for the right warehouse.

Ann pushed her head and shoulders through the window when the man grabbed her ankle and jerked her back inside. He pulled her down onto the desk. She kicked out with her free foot and struck the man in the face. He grunted and fell back. She twisted and tried to lunge back through the window, but Amira grabbed her by the back of the shirt and pulled her back down. Ann shoved Amira away, but the man struck Ann in the left side of the face. She was stunned from the blow and blood ran down the side of her face from a cut over her eye. He pulled her to the floor and held her down while Amira bent down with a syringe in her hand.

"I told you to cooperate or else." Amira jabbed the needle into Ann's arm.

Ann opened her mouth to scream but wasn't sure if any sound came out before the world went black again.

The two FBI agents pulled up in front of the warehouse listed as the kidnapper's last employment. They checked the front door but found it locked.

The two kidnappers lowered Ann's unconscious body into the backseat of the sedan and closed the door. The man opened the warehouse's rear overhead door.

Agents Ruiz and Kimbell walked around the exterior of the warehouse, checking doors. They worked their way around to the back and found an open rear overhead door. Looking at each other, they drew their weapons. They stepped cautiously around the corner and investigated the warehouse…. empty.

A block away the kidnappers sat at a traffic light.

---

**Washington Dulles International Airport**
**45020 Aviation Drive**
**Sterling, VA**

THE SLEEK PRIVATE jet touched down and taxied to a private hangar located on the airport property. After the engine's shutdown, the pilot exited the jet and was met by a U.S. Customs agent.

The agent was doing his routine job of checking flight manifests and passports. He'd checked the papers and documents of Mr. Ghazi and his people many times before. This day was no different. The agent noticed Ghazi exiting and went directly to a waiting limo.

"I see Mr. Ghazi came on this trip," said the customs agent offhand.

The pilot nodded. "Yes, he has some business to take care of in Washington."

"What's his business in Washington?"

"Mr. Ghazi is delivering an antiquity to the Smithsonian for an Egyptian exhibit."

The agent noticed several men downloading a large wooden box from the plane. It had FRAGILE ANTIQUITY printed on the side. He checked his manifest.

"Enjoy your stay in the U.S.," said the agent.

"Thank you, he will," answered the pilot.

------

**Industrial Complex**
**1521 6<sup>th</sup> Ave**
**Denver, Colorado**

IT WAS GETTING LATE, and the crime scene specialists finished up processing the warehouse area. They'd located the room with the mattress where Ann had been kept. They also found the broken window and the kicked-in door but weren't sure what to make of it.

Ruiz stood next to the head crime scene supervisor, "Anything useful, Jack?"

The senior crime scene technician, Jack Randall, at fifty-eight years old resembled an old hound dog. "We took some prints from the room with the mattress, the room with the broken window, and the over-head door. We found several blonde hairs on the mattress that we believe belong to Miss Campbell. I'll get them processed as soon as possible. Not to pour salt in a wound, Oscar, but from the looks of things you just missed them."

"Yeah, I know," Agent Ruiz said sourly. "I contacted Denver P.D. and they're sending out a broadcast. The only problem is we don't know what type of vehicle they were driving. It could be anything from a van to a Volkswagen bug."

Randall nodded and walked off to check on one of specialists.

Agent Kimbell drove up and Agent Ruiz climbed in. They drove back towards the area office in silence. They both knew Ann had slipped through their fingers.

# CHAPTER TEN

**Shady Oak Community Church**
**2203 E. Hollis Street**
**Shady Oak, Texas**

ELLIE AND MR. TILLON returned from Pecos with the used piano. After the long drive back, she was ready for a bath and a good night's sleep.

Pam, along with some of the men of the church arrived to help unload it and get it into the church's 1,000 square foot metal storage building. They stored holiday decorations, extra chairs and tables, paint cans, lawnmower, and boxes of miscellaneous items in the large storage building. It had a pull-down overhead door on one side and a regular door on the other. They manhandled the piano off the truck and rolled it through the large open overhead door into the storage building. It was placed in a corner of the building temporarily until it could be tuned and cleaned up.

Mr. Tillon and the other men said goodnight, pulled the overhead door down, and left while Pam stayed behind to help clean up the piano. Ellie locked the overhead door from the inside. They'd bought the piano at an estate sale where the piano had been sitting in a spare room for several years collecting dust and cobwebs.

They were not alone, however, because in the darkness a block away several figures were watching the building with glowing yellow eyes.

———

**J Double T Ranch**
**Sutton County, Texas**

JAKE FINISHED a long day's work. It felt good to be out working the cattle. He felt that someday the ranch would be a nice place to bring someone, maybe even someone like Ellie. He'd not heard from her yet but she was the pastor of a church after all and had many other responsibilities so she may not have time to call. Jake wished she would.

Later Jake was fixing himself a late snack when he heard Roscoe growl. He turned and saw Roscoe looking out through the screen door. Jake suddenly felt a cold chill as if someone had grabbed him with a cold hand. He walked over to the door and touched Roscoe's head. "What is it?" he asked as if he expected Roscoe to answer.

The big wolf growled deep inside his chest. Jake picked up his rifle, which he kept by the door, and stepped out on the porch.

He looked around but didn't see anything, but he could smell it. It was the distinct odor of ash and sulfur. Something was out there.

He heard his horse, Buck, neigh loudly so he walked over to the corral, reached over the fence, and stroked Buck. "Easy boy, I feel it too."

———

**Shady Oak Community Church**
**2203 E. Hollis Street**
**Shady Oak, Texas**

THE TWO CREATURES slipped quietly toward the church's storage building. Their master was with them tonight. After they'd tasted the chicken raiser's human flesh, they'd become bored with animal meat and craved more. As they crept closer, a startled cat yowled and fled.

Inside the storage building, Pam and Ellie were dusting off the piano. Pam had managed to get a face full of dust when she opened the lid to the piano, resulting in laughter from both women. Ellie heard the cat. "What was that?"

"Sounded like a cat to me," replied Pam. "Maybe a coyote came in too close looking for an easy meal?"

"Maybe it's the mysterious blood sucking goat monster of the desert looking for a victim," said Ellie in a pretend deep voice which brought more giggles from them.

The creatures approached the large overheard door. Their leader pulled on the door, but it didn't pull up. Both women turned at the sound. *Now who would be here this time of night,* thought Ellie? "Hello? Can we help you?"

No one answered, and then they heard scratching and sniffing. They moved along the side of the building sniffing and scratching. Ellie walked quietly over to the regular door and turned the thumb lock on the doorknob to lock it. She walked back over to where Pam stood beside the piano.

The doorknob rattled and their leader tilted back his head and laughed a horrid, shrieking laugh. Pam and Ellie froze at the sound. Whatever was outside didn't sound human.

"What's that smell?" asked Ellie.

"I'm not sure. It smells like rotten eggs, and ashes."

The creatures began clawing at the door, tearing chunks of wood out of the door. Pam picked up her cell phone and dialed 911.

The county sheriff's dispatcher answered. "911, what is your emergency?"

"Sarah, this is Pam from over in Shady Oak. We're inside our storage building next to our church and someone's trying to break in. We need a deputy."

"I'm sorry Pam, the only deputy on duty is Eddie Cole, and he's on the other side of the county talking to the Sims brothers again about some sort of UFOs. It'll take at least thirty minutes for him to get to you. Do you know who it is?"

"No, they wouldn't say and now they're trying to tear the door down," replied Pam.

"Are you locked in and safe?" asked Sarah.

Pam gave the phone a look of frustration. "Yes, for now, but they're ripping the door down." She hung up.

"Is any help coming?" asked Ellie.

The scratching was louder now.

"No, the cavalry is not available."

"Call Mr. Tillon."

Pam dialed, quickly told Mr. Tillon the situation, and hung up. "He's on his way."

Ellie pulled her cell phone from her pocket and dialed Jake's number.

---

**J Double T Ranch**
**Sutton County, Texas**

ROSCOE CONTINUED to growl but they couldn't locate the disturbing source. Jake carefully looked around, carefully examining every shadow for signs of an unwanted guest but still couldn't see anything. He closed his eyes, concentrated, and listened for every noise. He heard Roscoe growl, and then Buck snort and stomp. Jake tried to listen for something out of the ordinary besides the crickets chirping and a few birds rustling in a nearby tree. He sensed something else, so he tried to ignore the other sounds and concentrate on the other. It was quiet but heavy and had the sound of something moving. He sensed it was near the truck, and he smelled decaying flesh, ash, and sulfur. Jake opened his eyes and looked slowly toward the truck. He saw a dark spot that didn't seem to fit with the rest of the landscape. Jake always kept a round in the chamber of his rifle and cocked the hammer back. The sound was loud in the silence, the crickets stopped chirping, and the birds flew off. Jake watched the dark shape as it moved slowly, and a set of eyes turned their direction, a set of yellow eyes.

"Look out boy," yelled Ned.

The creature leapt out of the shadows onto the hood of the truck, caving in the hood. It had the appearance of a huge lizard the size of a small bull. It opened its snout and gave a screech that chilled Jake to the bone.

The creature leapt toward Jake who instantly raised his rifle and fired. The creature was struck in midair and fell to the ground. Jake and Ned walked over to where the animal had fallen but as they approached the thing tried to get up, so Jake carefully aimed and shot it through the head. He nudged it with his boot while Roscoe sniffed and growled. It was dead but before he could get a good look at it the thing started to decompose rapidly. Instinctively Jake knew it was some type of demonic being…and he'd killed it. Malachy said he would be given the ability to kill demonic creatures. *Perhaps this could be the answer to where the cattle had been going?*

"You ever seen anything like this, asked Jake. Ned shook his head. Jake's phone rang. *Ellie must be back from Pecos. I'll bet she's never seen anything like this,* thought Jake as he walked into the house.

————

**Shady Oak Community Church**
**2203 E. Hollis Street**
**Shady Oak, Texas**

PAM AND ELLIE stood in the corner by the piano as pieces of the door began to peel away. Jake's phone rang twice more before he finally picked up.

"Jake, Jake…help us," screamed Ellie into the phone.

"Ellie, what's wrong? What's going on there?"

"We're at the church's storage building. Something's breaking in. Hurry."

————

**J Double T Ranch**
**Sutton County, Tx**

THE PHONE SUDDENLY WENT DEAD. He dashed over to his truck with Roscoe on his heels. Jake started the truck, slammed it into drive, and peeled out toward town. His headlights passed over the decomposing lizard-like creature lying dead in the yard. He hoped he wouldn't be too late.

# CHAPTER ELEVEN

**Shady Oak Community Church**
**2203 E. Hollis Street**
**Shady Oak, Texas**

WITH ONE FINAL SWIPE, the doors collapsed, giving the two women a view of their attackers. Ellie had just called Jake and screamed for help but the shock and horror of seeing the creatures for the first time caused Ellie to drop her phone.

Two of the heathen creatures appeared to be huge 150 lbs. gray and brown lizards, but the third one in the middle stood on two legs. The feet and lower torso were lizard-like with a short tail, but the upper torso was human. The head and face looked part-human part-reptile except its jaw was too big and held jagged teeth. A belt around its waist held a large black sword.

"We have help coming, so stay back," yelled Pam defiantly.

The creature stared at them for a moment and a thin tongue flicked out of its mouth. "It will do you no good," said the creature. Its deep, scratchy voice seemed to come from hell itself. "It will be too late…for you."

The two lizard demons slowly crept closer. They slithered more than walked across the large room, knocking folding chairs and boxes aside with their tails. The creature's long tongues slithered out of their mouths and around their sharp teeth.

Pam inched around to the side of the piano, trying to put something between her and the creatures. One of the creatures moved closer for a better angle but Pam had worked her way behind the piano and reached out for Ellie just in time. The creature lunged for her, but Pam jerked Ellie back and down behind the piano. The creature slammed into the piano pushing it farther against the wall, with Pam and Ellie sandwiched behind it.

*Boom.*

A gunshot rang out. The sound startled both and they peeked from behind the piano to see Mr. Tillon standing just inside, armed with a pump shotgun. He'd fired a round at the demon and caused the side of its head to be torn to shreds by the shotgun's pellets. The blast knocked the creature around and it stared at Mr. Tillon with one eye hanging out of socket.

"Get out," yelled Mr. Tillon.

What happened next horrified and shocked them. The skin, muscles, and tendons on the demon moved and the wounds on the demon closed. In a matter of seconds, the monster was completely healed. The lizard-humanoid demon pointed at Mr. Tillon. "Kill him first."

The healed demon crept toward him with teeth bared and tongue slithering out, testing the air.

*Boom!*

Mr. Tillon fired again. Chunks of scale and flesh were blown off by the shotgun pellets, but it seemed unaffected as the wounds healed up almost instantly as it continued towards him.

*Boom! Boom!*

While Mr. Tillon fired at the beast, the other one attacked the piano. It clawed viciously at the old wooden music maker, ripping pieces of wood into the air.

*Boom!*

Mr. Tillon backed up, stood at the door's threshold, and fired his last round of buckshot. The monster at the piano clawed away the front panel covering the piano strings. When it jerked the large piece of wood loose, all the piano strings broke loose sending a cloud of dust and cobwebs into the air blocking its view for a moment. The creature became entangled in the piano strings. Mr. Tillon raised his empty shotgun like a club as the creature leapt at him, knocking him backward through the open door. The creature's momentum carried it through the door also, and they disappeared outside.

Once the air cleared the other monster wiggled free of the piano wires and renewed its attack on the piano, knowing it was about to feast on human flesh again. The last piece of wood came free of the top half of the old piano, and it looked down into the eyes of its two female victims hunkered down behind what was left of the piano. Nothing stood between them and those razor-sharp teeth. It was not going to be denied a meal.

Pam picked up one of the broken piano bench legs and held it like a club. "Grab a stick."

Ellie picked up a long piece of the broken piano to use in defense, even though they both knew it was useless. They were going to be its meal and there was nothing they could do.

The huge thing stared at them with its yellow eyes, shifted its weight, crouched down, and swiped at them with one large clawed arm. Both women swung their clubs in a feeble attempt to ward off the attack.

*Boom!*

The horrid creature was struck in the side and fell down against the piano. The demon was shaken by the blast and looked back at a gaping wound in its side. It was even more shocked when it didn't heal immediately. That had never happened until now.

Pam, Ellie, and the lizard humanoid demon turned to see a man standing in the doorway with a rifle. He was tall, wearing a Stetson, an old western work shirt, jeans, and worn-down cowboy boots.

"Am I late for the party?" asked Jake as he racked the lever of the rifle loading another bullet into the rifle's chamber.

The injured lizard beast tried to gather itself up from the ground. Jake aimed for the dying demon when out of the corner of his eye he saw the human-lizard like demon.

"Nooooo," screeched the devil as it leapt at Jake.

Jake spun around to fire at the thing, but it knocked the rifle out of Jake's hand and slid across the room. The monster's momentum forced both into the chairs and boxes. The two women saw them struggling and slowly came out from behind the piano. They stared at the large lizard thing, and it stared back at them in obvious confusion for a second before its eyes became still.

Jake kicked the monster backwards causing the repulsive thing to stumble backwards across the floor and fell into a pile of folding chairs. It leapt to its feet and looked around quickly to see the two women armed with their wooden clubs standing near the dead demon.

Jake climbed to his feet, bruised, cut in several places, but alive.

The creature pulled its black sword from its sheath and start towards Jake.

"You will die for this," it hissed.

Jake glanced across the room at the rifle lying on the concrete floor, but it was too far to reach. The monster would be on him in a second if he tried to get it. The demon stepped forward and swung the large sword at Jake thinking it was an easy victory, but Jake ducked and dodged out of the way. Jake knew he couldn't keep away from this thing forever and needed to end it quickly.

"You're good," it commented. "But I've been killing humans since the beginning of time." It leapt forward and swung the black sword in a deadly downward arch. Jake stepped forward, braced himself, and grabbed the monster's wrists as the sword came down. The blade stopped above Jake's head. They stood locked together, face to face.

"You can't win," it snarled.

Jake could smell its foul, sulfur-like breath. "Watch me." Jake head-butted the creature in the face causing it to stumble back. In that split second, Jake threw himself across the floor and grabbed the rifle. He spun around, aimed, and pulled the trigger. He heard a sickening click. The rifle jammed.

The creature stalked over to Jake and with a grin, raised his sword. A blur flashed across his vision as something attached itself to the creature's arm. It staggered back, stared down, and saw a dog attached to its forearm.

Roscoe.

The monster swung around with the hilt of the sword and struck Roscoe on the skull. Roscoe released his bite and fell limp onto the floor.

The momentary distraction gave Jake time to clear the jam from the rifle. The monster stepped forward and raised his sword again. "This will end now," it screeched.

Bent down on one knee, Jake fired from the hip and bullet struck the creature in the chest. It grunted, dropped the black sword, and stepped back in shock. It stared at the wound in awe as it didn't heal up as it should, so it put its clawed hand over the wound and looked at Jake as if to ask why or how.

Jake levered another round into the rifle and fired into the creature. The abomination's eyes widened in shock, and it gurgled up froth through its mouth.

Jake dropped his rifle and picked up the creature's sword, thrust it forward, and pierced the creature's torso completely through the middle. "That's for trying to hurt Ellie," said Jake. He jerked the sword out, and the creature fell to its knees. Jake pivoted and swung the sword down in an arch, severing the creature's head and shoulder from the rest of its body. The creature collapsed dead on the floor. "And that's for hurting my dog."

Jake tossed the sword aside in disgust and knelt next to Roscoe. The dog lay quiet and still on the floor. Jake stroked his fur and felt for a heartbeat and found it was beating strong. He was alive. He turned and looked at Ellie. "Are you ok?"

Ellie nodded, and looked over at Pam. She was covered in dust from head to toe but looked no worse for wear. "I'm okay too, Jake," Pam said sarcastically. "Thanks for asking."

Roscoe's eyes then fluttered and opened. He tried to get up but was shaky. Jake saw a nasty cut above Roscoe left eye. *If his skull wasn't fractured, he'll need a few stitches.* "I think he'll be okay," said Jake. "But I don't think your piano's going to make it."

"It served its purpose," replied Ellie. "But there's another one somewhere around. It went through the door after Mr. Tillon."

Jake picked up his rifle, and turned towards the door to go check on Mr. Tillon but suddenly stopped as Pam and Ellie screamed. A man stood in the doorway with golden brass colored skin, over seven feet tall, wearing all white with a golden sword. He held an unconscious Mr. Tillon in his arms who looked like a child compared to the giant. He ducked down to get through the door and set Mr. Tillon down softly.

"He'll be fine, just some scratches and a broken collar bone," said the giant in a deep calm voice.

"Thanks," said Jake with a smile. "Ellie, this is the man I told you about, this is Malachy."

The two women looked wide-eyed at the giant.

"There's another one like this outside," said Jake pointing to the dead lizard creature by the piano.

"I disposed of it," answered Malachy.

"Thank you, Malachy," said Ellie when she found her voice. "Bless you."

"Thank you, I am blessed. And may the blessings of heaven go with you in your mission, Jacob, Ellie, and Pamela." Then as if he had never been there, Malachy disappeared.

Pam stared with her mouth open at the spot where Malachy had been. "He knew my name." She turned to Ellie. "He called me by name."

Jake and Roscoe sat on the concrete floor while the two women helped Mr. Tillon.

"I thought demons couldn't come on church property," asked Pam.

Mr. Tillon had regained consciousness and Ellie helped him sit up. "Demons can't enter the church building itself because it's blessed, but this is just a storage building, not holy ground," explained Ellie.

They all stared at the destruction inside, wondering how they were going to explain it.

# CHAPTER TWELVE

**Ghazi Mansion**
**6322 Crosswinds Drive**
**Lake Barcroft, Virginia**

AFTER LEAVING THE AIRPORT, Ghazi's limo drove down I-66 west through Arlington, Virginia then south along winding roads near Lake Barcroft. The vehicle pulled in front of an iron gate, and the driver entered a series of numbers into the gate's keypad allowing the gates to open. Video surveillance cameras followed the limo as it followed a paved driveway for at least a mile through well-kept grounds to stop in front of the main house. The building was more than a main house; the multi-story gothic style mansion looked as if it came straight out of a horror movie. It could have been used for the set of a Frankenstein movie or the return of the Munsters.

Ghazi exited the rear door of the limo and glanced up at the gargoyles perched on the eaves of the grotesque mansion. Taking a deep breath of the humid Virginia air he felt relieved to be away from the dry desert of Arabia. He hated the sand and the dryness. Sand got into everything no matter how hard he tried to keep it out.

He strolled into the wide entry way to a fabulously ornate

wooden staircase directly in front of him. Several rooms fed from the entry way in both directions. The floors were marble, and the walls were polished panels of rosewood. A huge chandelier hung from the ceiling and priceless paintings hung from the walls.

Ghazi went directly to one of those doors and entered a room reminiscent of a turn-of-the-century library. The floor was stone, polished to a shine, and covered partially with rugs from China and the Orient. Two of the four walls were lined with open bookcases filled with classics writings of hundreds of authors. More priceless paintings hung on the other walls. The remaining wall had two windows covered with stained glass depicting hunting scenes. Between the windows were a set of French doors that led out onto a terrace overlooking well-kept gardens. Ghazi held private meetings here while in Virginia.

Ghazi approached a secluded door that stood between two of the bookcases. He entered a password into a wall pad and the door clicked open to a lit stone staircase leading down. Ghazi's footsteps echoed in the quiet as he followed the steps down that ended at the entrance to a grotto, a man-made cave.

One side of the cave sat a large wooden table on which sat many books. Most were books on the occult and witchcraft, while the rest dealt with history and vast ancient religions. The main attraction, however, was an altar sitting in the middle of the cave. It was sculptured out of solid granite. The top was flat with just a slight rise in the middle. A small channel was carved out along the edge of the stone. At intervals along the side, the channel emptied into a small hole in the back of several skulls carved in the rock. These gruesome heads faced outward. The skull's mouths were open, to allow whatever drained into the skull to pour out onto the floor. It was obvious that something or someone had been sacrificed there in the past. Behind the altar stood an alcove carved into the rock wall. The outer edge of the alcove was in the form of an arch and carved along the arch were skeletons in various positions and contortions. They appeared to being reaching out, trying to escape from the edge of the arch. Sitting under the arch was a throne. It also was made of stone with the arms and legs of the throne carved out to look like gargoyles showing various hideous glares.

Ghazi stepped up to the sacrificial altar and ran his hand across the top in an almost reverent manner. *Soon all my dreams will come true. Soon it will all come to past.*

————

**Shady Oak Community Church**
**2203 E. Hollis Street**
**Shady Oak, Texas**

THE COUNTY AMBULANCE service arrived and took Mr. Tillon to the regional hospital to treat his dislocated shoulder. Jake required a few minor bandages for his cuts, and one of the paramedics bandaged Roscoe's head until Jake could get him to a vet. A couple of church members arrived to help but were told not to go inside until after the sheriff's office arrived. Pam took notes and looked for a camera.

Deputy Eddie Cole finished listening to the Sims brothers' story of Martians and UFOs for the twentieth time. The dispatcher called and told him that someone was trying to break into the new church in Shady Oak, so he cut their UFO story short and headed towards the town. On his way, the dispatcher notified there had been a shooting at the church, so he stepped his response to code three.

After almost twenty minutes of high-speed driving across the county, he pulled up the front of the church. Several people were standing around the front of the church. He saw the new female pastor talking to a tall cowboy who looked as if he'd gone a few rounds with a heavy weight boxer. A wolf sat nearby with a bandage on its head.

*This ought to be a good story,* thought Deputy Cole. He parked his patrol car and walked over to the Ellie and Jake. "Evening folks, I heard you had a little trouble here," he said calmly.

Pam saw the deputy and came running over with notepad in

hand. "You're not going to believe this, Eddie. We were attacked by monsters. Creatures of the darkness, and they destroyed our piano."

Deputy Cole turned slowly toward Pam. "Uh huh, monsters destroyed your piano?"

"Don't look at me like that, Eddie. I know what I saw. They tried to eat us. The creatures are inside the church, but they're dead."

"Look, Pam, I just came from the Sims brother's house. I don't need any more science fiction stories tonight." He turned to Ellie. "Ma'am, you're the pastor here, right? Can you tell me what happened?"

Ellie looked at Pam and back at Deputy Cole. "Well sir, what Pam said was pretty much what happened. Three demonic creatures broke in and tried to kill us. They injured Mr. Tillon, and Jake's dog."

Deputy Cole rolled his eyes and looked at Jake. "Your name's Taft isn't it? So, what's your story?"

Jake knew that there was no explaining what happened, so he decided to show him. "Let me show you what's inside," suggested Jake.

The group trooped up to the front door. The first thing they experienced was the over whelming stench of decaying flesh. They covered their mouth and nose to help keep back the smell but what they found inside was not what they expected. Instead of two recently deceased corpses they found almost totally decomposed mounds of bones and flesh.

Deputy Cole glanced at the piles of decomposition, made a slight curse, and left the building. Pam and Ellie followed while Jake stayed for a minute or two. He stared at the remains, trying to make sense of it.

Outside, Deputy Cole was less than amused. "Ok, I'm not sure what's going on here. Those can't be the so-called creatures that attacked you thirty minutes ago. To be in that stage of decay they would have to have been there for at least a month. Could this have been some sort of prank that someone pulled on you?"

Pam and Ellie looked at each other. Ellie spoke up first. "Deputy, I know this sounds strange to you, but those things were alive thirty minutes ago and tried to kill us. I can't explain why they look the way they do. You have to believe us."

Jake had walked out and stood rubbing his chin in thought.

"So, what's your take on this?" asked the deputy.

"All I can figure is that these creatures have a different metabolism than we do which makes them decompose faster than humans. Perhaps an autopsy can help us?"

"If you think I'm ordering an autopsy on supposedly creatures from outer space then you're crazy" grumbled Deputy Cole.

"They're not from outer space," responded Ellie. "They're demons from hell."

Deputy Cole's face turned red. He'd lost his patience with this group of fanatics. "I don't care where they came from. I'm not ordering an autopsy. I got UFOs, a missing chicken farmer, cattle disappearing, and now monsters from hell." Deputy Cole shook his head and took a deep breath. "I'll call Doc Keller over at the vet. He can look at your creatures or demons or whatever you call them. He can fix up your dog too." With that, he turned and walked to his car to make the phone call. "This whole county is full of crazy people," muttered Deputy Cole under his breath.

Ellie watched him talking on the phone. He occasionally looked over at them and frowned.

"He doesn't believe a word of this," she said sadly.

"What did you expect?" said Jake. "He deals in facts. The fact is that normally there should be two corpses. It doesn't matter though; we know what we saw."

Ten minutes later the local veterinarian, Joe Keller, arrived to examine the corpses. He'd moved out to west Texas about ten years and was the only vet in the county. The tall, lanky vet spoke with Deputy Cole for a few minutes, and then examined Roscoe. He turned to the trio waiting by the church and explained that Roscoe needed an x-ray plus stitches but otherwise appeared healthy. He then looked at the ruined entrance to the church. "Eddie says ya'll killed monsters?" he said with a grin.

Pam frowned and opened her mouth but before she could say anything she'd regret, Jake stepped in. "Doc, we don't know for sure what exactly we've got inside. Can you take a look and see what you think?"

Doc Keller approached the doors to the church and was hit by the same overwhelming stench. "How long have these things been in here?"

"Almost an hour," answered Jake.

"Good Lord, they smell like they've been here for a week or more." Doc Keller opened a small bag he carried and removed a jar of Vaseline. He used his finger and removed a small amount of the Vaseline and placed it inside each of his nostrils. He noticed them watching. "It masks the stench." He then covered his nose and mouth with a surgical mask and entered. They waited patiently near the front while he examined the remains inside. After about fifteen minutes he emerged from the church, removed the mask, took off his eyeglasses, and rubbed the bridge of his nose. "You say those corpses inside were alive an hour ago?"

"Yes," snapped Pam defiantly.

"Well, it's nothing I've ever seen. They're in a state of advanced decomposition."

The three of them shook their heads in disappointment. "Is there anything you can tell us?" asked Jake.

Doc Keller thought for a minute before answering. "The little bit of skin that's left is lizard, but the bones are not right. It looks like someone mixed the bones of several animals together. I'm not trying to insult you, but could this be some prank that someone played on you?"

Ellie sighed in frustration. "Doctor, we were nearly killed by those things. It was no prank. Look at Jake. Did a prank put those bruises and cuts? Did a prank injure Jake's dog? Mr. Tillon is on his way to the hospital with a dislocated shoulder. This was real. We can't explain it, but we know what we saw."

Doc Keller looked at the three of them carefully. They had a look of determination that told him they were deadly serious. He nodded. "Ok, I'll take them back to the office and do some tests. If I hear anything I'll call." With that he returned to his truck, gathered two large plastic bags and went into the church.

"So where do we go from here?" asked Ellie.

"Malachy said to start in Florida," said Jake.

"Florida?"

"Do you still have those newspaper articles?" asked Jake.

"Yes."

Jake placed his hand on her shoulder. "Then it's time I go demon hunting."

# CHAPTER THIRTEEN

**The White House**
**1600 Pennsylvania Avenue Northwest**
**Washington D.C.**

JOHN WOHLMAN quietly entered the Presidential living quarters after knocking. President Campbell was sitting at the kitchen table eating a late snack.

"Excuse me, Mr. President, I have news from Denver."

"I hope it's good?"

"I'm sorry sir, but they haven't located Ann yet. The FBI was able to identify the dead kidnapper. They located his last known residence and work address. His apartment was vacant, so they went to his work address which turned out to be an abandoned warehouse. The kidnappers had been there but apparently moved Ann shortly before they arrived. Agent Ruiz still believes she's alive."

The President nodded his head. "At least she's still alive."

"The report says the deceased kidnapper was on a student visa. The FBI's checking all the visas for students in the Denver and Boulder area."

"These students can't be acting alone. There must be someone behind them."

"I agree. The dead man's employer is a company owned by a Hassan Ghazi."

"Have the CIA put together a file on him. It might be able to help us."

"It's already being done, sir."

---

**FBI Office**
**8000 East 36th Avenue**
**Denver, Colorado**

IT HAD BEEN a long night for Agents Ruiz and Kimbell. They'd spent most of the night working with Denver police and Colorado state troopers trying to check all the local airports, train stations, and major transportation outlets. They'd come up empty.

Agent Ruiz was nursing a cup of coffee, trying to jump start his tired body. Agent Kimbell was going through a stack of papers. "I never realized how many private airports, trains stations, and bus terminals there are in this area," he explained. "I don't know how we're going to check them all in time."

Agent Ruiz set his cup down on the desk. "I'm afraid your right. We could spend another day checking out all the transport businesses. For all we know they could still be right here in Denver and just moved her to another building. We need to narrow it down quickly. Time is running out."

Agent Kimbell got up and paced the room. "What about the guy that owns the warehouse? Ghazi? We could check his properties and buildings first and work out from there?"

"Good idea." Agent Ruiz began shuffling through the papers on his desk. He began going through a list of businesses and warehouses. "Let's see. It looks like he owns a private trucking company in Commerce City." Agent Ruiz gathered the rest of the papers together and got up to leave. "We can start there and look for any other locations on our way. Let's hope we aren't too far behind."

———

## Airborne over the Midwest, USA

ANN'S WORLD of darkness began to fade away and she was aware of the sounds around her. She heard voices quietly talking and the low hum of an engine. She tried to move but her arms wouldn't respond. Her head ached but she forced her eyes open and slowly looked around. She was in a well-furnished room with soft lighting. She noticed the oval windows and blinked through the mental fog. She realized she was on some sort of aircraft. A personal jet of some sort she surmised, and there were more people in the cabin. She didn't recognize one man, but she knew the other two. One was the man she'd kicked while trying to escape and the other was Amira. *Where am I going? Am I still in the USA?*

Amira noticed that Ann was awake. "Good, you're awake."

"My head hurts."

"Yes, that's a side effect of the sedative. If you hadn't been so uncooperative, I wouldn't have had to do it."

Ann shook her head to clear the cobwebs in her brain. "What do you expect me to do? Sit here and be your willing captive? You've taken me against my will and killed my friend. I heard you talking earlier about her...her dead body."

Amira came and sat next to her. "The plan was to remove you without anyone getting hurt. The Secret Service Agent and policeman were unfortunate obstacles that had to be removed."

Ann glared at her. "Obstacles? Police officer? You didn't kill the officer in the library too? These were people with families and friends. You morons killed them?"

Amira frowned but couldn't meet Ann's eyes. "In any war there are always casualties."

"What war?"

"Our holy war, the Jihad."

"You're nothing more than a terrorist," argued Ann.

"I'm a soldier in Allah's army."

"So, I either believe in your religion, do what you say, do as you want or you kill me? Sounds like a bad form of communism."

Amira stood up abruptly. "I'll get you something to eat and drink," she said coldly.

"You should be careful. It might be seen as consorting with the enemy."

Amira disappeared into another room. Ann's legs were free but both arms were tied to the armrests. She pulled and tugged on them in frustration. After a few minutes Amira returned with a soda and a warmed flight meal. Without saying a word, she lowered the tray from the seat in front, sat the food on the tray, and untied one of Ann's arms.

"Thank you," said Ann sarcastically.

"You're welcome," answered Amira coldly. She stood for a moment and watched the young American woman eat. Amira glanced at the others in the cabin then spoke very softly, "I don't know what you thought you heard but your secret service friend from the college is alive. She's recovering in a local hospital." She turned and walked away.

Ann didn't look up or respond, but her eyes widened. *Beth? Alive?*

# CHAPTER FOURTEEN

**I-20 east of Odessa, Texas**

JAKE DROVE Mr. Tillon's blue Chevrolet Suburban east on the interstate. Ellie sat in the front passenger seat while Pam took dibs on the middle seat. Roscoe was asleep on the far back bench seat. They were loaded down with suitcases and other gear. It looked as if they were on a vacation, except this was no pleasure trip.

Most of the congregation was supportive of their quest while some weren't total believers, even with Mr. Tillon's full support. He took over temporary pastoral duties while Ellie was gone, and Pam left her assistant editor in charge but would be emailing daily stories. She wasn't going to miss what she felt was the story of the century. Jake was reluctant to bring her along, but Ellie insisted.

Flying would have been faster but Jake wanted to come armed. He had brought his rifle and two Colt 45s along as well as a special footlocker full of items from his years in the military. He thought it might come in handy.

Pam had her laptop open and surfing the internet. "I've checked all the unusual stories like you asked, especially the one in Florida. The most recent one is a story about another attack on a couple not far from the first one. It says that a young couple was camping in the forest and some hikers found the man's body at the camp site. It doesn't go into too much detail except to say they think he was attacked by a bear. The woman is missing. Do you think it's the same one?"

"I'd make bet on it," said Jake. "If I was a betting man, that is," he added when he saw Ellie frowning.

"But why Florida? Why not one of the other places?" asked Pam.

"That's where Malachy said to start. There must be a reason."

"So, what's your plan?" asked Pam in an official journalist interview voice.

Jake frowned. "I plan on driving to Florida, hunt down this creature and stop it from hurting anyone else."

"And how do you plan to find it and kill it when the Florida authorities haven't been able to?"

"We'll work out the details when we get closer, but we have an edge that the authorities don't."

"And what's that?"

"We know what to look for," said Jake with a grin.

———

**Ghazi Estate**
**6322 Crosswinds Drive**
**Lake Barcroft, Virginia**

GHAZI SAT in an overstuffed leather chair in the mansion's study when his cell phone chirped. He looked at the caller ID and recognized it as a special number he'd set up, so he answered, "Yes?"

"Are we still on track?" asked the voice.

"Of course we are. I have the two packages that I need, and the lab is preparing my ace in the hole."

"We agreed that you would only use it as a last resort?"

"You do your job and leave the rest to me," grumbled Ghazi.

"I'm putting my neck on the line for this, Ghazi. I don't want to be a ruler of dead people."

"You do what we've agreed on and you'll have more riches and power than you can imagine."

"All I want is everything that I deserve."

"You will." Ghazi ended the phone connection and sat for a moment contemplating his conversation with his accomplice. The man was becoming impatient, but Ghazi needed to control him for a short time more, and then he'd have no need of him. He would make sure the man got exactly what he deserved.

———

**Circle G Trucking Company**
**4113 E 61$^{st}$ Ave**
**Commerce City, Colorado**

AGENTS RUIZ and Kimbell parked in front of the large building housing a trucking company with a large red G inside a circle painted on the side. They entered through the glass doors into a typical office reception area. The floors were polished tile, and the walls were covered with varnished paneling. Various photos of semi-tractors hung on the walls and an attractive young receptionist sat behind a wooden desk. She greeted them with a smile, and they identified themselves as federal agents. At their request, the office manager was called to the reception area, a Middle Eastern man in his mid-thirties named Mr. Ruhul. He appeared very pleasant and cooperative.

When asked about the nature of their business, Mr Ruhul went into his memorized speech about the trucking company. It appeared the business was a typical trucking company, transporting all types of goods all over the country and the two agents thanked him for his time then returned to the car.

Agent Kimble shook his head. "It didn't seem to be the right location to keep a woman captive."

"I agree. There are too many people and too much traffic in and out."

As they drove out of the parking lot, Agent Ruiz glanced over and noticed a helicopter pad set behind one of the buildings. "It's odd that Mr. Ruhul didn't mention they use helicopters?"

"Must have slipped his mind," answered Agent Kimbell sarcastically. "Should we go back and ask?"

"No, I doubt he'd tell us anything."

Agent Ruiz noticed a convenience store at the corner and told Agent Kimbell to pull in. The clerk was an older woman with a beehive hairdo and way too much make up. They purchased coffee and engaged her in some idle talk about the weather and the economy.

"You must get a lot of business from the trucking company?" asked Agent Ruiz casually.

"Yep, those trucker boys come in here pretty regular."

"I noticed they have a helipad too."

"Yeah, but they don't use it much. When they do, they're so noisy they could wake the dead. Like last night it took me forever to go back to sleep after it left. I need my beauty sleep ya know."

"Oh, I understand," said Agent Ruiz in a tone he hoped sounded sincere. "What time did it disturb you?"

"Oh, it came whipping in here about one o'clock this morning. Now who in their right mind would fly in here at that time of morning?"

"Who indeed?"

They thanked her for her time and left. In the car, Agent Ruiz immediately punched numbers on his cell phone. "I wonder who they'd be transporting that early in the morning?"

––––––––

**Budget Motel**
**9100 S. Hampton Ave**
**Houston, Texas**

JAKE RENTED rooms at a Budget Motel just off the interstate. They were all tired from the long drive and decided that after settling in they'd meet before turning in for the night. Ellie had noticed that

Jake had become quiet and seemed disturbed about something. They met in Jake's room. Roscoe had already claimed his side of the bed and was stretched out in total bliss. Jake was quietly sitting in one of the chairs next to the small table in the room. Ellie came over and sat in the other chair. "What's bothering you? You've been quiet for quite a while."

Jake looked up at her. "I can see all of them! I see these hideous creatures at gas stations, stores, everywhere. I see them whispering in people's ears, glaring, laughing, and snarling. I thought it would be simple. I'd just hunt them down and stop them, but when they are so many. I wonder if it too much."

They suddenly sensed someone else in the room and looked up to see Malachy sitting on the bed petting Roscoe.

Malachy smiled brightly, "Greetings from heaven."

Pam and Ellie smiled back but Jake simply nodded.

Malachy came over and stood next to Jake. The seven-foot angel placed a hand on Jake's shoulder. "You're upset about your ability to see these demons and creatures?"

Jake nodded. He wasn't going to ask how Malachy knew.

"I knew that having the ability to see them was going to be somewhat overwhelming. I've been around the fallen and their creatures since before the beginning of time. You see, I knew them when they were like me. I've watched over the centuries as they deteriorate into what they are today. You will adjust with time."

"But I thought they were supposed to be beautiful?" asked Ellie.

"They were beautiful in the beginning. Satan was the most beautiful, but his pride drove him to where he is now. As time progressed, they began to take on ugly characteristics from their behavior until they are what Jake sees them today. They do have the ability to change their appearance temporarily to look beautiful or look human, but it doesn't last. Their evilness shows through eventually."

Ellie could see the sadness in Malachy's eyes when he talked about the once heavenly angels. She could only imagine how he felt about fighting against those he once stood with side by side in heaven. "I'm sorry."

Malachy nodded and turned again to Jake. "You're not being

asked to do the impossible, just do what you can. Your mission is not to eradicate all of them, that would be impossible, just the specific task ahead of you. Focus on the task and do what you can in between."

"But how will we know what that task is?" asked Pam.

"You're headed to Florida. You're on the right track." With that said Malachy once again disappeared.

They sat in silence for a moment.

"Why can't he just use the door," commented Pam.

Ellie frowned at her sarcastic friend then looked over at Jake. He appeared to feel better as he smiled when he noticed her watching him.

"I'll be ok," he said. "Are you both sure you want to continue with me? This isn't going to be a cake walk?"

Ellie squeezed his arm. "This is not just your mission; we have a stake in this, so it's our mission too."

"Then ya'll need to get some rest. I have a feeling we're going to have a busy trip."

"Yep," said Pam as she and Ellie went out the door. "We don't want to be tired and grumpy when we meet the terrifying monster who wants to rip us to shreds."

Jake shook his head. *Why did I bring her along?*

———

**FBI Office**
**8000 East 36th Avenue**
**Denver, Colorado**

AGENT RUIZ SAT at his desk rubbing his eyes. He and Agent Kimble had been making phone calls to agencies to try to locate the destination of the helicopter once it left Circle G Trucking.

Earlier, they had received news that the student visa check in Boulder had come up dry. Most of the students were interviewed, none were thought to be suspects but some could not be located and would take some time to track them down. Time was one thing they didn't have.

"Now where would they take her, assuming they actually did take her by helicopter?" asked Agent Ruiz more to himself than to Agent Kimbell.

Agent Kimbell shook his head. "They could've taken her anywhere."

The door opened and his administrative assistant entered. A middle-aged woman, Susan Thompson had been working for the FBI field office for almost eight years. Ruiz trusted her explicitly and considered her one of the most dependable people on his staff. She had been working almost nonstop behind the scenes since the kidnapping.

Agent Ruiz looked up sadly, "More info to sift through?"

Susan responded with a tired smile. "I think I might have something for you."

Agent Ruiz stared at his short, brunette secretary. "I hope it's better than what we have, which is nothing."

"I have a friend that's an airline attendant. She knows several of the helicopter pilots around here," she explained. "I asked her to check around and she just called back. One of Ghazi's helicopter pilots mentioned they were headed to an airfield in Scottsbluff. Ghazi has a hangar there too."

Agent Ruiz smiled. "It's the Western Nebraska Regional Airport. It's close enough for a helicopter but far enough away not to draw attention. Suzie, get us on the next flight to Scottsbluff."

Susan went out the door to make the flight arrangements.

# CHAPTER FIFTEEN

**Mack's Steak House**
**10011 East I-10**
**Mobile, Alabama**

THEY STOPPED at a local restaurant for a nice break from the long drive from Texas, ate and discussed their game plan.

"How often are you updating your story with your assistant editor," Jake asked Pam, between mouthfuls.

"I plan to send him an update daily," replied Pam. "Pass me the butter."

"You need to make sure that he understands to keep locations and such out of it until later. I don't know how this is going to proceed or turn out. I'd like to be as quiet and under the radar as possible."

Pam nodded. "I understand. I'll keep it to general details but no specific locations for now."

Jake noticed a small demon sitting on the top edge of the booth next to a young man. It was an ugly little creature, about a foot tall and resembled a slimy slug with a long snout like an anteater. It was fat, and long strands of hair protruded from its fat body. It was whispering in the man's ear. Whatever the thing whispered, the man would repeat.

"I think I made a mistake in getting married," whispered the demon.

"I think I made a mistake in getting married," said the young man.

The young woman was on the brink of tears. The thing clapped its tiny claws together in joy. Slobber and slime drooled from the corner of its mouth.

The waitress brought Jake their bill which he paid, and they all got up to leave. He allowed Ellie and Pam to walk out first then as he passed the young couple's booth he reached out, grabbed the demon by the neck, and snatched it away. The young couple was startled by Jake's sudden movement and watched the tall cowboy walk out of the restaurant. The odd thing was his hand twitched occasionally as if he was holding an invisible, squirming fish. The young man turned back to his wife who reached out and held his hand. "Are you sure we can't try to make this work?"

He looked at her for a moment. The young man couldn't understand it, but for some reason he felt as if a load had been lifted off his shoulders.

"Let's try to make this work a little longer," he said.

They both smiled.

Outside, Pam and Ellie had watched as Jake came out of the restaurant with his hand shaking wildly. They couldn't see anything but watched as Jake appeared to wrestle with something. Jake used both hands, twisted them together, and they heard a sickening sound like bones breaking. Suddenly Jake was holding a large slug-like creature. It was dead. He carried it over to the dumpster and deposited it in the trash.

"Where did you find that thing?" asked Pam in disgust.

"It was sitting in the booth next to a young couple. It was causing problems between them, so I lent a hand."

———

**Ghazi Estate**
**6322 Crosswinds Drive**
**Lake Barcroft, Virginia**

A WHITE DELIVERY truck routinely drove onto the Ghazi estate, but rather than go to the rear of the building as a normal delivery truck, it drove under the front portico.

Amira climbed out of the cab along with the driver. They walked to rear of the truck and opened the rear door. Inside was another man sitting patiently with Ann. Her hands were bound; she was gagged and had a cotton bag over her head. The men roughly pulled her out of the truck and walked her inside the building.

Once inside they removed the bag and she was taken to a small bedroom upstairs. It was modestly furnished with a separate bathroom and one window. She was released from her bindings, the two men left, and locked the door.

Ann looked carefully around. She immediately went to the window and looked out. The glass was several inches thick preventing her from breaking it and climbing out. She looked out at a well-manicured lawn and tennis courts in the distance. She wasn't positive but thought she was still somewhere in the United States. Ann searched around but couldn't locate anything in the room that would identify her location, so she decided to take advantage of the shower to get off some of the dirt and grime from the warehouse.

After her shower she felt a little more human and she sat on the bed in a robe conveniently left in the bathroom for her. She was startled when there was a knock on the door which was then unlocked, and a maid entered accompanied by a mean looking guard. The woman left a bundle of clothes, gathered Ann's dirty clothes, and left without a word.

Ann picked up the clean clothes, a new pair of Khaki pants and a pressed white shirt. *How convenient. Not exactly my type, but at least they're clean.* After dressing, she continued looking around the room with only one thing in mind and that was to escape.

———

**Western Regional Airport**
**250023 Airport Terminal St**
**Scottsbluff, Nebraska**

THE CHARTERED AIRCRAFT landed at the small regional airport just outside of Scottsbluff. Agents Ruiz and Kimbell left the plane and went directly to the director's office. After identifying themselves as FBI agents, they were informed that G Enterprises had a hanger on the east side of the airport.

The two agents made the short walk to the row of private hangers and searched until they located the one with the large G on the side. They checked the doors but found them locked. At the rear of the building a metal ladder was attached to the wall leading to the roof for access to the air conditioning units. Without saying a word, they both climbed the ladder to the slanted hanger roof. At one end, the roof extended flat and contained the air conditioning units. On both sides of the slanted roof were several sky lights.

*Bingo* thought Agent Ruiz. They went over to one of the skylights and looked down. The skylight was frosted which allowed light in but kept them from seeing inside. Agent Ruiz removed a lock blade pocketknife and began pry away at one of the seams.

"Are you sure we can do this?" asked Agent Kimbell.

Agent Ruiz nodded as he pried part of the sky light loose. "We're not going to go inside I'm just going to take a peek."

"Isn't peeking illegal too?"

"When the President's daughter's life is at stake, I'm making it legal." Agent Ruiz pried up one corner of the frosted dome to allow them a small look inside. In the dim light coming in from the sun they were able to see a helicopter sitting inside on one side of the hanger. The other side was empty. "The helicopter's here."

"But are you sure it's the same one that flew in from Denver?"

"It's got to be. It's too much of a coincidence. Let's go talk to the tower, see if there was another aircraft in the hanger, and if it left."

The two federal agents climbed down and walked to the air traffic control tower. At the tower they learned that the helicopter had in fact flown in from Denver, but a small Lear jet had left the day before bound for Dulles International airport on the east coast. In the airport's coffee shop, Agent Ruiz called and briefed his superiors in Washington. After ending his cell phone conversation, Agent Ruiz sipped his coffee in silent thought.

"Now why would someone kidnap the President's daughter in Colorado and then take her back closer to home. That is assuming that she was on board?" asked Agent Kimbell.

Agent Ruiz shook his head. "It doesn't make sense but it's too much of a coincidence. She had to be on it. I'm getting tired of chasing right behind these people. I say let's get ahead and work our way back."

Agent Kimbell raised an eyebrow. "And how are we going to do that?"

Agent Ruiz gave him a sly grin. "I'm told that this Ghazi character is in Virginia on business, and the jet was headed that way. I intend to pay Ghazi a visit and see what I can shake loose."

---

**Budget Motel**
**2201 E. Silver Springs Blvd**
**Ocala, Florida**

AFTER RENTING two rooms they unloaded their suitcases and gear. Jake removed a small gun case from the back of the suburban and carried it into his room. He began emptying out the contents onto the bed. Ellie and Pam sat and watched. Jake removed two Colt 45 cal. Semi-auto handguns.

"My Winchester rifle is good in the country against coyotes and varmints, or for long shots but walking around carrying a rifle in a city can be very conspicuous. These can be concealed but provide us with some protection."

Pam reached over and opened her laptop. "I received an email from Doc Keller. He said he's been trying to figure out what those creatures at the church were. He said the DNA must have been contaminated. He said it was a mixture of lizard and some unknown species."

Jake chuckled. "I won't be surprised if he never figures it out. If he does it'll make history."

"I don't think demon DNA is in any data base yet," said Ellie with a smile.

Jake opened a map of Florida as well as a map of the Ocala National Forest on the table. Pam and Ellie joined him. They circled the areas where the known attacks had occurred.

"The news media is attributing the attacks to a rogue bear," commented Pam.

"Yes, but we know better," answered Ellie. "I just don't know how we're going to find this thing in a national forest."

Jake had been studying the map. "It appears the thing likes to hang around the St Francis Trail. It's an eight-mile trail that includes two swamps called the Bayhead and Riverine swamp."

Ellie shook her head. "But that's a big area. It could take weeks to cover."

"The reports said the authorities have covered the same ground with dogs and search parties but never found anything," added Pam.

"Yes, but they were looking for something human or animal. We're looking for neither. Remember, these creatures are invisible to humans unless they wish to be seen. Our edge is that I can see them all the time."

They all sat in silence for a few minutes staring at the map. Finally, Jake pointed to the locations of the attacks. "Do you notice that the attacks are within easy reach of the swamps? Maybe this thing likes to stay near the water?"

"And it seems to like the roads and campgrounds too," piped in Pam.

"I'm sure the authorities felt the same. It could be right under their noses, but they couldn't see it."

"The attacks then get blamed on bears or alligators that get too close to careless campers or teens," announced Ellie.

Jake nodded. "This thing isn't stupid. We'll check out the area near those campsites and parking areas first and work from there."

Pam and Ellie nodded. The plan seemed simple

---

**Ghazi Estate**
**6322 Crosswinds Drive**
**Lake Barcroft, Virginia**

ANN HEARD her door being unlocked, it opened and one of her guard's motioned for her to follow. She fell in behind him quietly while looking for any chance of escape. Overpowering the guard was out of the question as he was three times her size, so she followed him downstairs into a formal dining room.

It was a large gothic room with a single rectangular table. At one end sat a middle aged, bearded man wearing a dark suit. Sitting to his left was a younger Middle Eastern man dressed in traditional Muslim clothing. The older man stood and gestured for Ann to sit to his right, across from the younger man.

"Ah, Miss Campbell, I'm so glad you've come to dinner," he said with a grand smile.

"Like I had a choice," she replied sarcastically.

The man kept his smile, but it was strained. "Allow me to introduce myself. I am Hassan Ghazi." He pointed to the young man. "And this is my friend and associate, Azim Fawwaz."

The young man named Fawwaz simply stared at her in disgust.

"Please sit and eat. We'll talk about your situation."

Ann reluctantly sat down. Several servants brought out a full course meal. Over the next several minutes no one spoke as they ate. Ann was tempted to start a food fight as a sign of rebellion, but she kept remembering what Agent Sills had told her about keeping up her strength. The food was delicious and after only being given sandwiches this was a feast.

Ann would occasionally look up at Ghazi who was completely engrossed in his meal. She glanced over at the Fawwaz and was met by a glaring look of hatred. *What did I ever do to him?* While the two men were busy eating, Ann slipped one of the silver knives into her khaki pants pocket.

When dessert was served, Ghazi looked over at Ann and smiled. "I'm sure you're wondering why you were brought here?"

"I would imagine for ransom or extortion of some kind. That's what terrorists do," answered Ann rudely.

"Miss Campbell, I am shocked," he said as if insulted. "I am not a terrorist. I'm a simple businessman."

"So, what do you want?"

"I want nothing from you, Miss Campbell. You are merely a tool to achieve my true mission."

"Your mission?"

"Why yes. I intend to take over your government."

Ann stared at the man for a moment, waiting for a laugh.

He simply smiled.

"You can't be serious? How do you plan to achieve that? You couldn't take over by force and my father would never give up."

"That's exactly what I'm hoping he will do," answered Ghazi with a devilish grin. "Do you know what micro toxins are, Miss Campbell?"

Ann shook her head.

"Micro toxins are created by nature from mold and other sources. Mankind has made chemical micro toxins for years. They were used in Vietnam against the Viet Cong. They called it Yellow Rain. My friend Saddam Hussein used it in biological warfare against the Kurds in Iraq. He was kind enough to give it to me before the Americans invaded Iraq."

Ann felt her stomach tighten up in knots. "You can't be seriously thinking about using biological warfare?"

"I have every intention of using it, young lady. I'll distribute the toxins over Washington D.C., London, and Jerusalem while your father sits and watches. In a matter of days, the entire population will be suffering. Their lungs will fill with blood, and they'll drown in their own fluids. While the governments are in crisis, Azim and his people will simply rise up and take over."

Ann thought she was going to vomit. She was repulsed at how he could explain his plan for killing millions of innocent people over dinner. "We'll treat it. They'll find a cure. It won't work."

Ghazi continued to smile. "I have taken measures so that will never happen. And if they do find an antitoxin, it will be too late; we'll already be in place."

Azim spoke for the first time. "With the breakup of Russia, and the western countries under our control, the world will become a united Islamic world."

"But you'll poison Muslims as well."

Azim looked at her like she was a child. "True believers in our faith will understand the need for martyrs for the greater cause."

"And I will reluctantly step in as the leader of this new world order," announced Ghazi.

"With Allah as our ultimate guide," piped in Azim.

Ghazi's smile disappeared, "Of course."

Ann sat stunned.

Ghazi stood up. "Enough talk for tonight. I will let you return to your room as I'm sure you need your rest after your long trip."

Ann reached in her pocket and grabbed the hidden knife. As she stood up, she withdrew it from her pocket and lunged at Ghazi. With incredible quickness he grabbed her arm and twisted the knife away. He slapped her across the face with the back of his hand, knocking her to the floor. Blood trickled down her chin from a split lip.

"Stupid woman," he growled.

Ann glared up at him in defiance. "You'll never get away with this."

Ghazi bent down and looked directly at her. "Oh, I will, my dear. I certainly will," he sneered as his eyes went from brown to yellow. "Get her out of here."

Two guards jerked her to her feet, led her back to the room, and locked her in. She went into the bathroom and put a cool, wet washrag on her quickly swelling lip. She stared at herself in the mirror and thought about those yellow eyes.

# CHAPTER SIXTEEN

**Budget Motel**
**2201 E. Silver Springs Blvd**
**Ocala, Florida**

IT WAS late but Roscoe needed to go outside so Jake slipped his Colt .45 into the back of his waist band and went out with Roscoe. He waited around the pool area while Roscoe took care of nature's call. The pool area was vacant as it had closed at 10:00 p.m.

Jake casually looked around the vicinity and noticed something digging in the dumpster. It was a demon crawling through the trash. Its head was oblong and appeared to be too big for its body. The monster's upper lip draped over the bottom, and it had large nostrils. The body was about five foot tall when it stood to dig in the dumpster. It had short hair covering most of its body, but the hair was matted with bald spots. Where the hair had worn off, some of the spots had become sores and oozed. It reminded Jake of a hairy human with a dehorned rhino head. It dug through the trash, occasionally lifting its head to sniff the air. It ignored Jake's stare, knowing it was invisible to humans.

Roscoe came trotting back and they started back towards the

stairs. Roscoe suddenly growled deep in his chest about the same time that Jake sensed, rather than heard the creature approach. Thinking it was going to attack him, Jake spun around in a low defensive stance only to be knocked aside into a set of pool chairs by the thing as it lunged past. The creature snatched up Roscoe by the back of the neck, lifted him up over its head, grinned, and showed a row of broken, decaying teeth. It opened its mouth wide to apparently consume all or part of Jake's canine companion when Roscoe bit the protruding lip of the monster.

The monster jerked in pain, Jake slammed into it, and knocked everyone into the pool. The thing let go of Roscoe as Jake pushed it under the water. Roscoe surfaced and swam towards the edge of the pool as Jake turned his attention to the demon. *I'll teach you to try to eat my dog*, thought Jake as he held the thing under the water. It thrashed around for a moment then stopped. Jake looked down in the water and saw the yellow eyes staring up at him. *Why wasn't this thing drowning?*

In a second too late he realized his mistake. *These things don't need oxygen.* The creature grabbed Jake, pulled him under the water, and wrapped its arms around him tightly. In a panic, Jake squirmed and twisted to escape, but it only held on tighter. It could stay there all night, but Jake was quickly running out of air. *Calm yourself, Taft. There's got to be a way.* Then he remembered. *These things don't need air, but they bleed.* His upper arms were pinned but he could still reach his Colt .45. The creature was smiling, waiting for Jake to lose consciousness when Jake shoved the gun into its torso and pulled the trigger. *Eat this*, thought Jake as he pulled the trigger again and again, pumping .45 caliber slugs into the ugly thing. It released its hold in a vain attempt to avoid the bullets, but it was too late. It shook for a second, went limp, and slowly sank to the bottom of the pool. Jake lunged to the top, breaking the surface, and gasping for fresh air. After gulping several mouthfuls of air, he swam over to the side of the pool where Roscoe stood shaking in the cool night air. He pulled himself up on the side of the pool as Roscoe began licking his wet face. "You're welcome, buddy."

Ellie and Pam were in their room getting ready for bed. Ellie sat on the bed checking her email while Pam stood in the bathroom applying white face cream all over her face. "So how are you and Jake doing?" she asked.

Ellie looked up from the laptop. "What do you mean?"

"Oh, come on Ellie. I see how you two look at each other. You act like a couple of high school freshmen."

Ellie's face blushed. "We do not. Now just isn't the time to worry about relationships."

"Oh, I see, and when will it be time? Jake isn't going to wait forever."

Ellie was about to make a sarcastic remark when she heard a noise outside. She heard a squishing sound from someone walking in wet boots up the stairs. She peeked out through a crack in the curtains and to her dismay she saw Jake and Roscoe trudging along.

"What is it?" yelled Pam from the bathroom.

"It's Jake, and he's soaked."

"What?"

Ellie jerked the door open just as Jake and Roscoe plodded by. They were both soaked to the skin. Pam joined her at the door.

"What in the world happened to you?" asked Ellie.

"Roscoe and I went for a late-night dip in the pool," he grumbled.

"In your clothes?" asked Pam.

"Shush, Pamela. Now what really happened?"

Jake proceeded to tell the two women about the attack on Roscoe and the result. The two women looked over the railing and into the pool. The creature was already rapidly decomposing, and the water was turning a dark green with swirls of brown. Pam wrinkled up her cold cream covered face. "Oh, that's so gross."

"Should we notify the desk?" asked Ellie.

Jake shook his head. "No, we don't need the attention."

Pam peeked over the edge again. "I agree. There's no way we could tell the desk manager there's a dead demon in the pool. What did it look like?"

Jake looked at Pam. Her blonde hair was tied up on top of her head with her face covered in white cream. She wore a Texas Tech t-shirt, sweatpants, and bright purple fuzzy slippers. "It reminded me of….you."

"Funny, Jake. I'm going back inside." With that she turned and stomped back into their room.

"I just feel sorry for whoever finds the mess in the morning," said Ellie. She turned to Jake and began pushing him towards his room. "Go change before you catch a cold. I'll make some coffee and bring it over."

A few minutes after Jake had changed out of his wet clothes, he heard a light tap on the door. He peeked out and saw Ellie holding two cups of coffee. He let her in and accepted the warm brew. "Thanks. You didn't have to go to all the trouble. I would've been ok."

"Nonsense, you needed something to warm you up," replied Ellie.

Jake realized that even though the coffee felt warm, whenever he was around Ellie, he always seemed to be warmer than normal. "Aren't you afraid to be here alone in a motel room with a strange man?" he teased.

Ellie looked up at him over the rim of her cup and grinned. "Well, I'll admit you are one of the strange ones. Who else fights demons in a swimming pool in the middle of the night? Besides Roscoe can protect me, right?"

They both laughed. He loved to hear her laughter.

"I learned something important tonight," said Jake. "These creatures don't need oxygen. I held it under the water long enough for it to drown. There were no air bubbles."

"That's something worth knowing. Do you think it was after you because of what we're doing?"

Jake shook his head. "No, I don't think so. It was digging in the trash before it came after Roscoe. I think it was just after what it thought was an easy meal."

They both stood quietly sipping their coffee. Jake felt awkward. He wasn't sure if he was supposed to ask her to stay and talk or if she should leave. He wanted her to stay but didn't want to put her in an uncomfortable situation. After all, she was a church pastor. Ellie broke the silence. "Well, I...I...better be getting back. You never know what Pam might be scheming next door."

Jake laughed and opened the door. "Good night."

"Nite."

He watched until she was safely inside her room before he closed the door. Even though Roscoe was there with him, suddenly, the room felt empty.

---

**FBI Headquarters**
**935 Pennsylvania Avenue, NW**
**Washington, D.C.**

AGENTS RUIZ and Kimbell arrived in Washington. They'd taken the red eye flight from the Midwest and were met at Dulles International Airport by Agent Stephanie Williams. She was a veteran agent assigned to assist them in Washington.

On the drive into Washington, she briefed them on any updates they missed while flying in. "After your call about this man, Ghazi, being involved we sent a team out to his estate to set up surveillance," explained the 34-year-old, no nonsense career agent.

"Thanks. Do we have a file on him?" asked Agent Ruiz.

"The CIA is supposed to be sending it over this morning before we go pay him a visit. I talked to George Weldon over in Central Intel and he's saying there isn't much we know about him. He's apparently kept a low profile."

"That would make sense," answered Agent Ruiz with a nod. "It fits the profile. If he wanted to pull off something like this, he wouldn't want to be well known."

"Sounds about right," added Agent Kimbell sarcastically. "It's not the ones we know about, but the ones we don't know about that worry us."

"After you spoke with the Deputy Director, we called the Ghazi estate and surprisingly we were granted an appointment this morning at eleven."

"Great, that will give us time to shower and change clothes before we go rattle his chain."

————

## Budget Motel
## 2201 E. Silver Springs Blvd
## Ocala, Florida

IT WAS EARLY when Jake knocked on their room door. Ellie and Pam were already up and ready to go to breakfast and on their way down the stairs they saw the motel manager standing by the pool, talking to a local police officer.

"I tell ya, Bill, it's got to be a prank. Some of the high school kids must have thrown something into the pool," grumbled the manager.

The officer stood and rubbed his chin while looking at the murky water. "We'll get the fire department to come pump the water out and see what's down there. This is spring break weekend, so I imagine they threw something nasty in there. It stinks like rotten eggs."

"I tolerated the orange Kool-Aid last year, but this is too much."

Jake, Ellie, and Pam quietly walked by, got into their suburban, and drove to the nearest diner for breakfast. They sat in a booth and looked over the menu.

"So, what's our plan for the day?' asked Pam. She was always chipper and bright early in the morning.

"We scout the park during the day, so I'll know where to set up and wait tonight."

Ellie frowned at Jake. "What do you mean I? Don't you mean we?"

"I meant just me. It's going to be a long night or several nights. It's no place for you."

"You're not leaving us behind," argued Pam.

"Now ladies, it's not safe for you out there. I can't watch out for you and for the creature at the same time."

Pam raised an eyebrow and glared at Jake. "And who said we needed any watching. We can take care of ourselves."

"Like you did back at the church?"

"Hey, we were holding our own before you showed up."

"Now hold on you two," interjected Ellie. "No need to argue. Now Jake, we can be of some help. We can be an extra set of eyes and ears for you. I know we can't see the thing, but we can help keep an eye out for when or if it does show itself."

"No" growled Jake. "I don't want you in harm's way."

"What if we stayed in the suburban the whole time? We can still check the area. If anything happens, we'll be protected by the suburban. We'll keep Roscoe with us too. He can sense it before we'd ever see it."

Jake was going to object, but it did make sense and he saw the determination in their eyes. He dropped his head. "Alright, I'll agree as long as ya'll stay in the truck no matter what."

"It's a deal," announced Ellie. "Let's eat. I'm starved."

———

**Ghazi Estate**
**6322 Crosswinds Drive**
**Lake Barcroft, Virginia**

GHAZI SAT in his study checking the status of the laboratory's final processing of the micro toxins. His pharmaceutical company was an excellent cover for what he was planning. He looked up as Azim came into the room. "Will the helicopters be ready on time?" asked Ghazi.

"Yes. They're painting them now, especially the one to match the color of the U.S. helicopter. The hardware's being installed that will disperse the toxins."

"Excellent," said Ghazi with a grin. "I'm so pleased." His personal cell phone rang. "Yes?"

"The FBI is investigating you?"

"Good morning, Senator. Yes, I know. I have a meeting with them this morning."

"What? You're what? You knew? You already knew?"

"Calm down Senator. I have everything under control. Go back to your corporate sponsored lunches and answering constituent letters. I'll handle the FBI."

"Don't mock me Ghazi. My career is on the line. If this goes wrong, I'm in hot water. You can run back and hide in your country, but I have no place to go. Don't screw this up."

Ghazi's jaw tightened as he tried to remain calm. "My friend, everything will be taken care of. Don't fear. Your future is secure."

"Make sure it is." The phone clicked as he hung up.

"Why do you tolerate that vermin?" asked Azim.

"He's a useful tool to me right now. Soon I'll have no need for him, and he'll suffer the same fate as the rest of the American government officials."

"Good," answered Azim with a sneer.

Senator Amos Wilson slammed his cell phone down on his desk. A thirty-year veteran Senator from Ohio, he was angry at Ghazi's calmness. *How can that man be so calm while planning to take over the most powerful country in the world? I'll soon be sub-ruler of this part of the world. I can stop begging for votes and waiting for my measly retirement. I'll be rich beyond my dreams if that moron Ghazi doesn't blow it.*

He then picked up his phone and dialed a private number to his paid contact in the FBI.

———

**Budget Motel**
**2201 E. Silver Springs Blvd**
**Ocala, Florida**

THEY RETURNED from breakfast to pick up Roscoe and gather what they needed for their scouting party. A local fire engine was at the motel and had pumped the water out of the pool. In hip waders, they were down at the bottom of the pool shoveling out the remains of the decomposed demon and as they climbed the stairs, they heard them talking.

"This stuff's disgusting," commented one firefighter.

"No kidding. It looks like they threw a dead gator or something in here. They must have had it for a while cuz it's already soup."

Jake shook his head. If only they knew.

# CHAPTER SEVENTEEN

**Ghazi Estate**
**6322 Crosswinds Drive**
**Lake Barcroft, Virginia**

ANN SAT in her room desperately trying to figure a way out. Even though she had been exhausted she hadn't slept well. She stared out of the window at the beautiful landscape and part of the parking lot. She'd lain on the bed looking up at the ceiling half the night thinking about how she was going to escape.

*Wait a minute. The ceiling!*

She looked at the ceiling fan and light above the bed. *Too small!* She went into the bathroom and looked up at the rectangular fluorescent light fixture. *I might just fit!* She went back into the bedroom, looked around, and noticed the fancy handles on the desk in the corner. She grabbed one of the handles and began working it back and forth until she was able to break off the handle. Going back into the bathroom, she stood on the toilet, removed the light cover, and took out the bulbs. There was enough light from the bedroom for her to see to work. She used the tip of the handle to remove several of the screws. She pulled down part of the frame and investigated a dark empty space. *The attic!* Her room was on the upper floor and with the gabled roof there would be an attic. *Now all I must do is wait until dark.*

---

### Ocala National Forest
### Ocala, Florida

JAKE PARKED the suburban near one of the hiking trails in the beautiful national forest. The trio hiked through the forest while Roscoe ran and romped in the forest chasing anything he could find.

"The view is magnificent," commented Ellie.

"It would be even nicer if we weren't looking for a killer demon," answered Pam sarcastically.

Jake didn't say anything as they walked along the tall pine trees and across the wooden bridges that spanned the creeks and swamps. He concentrated on looking for tracks or other indications of the creature. Occasionally he stopped and studied a set of prints.

"Who do those belong to?" asked Ellie.

"A bear!"

"Like eight-foot-tall bears?" asked Pam as she looked around suspiciously.

"No," answered Jake. "You're thinking of Grizzlies. These are smaller bears. Most bears avoid humans, but some have grown accustomed to humans and rummage through tents or camping areas where careless campers have left out food."

They continued until they came to a campsite with a travel trailer where a family had set up camp. Three young children played in the area while the father gathered firewood. One of the children spied Roscoe and ran to tell his father. "Wolf, Daddy, wolf."

They approached the trailer as the children eyed Roscoe carefully.

"Is that a real wolf?" asked one of the boys about ten years old.

Jake smiled and explained that Roscoe was half wolf. The man introduced themselves as the Helms family. The father, Ted, said they camp there every year during spring break because it gave them time to get away from the city. Ted said he worked at a local drug research institute.

The smallest child was a five-year-old girl who looked out from behind her dad's leg. "Does he bite?"

"No," said Jake with a laugh. "His name's Roscoe and he loves to be petted."

The three children slowly approached Roscoe and carefully began petting him. They soon had him on his back, rubbing his belly while he enjoyed every second of it.

"Do you live nearby?" asked Ted.

"No sir. We're from Texas. The two ladies and I are out here on a little trip."

Before Ted had a chance to ask more questions his wife, Shirley, called them in for lunch. The trio said their goodbyes and left, but Roscoe was somewhat reluctant to leave. "Any idea of where to set up?" asked Ellie as they walked back to the suburban.

Jake nodded. "There was a spot we passed earlier that appears to be the area where the first two attacks took place. Y'all can set up down the road and watch in case it shows up where the other attacks occurred to the two campers."

"The Helms family seemed like nice people. For their sake a part of me doesn't want it to show up around here, but another part wants to see this thing gone," commented Ellie with a frown.

"I know how you feel," said Jake.

———

**Ghazi Estate**
**6322 Crosswinds Drive**
**Lake Barcroft, Virginia**

AGENTS WILLIAMS, Ruiz, and Kimbell pulled up to the gate of the Ghazi estate a few minutes before the scheduled appointment. The guard at the gate made a phone call to the security center to confirm their arrival. They were granted access and drove the mile long stretch to the main building.

"Did you notice all the security?" asked Agent Kimbell.

"Yes," nodded Agent Williams. "The two agents watching the house said it's covered with cameras, sensors, and foot patrols."

"Sounds like he's going to a lot of trouble to keep someone out," commented Agent Kimbell.

"Or to keep someone in," Agent Ruiz added.

They pulled up in front of the mansion and were met by a young Middle Eastern man. "I am Kateb. I am Mr. Ghazi's personal assistant. Please follow me."

They were escorted into the house and down the hall to a small conference room where they were left alone.

"Nice place," said Agent Kimbell off hand.

"Yeah, if you like mausoleums," replied agent Williams.

"When you're rich you can be afford to be eccentric."

Upstairs in her locked bedroom, Ann noticed a car pull up outside. She could only see part of the car as the corner of the house blocked her view. She watched as someone exited the vehicle and met with one of Ghazi's men. Even though she couldn't make out what was being said, she knew who the people were. After being the President's daughter and living around Washington she'd learned to spot them. Federal agents!

Ann's heart raced. She grabbed her self-made screwdriver and removed the remaining screws holding the bathroom's light fixture. She pulled it down, put her foot on the towel rack, and climbed into the darkness of the attic space.

Kateb escorted the agents back down the hall and into a lavishly decorated study. They got their first glimpse of Ghazi as he sat behind a large wooden desk. His hair was combed back, beard trimmed, and dressed in a grey business suit. He stood and smiled as they entered. "Ahh...welcome to my home. Please, be seated. May I get you anything to drink? Coffee? Soda?"

Agent Ruiz thought how Ghazi reminded him of a snake eyeing its prey right before it strikes. The three agents politely refused.

"Very well, now how can I be of service to you?"

*This guy is smooth… like slime* thought Agent Williams.

Agent Ruiz began. "I'm sure you've heard that the President's daughter was kidnapped several days ago. We're investigating possible leads as to her whereabouts."

Ghazi nodded. "Yes, yes, I've heard about that. I'm terribly sad about it, but how does that concern me?"

Agent Williams frowned. She thought his concern was a little too much.

"We tracked her to a warehouse in Denver," continued Agent Ruiz. "The warehouse belongs to your company. We were hoping you could shed some light on it."

"A warehouse in Denver?" Ghazi appeared deep in thought for a minute. "I have many buildings in many places. I would have to check and see what the status is of this warehouse. Perhaps someone used it illegally."

"One of the kidnappers was identified as an employee of yours."

"I have many employees around the world. I can't personally watch every one of them to ensure they obey all the laws. Did he confess to the kidnapping and give you more information?"

"He's dead," snapped Agent Kimbell.

"Oh my, then I'll contact my managers in the Denver area and find out about him and what we can do to help."

Agent Ruiz gritted his teeth. *This guy is too good.* "Unfortunately, his body was stolen from the morgue and one of our agents was killed. Someone didn't want us looking into who he was and what organization he might be tied to. Fortunately, we had he fingerprints already and were able to identify him."

"Oh, that sounds dreadful. I'm sorry about your agent. I'll do anything I can to help." Ghazi pushed a buzzer on his desk phone and stood up. "Please feel free to request anything you need from Kateb. He'll contact our corporate security who will be more than happy to provide you with all information that you might need."

Kateb entered quietly and waited by the door.

Ghazi smiled. "I do have a meeting in a few minutes so I can't stay any longer."

"Of course, we understand," answered Ruiz sarcastically. "You've been more than helpful."

"I'm glad I was able to assist you. I hope you find her quickly."

"We do too," replied Agent Ruiz. "And when we do, we'll prosecute whoever might be involved and whoever had knowledge, no matter how high up they may be." The three agents turned and were escorted out by Kateb.

It was dark in the attic. Ann waited a moment to allow her eyes to adjust to the dim light. It was hot and stuffy, but enough light came in from cracks that she could see to move around. She stepped from wooden beam to wooden beam, careful not to the step in between and fall through the ceiling. She worked her way across the attic until she was sure she was several rooms down and closer to the stairs. Her quickly devised plan was to sneak down the stairs, locate the agents, and obtain her freedom.

As best as she could figure she was in the middle of another bedroom. Hoping no one was inside she kicked on the sheet rock between the wooden supports and knocked a large hole in the ceiling. It appeared to be empty, so she dropped down, ran to the door, and cracked it open. From what she could see, the hallway was deserted so Ann slipped out into the hallway and walked carefully to the top of the stairs. It also was deserted. She descended the stairs halfway when she heard voices near the front entry way. The door opened and closed. *The agents must be leaving* she thought in a panic, so she bolted down the remaining steps and into the entryway. Her freedom was only a step away.

A large hand reached out and grabbed Ann by the hair and jerked her back. She screamed in pain as she was thrown roughly to the floor. One of her guards placed his knee in the middle of her back and pinned her to the floor. Ghazi walked calmly out of his study and stood over to Ann. "Going out for some fresh air?"

Ann refused to give him the satisfaction of an answer and glared at him from the floor.

"Did you think we wouldn't be watching you closely? You stupid woman! We've been watching you the whole time. It was very ingenious to use the drawer handle to remove the light fixture in the bathroom." Ghazi tilted his head and looked into her face. "There is no escape." With that he turned and went back into his study. Ann was jerked to her feet and dragged back to her room. A worker replaced the light fixture and left. She sat on the floor of her room, leaning against the bed. She looked around. *Hidden cameras? They've been watching me the whole time? Even in the bathroom?* Ann shivered, wrapped her arms around her knees, and for the first time since her kidnapping, she cried.

Ghazi sat sulking in his study. Things were not going as easily as he had planned so he called for Azim. The young man entered and took a seat.

"The FBI just left," said Ghazi obviously irritated. "I wasn't sure how much they knew so I allowed the visit to milk them of information. The FBI is getting too close. They identified your dead man in Denver."

Azim looked up into Ghazi's glaring face then looked away. "My men in Denver assured me they removed everything from the autopsy room."

"Your men were wrong," yelled Ghazi. "They were incompetent and allowed them to retain the fingerprints."

"The examiner must have had the fingerprint card with him."

"I don't care how they found out. The point is your men screwed up."

"We can make amends?"

Ghazi sat for a few moments in thought. "I want you to eliminate the three agents. Make it look like domestic terrorists."

"It will be done."

"And don't let them screw this up."

———

**FBI Headquarters**
**935 Pennsylvania Avenue, NW**
**Washington, D.C.**

AGENT RUIZ SAT in a chair against the wall in Agent Williams' office and fumed. "He's up to his eyes in this. I can feel it."

Agent Williams was going over the brief file on Ghazi the CIA put together while Agent Kimbell looked over her shoulder. "There's nothing in here to help us. It's like Ghazi appeared out of nowhere. There are no records of his birth, where he went to school, nothing."

"He was lying most of the time," added Agent Kimbell.

Agent Williams looked up at him. "Most? How about all of the time?"

"But we don't have anything to connect him to it," said Agent Ruiz. He thought for a moment. "I need a wiretap. Can you get us a court order?"

Agent Williams nodded. "I think I can get Judge McAdams to sign one."

"Good. I want to know when he leaves, where he goes, who he talks to, and about what."

Agent Williams' phone rang, and she picked it up. She listened and hung up. "The Deputy Director wants to see me," she explained while walking out. "I'll be right back, and then I'll start on the court order."

Agent Ruiz turned to Agent Kimbell. "We need to get a copy of every building, business, and vehicle that Ghazi owns in this area. She has to be in one of them." Agent Kimbell nodded and began typing on the computer on the desk.

Agent Williams returned wearing a serious frown. She flopped down in a chair next to the desk. "I've just been informed that Ghazi is off limits."

"What?" Agent Ruiz jumped to his feet. "That's not possible. He's in it up to his Taliban beard."

"I know but Deputy Director Sullens just advised me that as of right now Ghazi is not to be considered a suspect and to look elsewhere."

"Elsewhere? There is nowhere else to look," snapped Agent Ruiz.

"I know."

"Someone in high places must have pulled some strings to get the heat off?"

"It has to be someone in our government that has a lot to gain by the President's daughter being kidnapped."

"What if we went to the President and told him?" asked Agent Kimbell.

Agent Williams shook her head. "We don't know who pulled the strings. It could be someone working in the White House. We'd never get in to see him."

Agent Ruiz slammed his fist down on the desk. "I didn't come this far to be bullied away by some stuffed shirt politician with his or her own agenda. That girl's life is at stake."

"It could cost you. If they get wind that you're still investigating Ghazi, it could mean giving up your retirement," warned Agent Kimbell.

"How much would retirement mean if it cost that young woman's life?"

The three agents nodded together.

"Alright, so the wiretap is out but I say we keep the surveillance for now. We'll start checking into his business holdings as quietly as possible and go from there."

---

**Ocala National Forest**
**Ocala, Florida**

NIGHT HAD LONG SETTLED into the national forest. The darkness came alive with the sounds of frogs, crickets, and other nocturnal creatures. Jake, Ellie, and Pam had spent the rest of the day searching the area for supplies they needed. An ice cooler, sodas, and food to snack on, were a necessity for a long night of staying awake and Jake bought a set of walkie talkies so they could communicate. The trip was stretching everyone's budgets, but they knew how important it was to be prepared.

Ellie, Pam, and Roscoe parked along the road within sight of the usual teenage make out spot and near the scene of one of the attacks. They took turns watching the area with newly purchased binoculars.

Jake was a mile or so away sitting near the Helm's family trailer. He had chosen a large pine tree to set up and wait. It was now well after two in the morning, and they'd been there for several of hours already.

Pam looked through the binoculars at a car parked in the usual lover's spot. "Don't these people know there's a killer loose in this area? These kids shouldn't be out here at this hour."

Ellie was watching out the side window for any sign of the creature. "People have short memories. Nothing's happened for about a week. The Helms have been there for three days."

"Do you think it'll show up?"

"I'd like to say I hope so but I'm not sure we really want to see it."

"Maybe it moved on?"

"I don't think so. We noticed that it struck every week about the same time. It seems as if it's waiting for someone."

"I hope it's not waiting on us."

"Amen, sister."

"I wonder why there's not more police or federal people out here?"

"Jake and I thought about that too," said Ellie. "We figure the police have their hands full with everything outside the park and the forest service doesn't have the manpower to wait out the monster and besides they can't see it."

"You and Jake have been doing a lot of figuring lately haven't you?" asked Pam with a grin.

Even in the dark she could tell that Ellie blushed. "No, Pamela. Right now, it's business between Jake and me. We don't have time for anything else."

"Uh huh, and I'm the Queen of England. Speaking of Jake, it's about time to check in."

Jake had made them agree to radio him every hour and check in. Ellie picked up the radio. "Jake, are you there?"

"Go ahead."

"I don't suppose you've seen any sign of our unwanted guest?"

"Nope, it's been nice and quiet over here. Only one light is on in the trailer. The Helms family must be asleep."

"Ok, we're just checking in….as ordered." Ellie looked at Pam and winked. Pam giggled.

"This is for your safety and mine."

"Yes, we know, and we have Roscoe here to protect us." They both glanced into the back of the suburban where Roscoe was stretched out on the seat asleep. "He's on constant guard."

"He's asleep isn't he?"

They both giggled. "Yes."

"I'll talk to ya'll in an hour."

"Roger," Ellie giggled. "Over and out."

————

**Ghazi Estate**
**6322 Crosswinds Drive**
**Lake Barcroft, Virginia**

ANN HAD JUST FINISHED TAKING a shower, in the dark. She decided if they were going to watch her in the bathroom then they were only going to see darkness. She was sitting on the bed when someone unlocked the door. Amira entered with a smile and carried a tray of food. She sat the food on the dresser, came over, and sat on the edge of the bed. "I heard what happened today. You shouldn't have tried to escape. Mr. Ghazi is patient but don't push your luck."

Ann nibbled at her food. "What do you expect me to do? Sit here while he makes plans to take over the world after he kills millions of people?"

"No one is going to die," answered Amira with a shake of her head.

"Someone has died already."

Amira ignored her remark. "He's only using the biological warfare as a threat. He'll never use it."

"He told me he would," replied Ann harshly. "He intends to kill the entire population of Washington D.C., London, and Jerusalem and then take over like some king. All those people are going to die, including all the Muslims."

"You're wrong. He only plans to use it as a threat."

"Wake up Amira. He intends to kill me too. He can't allow me to leave here alive."

"He told me he's going to release you after his demands are met."

Ann shook her head in disgust. "It's no use. You don't see it. You're blinded by your faith in him. He's turned you into a kidnapper and killer. He's a psychopath. Who else would put cameras in this room and the bathroom so he can get some sort of perverted pleasure out of it?"

"No one is watching you. There are no cameras."

Ann pointed toward the bathroom. "He told me how I tried to escape. He hadn't even been upstairs. Do you want me to show you?"

"This conversation is over," said Amira coldly as she got up to leave. "I brought you some food to make you feel better. I didn't come to be insulted."

"If you walk around in a fog, you might get lost." Ann turned away. "Don't let the door hit you on your way out."

Amira left the room and walked downstairs. She didn't understand why the American woman could not understand. *Why did she make up lies?*

She went into the kitchen and found Akim sitting at a small table looking at aerial photos of Washington D.C.

"I took some food up to the American woman to try to appease her," explained Amira. "But she only insults me."

Akim looked up in disgust. "What did you expect? She's an infidel. Don't waste your time. She'll burn in hell."

Amira filled a cup of coffee. "She said there were cameras in her room and she was being watched. Why would she make up such a lie?"

"Because she isn't. There are cameras in her room."

"What? There are? Why?"

Akim stared at her as if he was looking at a small child. "Dear sister, we have to take precautions. She's an enemy and has to be watched. She has no rights or privileges and besides she's on borrowed time anyway."

Amira's eyes widened. "You're going to kill her?"

"She has to die for our cause. No one will listen and take us seriously if we let her live. It's all for the glory of Allah."

"Yes, of course it is," answered Amira. She turned her back on Akim.

*Ghazi said she was going to be released unharmed. What else haven't I been told that's going to happen?*

————

### Ocala National Forest
### Ocala, Florida

IT WAS EARLY in the morning, but the sun had not yet dawned. Pam was asleep and Ellie was watching the area. The car they'd been watching left hours ago. They'd checked in every hour but there had been no sign of the creature. It was fifteen minutes until the next check in time when Jake called on the radio. "There's something moving near the camper."

"What is it?" Pam awakened at the sound of Jake's voice.

A mile away, Jake was sitting beside a huge pine tree hidden from view. He had caught sight of some movement near the edge of the forest on the other side of the campsite. He raised his Winchester rifle and sighted along the barrel. "I don't know for sure what it is. It's still too far back in the trees."

"Do you want us to come over there?"

"No. Stay where you are." Jake followed the dark mass with the rifle sight as it emerged from the darkness. It moved towards a set of park trash cans and stood up. By the shape of the form and the movement, Jake knew what it was. "It's a bear."

"A bear? Are you sure?" asked Ellie.

Jake watched as the bear fumbled around the trash can but was unable to get the lid off. National Park trash cans have specially designed lids to prevent animals from getting into them. It dropped down on all fours and searched around for anything left by the campers.

"Yeah, I'm sure. It's looking for food."

"Maybe it's a demon disguised as a bear?" whispered Pam.

"Pam thinks it might be a demon disguised as a bear."

Jake stopped, raised an eyebrow for a second, and looked at the radio. "I know what a bear looks like. Tell her to go back to sleep."

"Jake says it's not a demon," whispered Ellie.

"I heard him," said Pam sarcastically.

Jake watched as the bear finally meandered back into the forest. "It'll be daylight soon. Let's call it a night. Come pick me up."

"Amen," said Pam.

# CHAPTER EIGHTEEN

**Quality Inn**
**7001 Spring Garden Blvd**
**Arlington, VA**

A DARK BLUE four door Ford Taurus was parked down the street from the hotel where Special Agents Ruiz and Kimbell were staying. It arrived shortly before sunrise to monitor the agents. The two middle eastern men waited patiently until a silver four door Impala pulled up to the curb. They watched as Agents Ruiz and Kimbell came out of the hotel and entered the vehicle. The FBI car dove off and they followed about a block behind.

"I spoke with the agents on surveillance at the estate," said Agent Williams as she drove toward FBI headquarters. "They said no one came or went all night. I explained that we're no longer officially authorized to be there, but they know what's at stake. They're going to rotate the surveillance as much as they can while working their cases."

"Good," answered Agent Ruiz. "I appreciate all their help, but I don't want to jeopardize their careers. If they get any heat, pull them off."

Agent Williams nodded. "I told them that. They know the score."

A block behind them sat the two men at a red light. As both cars entered Interstate 395, the passenger reached into the glove box and removed a small electronic remote. He flipped a small switch, and a green indicator light came on. "The timer's set," he said to the driver in Arabic.

"Good. Now all we do is wait and watch."

The three agents continued towards downtown Washington. Agent Williams glanced in her mirror a couple of times. She changed lanes twice.

Agent Ruiz, who sat in the front passenger seat, noticed it.

"What's wrong?"

"We have a tail."

Ruiz flipped down the passenger sun visor revealing a mirror and watched out the back for a minute.

"The Taurus three cars back in the other lane?"

"Yep."

Agent Kimbell glanced over his shoulder at the vehicle. Agent Ruiz picked up his cell phone and dialed into FBI headquarters.

"How far off are we?" he asked Agent Williams.

"Too far."

"Maybe we can lure them in?" Agent Ruiz gave the FBI operator their car information, their location, and direction of travel. "I gave her the information as best I could but there's a lot of static on the line. These cell phones stink."

Agent Williams changed lanes several more times and watched as the car followed but never came closer. She kept an eye on them as they crossed the Washington Channel. She told Agent Ruiz to call in, give their current location, and that they plan to take the 12<sup>th</sup> Street exit.

Agent Ruiz dialed again, spoke into the phone for a second time, and hung up. "I tried to give her the info as much as I could, but the reception was bad. Every other word was cutting out."

Agent Williams handed him her phone. "Try this one."

Agent Ruiz dialed again as they exited the freeway and onto 12<sup>th</sup>

Street. He spoke to the FBI operator then hung up. "I had the same problem. The towers must be acting up."

At the intersection with Independence Avenue, Agent Williams quickly changed lanes and made a sharp left turn to go west on Independence Avenue. She watched in her mirror as the Taurus continued straight. *Now that's strange* she thought. *They didn't even try to follow?*

Agent Ruiz noticed it too. "They didn't turn. How odd?"

Agent Williams thought for a moment. "What was the static like on the phone?"

"It was intermitted. It would come and go every second or so."

She turned south at Wallenberg Place and onto East Basin Drive to see if the followers had made the block to follow. The dark blue Taurus was nowhere in sight. As they drove by the Jefferson Memorial and onto Ohio Drive, she turned to the other two agents. "Now what would cause intermitted interference on our cell phones?"

It dawned on her at almost the same time as it did the other two agents, and they looked wide eyed at each other. She slammed on the brakes, jumped the curb, and came to a stop near the FDR memorial park. They leapt from the car and ran down towards the cherry trees along the man-made tidal basin. Ten seconds later a massive explosion shattered the early morning air as the car exploded and burst into flames. The concussion knocked the three agents to the ground.

A half a mile away the two men in the Taurus smiled at the sound of the explosion and the rising smoke.

The agents got to their feet. They were dirty and slightly singed, but alive. They watched the car burn as traffic came to a halt, and within a moment the sounds of sirens could be heard as fire engines responded.

"I think we're making someone nervous," commented Agent Ruiz.

Agent Kimbell nodded as he patted the dirt off his jacket. "I'll say."

Agent Williams stood with her hands on her hips and frowned at the burning car.

"Are you ok?" asked Agent Ruiz.

"No," she snapped. "My favorite jacket was in that car."

The other two agents stared at her, and then bellowed with laughter, more at having cheated death than at her.

---

**Ghazi Estate**
**6322 Crosswinds Drive**
**Lake Barcroft, Virginia**

GHAZI WAS ENJOYING his breakfast when his phone rang. He picked it up and listened.

"The three pests have been exterminated," said the voice in Arabic.

Ghazi hung up and smiled. *Breakfast was going to taste a lot better this morning.*

---

**The Italian Garden**
**7501 Old Keefer Rd**
**Ocala, Florida**

AFTER SLEEPING MOST of the day, Jake, Ellie, and Pam sat in a local restaurant and ate dinner in preparation for another night in the national forest.

Pam checked her laptop for messages and news while Jake and Ellie ate in silence. They were tired but determined.

"There's been another arson involving strange circumstances," explained Pam. "This time it occurred in Baltimore where a small health club was set on fire. Ten people died in the fire. They couldn't escape because the doors were blocked. A witness saw two men in dark clothes inside right before the fire."

"That's so tragic," said Ellie somberly. "I can't imagine how their families are dealing with it,"

"Sounds like the same two from the other arsons. I wish I knew why," commented Jake.

"Do evil, disgusting, low life demons have to have a reason?" said Pam.

Ellie nodded. "That's very true. They just spread hate wherever they go with no reason or thought for who they hurt."

"I hope we can deal with this problem here soon because I have a feeling, I have my work cut out for me," said Jake with a shake of his head.

---

**FBI Headquarters**
**935 Pennsylvania Avenue, NW**
**Washington, D.C.**

THE THREE AGENTS spent the rest of the day filling out reports. The FBI crime scene towed the burned-out shell of a car to their lab. The preliminary exam showed that an explosive device with a timer had been attached to the undercarriage of the car.

Agent Ruiz was reading over the initial report. "It's obvious that they attached the device sometime during the night, probably while it was parked at your home."

Agent Williams nodded. "I live in an apartment complex with a security gate; unfortunately, it's not hard to get past it. All they had to do was follow one of the residents in while the gate was open. They must've followed me to the hotel where I picked you up, waited until we were all in the car, and activated the bomb. I don't know why I didn't notice them earlier?"

"Don't beat yourself up about it," said Agent Kimbell. "You can't be on guard twenty-four hours a day. I hope we can trace the bomb parts back and prove Ghazi's behind this."

"The job of tracing the maker of the explosive and parts could take days or weeks. I don't think Ann Campbell has that long if it's not too late already."

"All we can do is keep up the surveillance at the estate and hope they make a mistake."

"They already made a mistake," added Agent Ruiz. "They think we're dead."

Agent Kimbell and Williams both smiled.

"That's right," said Agent Kimbell. "And that gives us an advantage for a while."

Agent Williams phone rang, she answered, and listened for a moment. "But sir, we can't...We're right in the middle of this investigation...Yes, sir...I know that but with all due respects...Yes sir." She slammed the phone down and pounded her fist on the desktop.

"Bad news?" asked Agent Kimbell sarcastically.

"Deputy Director Sullens wants us in a safe house until it blows over," explained Agent Williams.

"You mean he wants us locked away so we can't do anything," growled Agent Ruiz.

"He must be getting pressure from somewhere up high to keep us off it."

"Maybe?" said Agent Ruiz.

"But in the meantime, the trail gets colder," grumbled Agent Kimbell.

———

**Ocala National Forest**
**Ocala, Florida**

JAKE WAS AGAIN at his hiding spot while Pam and Ellie were parked under the same tree a mile away. They'd been there for several hours without any luck. Roscoe was in the far back seat dozing and Pam was asleep in the passenger seat while Ellie had kept watch on the area. She glanced down at the handheld radio then picked it up. "Jake, are you there?"

"Go ahead. Is something wrong?"

"No. It's just so quiet."

"Yeah, there's not much going on over here either. I think the campers are in bed."

"How long do you think this will take?"

"I don't know. If this thing keeps its schedule it'll show up soon. I hope in the next couple of days."

"Then what, where do we go from here?"

"I don't know. I guess we'll take one step at a time."

"You have a ranch to look after, and I have church responsibilities."

"I know. After this we'll reevaluate what we need to do."

"Okay."

"Ellie."

"Yes."

"Why did you pick Shady Oak to start your church?"

Ellie thought for a minute. "After college and seminary, I worked in several large churches in the northeast where I grew up. I felt that I was just going through the motions, like a machine, so I decided to go where I could start something new and build it from the ground up."

The radio was silent for a second.

"I'm glad you did."

Ellie blushed. "Me too."

"We better get off the radio and save the batteries but check in on time."

"Aye, aye, Captain."

"Are y'all through now?" grumbled Pam. "So, I can get some sleep."

"You've been ease dropping?"

"It was hard not to hear you two love birds chirp at each other."

"We are not love birds. We're just friends."

"Yeah, right. Wake me in an hour." Pam turned toward the window and drifted back to sleep.

"We're not," she said softly more to herself than to Pam, but even she didn't sound that convincing.

# CHAPTER NINETEEN

**FBI Safe House**
**Arlington, Virginia**

AGENT RUIZ SAT on the couch grumbling about being stuck in the safe house. The three agents were in a small brick house in an upper middle-class neighborhood just outside of Washington D.C. It had all the usual amenities that someone would need but Agent Ruiz felt it was like being in a prison. The five hours they'd been there already seemed to him like an eternity. Agent Kimbell was in the kitchen fixing a late-night snack while Agent Williams typed on her laptop she'd brought from the office. "I'm accessing the files at the office. I can still check on Ghazi's businesses from here," explained Agent Williams.

Agent Ruiz grumbled something she couldn't understand when there was a sound at the back door. Instantly the two agents hit the floor. Agent Kimbell ducked in from the kitchen and switched off the lights. They drew their weapons as Agent Ruiz slipped up beside the door. He slowly unlocked the door then threw it open and they pointed their weapons at the dark entrance.

"Agent Ruiz, this is Secret Service Agent Bill Meadows," said a voice from the darkness. "I'm coming to the door slowly."

They watched as a man appeared in the doorway. He had a flashlight in one hand and his badge case in the other. Several dark forms were behind him in the darkness.

"Step in nice and easy," ordered Agent Ruiz.

Once inside, Agent Williams examined his identification and found it was genuine. Agent Meadows motioned for the others to enter. Three more men and a woman came in quickly before shutting the door.

"What's this all about?" demanded Agent Williams. "This is supposed to be a safe house, not grand central station."

"Turn on the light please," asked Agent Meadows. "It should clear up your questions."

Agent Kimbell flipped on the lights again. Standing in the room were three male Secret Service agents along with Secret Service agent Beth Sills. The fourth man was wearing black slacks and a jacket with the Presidential seal embroidered on it.

"Mr. President?" blurted out Agent Williams.

"Agent Sills needs to sit down. She's still weak," said the President.

Agent Sills was thin and pale with her left arm in a sling. The agents helped her to the couch.

"Agent Sills called me and said she was out of the hospital and wanted to help. I told her she needed to rest but she refused. She said she was flying to Washington one way or another, so I had her flown here by military transport."

Agent Sills smiled weakly, but they could see the determination in her eyes. "I know I can't do much in my condition, but I thought I could help make phone calls and check out some things for you."

"It's good to see you up and moving again Beth," said Agent Ruiz. "We'll be glad to use your help, but I'm afraid we've hit a wall."

"They stuck us in this safe house to keep us out of the investigation," grumbled Agent Kimbell.

"How did you know we were here, sir?" asked Agent Ruiz.

"I have contacts inside the FBI," said the President with a wink.

"Director Chisom briefed me about the bombing and made a few indiscreet calls. I need your help."

They all nodded.

"Something's brewing in Washington. My daughter's been kidnapped and someone in Washington is involved. I don't know who it is or why."

The three FBI agents filled the President in on what they knew so far and what their suspicions were about Hassan Ghazi.

"The problem is, Mr. President," explained Agent Ruiz. "We don't have any real proof. Everything fits but we have no concrete proof."

The room was quiet for several moments before the President spoke. "Thank you all for your help and dedication. I appreciate it and I know Ann appreciates it wherever she is. I can't order you to do this, but I will ask. I'm asking you to go against your superior's orders and continue investigating Ghazi and his corporation. I'm asking you to find that concrete proof and if he's part of it I want him caught and punished." The President's eyes began to tear up. "But most of all I want you to find my daughter. I'll take personal responsibility for anything that results from this."

Agent Ruiz was the first to respond. "Mr. President, you don't have to ask. We never stopped; we're just trying to figure out how to do it without the resources of the bureau."

"I can offer you limited resources from the White House. Since we don't know who is involved, we'll have to keep it low key. Agent Meadows has already volunteered to be your contact man. He'll keep me briefed on your activities and give you what assistance he can." He stood to leave. "I can't tell you how much this means to me."

"You don't have to thank us Mr. President," said Agent Ruiz. "It's our job. It's what we do. We'll find your daughter."

The other two agents nodded in agreement. The President shook their hands before quietly slipping out the door. Agent Meadows gave them his personal cell phone they could call 24-hours a day. After they left, the three agents looked at each other.

"That was different," said Agent Kimbell who looked at Agent Sills and smiled.

"Yessss," said Agent Williams. "It looks like we are back in business."

"We can use my access codes and passwords," added Agent Sills. "This way no one at the FBI will know we're checking."

Agent Williams smiled. "Thank you for your help, but you need to rest and start in the morning."

Agent Sills shook her head. "I've been resting in a hospital bed for too long. I need to get to work." She stood up and slowly walked to the table and sat in front of the laptop where she began typing in passwords and accessing files.

"Suddenly I'm hungry," said Agent Ruiz with a huge grin. "Is anybody up for a late dinner?"

————

**Ocala National Forest**
**Ocala, Florida**

IT WAS DARK AND QUIET. Pam was on watch and had switched with Ellie three times already. She had watched every tree and bush until she knew them by heart. She even started giving each tree a name, *Fred, Wilma, Barney, Tiny Tim, Alvin*...but no sign of their unwanted visitor.

Jake was still sitting beside the same tree. He'd caught himself dozing off a couple of times and was fighting off fatigue. He watched the Helms family camper when a dark form appeared at the edge of the forest. It moved back and forth as if checking to make sure no one was around. "I've got movement."

"What is it?" answered Pam.

At the sound of Jake's voice Ellie's eyes came open and she sat up. "What's going on?"

"Jake sees something."

Jake eased his rifle into position and followed the dark form as it moved around in the dark. It came closer to the camper and lumbered into the clearing. "It's the bear again."

"Are you sure?"

"Yeah, it's trying to get into the trash can again."

Pam looked at Ellie and shrugged. "False alarm, it's the bear again."

Ellie rolled her eyes, curled back up in the front passenger seat, and dozed back off.

Jake watched the bear roam around looking for anything left to eat. When it didn't find anything, it wandered back into the dark. "It looks like he's going to look somewhere else. He's leaving."

"I copy that."

Jake lowered his rifle and settled back down. A minute or two later he saw the form reappear and lumber back into the clearing. "Looks like our bear came back. Guess he's hoping he missed something."

"Well, I wish Yogi Bear would go find someplace else to steal lunch baskets."

"He'll leave again when he doesn't find anything."

The form moved toward the trash can and then over towards the camper. It stood up by the door to the camper. *Wait a minute? This one isn't the bear; the form doesn't look right.* The dark form suddenly grabbed the door of the camper and ripped it open.

Jake jumped to his feet. "We got a problem. This one isn't the bear." He dropped the radio, grabbed his rifle, and ran towards the trailer.

"What? What is it?" yelled Pam into the radio. Ellie shot straight up in the seat, eyes wide open.

In an instant the creature was inside the trailer. Jake ran as fast as he could toward the trailer when he heard a woman's shriek from inside. He climbed into the camper and looked frantically around and was assailed by the smell of rotting flesh and sulfur. *It's a demon.* He heard another scream coming from the bedroom area of the camper and dashed down the tiny hall to the master bedroom where a dim light illuminated the bedroom.

Jake saw the creature.

It was tall and covered in maggots, insects, and other crawling things. It wore a huge black sword attached to a loop on its belt with rotting human appendages hung from the belt like trophies. It had thrown the bed aside and faced Ted and his wife who were hunkered down in a corner staring in terror.

"Leave 'em alone," yelled Jake.

It spun around and glared at Jake. It had a large snout and small eyes that glowed yellow. When it moved, huge clumps of maggots fell off it onto the bed. It growled at Jake.

Jake raised the rifle and fired. The sound of the gunshot was deafening inside the cramped trailer, and the impact of the bullet slammed the creature back against the wall. Jake racked another round into his Winchester and aimed at the thing. The creature lunged forward at Jake as he fired again, and another slug tore into its midsection knocking it sideways into the wall. *What's it going to take to kill this thing?* He levered another round into the chamber and fired at the monster as it shouldered into Jake, knocking him backward into the living room of the trailer. The blow knocked the rifle away and into the dark room. Jake rolled away to avoid any blows from the creature, but the thing continued out the door. Afraid of losing sight of the creature Jake was on his feet out the door without his rifle.

Ellie grabbed the radio. "Jake, Jake, what's going on?"

The women listened but the radio was silent, then Pam started the suburban.

"What are you going to do?" asked Ellie.

"I'm not sitting here and waiting. Hold on." Pam slammed it into drive and squealed the tires as she sped towards the camp site.

Jake looked around and saw the demon lumbering towards the forest. He knew his shots had injured the thing, but it might still get away, so he pulled his Colt 45 semi-auto handgun and fired several times into the creature. It stumbled but slowly kept going. *Something's not right.*

"Hey, freak. Why leave the party so soon?" yelled Jake.

The monstrous thing spun around on him, sending hundreds of insects flying off into the air. It drew its black sword and roared at Jake.

Jake was about to take another shot when he heard an engine racing accompanied by a set of headlights. *What the...?*

The creature turned toward the oncoming vehicle and was blinded by the headlights. It raised its arm to shield its eyes when it was struck head on by the suburban. The crushing blow sent the creature flying across the clearing as the SUV came to a screeching halt. Thousands of bugs and maggots were thrown in all different directions.

Jake ran towards the fallen creature. The demon, or what was left of it, was lying on its side. Most of its body was gone but the insects and other things knocked loose began crawling toward it to reassemble the creature.

"Not this time," spat Jake. He aimed carefully and shot it between the eyes. The thing went limp and died. The insects then seemed to lose interest and became a mass of disorganized individual creatures.

Pam and Ellie came running up to Jake.

"Are you ok?" asked Ellie.

"I'm fine."

They all looked down at the pile of rapidly decaying demon and the insects that were starting to disperse.

"It appeared to be a smaller demon covered mostly of insects that created a larger one," explained Jake.

"Yep, but it wasn't so tough against a couple of half crazed women in a suburban," said Pam triumphantly.

"You were supposed to stay put," growled Jake.

"And miss all the excitement?"

"You might've been hurt."

"But Roscoe was here to protect us."

Jake looked over and saw Roscoe sitting in the driver's seat barking out the window.

They checked on the Helms family in the trailer and found them with the children huddled inside around Ted and Shirley, but all appeared to be in good condition considering. They had the lights on inside and Jake retrieved his rifle.

"Thank you so much," said Shirley.

Ted rubbed his neck. "We don't know how to thank you."

Jake smiled. "There's no need to thank us. We just happened to be in the area."

"At this time of morning?"

"We were...uh...star gazing," answered Ellie.

They helped them put the door back in place as best they could. The kids kept looking over at what was left of the demonic creature.

"What was it?" asked Ted.

Jake shrugged. He didn't want to try to explain about an insect covered demon. "You might want to notify the park service."

"We already called 911 and they're sending a forest ranger out," explained Ted. When the family went back inside to clean up, Jake and the others slipped into the suburban and drove back to the motel.

"The Helms' will have one big story to tell the forest rangers," commented Pam.

"And the forest rangers will have an even harder time trying to identify the remains of the demon," added Jake.

After returning to the motel Jake took a shower then climbed into bed for some much-needed rest. Sleep didn't come immediately as he kept replaying the event over in his mind as there was something nagging at him that he just couldn't put his finger on it.

———

**FBI Safe House**
**Arlington, Virginia**

AGENT SILLS SAT at the laptop and checked Ghazi's business ties. She'd slept most of the night, but she still experienced the occasional pain in her chest. Her left arm was still in a sling, so she had to type with only her right hand which slowed her down.

Agents Ruiz was in the kitchen cooking breakfast when Agent Williams' cell phone rang. She answered and listened. "It's one of the agents on surveillance. He said Ghazi's on the move."

Agent Ruiz came in from the kitchen with burritos made of eggs, cheese, and sausage. "They're just like my mama used to make."

Agent Sills titled her head toward Agent Williams. "She's on the phone with another agent. He says Ghazi left the estate."

"I'm not surprised. He thinks were dead, so he probably feels free to come and go now."

Agent Williams hung up. "He's going to tail him and see where he goes."

"Excellent. Let's eat up. Where's Kimbell?"

"He's checking around outside. He'll be back in a few minutes."

Agent Ruiz had already stuffed his mouth with one of his burritos. "He'd better hurry or it'll all be gone."

--------

**The Breakfast Kettle**
**5401 S. Whitmore Ave**
**Ocala, Florida**

AFTER SLEEPING IN, the trio checked out of the motel and went for breakfast. They sat in a booth and ordered their meal while Pam sent several emails to her assistant editor earlier and checked the news. "It looks like the normal stuff, most of it bad," she said dryly. "Let's see...there was a high-level member of the Center for Disease Control found murdered in Los Angeles. They say it was an apparent robbery attempt. Here's a story about a car explosion in Washington near the Jefferson memorial. They don't what the cause is and it's under investigation. A suicide bomber in Baghdad killed nine people. The President's daughter is still missing, but there's nothing new on the kidnapping."

Ellie and Jake nodded as their food arrived.

"I hope they find her soon. It must be terrible for the First Family to have to wait, not knowing," said Ellie.

"So, what are our plans now?" asked Pam.

Jake shrugged. "I'm not sure yet, but something's been bothering me about last night."

"You mean besides a large half demon-half bug that broke into a trailer and attacked an innocent family?' added Pam with a smirk.

Jake frowned. "Yes."

"How about because it was a mean and didn't care who it attacked," added Ellie.

"But that's the issue. Why did it go straight for Ted and his wife first?" asked Jake. "It bypassed where the kids were sleeping and went straight for the master bedroom like it was looking for them. It was almost like it was on a mission."

Pam waved her fork. "Maybe it just wanted to get him out of the way first so it could do as it pleased with the rest of the family."

Ellie shivered. "That just sounds so morbid."

"Perhaps but I still can't get over the feeling that there was a method to its madness," added Jake.

The waitress came and filled up their coffee cups. She was a short middle-aged woman with a round face smiling face. "Are you visiting?"

They all smiled, and Ellie answered up first. "Yes, but we're leaving this morning. We've just been out to see the national forest. It's so beautiful."

The woman nodded. "Oh, it's beautiful, but did you hear about what happened last night?"

They all shook their heads.

"A family was attacked by a rogue bear. It was on the news this morning."

"A bear?" asked Ellie.

"Oh my, yes. They said it attacked a family inside a trailer. There was lots of bear tracks around. If it wasn't for an astrology professor, they might've been killed."

"Astrology professor?" asked Ellie.

"Yes, they thought he was from out west somewhere, like Arizona."

"Maybe it was just some kind of hunter that got lucky?" asked Pam with a grin.

Jake kicked her under the table.

The woman continued. "Oh no, Ted said he had a group of students with him and happened by at the right time. The group was watching the stars."

"You mean star gazing?" asked Pam with a giggle.

Ellie kicked her under the table.

"Well, I'm just glad that family's alright. They camp here every spring. They come in for breakfast occasionally. Nice family. He works for a research lab. He's the Vice President or assistant head guy. Maybe he'll find a cure for cancer or something someday. It's been nice visiting with you. Have a nice trip back." She turned and went back to the counter and took an order from another customer.

They continued eating for a few more minutes. Jake was deep in thought then looked up at Pam suddenly. "Can you check and see which research lab is around here?"

"Sure, but why.... professor?"

Jake frowned at her. "A lead.... maybe."

While Pam searched on her laptop, Ellie questioned Jake about his suspicions. "So, you think there might be some link between these attacks?"

"I'm grasping at straws. Maybe I'm trying to make sense out something that's senseless."

"I checked the area's businesses," Pam explained. "There's only one. It's called Martech Laboratories. According to their web site they do research on possible cures for the flu and other outbreaks. Let me see...yes, the father of the camping family is Theodore Helms, Vice President of Martech labs."

"Okay. Can you see if there have been any other unusual crimes or attacks near any other pharmaceutical companies or research labs?"

"But why would demons care about research labs?" inquired Ellie.

"I don't know, but I want to be sure."

"This might be something. The arson fire that claimed lives at a bar in Chicago was near a lab belonging to Martech. A gym fire was near two major drug research labs. One of them was Martech."

"So, you think demons are targeting people that work for Martech labs?" asked Ellie.

"I'm not sure what I think. All I know is that it seems odd, but I think it's worth following up on."

"Here's something else," said Pam. "That man in Los Angeles who worked for the CDC that was robbed and killed, I found the info from his obituary. He used to be a member of Martech Labs before he went to work for the CDC."

"Where's the nearest Martech lab."

"The web site says Atlanta, and it's the headquarters."

"Well, let's head to Atlanta."

# CHAPTER TWENTY

**FBI Safe House**
**Arlington, Virginia**

IT WAS AGONIZING for the agents to wait for any kind of news. Agent Sills rested in one of the bedrooms while the three FBI agents tried to stay busy. Agent Williams' cell phone finally rang; she answered it, talked with another agent for several moments, and hung up. "The surveillance team said Ghazi went to visit one of his helicopter manufacturing buildings. He went into one of the hangars for about an hour then went back to his estate."

Agent Ruiz thought for a minute. "Why would a helicopter plant be so important right now?"

"Maybe that's where they're holding Miss Campbell?"

"We need to go take a look at that hangar."

"I'll ask Sills if she can get us a vehicle."

Several hours later the three agents sat across the street from the G Helicopter Manufacturing Company. They'd been given a dark green Acura loaned to them by the Secret Service and were parked in the parking lot of a sprocket manufacturing company. They'd been watching the activity of the employees all afternoon and evening.

Most of the employees had gone home and it looked deserted except for the security guard.

They were about to give up and go back to the safe house when a van pulled up. On the side of it was printed the name G Pharmaceuticals. After entering the gate code, it drove to the hangar that Ghazi visited earlier. The security guard came out and opened an overhead door allowing the truck to enter.

"What do you think about that?" Agent Kimbell asked.

"A drug manufacturing van comes to a helicopter hangar after closing time?" explained Agent Ruiz.

Agent Kimbell snickered. "Maybe they're just visiting?"

"And maybe I'm the first female pope," added Agent Williams.

"Perhaps Ghazi is into drug running?"

"Maybe, but why do it after dark? It wouldn't be unusual for one of his other company vans to come and go during normal business hours."

"That is unless he didn't want the regular employees to see either."

After several minutes, the overhead door opened, and the van reappeared.

"Let's see where the van goes?" suggested Agent Williams.

They pulled out and followed the van. They hung back but kept it in view as it took a direct trip back to the company's drug manufacturing building. It entered the secured facility and drove around back and out of sight.

The facility was a small plant on a ten-acre lot. The main building was a single-story brick building with a lush landscaping. Another single-story building sat next to it that appeared to be a small warehouse. The complex appeared to be the same as any other industrial building in the area.

The three agents watched the facility for anything unusual but were disappointed. The business was quiet.

"Looks like a dead end," commented Agent Kimbell.

"Maybe not," Agent Ruiz answered. "Look at the air conditioning and heating units."

Kimbell sighted his binoculars on the four units on the west side of the building. "I see them, nothing unusual that I can see."

"How many do you think it would take to cool and heat that building?'

"I don't know. The four I see?"

"Look on the north side of the building," instructed Agent Ruiz.

Agent Kimbell focused on the north end of the building. Among the carefully placed landscape he saw four more units.

"There are four more units on the south end also," added Agent Williams.

"I would imagine there are four more on the eastside if we could see over there."

Agent Kimbell lowered his binoculars. "Now why would they need that many units to heat and cool a building that size?"

"They have enough power to freeze or cook a building three times that size," surmised Agent Williams.

Agent Ruiz raised an eyebrow. "Maybe there's more to the building than meets the eye."

"An underground complex?" asked Kimbell.

Agent Ruiz nodded. "That would be my guess. He's doing something he doesn't want us to know about."

"Do you think it's somehow tied into Ann Campbell's kidnapping?" asked Agent Williams.

"I'd bet Kimbell's retirement on it," answered Agent Ruiz with a grin.

"I still say he's drug running," Agent Kimbell added. "And bet your own retirement."

"We need to do some checking. Something smells rotten here."

---

**Interstate 75**
**Southern Georgia**

IT HAD BEEN a long drive towards Atlanta. They'd switched out drivers several times to break up the task, and Ellie now drove while

Jake navigated from the passenger seat. Pam was busy typing on her laptop as always while Jake stared out of the window.

"What do you see?" asked Ellie.

"It's just countryside."

"No. I mean do you see a lot of them?"

"Demons?"

Ellie nodded.

"Of course I do. Not so many in the country where there are less people but a lot in the cities."

Ellie glanced at him. *What a burden he must be carrying to see all those horrid things.* "You haven't said much about seeing them after we talked to Malachy."

"I don't want to say I'll get used to them because I don't think I ever will. I just try to get past them." Jake sighed heavily. "I try to stay focused on what we have to do. I'll worry about the rest of them later."

"You can always talk to me about it if you need to."

Jake turned to her and smiled. "Thanks. I'll do that. How are you holding up?"

"This has definitely not been what I call a pleasure trip. I never would've thought I'd be racing across the south looking for demons."

Jake chuckled. "I just wanted to have a small ranch and raise cattle."

"The important thing is we're here now doing what we know we're supposed to."

Jake nodded. "I agree. I just don't know where it will end or when."

"If you two are through over analyzing everything, I'm hungry," added Pam.

Jake rolled his eyes.

Ellie giggled.

---

**Ghazi Estate**
**6322 Crosswinds Drive**

**Lake Barcroft, Virginia**

GHAZI WAS FURIOUS. He called for Azim and when he entered, Ghazi threw several photos at him.

"Your men are incompetent," he yelled. "They're idiots. Can they not do anything right?"

Azim picked up the photos and carefully looked at them. The pictures were very grainy and not good quality.

"Those are still photos from a surveillance camera at the pharmaceutical building," snapped Ghazi. "Do you know who these people are?"

The photos were of three people in a car. Even though the photos were bad Azim could still recognize the three FBI agents who were supposed to be dead. Azim's stomach knotted. Ghazi did not take failure lightly. "These are the three FBI agents," answered Azim quietly.

Ghazi leaned over his desk. "And either they are very much alive, or their ghosts are haunting us. They're supposed to be dead."

"My men heard the explosion and saw the smoke. They assumed they were dead."

"Well, you men were wrong," he screamed again. "I want them dead. Do I need to do it myself?"

"No."

"Then see to it and try to use someone that's a little more competent this time."

Azim left the room totally humiliated. His men had let him down once again.

———

**Martech Laboratories**
**9312 Southwest Parkway**
**Mableton, Georgia**

THEY PULLED up near the entrance to Martech Laboratories in the city of Mableton, a suburb of Atlanta. After a brief reconnaissance of the parking lot, Jake located the parking space of the company's president, Gerald Farnswarth. They saw a Jaguar parked in the spot.

"So, what's the plan?" asked Pam.

"We contact the owner of the company and let him know what's happening," answered Jake.

"So, you're just going to storm in there and demand to see the owner of company then tell him demons are attacking his employees?"

Jake frowned at Pam. Ellie could see this was going nowhere. "What if Pam or I go inside and see if we can talk to someone?"

"No, I'll do it," said Jake. He suddenly climbed out of the truck and walked into the main building.

Pam shook her head. "This is not going to go well. I can just feel it."

"I know Jake seems rough on the outside but maybe he can show a more reasonable side when he needs to. He's not always a bull in a china closet."

A few minutes later Jake came out of the building, escorted by two unhappy looking security guards. Jake got back into the suburban.

"What happened?' asked Ellie.

"They wouldn't let me see him."

"Did you ask nicely?" asked Pam.

Without saying a word Jake started the suburban and drove out of the parking lot. They returned around closing time and watched the employees file out of the business. After an hour of waiting, an older man in a business suit came out of the building and climbed into the blue Jaguar and drove out of the parking lot. Jake shadowed the car to an affluent section where the jaguar pulled in front of a metal gate leading into a luxury home site. They watched from up the street as the gate opened, the vehicle pulled through, and the gate closed.

"So how do we get in?" asked Ellie before Pam could make a sarcastic remark.

Jake thought for a moment. "I can always scale the wall and go in?"

"Why not just ask to come in?" suggested Ellie.

"After what happened at the office, I don't think they're going to let me in."

Ellie smiled. "But if I ask real nice, maybe they will."

A few minutes later Ellie drove up to the entrance of the estate. Pam was in the passenger seat while Jake hid in the back. Ellie pushed the buzzer.

"May I help you," answered a metallic sounding voice coming from the speaker.

"Good evening, I'm Ellie Thompson from Shady Oak Community Church. I'd like to see Mr. Farnswarth, please."

A voice came back immediately. "Mr. Farnsworth doesn't see anyone without an appointment."

"But it's very important."

The speaker was silent.

"It's a matter of life and death."

The speaker remained silent.

Pam shrugged, and Ellie started backing up when the gate suddenly opened.

"Wow, maybe you do have the touch," said Pam.

They drove through the gate and up the long drive until their headlights lit up the front of the red brick, Victorian style house. They parked under a large tree with branches that hung over the drive. Ellie and Pam walked up to the door and rang the bell. Pam was the first to notice the door was cracked open and pushed it open.

"Helloooo," she called. The inside of the house was quiet. Jake peeked out of the side truck window and saw the women standing at the open door. The plan was for him to exit the suburban after they had contacted Mr. Farnswarth. He scanned the windows of the house looking for any movement then suddenly leapt from the vehicle with Roscoe at his side. He was at the open door in an instant.

"What's wrong?" whispered Ellie.

Jake pulled his Colt 45. "I saw three demons through the

window." He stepped inside the dark main entryway and carefully looked around but didn't see any movement.

"Call out again," whispered Jake.

"Helllooooooo."

When there was no answer Jake slowly worked his way along the wall to the left where a light shown under a closed door.

"Y'all stay there," ordered Jake. Both women shook their heads and stayed glued to Jake. With a heavy sigh of frustration, Jake opened the door and looked in carefully. The room appeared to be a study. Dark oak wood bookcases covered two walls that held numerous research books and scientific journals. A rock fireplace and a bay window that led out onto a side patio finished off the room. A couch faced the fireplace and an antique desk covered in papers stood in one of the corners.

Jake saw a pair of legs that protruded from behind the desk. He carefully stepped over and looked around behind it. Mr. Farnswarth lay on his back; his eyes stared straight up at the ceiling in death. His chest was ripped open, most of his internal organs appeared to be missing, and one arm was missing apparently ripped off. Jake heard a gasp and turned to look at Ellie and Pam. They both turned pale and quickly averted their eyes.

"We're too late," said Jake.

"So, who opened the gate?" asked Pam.

Before Jake or Ellie could answer they were hit by the smell of sulfur and ash. Roscoe growled as Jake spun only to be struck by a demon that knocked both into the antique table. The table turned over onto Mr. Farnswarth's corpse.

The demon had large wings, a long slim tail, and dark blue skin. The skin was smooth and shiny as it wrestled with Jake for the gun. It held the wrist of Jake's gun hand with one clawed hand while Jake held the demon's other hand to keep the sharp claws away. Roscoe took the opportunity and bit into the tail causing the thing to screech.

Ellie and Pam backed away until they saw another one stroll into the room. It was at least seven feet tall, muscular, with bright green skin and large spiral horns protruding from the top of its head. The thing held Mr. Farnsworth's bloody arm in one clawed hand. Its mouth was covered in blood, and it grinned showing sharp teeth. The two women stood, frozen while Jake and Roscoe wrestled with the other. The huge green demon looked at the women carefully, glanced at the severed arm in his hand, tossed it away and rubbed its talons together as if preparing for another meal.

"Jake," yelled Ellie.

"Your friend's busy," said the thing in a scratchy deep voice. "I'll take care of you two and then I'll take care of Jackson."

Jake could see the green demon out of the corner of his eye. The demon he was wrestling was on top and trying to push the gun towards him while Jake pushed up toward the demon. Jake suddenly relaxed which caused the demon to lose his balance and slump forward. Jake arched his back and twisted his hips up. The demon held on, but the move allowed Jake to pivot his arm and aimed straight at the huge green demon. Jake pulled the trigger three times and struck the huge beast. The green creature suddenly stared at the women with a puzzled look and fell face forward on the floor.

The blue demon went wild and started kicking; trying to shred Jake with its hind legs despite Roscoe's hold on its tail.

With the other demon dead, Ellie stepped over, grabbed a metal fireplace poker, and swung it at the heathen fighting with Jake. The hook side of the poker struck the thing in the shoulder and caused a gash. She swung again and again to get the creature off Jake. The demon finally turned and hissed at Ellie. The injuries immediately healed almost as soon as she struck but Ellie continued to swing again and again. The degenerate devil released its hold on Jake's free hand and grabbed the metal poker. Ellie tried to hold on but with little effort it jerked it away. It hissed at her, turned and raised the poker over its head.

When the thing released Jake's free hand he reached over and grabbed the gun from the hand the creature still held. He rammed the barrel under the thing's chin and pulled the trigger. The impact blew off the back of the demon's head, spreading skin, meat, bone, and demon fluid across the room. Jake shoved the dead demon off and jumped to his feet. "Are y'all ok?"

Both women nodded as they stared at the dead demons.

Pam looked around suddenly. "Didn't you say you saw three?"

Jake dashed to the door and looked into the hallway, but it was empty. They listened carefully and heard scratching and slurping coming from upstairs. He checked his gun's magazine too make sure he had enough ammo and still had four shots. He hoped it was enough and headed up the stairs with the two women close behind. At the top of the stairs, he motioned to the end of the hall. He waved for them to wait but they stayed right with him, more afraid of being left behind than of what they might find.

At the door Jake pushed it open slowly and quietly into what appeared to be the master bedroom. In the doorway leading to the bathroom a demon squatted over what looked like a human body. As they stepped into the room, they saw a smaller yellow colored demon with rough skin like a gator with a muzzle covered in blood. Roscoe growled a warning which got the hellion's attention. It stood up and snarled at Jake. It took three quick shots to kill the thing as Pam and Ellie stared in horror at the human form on the floor. The body appeared to be a woman, probably Mrs. Farnswarth. The top part of her skull was peeled back which had allowed the beast to feast on the soft tissues of her brain.

After killing the beast, Jake shoved Ellie and Pam out into the hallway. "Get out of here, now."

They went down the stairs, out the door and into the suburban. Ellie sat in the front passenger seat; her face drained of color. Pam sat in the back, shook her head, and petted Roscoe. Jake drove several blocks when Ellie grabbed his arm. "Stop the truck, now." Jake pulled over to the side of the road. Ellie opened the passenger door, got out, and vomited. Pam sighed heavily while Roscoe licked her face. Ellie climbed back into the suburban. Pam passed her a bottle of water from the ice cooler, and she drank some water.

"Are you ok?" asked Jake.

Ellie nodded. "I've seen deceased people at funerals, but never like that."

"Unfortunately, I have," said Jake. "But it was during combat, not innocent people."

"I grew up on a ranch," added Pam. "I've seen dead animals but that was almost too much for me too."

Jake slammed his fist on the steering wheel. "I failed. I should've done something more."

"It's not your fault," said Ellie as she placed her hand on his shoulder. The color was returning to her face.

"I think you two should go back to Texas. This is more than you bargained for.'

"We're in this together. This is our mission too."

"Don't get macho on us, Taft," added Pam.

Jake turned and looked at Ellie and then back at Pam. "Are you sure you want to stay with this? I wouldn't blame you if you wanted to go home."

"No, we're with you, no matter what happens."

"So, what are we going to do now?" asked Pam.

Jake took off his Stetson hat and ran his hand through his hair. "I don't know."

"Maybe we can still save Jackson," said Ellie.

"Who's Jackson?" asked Jake.

"I don't know. That demon said he'd take care of Jackson too."

"But is Jackson his first name or last? We don't know where to find him?"

"Wait a minute, I don't think he meant a person," exclaimed Pam. "I think he meant a place." She grabbed her laptop and started typing. "I remember seeing Jackson somewhere in my research of Martech. Here it is. Martech has a lab in Jackson, Mississippi."

"But what about those poor people back there?' asked Ellie with a shudder.

"We can't do anything for them, but we can do something for the people in Jackson. Pam can call an anonymous tip in while we head out," said Jake. "It may take a while before whoever's running this nightmare to figure out the hit squad isn't going to Jackson."

"Can we get there in time?" asked Ellie.

"We have to," said Jake.

# CHAPTER TWENTY-ONE

**FBI Safe House**
**Arlington, Virginia**

AGENT RUIZ and Kimbell were busy on one of the laptops trying to locate more information on Ghazi's lab when Agent Sims phone chirped. She answered, listened, and hung up. "That was Agent Meadows. He said they found the car that followed you. It was a rental that came back to a fake corporation credit card, but they gave a valid address He thinks the two might still be there, so he secured a search warrant."

The FBI agents looked up at her with smiles.

"But he said you can't go"

---

**Meadowside Apartments**
**1701 Benfield Blvd**
**Arlington, Virginia**

AGENT MEADOWS SAT in the rear of a van disguised as a plumbing truck. He spoke into the radio to several agents stationed around the apartment complex. "Can Thompson tell if anyone's there?"

"No sir. The door is in the middle of a walkway and faces across from another apartment."

"The manager gave Agent Grainger a key to the apartment. Give us a minute to get there and come in on the other side."

Agent Meadows and two other secret service agents exited the rear door of the van and quickly made their way to one side of the apartment door. Several agents came in from the other side. Agent Meadows knocked on the door. "U.S. Secret Service, open the door." When there was no answer, he nodded to Agent Grainger who carefully inserted the key into the lock and turned it. *Click*. He turned the knob and shoved the door open.

"Secret Service, we have a search warrant," yelled Agent Meadows as he dashed inside the apartment followed by the rest. They quickly spread to either side of the doorway but came to an abrupt halt. What they saw might have been a B grade horror movie set gone bad except it was real. The furniture was shredded and torn to pieces with blood splattered on the walls.

"Is that what I think it is in the hallway?" asked Agent Grainger.

They all looked down the hall at a severed human head, mouth gapped open, and eyes wide open staring back at them

"Check everywhere," said Agent Meadows. "And be careful."

The agents carefully worked their way down the hall. They found one corpse in the bedroom. The torso was on the bed while the remaining appendages were strewn around the room. The other man was found in the bathroom. He'd apparently tried to barricade himself in because the door was crushed in. One half of him was on the floor and the other half was in the bathtub.

"Who on earth could have done this?" asked Agent Thompson.

Agent Meadows shook his head. "I don't know but they must've been angry."

Another agent spoke up. "I was stationed in Baghdad when several car bombs went off and didn't cause this kind of damage."

"Alright, everyone out," snapped Agent Meadows. "We'll turn this over to crime scene and let them piece this together."

"Good luck," said Agent Thompson sarcastically.

———

**Ghazi Estate**
**6322 Crosswinds Drive**
**Lake Barcroft, Virginia**

ANN FELT like she was going stir crazy. She'd lost track of the number of days she'd been held captive. She tried to keep busy with exercises and looking for a way out but that was wearing thin. They treated her decent though, providing meals and clothes but it was all growing very tiresome. *Maybe they're trying to break me down mentally,* she thought. As if on cue the door was unlocked, and Amira came in. "I came to see if you needed anything," she asked.

"How about a taxi ride out of this place?"

"You've been treated humanely," snapped Amira.

"Like a caged animal?"

"Why do you have to be so rude? I thought your religion taught peace and kindness?"

"And I thought yours taught love and tolerance instead of murder and kidnapping?"

Amira went and sat in a chair next to the bed. "I thought I could convince you to see our side of the situation, but I guess I was wrong. Just like your ancestors, you think your way is the best no matter what."

Ann stared hard at her female kidnapper. "And what are you doing? Forcing people to convert or die? You give a bad name to millions of peace-loving, law-abiding Muslims."

"That was the choice your ancestors gave mine."

"That was hundreds of years ago. That was during the dark ages when most people were ignorant and uneducated. They had no idea of different cultures and prior history. If you're emulating their ways, then you're as ignorant as they were? Are you trying to return us to the dark ages?"

Amira got to her feet. "I need to go."

"Amira, you can't solve the world's problems with violence. If we don't learn from history then we're doomed to repeat it over and over. That's not the answer. Violence only brings more violence. There's got to be a better way."

"Are you trying to convert me to your way?"

"No. I'm trying to get you to see a better way. It's common sense more than religion."

Amira walked to the door to leave. "I'll check in later if you need something." She left and went downstairs. Azim was waiting. "I don't want you to visit the American woman again."

"What? Why not?"

"She is trying to corrupt your mind with her lies."

"You were spying on me?"

"I was just listening to ensure that she didn't do or say anything to harm you. You need to stay away from her."

Amira turned and walked down the hall to her room. *My own brother is spying on me!*

---

### FBI Safe House
### Arlington, Virginia

THE FOUR AGENTS were briefed on the gruesome discovery at the bomber's apartment.

"Sounds to me like someone is getting nervous," said Agent Williams.

"Maybe he's trying to cover his tracks?" added Agent Kimbell.

Agent Ruiz nodded. "Yeah, and maybe send a message to someone?"

They kept busy planning how to set up surveillance at Ghazi's pharmaceutical company and helicopter plant. Their hope was to find any evidence he was involved in Ann Campbell's kidnapping. Agent Ruiz's cell phone rang. He answered it and listened for a few moments. "Yes sir, we'll be there." After disconnecting, he explained that Deputy Director Sullens wanted them to come to the office. The bureau found evidence on the deceased bombers and wanted them to examine it.

"Can't they just send us an email or photo?" asked Agent Kimbell.

Agent Ruiz shrugged. "I guess not. He was very insistent that we come to the office, and a car will pick us up shortly. Maybe this is the breakthrough we've been looking for?"

"I hope so," said Agent Williams. "I'm getting tired of hiding out."

"If this is a major break then we can come out of hiding."

"I'll call Agent Meadows at the White House and let him know," Agent Sills added.

Thirty minutes later, another FBI agent, Tim Walls, arrived and picked up the three FBI agents. After turning onto North Glebe Road, they traveled towards Interstate 66 which led into Washington D.C. but came upon a construction detour. Traffic was backed up and moving slowly.

"Just our luck," grumbled Agent Ruiz. "We're in a hurry to get into downtown and traffic's a mess."

For the next fifteen minutes they inched along in the slow-moving traffic. They stopped again while a flagman waved traffic through from the other direction.

"We should've gotten breakfast first," complained Agent Kimbell from the back seat. Agent Walls smiled and turned to him. "You can jump out and run get us something. We'll be right here."

Several cars behind them sat a white panel van with "Charlie's Painting and Restoration" painted on the side. Two men in white painter's clothes sat in the front. The passenger reached back and knocked several times on the metal panel between the front and rear compartment. The two men then reached down and removed two black ski masks from a bag on the floor and pulled them over their heads. The passenger removed two semi-auto rifles and knocked again on the metal panel. The back doors flew open and two more armed men in painter's clothes climbed out. The astonished motorists sat and watched the four-armed gunmen dash towards a four-door government-type vehicle. Agent Walls was still turned towards the back passengers when his eyes widened. "Oh, my g..."

Agents Ruiz and Williams saw the startled look on his face and turned to see the armed gunmen running towards them.

"Out...out...everyone out...gun...gun," yelled Agent Williams as they forced their car doors open.

The armed gunmen saw the doors to their target open as the FBI agents tried to exit their car. Knowing that their surprise was blown, they opened fire while still a few car lengths away. The government vehicle was quickly riddled with 9mm rounds.

Agent Ruiz rolled onto the ground and drew his weapon while Agent Williams dove headfirst in front a car stopped in the next lane. Agent Kimbell spun around in the back seat and fired through the back window, shattering the glass. Agent Walls was slower than the rest as he tried to climb out from around the steering wheel and was struck several times by enemy fire. Agent Kimbell glanced at him as he slumped over the steering wheel. Several more rounds came through the back window and struck Agent Kimbell. He felt the pain in his neck and slid farther down in the seat as everything started to go black.

Agent Ruiz glanced up over the bumper of a car occupied by a terrified motorist who was scrambling to exit their car. Most of the surrounding motorist also fled their vehicles in a panic. Agent Ruiz fired several rounds at the gunmen and saw one of them fall. He ducked back down as a rain of bullets struck the car. Agent Williams was trying to hold off two gunmen, but it was looking glum. They were out gunned and too many innocent civilians were still nearby.

One gunman huddled behind a recently vacated car directly behind the FBI vehicle. He kept Agent Williams pinned down with gun fire while another one circled around behind her.

Agent Ruiz was busy keeping the last gunmen at bay. The assassin was two cars back behind a Pontiac with a female driver hunched down behind the wheel. He wanted to glance into their car and see why Agents Kimbell and Walls weren't returning fire but didn't want to take his eyes off the gunmen's location.

Agent Williams fired once more at the armed man when her slide locked back. She reached for her full magazine on her belt when the other gunman stepped from behind her. He'd managed to creep around behind her while she was distracted with the other gun man. She spun and tried to ram her magazine into the gun as the hooded man aimed his weapon at her. She could see his eyes wide and his mouth in a broad grin. She seated her magazine and hit the thumb release that forced a round into the chamber, but she knew it was too late. She braced for the impact and heard the shots. She blinked twice and realized she hadn't been hit. The gunman had a startled look on his face as he crumpled to the ground. Agent Williams spun around to confront the other gunman and saw him firing away from her, back behind him. She took careful aimed and shot the man.

The last gunman knew the plan had gone badly. It had been a simple plan. They were to rush up and kill all the agents in the car before they could react but had been spotted by the FBI agent who'd been driving. He felt it was time to escape. He jerked open the door of the car he was hiding beside and pulled a terrified women from the car. He used the woman as a shield and backed away.

Agent Ruiz was about out of ammo. He knew he only had a round or two left before he had to reload. He wanted to try to save them for the best shot he could make before making himself vulnerable while reloading. He could hear gun fire and knew at least one of his fellow agents was still in the fight. The hooded man used the woman as a human shield and fired at Agent Ruiz. *The coward.* The man backed up about ten feet when another shot rang out. The gunman released the hostage and slowly fell to the ground.

Movement caught Agent Ruiz's eye and he turned to see two men in plain clothes with handguns appear from behind a car. He noticed badges attached to their belts. *Secret Service badges.*

Agent Williams caught sight of the man that had saved her life. He was in civilian clothes but had a Secret Service badge. *Thank God, Secret Service agents.*

One of the agents approached her and asked if she injured.

"No, I'm fine," she answered. "I'm glad the cavalry showed up."

He smiled a grim smile. "Sorry we're late. Agent Meadows thought it would be a good idea to keep your safe house under surveillance. We followed you from the house but got stuck back in this construction traffic. We heard the shots and came as quick as we could."

After seeing the Secret Service agents, Agent Ruiz leapt to his feet and ran to the car. He checked on Agent Walls but he was dead. He quickly checked Agent Kimbell and found a weak pulse. "I need an ambulance...now."

An hour later, the area was full of law enforcement officers, ambulances, and news crews.

Agent Kimbell had been rushed to Georgetown University hospital and was listed in critical condition. Four citizens had been injured in the fire fight but nonserious. Crime Scene officers arrived and collected evidence and photographed to the scene. It would take hours to mark and collect all the shell casings and photograph everything. The coroner's office arrived and examined the dead assassins. They were all men of Middle Eastern descent.

The two remaining FBI agents, Ruiz, and Williams, sat in the FBI mobile command post that had been brought to the scene.

"This was a total set up," grumbled Agent Ruiz.

"Someone is going to pay for this," said Agent Williams. "Tim was a friend of mine. We used to work cases together."

"Did he have any family?"

"He wasn't married, just a girlfriend but I think they were planning to get engaged though. How could this happen? You took the call from a Deputy Director?"

"I called him back and demanded how he got his information. He said he received a note about it this morning, and assumed it was reliable. He didn't seem so happy about my tone of voice."

"I wouldn't care. He's got a lot more to worry about right now than your attitude. He set us up, accidentally or intentionally."

Agent Ruiz shook his head. "I don't know, but I intend to find out."

# CHAPTER TWENTY-TWO

**Martech Laboratories**
**12001 W. Pearl Blvd**
**Jackson, Mississippi**

AFTER CHECKING into a hotel in the middle of the night, they slept late into the day. Since it seemed that the demon's method of operation or M.O. was to wait until after dark and hit somewhere away from the research labs, they figured they had some time for rest.

At the end of the day, Jake, Ellie, and Pam drove to the Martech Lab building located in one of the industrial areas of Jackson. It was a large multi-story building with large exterior glass panels. They watched as the employees left work for the day.

"How are we going to know where these demons were going to strike? We're not even sure when?" asked Pam.

Jake glanced into the back seat where she sat. "If we're right, they're on some type of schedule, and they seem to be hitting as quickly as possible."

"Okay, but how do we know where they're going to hit here in Jackson?" asked Pam.

They were all silent for a moment.

"We could follow several of them around and see where they go?" suggested Ellie.

Jake shook his head. "That would take too long."

"They seem to hit places where several of them gather. Besides attacking the two leaders of the company, the attack sites were bars and gyms," Ellie interjected.

"But how do we know where most of them go?"

They sat in silence once again watching the employees file out of the building. A convenience store sat at the end of the block from the building and many of the employees stopped off there before heading elsewhere.

"Pull into the convenience store. I have an idea," said Pam.

Jake pulled into a parking space in front of the store. Pam climbed out of the suburban and went inside. They watched as she bought a soda and talked to a couple of young male employees. The two men seemed to be more than happy to talk to the attractive blonde woman. After a few minutes she came back to the suburban.

"What was that all about?" asked Jake.

Pam smiled brightly. "I simply told the two men that I was new to the lab and wanted to know where they went for some fun after work. They were more than happy to tell me where most of the employees hang out."

"And?"

"They all go to a place called Lenny's Sports Grill. It's across town."

They drove over to the sport's bar and grill and found the parking lot was full.

"This must be the place," said Pam.

"So, what now?" asked Ellie.

"We wait," explained Jake.

"What about the back door? We can go watch the back."

"No. It's too dangerous."

"But we can help watch out for them. Three sets of eyes are better than one."

Jake frowned. *Not again.* "Are we going to have to argue about this every time?"

"No," said Ellie. "You can stay here, and we'll just drive around back and watch."

Jake frowned. "I know. And Roscoe can protect you." He didn't like it, but it did make sense. "Okay, go around back and park. Don't do anything but watch, and I'll call you in a few minutes." Jake climbed out of the suburban. Ellie climbed in the driver's seat, waved at Jake, and drove around back. Jake looked around for any sign of trouble. This section was dotted with bars and small restaurants. The street was not overly crowded but busy. People were coming and going from several of the establishments.

Having the ability to see demons, Jake saw more demons than normal in the area. There were several demons of different sizes and shapes following humans around, whispering, laughing, taunting, and trying to manipulate each person for their own devious reasons. It reminded him of a science fiction movie on a distant planet with humans and aliens mixed, except none of these aliens were nice. No matter how much he tried to stay focused on one objective, he had the urge to wade into them and start swinging.

His cell phone rang. It was Ellie.

"Yes?"

"It's pretty quiet back here, and dark. There's a small light over the back door but not much else. I'm not sure you could see one even if it was here."

"Okay. Y'all come out then and we'll keep an eye from here."

"We'll stay for a few minutes and see first."

Jake stared at the cell phone and grumbled. He didn't like the idea as he waited impatiently in a doorway across the street and looked at his watch. Ten minutes seems like an hour. He watched the door as happy customers came and went then movement caught Jake's eye. He looked over towards a dark alley a couple of doors down and saw two sets of glowing yellow eyes staring out from the alley. More demons. He turned back and continued to watch the bar, but after a few minutes he noticed that the two seemed to be watching the sports bar and grill intently. He then noticed that none of the demons went into the sports bar, and were out in plain view, not being as discreet as these two. Why hide if no one can see you?

He removed his Colt 45 semi-automatic handgun from the back of his jeans, checked the magazine to make sure it was full and strolled across the street.

Upon entering the darkened alley, Jake could just barely make out the two forms. They wore matching cloaks and hoods which made it hard to see them completely. "Howdy boys, see anything interesting at the bar?"

The two looked at Jake not sure what to make of the human that could see them.

"Stay right where you are and don't do anything stupid. I have a few questions for you two," ordered Jake and pointed his handgun at them.

One of them took a couple of steps to the right to create distance between them. Jake didn't like that. "Get back over there with your twin."

The one farthest away raised its arm and pointed at Jake. Expecting some sort of weapon, Jake shot the creature. The thing was thrown backwards into the wall and as Jake turned on the other one it raised its arm as well. He saw several small tentacle-like extensions slither from the end of the sleeve, and the ends began to glow. Jake instinctively stepped forward, grabbed the sleeve, and jerked it away as streams of flame spewed from the end of the tentacles. The flames hit the far wall and dumpster, igniting the trash, and casting the alley in an eerie glow of firelight. Jake held the creature's sleeve, swung his Colt 45, and struck the thing in the head. The blow stunned the demon for a second allowing Jake time to swing the gun up under its arm striking at where he thought an elbow would be if it had an elbow. He felt something snap, and the creature screeched. It tried to pull away, but he held tight as more flame shot out from the small tentacles. Jake shoved the barrel of the gun against the end of the sleeve and fired again. Several of the tentacles were blown off and left a massive hole where a liquid-like flame oozed out. The creature screeched again.

The other flame throwing demon was injured but not dead, stumbled to its feet, turned, and aimed a tentacle at Jake.

Jake saw the ends glow and spun the injured creature in front of him as a shield. A blast of flame shot out of the slithering squid-like arm at them, and the twin creature took the blast head on while Jake stood behind it. Even being protected by the freak's body, Jake could feel the heat. After dosing them with liquid fire the demon turned and ran down the alley. Jake shoved the other demon away while it tried to raise its broken, injured arm at him, but received a bullet in the head instead. Jake sprinted down the alley after the other one, turned the corner of the building, out of the glow of the burning trash, and into more darkness.

Ellie and Pam were still watching for anything abnormal when they heard gunshots and Roscoe started barking. Ellie's eyes widened and she quickly drove around to the front of the bar where they saw the burning dumpster and trash in an alley down the street. A nosey crowd began filling in to watch the dumpster fire and the sounds of sirens filled the air as the fire department responded.

"What do you think happened?" asked Pam.

"Jake happened," said Ellie. "I'm going around to the other side of that alley so we can help Jake."

"Are you sure it's Jake's doing?"

Ellie turned and stared at Pam.

"Never mind," said Pam. "Drive on sister."

Jake was cautiously walking down the dark alley because the last thing he wanted to do was to be cooked by one of the creature's tentacles. Halfway down the alley Jake stopped, listened as carefully as possible and heard the slightest sound of cloth rubbing on cloth behind him to the left. He spun and fired as the creature stepped out from a recessed corner of the building. Jake missed hitting the thing and the next round jammed. Jake could see in the dim light the empty shell case wedged in the slide, commonly called a "stove pipe" jam. He brushed his hand over the slide to clear the jammed bullet as the thing spoke for the first time in a high pitched, whiney voice. "You'll pay for this."

Jake watched the demon's tentacles glow as he pulled the slide back on his weapon to load a new round. Suddenly a huge fist appeared out of nowhere and slammed into the side of the creature's head, knocking it back against the wall. Flames shot up into the air, and in the glow, Jake saw a giant man in white with skin the color of golden brass.

Even though stunned, the creature pointed its arm at Malachy who simply raised his golden sword and severed the fire spewing arm from its owner. The creature screamed in pain.

Jake stared at the two nonhumans. It seemed suddenly sad how two beings that had started together in heaven could end up so different. One was an angel dressed in white with a golden sword and the other a disgusting fire emitting creature from the depths of hell.

Jake finished racking a round into the chamber and pointed it at the thing. The creature held up its remaining hand that wasn't a squid-like aperture, but instead a pitiful hand with burned, flaky skin.

"Please don't kill me," it whined.

"Then tell me why you're attacking innocent people, especially ones that work for Martech labs," demanded Jake.

The thing remained silent.

Jake aimed the gun at the thing's head.

"Wait," the thing pleaded. "If I tell you he'll kill me."

"If you don't, I'll kill you."

The thing hesitated a moment. "Tarnac. Seek out Tarnac."

The sound of sirens, voices shouting, and running began getting closer.

"You must hurry," urged Malachy.

In that brief second, several small tentacles slithered out from the front of the creature's cloak and were pointed straight at Malachy. Jake shot the creature several times, killing it. The gun shots brought more voices and running.

"Go that way and your friends will be waiting," said Malachy as he pointed down the alley.

Jake started down the alley but stopped and turned back. "Any idea where to find this Tarnac person?"

Malachy nodded. "Hell's Corner, New Orleans."

Jake ran down to the end of the alley and emerged on a side

street. He saw their suburban turn the corner and waved them down. They stopped at the curb and Jake climbed in.

"Are you okay?" asked Ellie.

"Yeah, I'm fine, just a little singed."

"How did you know where we were?"

"A large friend told me."

"What about the demons?" inquired Pam.

"Those two won't be torching anything ever again."

"Good, but what now?"

"We go to New Orleans to a place called Hell's Corner and a thing called Tarnac."

Pam raised one eyebrow. "A place called what?"

"Who?" asked Ellie.

Jake turned to Ellie. "Head back to the hotel and I'll explain it all on the way."

————

**FBI Headquarters**
**935 Pennsylvania Avenue, NW**
**Washington, D.C.**

AGENTS WILLIAMS and Ruiz sat in a conference room at FBI headquarters. They'd been up over twenty-four hours completing reports and interviews by investigators and were exhausted. Two attempts on their lives in a week and they were no closer to finding Ann Campbell than before.

The door opened and a tall Black man in a blue suit entered. His hair was dark with streaks of grey, walked ramrod straight, and gave the air of authority. Without saying a word, he sat and began laying out documents and photos.

"Agent Williams and Agent Ruiz," he said finally.

"Deputy Director Ross," answered Agent Williams.

Agent Ruiz simply nodded.

"As you know I am the supervisor of this internal investigation. My job is to determine what happened and if there were any mistakes made that caused the death of one agent and injury of another."

"His name was Timothy Walls," corrected Agent Williams.

Deputy Director Ross raised an eyebrow. "Yes, I read that."

"How is Agent Kimbell?" asked Agent Ruiz.

"The last information I received was that he was in critical condition."

Agent Ruiz nodded again.

"Let's get down to the matter at hand. I have reviewed all the statements, but I have a few questions. First, did you think it was suspicious that you were summoned while staying in a safe house?"

"I thought it was a little odd but when Deputy Director Sullens insisted, we had no choice," answered Agent Williams. "We were set up."

Deputy Director Ross stared hard at her. "What I want to know is how did the assassins know where to find you?"

"Why don't you ask Deputy Director Sullens?" grumbled Agent Ruiz.

"I will. Are you accusing him of being the one who set you up?"

"I don't know, sir," answered Agent Ruiz between gritted teeth. "I'm saying that someone sent Agent Walls to get us, someone tailed him to us, and so someone had been given advanced warning."

"And if it hadn't been for the Secret Service," added Agent Williams. "We'd all be dead."

"Yes, it was quite a coincidence that they were right there," Deputy Director Ross said questionably.

"They said they were coming back from an interview with a suspect and heard the commotion," answered Agent Ruiz. They wanted to keep their alliance with the President secret for now.

"Could someone at the safe house have been careless and led the killers there?"

"No, sir," Agent Williams said curtly. Her face was getting red. "We were careful not to give away our location. And besides, if they knew where the safe house was, they would've come there and wouldn't have had to lure us out."

"Good Point."

"Shouldn't you be asking Deputy Director Sullens these questions and finding out who gave him the information?"

Deputy Director Ross' face went cold. "Agent Williams, are you telling me how to do my job?"

"No, sir," said Agent Ruiz to take the heat off Agent Williams. "Sir, in the last week we've been shot at and nearly blown up. We're a little edgy and we'd like some answers too. We're no closer to finding the President's daughter than when we got here."

Deputy Director Ross nodded, and his face softened. "I know you've had a rough time lately." He gathered his notes, photos, and documents. "That's all I have for now." He rose and went to the door. "I'll keep in touch." He quietly closed the door behind him.

"I'll keep in touch," Agent Williams said in mock imitation of his voice. "I'll bet you will."

Agent Ruiz sat and rubbed his temples. "He's just doing his job. It's hard enough investigating the disappearance of the President's daughter with a target on our back, and now we have this."

The door opened again, and Director Bill Chisom entered. They both stopped and acknowledged him. Both agents admired him because he'd worked his way up from the bottom to become the Director of the FBI. Director Chisom walked to a side table and poured himself come coffee. "I'm sorry about Agent Walls. He was a good agent. Just the other day I read a commendation on him for a bust he made. He'll be sorely missed."

Both agents nodded. Director Chisom sat in the same chair the deputy director had vacated. "I understand you just spoke with Deputy Director Ross?"

"Yes, sir," answered Agent Williams. It was hard keeping the frustration from her voice.

Director Chisom smiled slightly. "I know he can seem cold and harsh, but that's his job. He's a good man. It's a difficult job investigating the investigators."

"With all due respect, sir, we were ambushed."

"I know," he said softly.

"And we're no closer to finding the President's daughter," added Agent Ruiz.

"I know that too."

"And being cooped up in that safe house hasn't helped any...sir."

Director Chisom sipped his coffee for a minute. "It was very fortunate that the Secret Service was nearby. It was almost like they were following you."

Agent Ruiz glanced sideways at Agent Williams. "Yes, sir, it was a lucky break."

"I sent a note over to them, thanking them for their help, but now, to other things. I don't like my agents being shot at or blown up and I want to find out as bad as you do." He stopped and stared at them both. "From here on out, none of this information leaves this room?"

Both agents nodded.

"Good. It's obvious we have a traitor in the bureau. If there is one thing, I detest more than anything is a turn coat. I can fight the enemy and even respect them if they are open about it, but I can't tolerate a traitor. The note that was given to Deputy Director Sullens is missing. I've since found out he told you to back off investigating Hassan Ghazi. I also checked with the other agents working the Campbell kidnapping since you've been in captivity, but they've come up dry too.

"There are some serious questions that have not been answered. I have put Deputy Director Sullens on administrative leave pending the outcome of the investigation.

"Now I can't order you to resume the investigation and knowingly put your lives in danger, but if you're willing, you'll be given full access again."

Agent Williams smiled and Agent Ruiz's eyes widened.

"You don't have to order me sir, I want to resume the investigation," piped in Agent Williams.

"Agent Ruiz?"

"And miss the look on Ghazi's face, no way, sir."

"You'll be working in full knowledge that you're in constant danger?"

"Yes, sir," they both said.

"You really think he's behind her kidnapping?"

"I'd stake my life on it," answered Agent Ruiz.

"I think you already have," said Director Chisom with a grim smile. "Very well, the investigation will be reassigned to you."

"Thank you, sir," answered Agent Ruiz.

"Yes, thank you, sir," added Agent Williams with a smile.

"Until we root out this person, you answer only to me. If you get a message, confirm it with me. If you get some information, confirm it with me. You will be a target for them until we find them out. I feel certain Deputy Director Ross will find them, but until then you have to be careful."

"We will, sir," answered Agent Ruiz.

Director Chisom left quietly.

"Yessssss," Agent Williams said through a big smile.

"We're back in business," answered Agent Ruiz.

"It's time to put the heat on Ghazi."

# CHAPTER TWENTY-THREE

**New Orleans, Louisiana**

SINCE 2000 TO the present there have been at least 20 hurricanes or tropical storms that have struck the New Orleans area. Most of the area has slowly rebuilt and most of the "Big Easy" recovered. It returned to the way it was, a mixture of the old style with modern, jazz with rock, and Cajun with fast food.

There was, however, an area that never recovered. This section had never been rebuilt, and the remnants of houses were still stacked up and down empty streets. Abandoned, overturned cars lay rusted where the flood waters had left them.

It was a buffer to something worse that lay just outside the city limits. Old rundown buildings and bars had been taken over by drug dealers, prostitutes, and other dredges of society. This became known as "Hell's Corner."

The local parish law enforcement made many attempts to clean up the area but being understaffed and having too large of an area to patrol kept them from properly controlling the crime. By the time any law enforcement vehicles crossed the buffer zone and into "Hell's

Corner" the area appeared to be empty and quiet. Eventually it became off limits to most law-abiding citizens.

Jake booked two rooms at a motel off of Interstate 10. After a few stops at local stores, a few well-meaning warnings, and a few unusual stares, they were given directions to "Hell's Corner." They turned off the highway and drove across the buffer of empty, decaying buildings, downed trees, debris covered lots to the entrance to "Hell's Corner". It oozed darkness and evil.

Most buildings had been partially repaired and displayed signs advertising bars, tattoo parlors, bordellos, smoke shops, voodoo shops, tarot reading, and many others. Other buildings were nearly collapsed and in need of repair but were occupied. Amazingly the traffic in the area was more than expected by young people or college students looking for excitement while others were there because they were in need. Unfortunately, their needs included illegal narcotics, unusual sexual desires, and other bizarre fetishes which the residents of "Hell's Corner" were more than happy to provide.

Jake drove the suburban slowly down the street, eyeing the residents and visitors. Pam and Ellie looked sadly at the total depravity that lay before them. Scantily clad women flagged down carloads of young men while drug addicts sat on building steps shooting up, smoking, and snorting their drug of choice in plain view of everyone. Amongst all of it Jake saw demon after demon. Ellie looked over at Jake and could see his look of disgust.

"This is horrible," she said sadly. "I can only imagine what you see."

"Take what you see and double it. This is a devil's paradise. They're enjoying themselves, preying on the underside of mankind."

"I can't believe these creatures get pleasure out of this."

"They left heaven for this?" Pam asked in disgust.

"It was their choice."

Apparently, there were sections to "Hell's Corner". The outskirts were for the curious, casual visitor but the farther in the deeper into debauchery they went.

"Oh, my," gasped Pam.

"What is it?" asked Jake.

"I can see the demons."

Jake glanced at Ellie, and she nodded.

At this level into "Hell's Corner" the demons didn't attempt to hide or remain unseen. This was for the hard core, the desperate, and the bottom of society.

A hugely obese degenerate creature with skin like leather sat on the sidewalk next to a deceased human drug addict. Its yellow eyes were deep sunk and small. The folds of its skin quivered every time it moved, and its two large arms held the corpse's leg while it chewed on it like fried chicken. Two smaller arms protruded from its side and picked up small pieces of human flesh that fell onto its huge abdomen.

Three smaller almost birdlike demons stood around the corpse. Their heads were triangular shaped with three points. Their eyes were large and bulged from their bodies. Small claws grasped the vital organs of the corpse through an open wound in the chest and feasted.

Across the street several long necked demons pushed and shoved a skinny, gaunt, zombie-like man back and forth like he was a toy. A large purplish colored demon with large spikes protruding from its back lumbered down the sidewalk. It dragged a half-dressed woman who seemed oblivious to her situation.

Jake looked on in horror, Ellie stared in shock, and Pam closed her eyes while Roscoe growled. As they continued down the street, they witnessed more savage, unbridled evil. Three demons had a large fire pit and were cooking something on a spit, and it obviously had been human at one time.

They saw at the end of the street the capital building, the head-quarters of this horrid place. It was an old southern mansion, or at least it used to be. The three storied home looked specially made for every horror movie. It reminded them of the house from the movie *Psycho*, or *The Munsters* mansion.

The paint had long faded and peeled off, window shutters were hanging askew or totally gone, and the tall columns in front were vine covered. The cobblestone driveway led past trees covered in Spanish moss. Lights were on inside the mansion and laughter, screams, and music were heard coming from inside. Foot traffic of human and demon could be seen coming and going.

"I think this might be the place," said Jake.

"I think you're right," said Ellie.

"I want to go home," Pam added.

————

**Ghazi Estate**
**6322 Crosswinds Drive**
**Lake Barcroft, Virginia**

ANN FINISHED DOING PUSHUPS. She was trying to keep busy and not let her mind wander. She knew isolation was one of the first ways kidnappers used to break down someone, and she was determined not to break.

It was getting close to mid-morning when one of her guards opened her door and motioned for her to follow. She was led downstairs to a room that appeared to be a study of some sort. Upon entering she saw Ghazi sitting behind a large wooden desk.

"Good morning, Miss Campbell. Please have seat."

"I'll stand."

Ghazi looked at her guard and made a slight movement with his head. The guard grabbed her and shoved her into a chair.

"Leave us," Ghazi ordered, and the guard quietly left.

"I hope that you've been treated well?"

"Oh, yeah, great."

Ghazi smiled. "That's good. It won't be much longer, and everything will be over."

"And then you can kill me?" said Ann.

Ghazi leaned back in his high-backed chair. "It doesn't have to be that way." He got to his feet and walked over to a door between two bookcases. "I'd like to show you something."

"I'll pass."

"Please don't make me force you. I can have your guard help you?"

Ann reluctantly got to her feet and followed him.

Ghazi entered a series of numbers in a wall keypad, and the door clicked open. She noticed a set of stones steps that led down.

"Is this your secret dungeon?"

Ghazi laughed. "No, this is my private piece of heaven." He motioned for her to lead.

She took a deep breath and carefully walked down the steps into the man-made cave. At the bottom she saw the carved altar and throne, and next to it sat a square shaped box with a tarp over it. Across the room sat a television camera of some sort. She froze.

Ghazi pushed her into the room. "This is my private temple."

Ann's skin crawled and she shivered. "What a ghastly place."

"Why thank you. I designed it myself."

Ghazi approached the altar and ran his hand over the top. He then went and sat on his stone throne.

Ann could see the joy and happiness in his face. "I'm afraid to ask but what is this for?"

"This is where I will be when I take over the United States, and ultimately the world."

"You're insane."

Ghazi smiled. "Sanity is just a matter of perspective, my dear."

"You'll never get away with it."

"I can and I will." Ghazi pointed to the tarp. "Feel free to pull the tarp off."

Ann remained where she was.

"It's ok, it won't hurt you. Go ahead."

Ann slowly pulled the tarp off the object. She stared at the golden box-like item.

"Do you know what it is?"

She shook her head. It looked vaguely familiar, but she wasn't sure.

"Do you remember your Sunday school lessons?" he asked. "It's very important to those cursed Jews. It's their precious Ark of the Covenant."

Ann stared at him and then back at the beautifully decorated box. The large chest-like box with the winged angels on top shined in the light. She was amazed it still existed.

"Impressive isn't it?"

Ann remembered hearing stories about it and of course she'd seen the movie with Harrison Ford. She remembered Indiana Jones found it and how precious it was. "It doesn't belong to you."

"I paid highly for it."

"What are you going to do with it?"

"The question is what are you going to do?"

"Me?"

Ghazi leered at her with lust filled eyes. "I've been watching you in your room and I've been impressed by what I've seen."

Ann thought about him watching her in her room, wrapped her arms around herself and shivered. "You're perverted."

Ghazi laughed a deep, malignant laugh. "I need someone who can serve with me. I need someone who can sit at my side while I rule my new empire. You can be that person."

Ann eyed widened. She wasn't sure she heard what he said. "You want me to become your wife?"

"No, you can become my queen."

"Queen?"

"Imagine sitting at my side with this at our feet, ruling over the world. Who would serve my empire better than the daughter of the previous President?"

Anger flared in Ann's eyes. "Previous President? My father is still the President. He will not give in to you or your scheme. I would rather die than have anything to do with you."

Ghazi looked at her for a moment and she could see the disappointment in his face, but it lasted for only a minute. "Very well, it's your choice."

**23 Sandhill Drive**
**Arlington, Virginia**

DEPUTY DIRECTOR SULLENS sat behind his desk at his home and shredded papers. He knew he was in trouble after the ambush had gone wrong. The Senator had assured him that everything would be fine as soon as the agents were out of the way, but the assassins botched the job. The promise of riches and glory in the new world order compared to a government pension was too much to pass over, but now it was in jeopardy. Destroy any evidence. Without evidence there's no way they can prove anything. His government pension was looking better than ever now.

While the shredder whirled and buzzed, Deputy Director Sullens poured himself a small glass of Whiskey. As he lifted the glass to his lips, he saw two of the most horrible looking creatures standing in front of the desk. He dropped the glass on the desk and reached for the gun in his desk, but it was too late. The things were on top of him in a split second. The last thing he saw were yellow eyes and the last thing he heard was his own scream.

———

**Hampton Inn**
**4356 LaSalle Ave**
**New Orleans, Louisiana**

JAKE, Ellie, and Pam sat in one of the hotel rooms. They skipped dinner after leaving "Hell's Corner" because no one had an appetite.

Pam sat and read the latest news clippings as well as her email. "I checked the Atlanta news. There's an article about the Farnsworth's murders. It mentions a possible suspect that caused a disturbance at the company's headquarters earlier in the day. He was last seen driving a dark colored SUV type vehicle. You know this means we're suspects."

"I would imagine we are," said Jake. "But there was no way we could've stayed behind. We were lucky we got to Jackson in time.

We'll have to be careful. What does it say about out trip to Jackson?"

Pam pulled up Jackson's local news. "It says there were two homeless men burned in a dumpster fire. The bodies were so badly burned they couldn't identify them."

"What it means is they couldn't explain two dead rapidly decomposing demons so they wrote it off as best as they could."

Pam nodded, went back to her laptop as Jake and Ellie returned to their discussion on how to get inside the mansion.

"Absolutely not," bellowed Jake. "After what happened in Atlanta and Jackson there's no way I'm going to let you go inside. It's too dangerous."

"So, what're you going to do? Storm inside like you usually do? It didn't help us in Atlanta and now you're a murder suspect," yelled Ellie. "A Texan in a Stetson hat walking into the mansion is going to attract a little too much attention."

"The answer is still no."

Ellie jumped to her feet. "And since when do you tell me what to do? I'll go if I decide to."

Jake stood up and towered over her. "When it comes to your safety, I decide. You're not going."

Ellie straightened as much as her five-foot four frame could, and with hands on her hips, she stared up to his six foot three inches. "I'm going."

Jake bent down so that they were nose to nose. "No, you're not."

"Give up, Jake," interrupted Pam without looking up from her laptop. "I know her, she won't give up."

Jake glanced over at Pam. "You're a lot of help."

"I'm just saving you the trouble of arguing," she answered with a shrug.

He looked back at Ellie who was still standing firm. Jake shook his head and stomped out of the room.

Ellie stood with her arms folded. "Men, why do they have to be so hardheaded?"

"He cares about you."

"You're a lot of help, Pam."

"Give him a few minutes to calm down and he'll be ok."

Ten minutes later Ellie stepped outside where Jake was sitting on a wooden bench. He turned and smiled slightly.

"I'm sorry I yelled at you," he said.

She went and sat next to him. "I understand. You have a big responsibility."

"It's not just that. I don't want you hurt. I'm beginning to... become attached...I mean, care about you."

"And I care about you and Pam."

Jake was staring down at the ground. He'd never felt this way before about anyone. Ellie was different from anyone he'd ever met, and he wanted her with him all the time but wanted her far from here where it was safe. "That's not what I mean. I care about you differently."

Ellie blushed and smiled. She reached over and put her hand in his. "I know. I feel the same way too."

Jake looked up into her eyes. "Ellie, I'm not very good at intimacy. Being in the military unit I was assigned to my relationships were usually short. My career required constant moving so I never built lasting relationships, and because of my job, those I did get close to usually ended up dead. I never wanted to get close to anyone...until now."

"I'm not going anywhere. When this is over, we can work it out."

"But when will it be over? This has been going on since the beginning of time and may go on until the end of time."

"And I'll be right here until then." She looked at Jake, and saw the worry in his handsome, chiseled face. "We'll face it together."

"I don't want anything to happen to you."

She squeezed his hand. "You can't lock my up like a china doll. I won't break. Where you go, I go."

Jake didn't say anything. He just squeezed her hand back and smiled.

"Now, you just need some help," he said. "And I have an idea."

———

**FBI Headquarters**
**935 Pennsylvania Avenue, NW**
**Washington, D.C.**

AGENTS RUIZ and Williams returned to the safe house and removed their belongings. Agent Williams had an aunt who lived in Sleepy Hollow, Virginia. She was a retired schoolteacher who traveled abroad and didn't mind Agent Williams using it for a while. They moved Agent Sills into it and set up shop.

At FBI headquarters, they entered Agent Williams' office with a document signed by a federal judge authorizing a phone tap on Ghazi's mansion. They were surprised to see Deputy Director Ross sitting behind her desk.

"Good morning, sir," said Agent Williams.

"It's morning, but it's not a good one," he snapped.

Agent Williams glanced at Agent Ruiz who simply shrugged.

Deputy Director Ross waited for them to sit. "Deputy Director Sullens was ordered to contact us every morning from his residence. When he didn't call in early this morning, agents went to his home. They found him dead in his study."

"We're sorry to hear that, sir," said Agent Williams.

"Deputy Director Sullens' file drawers were open but empty. His shredder was full of shredded paper. All indications are he destroyed whatever incriminating evidence he had and then was killed."

The two agents nodded.

"I find it hard to believe he's a traitor. I've known him for at least twenty-five years. The lab's going over his house as we speak. Maybe they can find some answers."

"Yes, sir, we hope so," was all Agent Ruiz could think of to say.

Deputy Director Ross got up from the chair and headed for the door. "I hope you find President's Campbell's daughter soon. We have one agent in critical condition, two good agents dead and a deputy director dead because of this. I don't want to lose any more."

"Yes, sir, we agree," answered Agent Williams.

Deputy Director Ross nodded and left.

Agent Williams shook her head. "I can't believe Deputy Director

Sullens was involved. I just thought he'd lost the note or threw it away. I never would have thought he'd be in deep."

"Everyone has their price," answered Agent Ruiz.

"Then let's slam the door on this thing before anyone else gets hurt."

# CHAPTER TWENTY-FOUR

**Hell's Corner**
**New Orleans, Louisiana**

"I WANT to go on record as saying I think this is a very bad idea," said Pam from the backseat of the Suburban.

"Think positive," answered Ellie.

"I am. I'm positive this is a bad idea."

Jake chuckled. "Let's wait and see what happens."

"That's what I'm afraid of."

It was dark and quiet as Jake drove through the deserted buffer zone, the no-man's land between the rest of the world and "Hell's Corner." They reluctantly went back into the den of demons. They drove up and down several streets, trying not to look at the indecency and wickedness occurring everywhere. Jake apparently saw what he wanted and pulled over to the side.

"Stay in the truck."

He climbed out, walked across the street towards two women, obviously prostitutes, who stood on the corner. One of them, a bleached blonde with sunken, deep set eyes smiled at Jake.

"Hi, handsome, want a date?"

Jake tipped his hat, "Evening, ladies."

The other woman, a pink haired woman with scars and needle marks on her arms, stepped up and spoke.

"We can make a deal for the two of us. You look more than man enough."

Jake shook his head. "Sorry, ladies, but I'm looking for the gent behind you."

The two women glanced behind him at the ugly demon turned pimp that stood in the shadows. It was tall and thin with a bulbous head covered on the side with a frilly flap. Its neck was thin and long that led into a thin, almost snake-like body with long scaly arms.

The blonde woman tilted her head at the demon and spoke to Jake. "Honey, you make the deal with us, and he takes his cut later."

"I wasn't talking about him," said Jake. "I was talking about the other one." Jake pointed at a pitiful demon at the pimp demon's feet. The tall one held down a smaller demon with a clawed foot. The small demon was only about a foot tall and purple in color. It had a frog-like head with large protruding eyes that seemed to work independently. The creature's head and body were covered in scars from obvious beatings and abuse. Its arms were thin and frail with two small wings on its back that were shriveled and distorted. The large one held it down and constantly thumped the little demon's head with one of the claws in a nervous twitch. If it wasn't a demon, Jake could almost feel sorry for it.

The tall demon stretched it head out and looked Jake up and down with its yellow eyes. "What do you want, human?" it said in a raspy voice. "Are these two females not good enough for you?"

Jake glanced down at the pitiful demon under foot. "I want him."

"He's not for sale."

"Good, then you can give it to me."

The demon twisted its head back and forth at Jake, causing the flaps to shake like elephant ears.

"You stupid human, you have no idea who you're dealing with."

"Neither do you." With that Jake struck the thing between the eyes with his fist, knocking it backwards and it released its hold on the smaller one. Jake grabbed the little one by the back of the neck, turned, and began walking away.

The tall demon shook its head, roared, and lunged out of the darkness at Jake.

Anticipating this, Jake drew his Colt .45, and shot it several times as it charged. The creature dropped dead on the sidewalk. Several pedestrians stopped for a moment and stared but moved on. Apparently, violence was an everyday occurrence here.

The two prostitutes watched wide eyed as Jake walked across the street and climbed into the suburban. He sat the little demon on the backseat.

"Hand me that rope in the back."

Pam reached behind her, grabbed a small length of rope, and handed it to Jake. He promptly tied the little creature's arms and legs. "Don't do anything stupid," ordered Jake. "Or it will be the last thing you do."

The little demon struggled and fought against the ropes. He gnawed at the rope but couldn't bite it in half. He grunted and strained but couldn't disappear.

Jake looked into the rear-view mirror. "Roscoe, watch him for me."

Roscoe had already leaned over the backseat to look at the little creature.

It looked up at the wolfdog.

Roscoe growled.

The thing looked over at Pam who'd moved farther across the seat away from it.

One of its eyes watched Roscoe while the other looked at Pam. "Hi, sweets."

"Oh, gross," was all Pam could say. "Jake, what're you going to do with it?"

Jake smiled. "He's going to be our ticket inside."

---

**Ghazi Estate**

**6322 Crosswinds Drive**
**Lake Barcroft, Virginia**

ANN WAS AWAKENED by the sound of hammering and drilling. She looked out of her window and saw several work vans in the parking area. She saw several workmen coming and going apparently doing some type of renovations. *What is that maniac up too now?*

———

**G Enterprises Helicopter Facility**
**6411 Lincoln Parkway**
**Springfield, Virginia**

GHAZI STEPPED out of his limo and walked quickly into the office inside one of the main hangers of his helicopter plant.

Azim was waiting.

"Are the helicopters ready?" asked Ghazi.

Azim nodded.

"Good, let me see them."

He followed Azim into the huge hanger. Three helicopters sat inside, and Ghazi gazed at them with pleasure.

Two of them were the G-60, a small commuter type built by his company, but the third was special. It was an EH101 helicopter. Designed as a highly agile and maneuverable helicopter, the Lockheed Martin built aircraft has three engines to propel the aircraft up to altitudes of 15,000 feet. Currently the US101, the American variant of the EH101 is used as the Presidential helicopter, known as "Marine One."

"Very good. Are they ready for deployment?"

"Yes," answered Azim. "All three are ready to be shipped out."

"And the payload?"

"All three have been retrofitted with the canisters for the micro toxins. All three are mission ready."

Ghazi nodded and beamed at one of the helicopters. It was the one that had the words "United States of America" painted across the tail section. It was an exact replica of Marine One.

"Send them out."

----

**Hampton Inn**
**4356 LaSalle Ave**
**New Orleans, Louisiana**

BACK IN THE HOTEL ROOM, Jake tied one end of the rope around their new captive's neck like a leash and the other end to the edge of the bed. The purple skinned, yellow eyed creature sat and chewed on the rope.

"What kind of rope is this?" it finally asked when it couldn't chew through.

Jake and Ellie were sitting at the small hotel room table watching. Pam had taken a photograph of the creature and was emailing it to her assistant editor. She looked up. "I'm curious too."

"I figured since the weapons I use have a different effect on demons, I thought perhaps a rope would be too and apparently I was right," answered Jake.

The creature continued chewing on the rope, occasionally moving its distorted, deformed little wings.

"I wish that Malachy would have given me an instruction manual so I'd know what I can do and can't do," Jake said to Ellie with a chuckle.

The little demon stopped chewing, looked at the rope as if it was poison, and jumped back against the bed frame. "MALACHY?" it screeched.

They watched as the thing squirmed around on the floor and finally managed to crawl between the bed and the nightstand.

Jake looked between the bed and nightstand where the thing had the edge of the bedspread over its head.

"Do you know him?"

"No, no, no, no...but don't let him see me."

Jake reached over, pulled the rope, and dragged the thing out into the open. It tried to stay hidden and clawed at the carpet.

"No, no, I must hide," he pleaded.

Jake kept a tight hold on the rope. "Malachy is not here right now." Jake looked at Ellie and winked. "If you cooperate Malachy might not hurt you."

It sat on its haunches. Both of its eyes were going into different directions, looking around. "What must I do?"

"Do you have a name?" Ellie asked.

The frightened little monster looked around. "Mobak," he answered quietly.

"That's a nice name," said Ellie. "My name is Ellie, and this is Jake. We need your help."

Mobak frowned. "What kind of help?"

"We need you to guide us into the mansion in Hell's Corner, to see Tarnac," explained Jake.

"No, no, no, I cannot do that."

"You will, and you are," added Jake.

"He will kill me," he whined. "And you too."

"I'll protect you."

He shook his head. "You cannot. You are only human."

"I'm not just a human," explained Jake. "As you saw earlier, I can kill your kind."

The little thing looked Jake up and down. "Yes, you did kill Obnarey."

"Was that the long necked one with the flaps on its head?" asked Pam.

"Yes."

"You'll escort us into the mansion to see Tarnac. After that I'll release you...Deal?"

The thing looked up at Jake with both eyes. "You would do that? You won't kill me? You will let me go if I help you get inside?"

"Yes."

Mobak sat for a second and thought. "Deal."

"If you break the deal or cross us," explained Jake. "I'll kill you and feed you to Roscoe. Or maybe I'll just give you to Malachy."

Mobak looked over at Roscoe who was sleeping on the floor by the bathroom door. It shivered. "I understand."

"Good." Jake looked over at Ellie who nodded.

"Now that y'all have that settled, I'm hungry," added Pam.

Thirty minutes later they sat in the hotel room eating fast food hamburgers. Jake got a kid's meal and gave it to Mobak. He devoured his meal. Table manners were not his specialty as food dropped on the floor as he drooled and slurped. Pam looked over the edge of the bed at him.

One eye glanced up at her. "Hi, sweets," he said with a mouth full of food.

"My name is Pam."

"Ok, sweets."

Pam rolled her eyes and went back to eating.

"Why did you leave heaven?" asked Ellie.

Mobak frowned at her. "We were thrown out."

Ellie shook her head. "No, you were cast out after you rebelled."

"How do you know so much?"

"I'm a pastor of a church."

Mobak frowned again. "Great, I'm being held hostage by a demon killer, a preacher woman, and a wolf. What luck?"

"But you had everything you wanted in heaven?"

Mobak put the hamburger down and lowered his head. "We were told by Lord Satan that we could all become gods. We believed that we could all be God. It didn't turn out that way."

"And now you can never return?"

Mobak nodded.

"Why do you have so many scars?" asked Pam.

"As you can see, I'm small. The others use me for entertainment and amusement."

"What were you in heaven?"

"I was what you call a seraphim."

"A six-winged angel?" asked Ellie.

Mobak pointed to several stubs protruding from his back just below the deformed wings. "I used to have all six, but not anymore."

"I'm sorry," said Ellie. Even though he was a condemned demon, she felt sorry for him.

Mobak shrugged and went back to eating.

Pam looked up at Jake, "Any idea how we're going to get into that mansion? It'll be hard, even with our little helper?"

"I'm not real sure yet," answered Jake. "We'll come up with something."

"I have an idea," added Ellie, "but we need to find a costume store."

# CHAPTER TWENTY-FIVE

**Hampton Inn**
**4356 LaSalle Ave**
**New Orleans, Louisiana**

"THIS IS INSANE. It'll never work," said Pam.

"Have a little faith," said Ellie.

After a trip to a local costume shop, they returned to their hotel room and put Ellie's plan into action. Ellie painted their faces with light gray make up to give them an ashen, pale appearance. She added dark lines under their eyes and highlights to make them look sullen and zombie-like. Jake dressed in black clothes and a dark robe with a hood. Ellie and Pam both wore short skirts, fishnets stockings and halter tops to look like street prostitutes.

"If you ever tell anyone about this," warned Pam.

"Sometimes we have to do the unusual to accomplish our task," said Ellie. "I think we'll be forgiven for this considering our circumstances."

Mobak sat on the floor, still attached to his leash, and watched them with his yellow eyes. One of his eyes rotated toward Pam. "Lookin hot, Sweets."

"That's it, I'm not going," replied Pam.

Jake chuckled and headed for the door. "I'll be right back." A few minutes later he returned carrying a large footlocker. It had been in the back of the suburban the entire trip. Jake sat it on the floor and began removing various items and laying them on the bed. He had camouflage ACU's or Army Combat Uniforms, mesh netting, electronics, and other military gear.

"What's all this?" asked Pam.

"Most of this I've bought over the years from army-navy surplus stores around the country but some of its left over from my military days."

At the bottom was a dark green hard plastic case. He opened the case and removed a semi-auto assault rifle.

"What is that?" Ellie asked.

"It's a lightweight, air cooled, magazine fed, shoulder fired AR-15 with a scope," answered Jake with a smile. There were several magazines in the case.

"Were you planning to start your own little war?" asked Pam with raised eyebrows.

"I kept this just in case I ever needed to run off rustlers or annoying news people."

"Oh, of course," said Pam sarcastically.

"I didn't think my Winchester will be adequate for this job."

———

NO ONE SPOKE during their drive through the buffer zone and into Hell's Corner. Jake parked the suburban around the corner from the front of the mansion. It was just after dark and a light drizzle started falling. The usual crude, indecent activities were already at full speed. The group walked slowly up the sidewalk towards the mansion.

Jake was armed with a Colt .45 and his AR-15 which hung from a sling under his ankle length robe. He pulled his hood over his head to keep his face in shadows while he held the rope attached to Mobak who walked along side. Ellie and Pam followed behind them.

Jake had compromised with Pam and allowed them to wear capes with hoods because of the weather. They also kept their hoods over their heads to hide their faces. Ellie held Roscoe on a leash, but Roscoe wasn't wearing any makeup as his wolf-like appearance blended perfectly.

"This isn't going to work," whispered Pam as they walked.

"Shush, Pamela," said Ellie. "Yes, it will."

Mobak didn't seem to be bothered by the drizzle. "They'll see through your disguises eventually."

"I don't want to fool them forever, just a few minutes," explained Jake.

Their trip up to the broken gates of the mansion went without a hitch. They drew a few glances from demons, ghosts, and human alike, but in that decrepit atmosphere nothing was abnormal.

"Now what?" asked Ellie.

"Now we go inside and ask," said Jake.

They walked up the walkway to the large wooden doors. One door was cracked open which allowed them to hear music and talking coming from inside. Jake pushed the door the rest of the way open as they entered.

They stood in the circular entry way of the old southern mansion. The inside was as bad as the outside. Plain light bulbs illuminated the bare floors. A few old pictures and paintings hung from the stained walls. A water line could be seen along the walls where the hurricane flood waters had been. The paint and wallpaper were replaced by mold and dust. A large staircase allowed access to the second floor, and a hallway led left and right to more rooms. They heard sounds and noises coming from side rooms, but they dared not investigate for fear of what they might find. Wandering in this place could be dangerous if not fatal.

"Have you ever been in here before?" Pam asked Mobak.

"No."

"Now he tells us."

"Shhh," whispered Ellie. "What now, Jake?"

"We ask directions?" answered Jake. He glanced down at Mobak who nodded in agreement.

Two people sat against a wall and smoked crack cocaine from a glass pipe. A medium sized, lime-green colored demon with sores covering its torso clapped and cheered the two on. It glanced at the group for only a second and then returned to its two human victims.

A six-foot demon came out of a side room. One eye was missing and only a dark empty socket stared back. It had large arms that hung almost to the floor but had short legs. It limped as it walked past with a woman in tow. She was skinny with bite marks and needle marks on her arms and legs. Several patches of her hair was missing, and her eyes were swollen.

Mobak stepped forward and made several unrecognizable squeaks, clicks, and grunts. The ape-like demon stopped and grunted. For a moment the two grunted and squeaked in some sort of strange demon language like dolphin sounds. The woman remained silent. Her eyes were glazed over in an apparent drug induced stupor. Finally, the large one grunted, looked at them, snorted, and continued past with the woman still in tow.

"What's with the strange language?" asked Pam.

"Long story, sweets," explained Mobak.

"That poor woman," whispered Ellie.

"I wonder how that thing lost an eye?" asked Pam.

"He made Tarnac upset," answered Mobak. "Do you still want to go?"

Ellie took a deep breath and nodded.

Jake also nodded, "Where to now?"

Mobak pointed up, and they started up the stairs. There were several people lying on the stairs, and they had to carefully step around them. One young man had fresh blood oozing from a needle mark in his arm. As Pam stepped past him, he reached out and grabbed her ankle.

"Hey, baby, let's go for some fun," he mumbled.

Roscoe growled. Jake reached down and pulled the man's hand away.

"She's with me."

At the top of the stairs a hallway went left and right. The section of the mansion was busy with activity. Demons of all shapes and sizes along with humans wandered the halls. Mobak pointed left to a door down the hall where a single demon leaning against the wall.

"So that's the place?" asked Jake.

Mobak nodded.

They started down the hall when Jake felt Mobak's rope tighten. The demon had stopped.

"Are you sure this is a good idea?" asked Mobak.

"No, but it's what we have to do."

"Tarnac may not be happy that you're here."

"I know, but I'm going anyway."

Mobak hesitated a moment but then followed. "You people are either very brave, or insane," he muttered.

They weaved their way through the crowded hallway. At the door, the large ugly demon guarding the door glanced at them. Its head was large but flat on top. Its small yellow eyes stared out at them from under a thick forehead. It had no neck as its head came straight from its massive shoulders. A large black sword hung from a belt around its huge waist.

Bodyguard?

Mobak began another strange conversation with the guard using the same type of grunts, clicks, and squeaks. The guard shook its head and grunted. Even Jake knew that meant they were being denied entry. Mobak pointed to Jake and renewed his conversation. After a few more minutes of odd conversation the guard looked at Jake strangely and nodded. It turned, knocked, and entered the room. The group waited outside.

"What did you say?" asked Jake.

"I told him you were a half-son of one of the princes of the air."

"I don't know what that means but it doesn't sound good."

"I know what it means and it's impossible," whispered Ellie.

Mobak smiled. "We know that, but the guard doesn't. They are strong and obedient but stupid."

"Tarnac will know it's a lie," said Jake.

"But he'll be too curious not to see for himself. I'll get you inside, but the rest is up to you. That's our deal, right?"

Jake nodded.

The guard returned and motioned for them to enter. Jake handed Mobak's rope to Pam in case something went wrong, and he needed both hands. As they started inside, the guard held up his hand and looked down at Mobak.

Jake looked at the demon guard. "He's with us."

The guard glared back for a five count, then shrugged and motioned for them to enter. They quickly stepped into the room as Roscoe growled at the guard. After everyone was inside and the guard closed the door, they realized they had just entered what could only be described as a bad nightmare.

The room was an old ballroom with boarded up windows. The walls were painted black with various satanic symbols painted in red or white. Attached to the walls were shackles, chains, and all types of torture devices. Several large cages sat around the room but were temporarily empty. Candles and incense burned throughout the room, but the stench of death still hung in the air.

Pam was speechless and Ellie covered her mouth with the edge of her cape. Jake subtly reached inside his robe and gripped the handle of his AR-15.

A six-foot, thin built demon stepped up to meet them. Its face almost seemed human, but its skull was enlarged and deformed. The skin was stretched tight against its skull, and its arms and legs were thin.

"You came to see Tarnac?"

Jake nodded.

The creature turned and pointed to a darkened corner of the room.

On an upraised platform in a large, overstuffed chair sat the demon called Tarnac. Even in the dim light he looked horrifying. He had a large oval shaped head with the usual yellowish glowing eyes, and one eye had a vertical scar through it. Its snout was like that of an alligator with large teeth that protruded below its jaw and curved around in a semi-circle. Its body was large and muscular with smaller horn-like points along its arms and legs. Its hands were clawed with the thumb claw curved and honed to a point. Bones and skulls of animals and humans alike were scattered around the feet of the chair. To one side sat a large bong used to smoke narcotics. Tarnac held a large meat covered bone in one hand and a tube connected to the drug bong in the other. A large black sword rested against one arm of the chair.

The group slowly approached the thing. Tarnac carefully looked at each member of the little hooded group. Roscoe growled and Ellie kept a tight hold on his leash. Tarnac tilted his head and looked toward Pam. Mobak had slipped under her cape and wrapped a piece of it around his head so only his face showed.

"Mobak?" asked Tarnac. The monster's voice was deep and low, adding to its already frightening appearance.

Mobak timidly stepped out from under Pam's cape. He grunted, squeaked, and clicked through a brief conversation with Tarnac. He held up the rope attached to his neck, and in English said, "I didn't have a choice. They made me."

Tarnac made few clicks and squeaks in their strange language and Mobak slinked back under the cape. He turned to Jake. "Why are you here?"

Jake pulled back his hood. "We came for information."

Tarnac looked at Jake for a moment, saw the make up and let out a deep, bass chuckle. "It's a little early for Halloween." He ripped off a piece of meat from the bone and chewed it slowly. Tarnac then inhaled whatever narcotic was in the bong and looked down at Jake. "And I don't give out information."

The thin demon stepped out from behind them with a curved, spiral shaped knife. Jake sensed the movement and withdrew the AR-15 and pointed it at the demon.

"Go ahead, if you feel lucky," sneered Jake.

The skinny demon glared. "You stupid human, you can't hurt me."

Jake pulled the Colt 45 and pointed it a Tarnac without taking his eyes off the would-be executioner. "Tell it to your lizard friend, the two arson twins, just to name a few."

The demon hesitated.

"You killed Yeknar, Rontat, and Utret?" asked Tarnac.

"If that's what you called them, yes, and as I said several more."

Tarnac made a slight movement with his head and the other demon replaced the knife and moved back into the shadows. Jake didn't budge.

"You can put your weapons away now human. Radnor will not harm you."

Jake lowered the assault rifle but kept the Colt 45 pointed at Tarnac.

Tarnac chuckled. "I like your mistrust. That's good. I've heard rumors that someone's been killing us. What information do you want?"

"I want to know why they've been killing people, specifically those who work for Martech pharmaceuticals."

Tarnac drummed his claw on the arm of chair. Jake glanced at Ellie. She looked pale even under the makeup, and her lips were moving without sound. Praying.

"Even if I tell you," Tarnac said suddenly. "How do you plan to get out of here?"

"The same way we came in."

"But what if I object?"

"You'll be dead."

Tarnac's frowned, but then threw back his head and laughed. The sudden outburst startled Pam, Ellie continued her silent prayer, and Jake kept his weapon trained on Tarnac.

"I assume whoever told you to come see me thought I'd kill you immediately, but I like you, human. The one you seek is named Hassan Ghazi. He can be found in Virginia."

"Why?"

Tarnac picked a piece of meat from between a tooth before answering. "It's something to do with his insane plan to take over the world."

Jake was shocked but kept his face stoic.

"You may leave now," said Tarnac casually. "I will allow you safe passage out of here."

Jake nodded but kept his weapon aimed at Tarnac.

"Radnor, please allow them to leave."

Radnor opened the door and motioned for them to leave. The group backed away out the door. Jake was the last to leave.

"Remember one thing, demon killer," growled Tarnac. "The next time we meet I won't be so hospitable."

"I'll be waiting," sneered Jake.

The group made their way down the hall to the stairs.

"I don't trust him," said Ellie. "He can't let us go so easily."

"I don't either but let's just get out of here," said Jake.

They went down the stairs to the main entryway.

Upstairs Radnor approached Tarnac. "Your most wretched highness," he said in squeaks and clicks. "Forgive my ignorance but do you think it wise to let the humans leave unharmed?"

Tarnac smiled. "I told them I would give them safe passage out, but once outside it's a different matter."

Radnor smiled, nodded, and went out into the hallway.

The small group went out the front doors and down the walkway.

"So far so good," said Pam.

Jake bent down and untied the rope from around Mobak's neck. "You're free now."

Mobak rubbed his neck. "You kept your word?"

Jake nodded. "A deal is a deal."

Mobak smiled and turned to Pam. "Bye, Sweets."

Pam rolled her eyes.

A ghost wearing a confederate uniform approached them. "Pardon me for intruding, but those heathens are about to come out of the house like huntin' dogs after a racoon. You better high tail it."

They heard numerous sounds of grunts, clicks and squeals coming from the mansion. Mobak ran off into the bushes.

Jake glanced back and saw several demons run out of the mansion towards them. "Run, head to the truck."

"Hurry, we'll try to hold them off," yelled the confederate soldier. He pulled his saber and charged the demons. "C'mon boys, let's give these monsters a good ole southern whipping," he yelled to the other confederate ghosts. A group of confederate ghosts tried in to vain to stop the horde but unfortunately there were too many.

The group ran down the walkway and onto the sidewalk as more demons poured out of the mansion. Jake kept the two women ahead of him as they ran. One demon leapt over the Iron Gate and directly in front of Jake. He shot it twice before it went down. This caused several of the demons to hesitate but were urged on by the mob.

The group arrived at the suburban only seconds ahead of the demons. Ellie climbed in the front passenger seat while Pam climbed into the rear passenger side. Jake stopped, fired into the crowd with his AR-15 and killed several demons, but more took their place. Roscoe stood his ground beside Jake and barked.

One demon dove past Jake and slammed into Ellie's door leaving a huge dent. Jake brought the butt of the rifle down and cracked the creature's skull. Another demon grabbed his arm, but Jake shot it through the neck.

An orange-colored demon smashed the glass on the rear passenger window and grabbed Pam by the hair. She screamed and Roscoe bit the creature's leg. Another demon leapt on top of the suburban and Jake shot it. Pam struggled to get free while the thing tried to pull her through the window of the vehicle. Roscoe growled and continued to bite the orange demon's leg. Jake was busy firing at approaching demons and couldn't help. A small purple demon leapt through the air and landed on the orange demon's head.

"She's with me," yelled Mobak as he clawed at the other demon's eyes. The large creature released its hold on Pam and frantically tried to pull Mobak off.

"Roscoe, get in now," yelled Jake as he fired a shot into an obese, putrid smelling demon. Roscoe jumped up through the window into the back with Pam. "Ellie...drive." The rifle clicked on an empty chamber. *Oh great. No time to reload now.* Jake fired his remaining Colt handgun at a tall demon towering over him.

Ellie climbed over into the driver's seat and started up the suburban. Jake climbed onto the running board of the suburban and yelled for Ellie to go.

Mobak fought with the creature that had attacked Pam. Unfortunately, it had long arms and grabbed Mobak, pulled him off, and slammed him to the ground. It stomped on Mobak's back which caused a sickening crunch sound. Jake shot the demon, reached down, scooped up Mobak, and handed him to Pam through the broken window as Ellie slammed on the accelerator. The suburban's tires screeched as Ellie raced down the street to get away. Jake jerked open the front passenger door and climbed in. The mob of demon's kept up the pursuit, and several of the faster ones stayed close. A demon jumped onto the back of the suburban, clinging to the bumper and luggage rack.

Jake loaded a magazine into the assault rifle. "Duck," he yelled at Pam, and fired through the back window of the suburban, shattering the glass, and knocking the thing off. They raced through the different levels of Hell's Corner with an ever-growing mob of demons in pursuit.

In minutes they were clear of Hell's Corner and racing across the buffer zone with a mass of demons still on their heels. The top of the suburban caved in when several jumped onto the top of the truck and three more climbed onto the back. Their weight was slowing them down and more demons were catching up.

Jake fired through the roof.

"We're slowing down," said Ellie. "Their weight's dragging us down."

"I don't have enough ammo for all of them," said Jake. "Keep going. Maybe we can lose most of them."

Ellie looked in the mirror and saw hundreds of demons in pursuit. She kept the gas pedal to the floor.

Jake poured round after round through the back window and rear portion of the suburban, killing demon after demon. The sound of the shots was deafening inside the suburban. As soon as one fell off, two more climbed on top. One pounded on the top and was able to puncture a hole in the roof. Jake shot it several times.

The suburban was slowing down as more demons climbed on. One landed on the hood and Ellie could barely see. Jake used the last of the .223 rounds from his assault rifle and was down to what he had in his handgun.

They passed an intersection in the buffer zone when the suburban shuddered. The demons were suddenly gone.

The suburban was immediately lighter and since Ellie had the gas pedal floored, the vehicle catapulted forward and away from the vacant buffer zone. All three looked back to see the mass of demons disappear in the distance as they sped away.

"What happened?" asked Ellie.

"I don't know," answered Jake. "But I'm glad it did."

"What about Mobak?" asked Pam.

Jake looked into the back seat and saw the limp form of the little demon. "I'm not sure. Let's go back to the hotel."

At the mansion, Tarnac stood at the door and watched the demons return. Radnor stood beside him and slightly behind. "They were unsuccessful," explained Radnor.

"I can see that."

The mansion sat on a slight hill and Tarnac could see past hell's corner toward the buffer zone. They could see what the humans couldn't.

At the intersection where the demon's stopped was a huge line of thousands and thousands of armed angels with one standing in the front.

Malachy.

"What about Ghazi?" asked Radnor. "Should we warn him about them?"

"No. Let Ghazi deal with him, and if he kills the human then it's better for us. If not, then with Ghazi gone, it will be better for us. It'll give me more room to expand, so either way I win."

Radnor nodded and smiled.

At the hotel, they laid the little demon on the bed. Mobak opened his eyes and looked around. "Hi, Sweets," he said weakly.

It was obvious that the little creature was seriously injured. His left side was limp, and he had trouble moving the other, but he reached up with a small, clawed hand and placed it on Pam's arm.

Pam looked sadly down at him. "You helped me? Why?"

"You kept your word." One eye rotated around and widened.

They all looked up to see Malachy standing over them. He looked down at the injured demon.

"Mobak."

"I tried to save your friends, Malachy."

Malachy nodded sadly. "You did fine."

"Isn't there anything you can do?" asked Pam.

Malachy shook his head.

"But can't we get him some help? Can't we take him somewhere?"

"There's no place to take him," said Ellie quietly. "He's a demon. We can't just take him to a hospital."

"It's ok, sweets," Mobak said. "There's nothing you can do for me. I made my choice, and it can't be changed." His voice was getting softer.

"You did a good thing," said Jake.

"I did, didn't I? I haven't done anything good since..." His eyes rotated then stopped, and his body became still.

No one spoke or moved.

Pam finally spoke. "This is crazy," she said with tears in her eyes.

Malachy placed his hand on her shoulder. "Mobak might not have been as evil as the rest, but he made his choice eons ago."

"What should we do with him?" asked Ellie.

"Give him to me," answered Malachy. "I'll take care of it."

Due to the rapid decomposition, they quickly wrapped Mobak's body in hotel towels and handed him to Malachy. The gold-colored giant looked strange holding the tiny body of the fallen angel, and then he disappeared.

Ellie moved over, put her arm around Pam, and looked at Jake. "What do we do now?"

"I'm going to Virginia," answered Jake. "I've got to find Ghazi and stop him."

Pam looked up. "You mean we're going to Virginia," she said determinedly.

Jake nodded.

# CHAPTER TWENTY-SIX

**Ghazi Estate**
**6322 Crosswinds Drive**
**Lake Barcroft, Virginia**

AMIRA WAS NOT HAPPY, and Azim had become sullener and angrier. It was obvious that he and Ghazi were not getting along. Amira needed time to think and walked quietly down the hall towards the front door to get some fresh air to clear her head. Ghazi's study door was cracked and as she passed by, she glanced in and what she saw horrified her.

A hideous creature sat at Ghazi's desk. It was dark red fur with brown swirls along its skin. It had a massive head with two large yellow eyes set in front. It had large teeth and huge leathery wings. Its arms were muscular and large hands. Amira gasped out loud without realizing causing the creature to look up.

"Who's there?"

It was Ghazi's voice. Amira closed her eyes for a second, opened them, and looked inside. She saw Ghazi sitting in his chair wearing polo shirt and khaki slacks.

"Amira, is that you?" he asked.

Amira pushed the door open slightly. "Yes, Mr. Ghazi. I was going out to get some fresh air."

Ghazi stared at her for a moment. "I think that would be appropriate. You look pale."

Amira nodded and hurriedly went outside. She shook her head again. Did I see what I thought I saw? Am I seeing things? She glanced back and saw Ghazi at the window watching her. She walked down the path and into the nearby flower garden. Amira had some serious thinking to do.

The next morning Ghazi stood in his lush master bedroom getting ready for his morning meetings when his phone rang. He answered and heard Senator Wilson ranting and raving.

"Ghazi, you imbecile, do you have any idea what's going on?"

"Good morning, Senator, please hold one moment." Ghazi put him on hold and flipped a switched attached to his phone. He picked the phone back up. "And what do I have the pleasure of knowing now, Senator."

"What were you doing? Are you trying to insult me by putting me on hold?"

Ghazi sighed heavily. "Senator, I simply engaged my scrambler and jamming device on my phone. I'm sure by now the FBI is taping my phone lines. This will ensure our conversations are private."

"But they can unscramble them, you idiot."

Ghazi was trying not to get angry. "My dear, Senator," he said through gritted teeth. "By the time they decipher the scrambled phone tapes, it will be too late. Now what is the problem?"

"The problem is all the bungling going on. This was supposed to be a smooth operation. Those so-called assassins screwed up again in their attempt to get rid of the FBI agents. The first ones didn't blow them up and the second ones only killed the wrong agent. Now my contact in the FBI is dead. It won't be long before they trace it all back to me."

Ghazi was growing tired of this ignorant human. "Everything's going as planned and I've simply moved the timetable forward. As far as your contact in the FBI, he was careless. The bombers were deleted to show that failure is not an option, and the assassins were killed by the FBI agents during their attack. These potential problems have been resolved."

"Deleted? Potential problems?" screamed Senator Wilson. "Killing a Deputy Director of the FBI is not deleting potential problems. You knew he was my contact?"

"Yes, I knew."

"Have you been spying on me?"

"Of course not, Senator, I have other contacts who keep a watchful eye out for me."

"There are too many coincidences to be safe. If I go down on this, I'm taking you with me. Don't forget that."

Ghazi's eyes began to glow yellow. "The plan will not fail. You do your part and try not to screw up and everything will be fine. Now, go back to your law making or whatever you do and let me handle this. I will see to it that the FBI agents are taken care of."

Before Senator Wilson could reply, Ghazi hung up. He gathered himself and calmed down. He was not going to let a lowly human like Senator Wilson ruin his day. One of his underlings was keeping a close eye on Senator Wilson, much closer than he even knew.

---

**FBI Headquarters**
**935 Pennsylvania Avenue NW**
**Washington, D.C.**

AGENTS WILLIAMS and Ruiz were sifting through phone records and financial reports on Ghazi's companies. They delegated more of it to other agents to assist in trying to find a needle in a haystack that could break the case.

Agent Ruiz slammed down a stack of papers. "Damn, there's nothing here that we can tie to Ghazi and the President's daughter."

Agent Williams held her head in her hands. "So far, we have small pieces of nothing. Ghazi must be on to our phone tap because he's scrambled his phone lines. It'll take weeks to decipher it all."

Agent Ruiz got up and walked over to a large writing board

they'd placed on a stand. It had photos, notes, names, dates, and locations written on it. "This is what we have right now. The President's daughter is kidnapped but no ransom or contact has been made. We believe the kidnapper is Hassan Ghazi, and we think she's somewhere in the eastern United States. We know that Ghazi is doing something secret in a pharmaceutical lab, maybe making illegal drugs of some type, and it ties into his helicopter plant somehow. And we have a string of dead agents along the way, not to mention the death of a Deputy Director."

"Maybe he's just using the helicopters to move his drugs. He could just be a major drug dealer?"

Agent Ruiz shook his head. "I get a feeling that there's more to this, but I can't put it together."

The door opened and Director Chisom entered quietly. He nodded to the two agents. "I have some bad news." He hesitated for a moment. "Agent Kimbell passed away last night. I'm sorry."

Agent Williams simply held her head in her hands. Agent Ruiz threw a handful of papers across the room and cursed.

# CHAPTER TWENTY-SEVEN

**Midwestern Virginia**

THE LONG DRIVE towards Virginia had been uneventful so far. They hid the Suburban until Jake was able to repair the damage as much as possible so it wouldn't attract attention. He put epoxy putty over the bullet holes and spray painted it primer gray. They taped plastic over the shattered windows. It was now a flat gray and blue colored SUV with dents and claw marks all over that still looked like it had been through a small war.

Pam had just finished sending her latest update to her assistant editor back in Shady Oak. "It seems like an eternity since we left Shady Oak."

Ellie nodded. "A lot happened since we left, and much more than I ever would've imagined."

"Do you regret it?" asked Jake as he drove through the heavily wooded hills of Virginia.

Ellie reached over and put her hand on his shoulder. "No, no regrets."

"Do you have any idea how we're going to find this Ghazi person?" asked Pam. "I looked up all the companies in the area that belong to him. He has a research lab, trucking company, and helicopter manufacturing plant in Virginia, but no idea where he is right now."

Ellie looked over at Jake. "Maybe we can call someone and warn them? Is there an agency we can call?"

"I doubt it," said Jake. "Besides, what're we going to do, call and tell them that we believe a demon that looks like a human is planning on taking over the world? And don't forget, I'm a murder suspect."

"I see what you mean."

"And we don't even know what he's planning?" added Pam.

Jake smiled. "I guess I'll have to ask when we get there."

"I hope it doesn't involve running, shooting, burning, or destroying anything."

———

**FBI Headquarters**
**935 Pennsylvania Avenue, NW**
**Washington, D.C.**

THE DAY HAD BEEN long and tedious especially after the news of Agent Kimbell's death. They increased their efforts by digging through files and print outs on Ghazi's companies. They were squeaky clean, and that was frustrating.

Agent Ruiz tossed down his stack of print outs. "His shipments and receipts are impeccable. This guy doesn't screw up."

Agent Williams nodded without looking up. "Yep, he definitely covered his tracks."

"Anything from the surveillance team?"

"Just their report about the last shipments that said two small helicopters and one large were shipped out on flat beds. It seems to be routine things."

Agent Ruiz grunted. "That's wonderful, another dead end."

They went back to reading, but something kept nagging at him. He looked up at Agent Williams. "Let me see that handout on the helicopter shipments?"

She handed him the file. "What are you thinking?"

Agent Ruiz frowned. "I don't know." He read through the report. "What kind of helicopters do they make there?"

Agent Williams shrugged. She looked through a stack of papers to a pamphlet. "It says here they produce the G-60. It looks like the usual civilian helicopter like the Sikorsky S-76 or the MD Explorer. Why?"

"Those are all the regular size commuter type helicopters, about the same size, right?"

"Right?"

"So why was there one large helicopter?"

Agent Williams raised her eyebrows. "I don't know, because he wanted a bigger one?"

"Exactly, and it may be nothing or it may be something. Where's the shipping receipt?"

The two agents dug through stacks of documents until they found the receipt.

Agent Ruiz read it and handled it to Agent Williams. "This is interesting."

She looked at it but didn't see anything unusual. "It shows two G-60s and one EH101 helicopter shipped out. So?"

"Think, Williams, think. What is unique about it?"

"It's bigger than the other two?"

"Who else uses the EH101?"

Agent Williams shrugged. "The military, among many, and it's also the..." She raised an eyebrow and looked at Agent Ruiz. "It's also Marine One."

"Correct. Now why would he want that type of helicopter right now?"

Agent Williams shook her head. "I don't know, but we need to find that helicopter."

The door opened and an agent stepped in. "I got some news for you."

"I hope it's good," said Agent Williams.

The agent handed her a piece of paper. "It's a tip from the hot line. An anonymous female called and said that G Pharmaceuticals are creating biological weapons at their plant. Will this help you?"

Agent Ruiz grabbed the sheet. "Hell yes, thanks. This is just what we were hoping for. I could kiss you if weren't so ugly."

"In your dreams, Ruiz," answered the agent with a smirk.

"Do you think this will be enough for a search warrant?" asked Agent Williams.

"I think it can be if we word it just right."

"Now, who do you suppose would call this in?' asked Agent Williams.

"Maybe someone with a conscience?"

————

**Ghazi Estate**
**6322 Crosswinds Drive**
**Lake Barcroft, Virginia**

ANN WAS SUMMONED ONCE MORE to the dining room of the estate. She'd lost all track of time despite her efforts to keep busy with both mental and physical exercises. She had no idea how she was going to escape before Ghazi killed her. The only contact she had with anyone was the maid when she came to clean, and she didn't talk.

She entered the dining room and saw Ghazi, Azim, and Amira waiting for her at the huge table. What caught her attention the most was Amira. One of her eyes was badly swollen, her lips were swollen, and she had numerous bruises. Someone had obviously beaten her badly.

"Welcome, Miss Campbell, please have a seat. We're about to have dinner. Join us," said Ghazi with a smile.

Ann hated how cheerful he was, knowing the madness beneath. She sat across from Amira, who never looked up. She stared at Amira, but she sat quietly and refused to look up.

"Are you wondering what happened to Amira?" asked Ghazi. He looked over at Amira in mock sadness. "Tsk, tsk, tsk. She had to be punished. Amira made a phone call to the FBI hotline about my laboratory. It doesn't stop my plans, but I had to make some sudden changes to fix the problem."

Ann glared at him and then looked over at Amira. "Are you ok?"

"She can't answer you my, dear. I can't have her talking to the FBI again, so I cut her tongue out."

Ann sat back in shock and put a hand to her mouth. She glared at Ghazi. "You're an animal."

"I detest disobedience." Ghazi got up and walked over to Amira. He stood next to her, removed a tape recorder from his pocket, and tossed it across the table where it landed in front of Ann. "I need you to record a few things."

"Forget it."

"I thought you might be reluctant. I brought Amira here to show you what happens to those that disobey, but I also needed her to persuade you."

Ann frowned at him.

Ghazi reached into his pocket and removed a lock blade knife. He opened it, jerked Amira's head back, and put the knife to her throat. "I have no more need for her. If you say exactly what I want you to say, I'll let her live, if not, I'll cut her throat here and now."

Even after everything, Ann was still shocked at his brutality. She looked at Amira who stared wide eyed at Ann with her one good eye. Her eye was almost pleading for Ann not to give in. A single tear ran down Amira's face.

Ann lowered her head. "I'll do it."

Ghazi released Amira and walked back to his seat at the table. "Wonderful! Let's eat and then you can record what I dictate to you." He looked up at Azim. "Get her out of my sight."

Azim quietly got up and escorted Amira out of the room.

Ghazi watched them leave. "Azim hates you. He blames you for Amira's current situation. He thinks you corrupted her."

"I only told her the truth," replied Ann.

Ghazi nodded. "The truth is a matter of interpretation. Azim is a simple-minded fanatic that can't get past his own hatred for the western world. I, on the other hand, embrace the western world."

"He doesn't know about your…alternate plans?"

"Of course not, he thinks the world will be perfect under Islamic law. He has no idea, but enough of this, let's eat."

---

### G Pharmaceuticals and Research Laboratory
### 3571 Vermont Rd
### Alexandria, Virginia

AGENT WILLIAMS and Ruiz sat in an unmarked car up the road from Ghazi's pharmaceutical company. She held a newly signed search warrant. It had taken some convincing and hints of homeland security to get the federal judge to agree to sign it.

The FBI tactical team made a recon run and returned reporting all was quiet. The business was closed for the night, and only one security guard was stationed at the gate. They choose to wait until after the plant closed to avoid any potential problems with employees that may or may not be involved.

Agent Williams radio squawked.

"We're in position," said a tactical FBI agent calmly.

"I copy," said another. "We have a perimeter set and wait for your go."

"Everything is a go. All we need is for the final word from Williams," said the lead tactical agent.

It always amazed her that in stressful, dangerous situations these men talk as if they were at a dinner party. She picked up the radio and pressed the button. "I have the warrant, it's a go."

Two dark vans pulled out slowly from down the street and drove quickly passed Agent Ruiz and Williams. The two vans drove up to the gate without headlights. Two federal agents leapt from the back of the van and confronted the security guard. They identified themselves as federal agents and ordered him to open the gate.

Once the gate was open the two vans, along with the car containing Agent Ruiz and Williams, quickly pulled into the parking lot. The vans stopped, the back came open, and several federal tactical agents jumped out and ran to find cover in directions covered previously in the pre-mission briefing. Agents Ruiz and Agent Williams waited outside their car. Both were wearing their bullet-proof raid jackets and watched as the tactical team moved swiftly and quietly around the building.

The front door was a typical metal frame door with safety glass. One agent yelled, "Federal agents, we have a search warrant," and smashed the glass. The silent alarm system was activated as the agents slipped through the opening and inside the building. They quickly worked their way from room to room, clearing each room. They came to a metal door and opened it. It led down to the basement.

"Hey, Williams, we found the stairwell leading down. Looks like we found your secret lab," said the entry team's lead agent named Best.

"10-4, keep us posted when it's clear," answered Agent Williams. She turned to Agent Ruiz. "Chad Best's one of the best tactical officers at the bureau. I've known him for years and he's more than competent."

Agent Ruiz nodded. He'd heard rumors a couple of years back that they'd been more than friends at one time.

The team moved down the stairs to another door. They didn't like being confined to a stairwell without another exit but didn't have a choice. They opened the door to the basement. The interior was quiet and dark. A few emergency lights showed a huge underground complex of glass enclosed rooms on each side of the hall.

"You take the left, we'll take right," he said to his second in command. The team split and worked their way down the hall. The last member of the entry team let the stairwell door close, and it made a loud click. Several agents looked back, and the last agent shrugged. They continued their search as the teams entered each room and found it empty of employees. No one appeared to be working late.

"What's the status?" asked the agent in charge of the outside perimeter.

"So far so good," answered Agent Best. "This place is full of lab equipment and volatile chemicals. We're going to need Haz Mat down here after we clear this place."

They continued to clear the laboratory. They checked the last office, but no one was inside.

"All clear," said Agent Best. "It's all yours, Agent Williams."

"10-4," radioed Agent Williams. She turned to Ruiz. "Let's go see what Ghazi has been up to."

In the basement, one of the agents closed an office door farthest from the exit and heard a distinct click above him. He looked up and saw a wire leading from the door frame into the wall. Soon a ticking sound could be heard throughout the basement.

"That doesn't sound good," said the agent sarcastically.

Agent Best listened for a second as the ticking sound began to get faster. His face went pale. "Get out, get out," he yelled into his throat mic. "The basement's been rigged. It's a trap. We've been set up."

The entry team dashed to the exit only to find it locked. A demolitions man quickly put an explosive device on the door lock and blew it off as the ticking sound sped up even more. The team dashed up the stairs to find the other door locked requiring another explosive. It took precious seconds.

"We're almost out," yelled Agent Best. "Get clear of the building. Don't wait for us."

Outside, the agents surrounding the perimeter started falling back. Agents Ruiz and Williams were already far enough away.

"C'mon, Chad, run faster," said Agent Williams through gritted teeth.

They could see the team's flashlights bounce around as they dashed towards the door. The first explosion came from the basement, shook the floor, and knocked two agents to the ground. They were helped up and ran as several more explosions rocked the building. As they rounded the corner and headed towards the main doors, the basement door blew off its hinges and a huge ball of flame erupted.

"Go, go, go," yelled Agent Best as he dove out through the glassless door into the night air. Several more team members ducked and dove through the door, but several didn't as the huge ball of fire barreled through the building and engulfed them. They screamed in agony as the windows blew out of the building and flames shot out through every opening. The agents outside ducked behind vehicles as glass and debris shot in all different directions.

The explosion died out, but several fires burned and small explosions could be heard inside. The agents outside ran toward those on the ground. Some of their clothes had caught fire and were quickly extinguished. Agent Williams rolled Agent Best over to find him staring up at her.

"Chad, are you ok?"

He looked at her but didn't answer.

"Chad, are you ok?"

He frowned at her. "Speak up, woman. I can't hear you."

Agent Williams smiled and hugged him. The explosion had deafened him temporarily, but he was alive. She helped him up as the other agents were also helped clear of the building.

Within moments sirens wailed as the fire department came to fight the blaze.

Agent Ruiz shook his head. "He knew we were coming."

"I know," said Agent Williams.

Several ambulances arrived to care for the injured agents. Six were treated for cuts and scrapes but two were not so lucky and were killed. The building was a total loss. The main level collapsed into the basement.

Much later the two agents drove back towards Washington on interstate 495. "Once everything cools, we'll have crime scene and arson look for anything left," said Agent Ruiz.

"I wouldn't bet on finding anything though," said Agent Williams sadly. "I would think he'd move everything before wiring the building, but you can never tell."

Agent Ruiz's head was back against the headrest and his eyes were closed. "My, god, two more agents are dead. When will this end?"

"I don't know. He seems to always be one step ahead of us."

"He's got to make a mistake sometime.'

"Yep, and I'm going to nail the asshole when he does."

———

**Ghazi Estate**
**6322 Crosswinds Drive**
**Lake Barcroft, Virginia**

GHAZI WAS in his room reading and watching the news when there was a knock on the door, and Azim entered.

Ghazi looked at him briefly. "What is it?"

"I just received news that the booby trap worked at the lab. The Americans lost some of their men and will come up empty."

Ghazi nodded. "Good, it should keep them busy for a while."

He stared at Azim for a few moments.

"Is something wrong?" asked Azim.

"No," Ghazi answered. "I have something I need you to do. I want you personally to fly with the pilot over Washington and deliver the toxins."

Azim's eyes widened and he smiled brightly. "Yes, yes, I would be honored to personally strike a blow against the Americans. Thank you."

"Good, then it's settled. You'll leave soon to meet with the pilot."

"Allah has blessed me," said Azim as he left.

Ghazi smiled and changed the television station to the comedy channel.

Ann sat on the edge of her bed holding her head in his hands. She was worn out and didn't know how much more she could take. There was a slight knock on the door before it was unlocked. Ann looked up and Amira entered as the guard behind her glanced at her with a sympathetic shake of his head.

"Amira," Ann said as she jumped up. She led Amira over to the bed and they both sat on the edge. "I'm so sorry." Tears welled up in her eyes.

Amira could only shake her head. She removed a small pad and pen from her pocket and wrote a note. "Ghazi is a monster."

Ann looked at the note. "Yes, he's a very evil man."

Amira shook her head and wrote another note, "No, a demon."

After reading the note Ann nodded her head. "I can think of a lot more ways to describe him."

It was obvious that Ann didn't understand, and Amira started crying. Ann held her, stroked her hair, and they both sat while she cried. Amira went into the bathroom for some tissues and left her notepad on the bed. Ann picked it up. She had long since located the tiny cameras in her room and turned her back to it. She wrote a series of numbers on the pad, ripped off the paper, and stuffed it in her pants pocket. Amira returned and wrote another message.

"I cannot leave. I was caught. They will kill everyone."

Before Ann could answer there was a knock at the door. Time was up, and Amira got up sadly to leave. Ann grabbed her arm as she was leaving. "You must get away. You must try to leave."

Amira only stared at her with her one good eye and left.

Ann sat on the bed and stared at the floor.

# CHAPTER TWENTY-EIGHT

**Northbound, Interstate 495, Virginia**

IT WAS GETTING LATE as they traveled toward northern Virginia.

"Are you going to stop soon?' asked Pam. "Roscoe and I are getting tired of riding."

Ellie looked over at Jake. "I think we should go a little farther and then stop."

"I agree. That'll give us a fresh start in the morning," added Jake.

A storm front moved in and a steady rain saturated the area as Agents Williams and Ruiz rode north on Interstate 495 toward Washington. They were quiet, both deep in thought when their unmarked car jolted.

"What was that?' asked Agent Ruiz.

"I don't know?"

"Did you hit something?"

"I don't think so. I didn't see anything."

Agent Williams continued driving when something huge and dark leapt out in front of the car's headlights. Both agents saw it at the same time, and Agent Williams swerved to avoid hitting it. The car slid on the wet pavement, but she brought it back under control.

"What was that?" said Agent Williams.

"I don't know, but it was big."

Something landed on the top of the car.

"What the...," said Agent Ruiz but before he could finish a huge, clawed hand punched through the roof of the car and began trying to grab the occupants. Agent Ruiz ducked and pulled out his gun while Agent Williams tried to keep the car on the highway and received several lacerations on her face for her efforts. Agent Ruiz fired three rounds through the roof, and all went quiet.

The two agents looked at each other in wide eyed confusion when something slammed hard onto the hood. The agents jerked back to see a huge black creature on the hood. It was as large as an ape with muscular arms and huge wings that flapped in the wind. Its face was blunt with no nose, yellow eyes that glowed, and ragged teeth protruding from its mouth in awkward angles.

Agent Williams swerved left and right to throw it off, but the monster hung on. Agent Ruiz shot it several times through the windshield but saw the bullet wounds miraculously close. The thing rammed a clawed fist through the windshield and grabbed the steering wheel. Agent Williams and the creature fought for control of the car, and as the car slid back and forth across the wet freeway it side swiped a delivery truck. Agent Ruiz fired several more times into the creature only to have them heal in seconds. The only effect the rounds had was to irritate it. The car was jolted again as another creature leapt upon the trunk. The weight caused the car to spin out of control, sideswiped the cement median, and stopped.

Agent Ruiz leapt out of the passenger side and fired several more times at the one on the back. This one was different. It was almost seven feet tall, thin, but its skin was a burnt orange color. Its arms, legs, and neck were thin making it look like a deformed grasshopper with teeth.

It took the bullets the same as the other and kept coming. It climbed off the car, swung at Agent Ruiz, and caught him on the shoulder which tore skin, spun him around, and knocked him to the ground.

The other demon climbed on to the roof of the vehicle. The

driver's side doors were wedged up against the cement barrier so Agent Williams could not escape. She drew her gun and fired several times up through the roof and into the monster. The demon peeled back the roof of the car like it was tin foil and grabbed her by the back of the jacket. The only thing that saved her from the claws was the thickness of her bullet proof raid vest. It pulled her up through the car as she fired into the monster as fast as she could.

The thin one leapt at Agent Ruiz as he tried to crawl under the car to escape its claws. He reloaded his 9mm handgun as the thing tried to lift the car up to get to him. Agent Ruiz fired several more times with no effect, but fortunately the creature couldn't lift the car up because the other one was on top holding Agent Williams.

Both agents knew there was no help coming from the Secret Service this time. Since they had been accompanied earlier by the two tactical vans, the secret service agents had taken the night off. They were on their own.

The thin one screamed, clicked, and squealed at the other in their bizarre language but the other simply ignored him. He was busy holding up Agent Williams like a fisherman would a prize fish. She continued to fire at the thing while yelling at it to put her down. It moved closer and she could see the rain dripping off its jagged teeth and smell its sulfur fetid breath. She fired her last round and reached for new ammo magazine but knew she'd be too late. The thing smiled and opened its mouth to engulf her entire face.

Jake was also northbound on Interstate 495 when he came upon a traffic jam.

"Must be an accident," said Ellie.

"Looks like the two left lanes are blocked but the far-right lanes are open," added Pam as she tried to see through the rain.

About that time several people ran past them in an apparent attempt to flee the scene.

"What the..." said Jake as he climbed out of the truck and pulled on his rain slicker. "I'll go see what's going on."

They heard several gun shots.

"Quick, hand me my rifle."

The thin creature had managed to grab Agent Ruiz's leg and

pulled him from under the car. He continued to pump bullets into the thing, but once out from under the car he looked up into the pouring rain at the monster. He came eye to eye with the yellow eyed demon and it smiled showing sharp teeth. Agent Ruiz's eyes widened.

Another shot rang out and knocked the thin creature back, causing it to release Agent Ruiz. He looked back toward the rear of the car and saw a tall cowboy in a rain slicker running towards them armed with a rifle.

"Get away from them, scum."

Jake had fired while running and his shot was off slightly which only hit the thing's shoulder. He levered another round and turned to the one on the roof of the car. "Drop her," he yelled as he snapped off another shot. This one tore through the mid-section of the behemoth and it dropped Agent Williams, who fell back through the opening in the roof.

Since the wound in its shoulder didn't heal, the thin one looked down in shock, and panicked. It darted to the left as Jake levered another round into his rifle and was gone into the darkness before he could get a good shot. He spun back at the other as it stepped onto the concrete median. Cars screeched as it leapt into the air and flew across the interstate. Jake aimed as best he could and fired once more before it disappeared into the dark, rainy sky.

"Are you ok?" asked Jake as he approached the man on the ground.

"Yes, thanks, I'm an FBI agent but my partner's in the car," answered Agent Ruiz as he climbed to his feet.

Jake looked through the window and saw Agent Williams in the car. She sat sideways in the front, soaked from the rain pouring in through the open hole in the roof with blood running down her cheek, but alive. She forced a thin smile.

"What were those things?" asked Agent Ruiz.

"Demons," answered Jake calmly.

"What?" said Agent Williams as she climbed out through the vehicle's passenger side.

"Who are you?" asked Agent Ruiz.

"My name's Jake."

"Jake, I'm Agent Oscar Ruiz."

"You need medical treatment," said Jake as he pointed to Agent Ruiz's shoulder.

Ruiz nodded and pulled his cell phone from his jacket pocket, called 911, and asked for additional agents as well as an ambulance. He hung up and turned to Agent Williams who was examining their ruined car. "Are you alright?"

"Yeah, just some scratches, but where's your new friend? I need to ask him a few questions."

They looked around for Jake, but he was gone.

"I don't know where he went but I'm glad he was here."

Agent Williams shivered. "Let's try to get out of this rain."

Jake climbed back into the suburban and drove around the cluster of stopped cars. They blended into the rest of the slow-moving traffic as the rain helped mask their departure.

"What happened?" asked Ellie.

"Demons," answered Jake.

"What did they want?" asked Pam as they passed the wrecked car with the roof peeled back.

"I'm not sure, but they attacked two FBI agents."

"FBI agents?" asked Ellie as she turned and stared at Jake.

"The FBI?" asked Pam from the backseat.

"I was able to chase the demons off before they killed them," explained Jake.

"And we're just going to drive off?" asked Pam.

"Yep," said Jake. "We can't stay and try to explain that we're hunting demons. It might be too late already."

Ellie nodded in agreement. "I'm sure they have questions, but I agree with Jake. We can explain later."

Pam shook her head. "We're so in trouble. First a murder suspect and now the FBI will be looking for us. I'm going to federal prison for this. Pamela Martin, inmate number 503."

"Maybe they'll give us adjoining cells," said Ellie with a grin.

———

**Ghazi Estate**
**6322 Crosswinds Drive**
**Lake Barcroft, Virginia**

GHAZI SAT in his overstuffed chair at his desk in his study and fumed after he heard the results of the attack on the FBI agents. Those two agents have more lives than a cat, but now they'll have to wait. What concerned him now was that someone intervened.

He'd sent two of his trusted underlings to handle the agents. They'd eliminated the failed bombers and Deputy Director Sullens but now one was wounded and the other died shortly after returning. Someone or something was out there that could kill them. Teftrol only had a shoulder wound and was able to describe the demon killer. A human! A tall cowboy armed with a rifle. This was new to Ghazi as he sat back in his chair and tented his fingers in thought. There were so many questions but no answers. He decided he would keep his plans on schedule and keep a lookout for this cowboy.

———

**FBI Headquarters**
**935 Pennsylvania Avenue, NW**
**Washington, D.C.**

AGENTS RUIZ and Williams sat in a conference room as the sun rose behind cloudy, rainy skies. They were wrapped in blankets and drank hot coffee.

Agent Ruiz thought it was not going to go well as FBI Director Chisom and Deputy Director Ross entered the room. They both arrived wearing casual clothes after being called while at home.

Director Chisom nodded and asked if they needed anything before they began while Deputy Director Ross simply put down a stack of files without speaking.

Both agents said they were fine.

Deputy Director Ross looked at each of them with a frown. "I've read the after-action report on this incident which I prefer to call a fiasco. This reads like a science fiction novel rather than a report."

Agent Williams sat up abruptly. "Sir, we didn't make this up. We put down everything that happened."

Deputy Director Ross raised an eyebrow. "A building blows up while you're searching it and then you get attacked by aliens on the way back?"

"We didn't blow it up," answered Agent Williams. "It was a trap. We were set up. Ghazi knew we were coming...sir."

"And how do you suppose Ghazi knew you were coming?"

"I don't know, sir. Perhaps the phone call was a set up to lure us out there. I don't know."

Deputy Director Ross shuffled some papers. "Now, how about these things that attacked you on the freeway? Do you expect me to believe these were aliens or monsters?"

Agent Ruiz could see Agent Williams getting frustrated, so he spoke up first. "Deputy Director, sir, we're not sure what they were. All we know is we were attacked. We gave a description of what they looked like."

Deputy Director Ross nodded. "Could they have been men with body armor and disguises?"

"Yes, sir, they could have been, except they leapt onto a moving car, peeled back the top of the car like it was a sardine can, and threw us around like rag dolls."

Deputy Director Ross shook his head. "And then a cowboy came out of nowhere and saved you?"

"And they both flew away," added Agent Williams.

Agent Ruiz nodded. "The man said his name was Jake."

"And he too flew away?"

"I think he drove off," answered Agent Ruiz through gritted teeth. "Maybe he was just a hunter that happened by."

"How can you explain the fact that you both fired almost thirty times at your attackers with no effect, but yet this mysterious cowboy scared them off with a couple of shots?"

"We don't know, sir," said Agent Williams. "The rifle ammo would've penetrated body armor while our handgun rounds won't.'

"Perhaps, but overall it sounds too preposterous."

Agent Williams jumped to her feet and leaned over the conference table. "We've been shot at, almost blown up, and attacked by who knows what." She pointed to the stitches on her face. "Do you think I got these by mistake? Agent Ruiz has stitches in his shoulder from them too. We're getting sick and tired of being called liars. I'm telling you that's what happened and that's what we saw, and if you don't like it, sir, you can shove it all the..."

"Agent Williams," snapped Director Chisom. "That's enough. Sit down."

Agent Williams sat down slowly and reluctantly while she glared at Deputy Director Ross.

Director Chisom glanced at Deputy Director Ross and nodded slightly. Deputy Director Ross gathered the files on the table and left.

As soon as the door closed, Agent Ruiz spoke up. "Director Chisom, sir, we know what we..."

Director Chisom held up a hand. "Calm down. Believe it or not we're on your side."

"I can't tell," mumbled Agent Williams.

Director Chisom ignored her remark. "Agent Dutton, one of the two tactical agents that were killed tonight was Deputy Director Ross' nephew."

Agent Ruiz and Williams looked at each.

"We didn't know, sir," said Agent Ruiz sadly.

"Of course not," answered Director Chisom. "Deputy Director Ross was the one who recommended him for the position, and now he has to go tell his sister that her only son is dead. He wants to find out who did this as much as you do, but you have to agree that it does sound bizarre."

Agent Ruiz nodded. "Yes, sir, I know but we can only tell you what we saw and did."

Director Chisom sat quietly for a moment. "We don't know for sure what happened, but I think we're getting close. I believe Ghazi found out somehow that we were onto his lab and either moved his operation or finished what he needed, and booby trapped it to cover it up. It'll take weeks if not longer to uncover what was in that basement, but I don't think we have that long to wait."

Both agents nodded in agreement.

"I have the feeling everything is beginning to escalate, but we're still far behind. I briefed the President yesterday about everything that we knew, and he confided in me that he's been in contact with you two through Agent Sills and Agent Meadows."

Both agents glanced at each other.

"I appreciate your loyalty to the President, and I admire that in an agent. I just wish all my agents were that loyal." He paused a moment and pointed to the claw marks on Agent Williams' face. "Deputy Director Sullens' body or what was left of it had the same type of claw marks."

"Someone is being very thorough," said Agent Ruiz.

"After they found him, the medical examiner found several claw marks that can't be explained. Something chewed on him, and Deputy Director Sullens didn't own a pet. Deputy Director Ross and I believe the same ones that attacked you killed him."

Agent Williams sat back and sighed. She felt better that someone at least started believing their story.

"I don't know what attacked you. Ghazi may have a hit squad or something worse, but right now that must take a back seat to other things. Tell me about this helicopter idea."

Agent Ruiz spoke up. "Ghazi manufactures his own type of helicopters, but he recently purchased an EH101 and had it shipped out."

"The same type as Marine One?"

"Yes, sir, and we felt it was too much of a coincidence. We think he's holding the President's daughter somewhere close by and now purchased the same transportation as the President. He's up to something."

"So, you think she's still alive?"

"Yes, sir, I do. I think if she wasn't we would know by now. He's keeping her for some reason, but we don't why."

"Very good, then you need to find out how the helicopters are involved, where they went, and maybe we can break this thing open."

"We will, sir," they both answered.

Director Chisom got up to leave. "Oh, by the way, we identified the hit men that attacked you the other day. They were foreign terrorists that came in on fake passports. They were known associates of a man called Azim Fawwaz. He's a fanatical Islamic extremist. We'll send over his file. Keep an eye out for him."

"Yes, sir," answered Agent Williams.

"I speak with the President every day, so he'll keep me briefed on your activities." He chuckled to himself. "It sounds odd. It's usually the other way around." He turned and left.

Agent Ruiz stood and stretched. "I have a change of clothes in the locker downstairs. I'll take a quick nap and start looking for those helicopters."

"I got dibs on the office couch though," answered Agent Williams tiredly.

# CHAPTER TWENTY-NINE

**Ghazi Estate**
**6322 Crosswinds Drive**
**Lake Barcroft, Virginia**

THE MAID OPENED Ann's door, brought in her breakfast tray, and as usual sat it on the dresser then left without speaking.

Ann had not slept much the night before after learning what had happened to Amira. She also had a foreboding feeling about her own fate. Her eyes were blood shot and swollen.

She looked at the scrambled eggs and toast. She lifted the napkin and a small metal object fell out. She quickly shifted around to block the hidden camera and hoped no one saw it. She picked up the item that was slightly smaller than a cigarette lighter. A thumb drive, a portable disk drive that could be plugged into any USB computer port. She turned it over and over in her hand. Ann wondered who would send her a disk drive, and then her eyes lit up. Amira! She smiled slightly and slipped the disk drive into her pocket. She was suddenly very hungry.

———

**Three Stallions Bar and Grill**
**2378 East Wesley Ave**
**Arlington, Virginia**

AFTER STAYING the night at a local hotel, Jake scouted the area to find a local bar where he might find information. Bars were always good for information. Bartenders knew everything about everyone, and if not there was always a patron that did.

Jake found one he thought was right. It was one of many old run-down bars that dot the map all across the United States. The one story, windowless building was painted a dark blue with a faded painting of three horses on the outside wall. The sign read, Three Stallions Bar, and in the rain it looked gloomier than normal.

Jake opened the door and entered the dimly lit bar. He was hit with the usual smell of alcohol, smoke, and sweat. It was a single large room with a bar along one wall, and a small empty dance floor in the middle. A five-by-five-foot wooden karaoke stage stood against another wall.

Several small tables where set about the room, and an elderly man accompanied by an obese woman sat at one table drinking beer. Two trucker type men sat at the bar near the door. A juke box blared out the latest country song while the bartender washed glasses behind the bar and watched a television mounted on a stand above the bar with the local news on.

Jake walked over and sat on a bar stool at the other end of the bar. One bar stool stood between Jake and the far wall.

The bartender walked down to Jake and asked what he wanted to drink. Jake asked for a beer and the bartender brought him a cold bottle of beer. Jake left it untouched and turned toward the empty bar stool next to the wall. What the others didn't see was the ugly shaggy demon that sat there.

It was a short, stocky built monster with long, shaggy, smelly hair covering its body. It stank of sulfur, sweat, and alcohol. The creature drooled as it sat and stared straight ahead, oblivious to Jake.

"I need a little information," said Jake.

The bartender stood at the other end of the bar where the two men sat, but heard Jake speak to the empty bar stool. "Can I help you?" asked the bartender.

Jake turned to him. "No, thank you."

The bartender looked at the other two customers and shrugged.

The monster didn't respond. Jake leaned closer to it and tried not to gag from the stench. "I need to find out where I can find Ghazi?"

The creature looked over at Jake with its red rimmed, blood shot, alcohol glazed yellow eyes. It wasn't sure who Jake was talking to as no one had ever seen him.

Jake tried again. "I've been to New Orleans and talked to Tarnac."

The hair on the creature began to shiver and if it was possible for a demon to turn pale, it did. "You can...can see me?" it muttered. "You know of Tarnac?"

Jake nodded. "Yes. I'll be glad to give him your regards if I see him again."

The thing started shaking and almost fell off the stool. "No, no."

Jake leaned over even farther. "Then tell me where to find Ghazi."

The bartender and the other patrons were staring at the tall cowboy talking to an empty bar stool. "Mister, do you need any help?" asked one of the men.

Jake glanced back at them. "No, I'm fine."

They all looked at each other. One man tapped his finger against his head indicating the strange cowboy might not be of a right mind, and the other man snickered.

Jake ignored them.

"I can't. Ghazi will kill me if I tell you," said the hairy demon.

Jake glared at the creature. "I survived seeing Tarnac, and I can see you? Would you like for me to show you how I survived?"

The thing stared at Jake for a second. "No, no, but I can't tell you."

Jake was about to lose his patience when he heard Ghazi's name on the television above the bar. He looked up to see a news reporter talking. "Can you turn the television up, please?" Jake asked the bartender.

The bartender looked at Jake and then at his two buddies at the bar. He shrugged again and turned up the TV using the remote.

A female announcer was reporting an explosion at a pharmaceutical plant owned by Ghazi. Behind her, Jake could see the fire department tending the dying fire that was once the laboratory. Jake caught the end of her broadcast.

"And fire officials are still speculating as to the cause of the fire," said the reporter. "Again, an explosion occurred at this pharmaceutical plant after a late-night raid by the FBI. Two agents were killed in the explosion, and the whole incident is currently being investigated. Now, I'll turn it over to Tom Young who is standing by outside the Ghazi estate. Tom?"

The picture switched to a middle-aged news reporter standing in front of a large, gated estate. "Thanks, Sharon. I'm standing in front of the Hassan Ghazi's estate on Lake Barcroft. We've tried to speak to a representative from the company but so far, we've only been given a written statement. It states that G Pharmaceuticals has done nothing wrong and will be filing suit against the FBI and the US government for destroying the company's valuable plant."

The reporter went on to explain about the investigation, but Jake stopped listening. He'd learned what he needed to know and got up to leave. "You're lucky. I found out what I needed without you." Jake walked past the three men at the end of the bar.

"You never touched your beer, mister. You want your money back?" asked the bartender.

"No, thanks, the demon I was talking to drank it," answered Jake as he went out the door into the rain.

They watched him leave and then all three walked down to the end of the bar where an empty bottle of beer sat. The bartender picked it up, looked at the empty bottle, and scratched his head. "How did he do that?"

The other two men looked at each other. "I dunno, but I swear he never drank it."

The three men looked at the empty bar stool next to wall. That part of the bar seemed to reek of sweat, alcohol, and smoke more than normal.

---

**FBI Headquarters**
**935 Pennsylvania Avenue, NW**
**Washington, D.C.**

AFTER TAKING A SHOWER, Agent Ruiz changed the bandage on his shoulder. He put on a new set of clothes he kept in a locker and went upstairs for a couple of hours of rest. He entered Agent Williams' office and found her already asleep on the office couch but was surprised to see Agent Sills in the office.

"Beth, what are you doing here?"

She smiled from behind the desk and looked much better despite keeping her arm in a sling.

"I was getting tired of sitting around that house, so I had one of the Secret Service agents bring me here. I need to be closer to what's going on."

"Okay, then while we're napping you can try to track down where they shipped those three helicopters from Ghazi's plant."

"I'm already on it," she said and pointed to Agent Williams. "Stephanie already briefed me on what we're looking for."

Agent Ruiz pulled two chairs together and stretched out. "Great, then wake me in a couple of hours."

"I've already tracked two of them to the airport where they're scheduled to be flown overseas," explained Agents Sills. "I'll try to pinpoint where and wake you up." When she didn't get an answer, she looked over and saw Agent Ruiz was already sound asleep.

---

**Ghazi Estate**
**6322 Crosswinds Drive**
**Lake Barcroft, Virginia**

ANN WATCHED out of the window and saw that the crew working on the house had finally finished. They'd run wiring around the outside and inside as she'd heard drilling and banging from within for several days.

She watched a white van pulled up, a man climbed out, and went inside. Ann had gotten accustomed to watching out the window for anything that might give her hope and to keep her from going stir crazy. She couldn't see all the van, just the front half. A few minutes later she watched Azim and the driver get in the van and leave. She was glad to see Azim leave.

The van pulled out of the estate, past the news crews, and drove down the winding lakeside road and past an old beat up gray and blue suburban with fishing poles sticking out of the side window. Neither one paid it any attention, but a fisherman nearby was watching them closely.

Jake watched through his binoculars as the van continued down the road while Ellie sat nearby with a fishing pole, trying to look like she was enjoying a day of fishing in the rain. After he left the bar, he picked up Ellie, bought some items at a local sporting goods store, and drove out to the lake. After they located the Ghazi estate, they set up their charade and waited. They'd left Pam and Roscoe back at the hotel as too many people might have brought on suspicions.

He'd switched from his Stetson to a fishing cap to try to blend in as a local fisherman. For the past several hours Jake had been watching the estate, take photos with Pam's digital camera, noting the guard's movements and the security systems placements around the property.

Despite the rain gear Ellie was soaked but was not going to complain. She knew how important it was for Jake to get as much information as possible, and she just enjoyed being with him, even in the rain.

Jake glanced over at her, and she forced a smile.

"You look about as happy as a soaked kitten," he said with a grin.

She didn't know if that was an insult or a compliment, so she just kept smiling.

"I have all the information I need for now. I don't want to stay too long and attract any attention from the other car."

"What car?"

Jake pointed to a car up the road just within sight, parked on a side road. "That's a surveillance car of some type. The news said the FBI raided his lab, so I imagine it's them. Are you ready for some warm coffee and dry clothes?"

"Oh, yes," Ellie said a little too quickly.

Jake laughed. "You didn't have to come out here."

"I know, but I wanted to keep you company. You might've wandered off and got lost."

—————

**FBI Headquarters**
**935 Pennsylvania Avenue, NW**
**Washington, D.C.**

BOTH AGENTS WERE awake and busy. Agent Sills had traced the two smaller helicopters to cargo building four at Dulles International Airport. Due to the helicopter's small size, they were placed in metal containers to be loaded on a commercial aircraft to delivery overseas. Agent Williams had contacted the airport authorities who were going to delay them.

Agents Williams and Ruiz drove out to Dulles and met several customs officers where they briefed them on the situation. The party of agents, customs and transportation officials descended on the large crate that was already outside and ready to be loaded. The customs and shipping papers showed the helicopter in the container to be going to Columbia in South America. The customs official ordered the large metal container opened for routine examination.

The airport loading worker was reluctant. It was raining and it would run everything else late, including his coffee break. "It's already passed through customs for shipping. It's just a helicopter."

The older customs official frowned at the man. "Open it or explain it to the FBI."

The man looked over at the two FBI agents getting wet in the rain. The female agent had several stitches along the side of her face and the other man didn't look like he was in the mood for any arguments either.

He removed the customs seal from the handle, pulled the handles to release the large door and opened it. The airport worker turned pale. The container was filled with tractors, not a helicopter.

"Already passed customs, huh?" asked the customs official.

While the custom's official and loading worker broke out into a verbal argument over who was responsible, Agent Ruiz called Agent Sills back at the office.

"Beth, we've been scammed again. The helicopter isn't here. I imagine the other one is not there too. Where was the other one going?"

Agent Sills checked the shipping records on the computer. "It shows to be going to Pakistan."

Agent Ruiz shook his head while they walked back into the building. "Is there any place else they could have shipped them?"

"No, there are no helicopter deliveries anywhere else."

"Thanks but keep checking for any large shipments that could be disguised as helicopters."

---

**Quality Inn**
**6510 High Crest Blvd**
**Arlington, Virginia**

JAKE TOOK A HOT SHOWER, drank some hot coffee, and went next door to the women's room. Ellie had already explained everything to Pam, and she was looking through the photos in the camera.

"What an impressive set up he has there," said Pam.

"Yeah, it's definitely not set up for casual visitors," answered Ellie who was still sipping her coffee.

"So, what's your plan?"

Jake sat in one of chairs at the small motel table. "It's going to be a challenge. There's no way we can just walk up and knock, and Halloween make up isn't going to fool anyone or get us in. This is going to have to be a covert, one-man stealth operation." He looked over at Ellie, expecting a rebuttal, but she just sat on the bed and remained quiet.

Pam nodded. "I agree."

Ellie looked up at Jake. Her face was obviously worried. "I know that we can't go on this one. We don't have the skills to get through the security, but can you?"

"I hope so," said Jake. "It won't be easy, but I think I found a few weak spots in their system, and the rain should mask a lot of movement.

---

### Interstate 495
### Merrifield, Virginia

AGENTS RUIZ and Williams drove back from the airport in unhappy moods.

"He did it again," said Agent Ruiz. "He's always one step ahead."

"I know," said Agent Williams. She drove and watched carefully for anything unusual. They didn't need another ambush.

"Let's assume for a minute that the Marine One look alike was staying here. There wouldn't be any reason to send it elsewhere. Now where would you send the other two?"

"To two other large cities?"

"But which ones?"

"Here in the United States?"

Agent Ruiz shook his head. "No, I don't think so. If the lab was making bioweapons and you wanted to use bio-terrorism, where would you strike?"

"Our allies?"

Agent Ruiz thought for moment. "If you were a Middle Eastern terrorist, who would you target?"

They both sat in thought listening to the windshield wipers keep the windshield clear.

"England?" asked Agent Williams.

"I think you're right and that would mean London, but who would be the other?"

"Who do Islamic terrorists hate the most, besides us and England? It has to be Israel."

Agent Ruiz nodded and called Agent Sills at the office. He asked her to check any large containers flown to England or Israel from this area by Ghazi enterprises. "Now where would I hide a large helicopter?"

Agent Sills called back a few minutes later with the information. "I found where two containers were flown out yesterday. One was sent to London's Heathrow Airport and the other went to Ben Guiron International airport in Israel. The shipping documents said it was loaded with semi-tractors."

Agent Ruiz smiled. "Alert Interpol and let them know. Good work. We may be able to nab them before they get away." He hung up and explained everything to Agent Williams.

"Now, we just have to find the big one," she reminded him.

Agent Ruiz frowned. "You have a way of raining on my parade."

"If you haven't noticed, it's already raining."

# CHAPTER THIRTY

**Ghazi Estate**
**6322 Crosswinds Drive**
**Lake Barcroft, Virginia**

THROUGH THE HEAVY rain clouds and rain, they made the drive to Lake Barcroft. They drove in silence as they all knew the dangerous task Jake had ahead. Pam fiddled with her laptop to stay busy. Ellie drove while Jake went over his gear for the twentieth time.

His face was covered in black and grey face paint, and his night vision goggles were pushed back on top of his head. He wore dark grey, brown, and black colored camouflage ACU's along with a mesh vest with extra ammo. His weapons consisted of his holstered Colt 45, an army survival knife strapped to his boot, and his assault rifle.

Ellie pulled up and stopped a half a mile from the estate. She looked over at Jake and could see he already had his serious game face on.

He looked at her worried face. "It'll be okay," he said firmly.

She nodded and pushed a loose section of hair behind her ear. Tears welled up in her eyes. "Please be careful."

He smiled slightly. He leaned over and looked into her tear-filled eyes. "I promise." He looked back at Roscoe. "Take care of them for me."

Roscoe barked.

Jake turned off his cell phone and put it in his pocket. "I'll call you when I'm done." He reached for the door handle when Ellie grabbed his arm.

"Come back safely," she said.

They stared at each other for a moment.

Pam looked at them. "Oh, for pete's sake, Taft, just kiss her."

Ellie blushed then kissed him on the cheek. Jake smiled and kissed her on the mouth. Ellie's eyes widened.

"Keep the home fires burning," he said and climbed out of the truck. In an instant he blended into the dark and was gone.

Ellie sat for a moment and stared into the darkness. Pam reached up and put her handle on her shoulder. "He'll be fine, Jake knows what he's doing."

As the suburban drove off, a dark form emerged from the darkness and two glowing yellow eyes watched the taillights grow smaller. A second later, it took to the air and followed.

————

**Interstate 66**
**Washington, D.C.**

THE TWO FBI agents drove easily towards downtown Washington as most of the heavy traffic was headed out. They crossed the bridge near the Lincoln Memorial, but Agent Ruiz couldn't see the building because two eighteen wheelers were stopped in traffic and blocked his view. His eyes suddenly widened.

"Turn around now," he blurted out.

Agent Williams slammed on the brakes thinking they were under attack again and nearly hit the car next to them.

"What? Why?"

"It's so simply," said Agent Ruiz.

"What is? What the hell are you talking about?"

"I know where the helicopter is," he said. "It's hidden in plain sight."

Agent Williams looked at him with a puzzled frown. "What?"

"It's at his trucking company. Where else can you hide something that big and no one would notice? A helicopter on a flatbed sitting amongst other eighteen wheelers wouldn't even be noticed."

"But how is he going to fly it?" she asked.

Agent Ruiz smiled. "When I went to his trucking company in Colorado, he had a helipad there. We think that's where they transported Ann Campbell out of the state, and I'll bet he has one here too. If he doesn't, they could just take off from the flat bed of the truck."

Agent Williams made a U-turn at the next light. "It's going to take us awhile to get there in this traffic even with lights and sirens." She reached up, turned on their dash mounted red strobe light, and activated their siren.

"I'll call ahead and have a Fairfax Deputy stand by."

———

**G Trucking**
**508 Old Tennessee Rd**
**Tysons Corner, Virginia**

AZIM STOOD on the helipad at the trucking company and smiled at the large helicopter. It looked beautiful to him.

The pilot was doing his preflight checks before they took off while Azim climbed aboard and went directly to the cockpit. He sat in the co-pilot's seat of the dual seated cockpit and looked down at a series of tubes that ran from the rear compartment to the cockpit. He removed a small, curved handle from his pocket and attached it to a nozzle protruding from the tubing. It was the release handle for the micro toxins he would soon release over Washington.

He believed it would begin the end of the United States government and the beginning of an Islamic state that would sweep the world. The pilot climbed inside and started his checklist.

"I've been briefed on our mission," said the pilot in Arabic. "But how do you plan to keep the defense forces from shooting us down?"

Azim smiled and pulled a tape recorder from his pocket, "Insurance!"

---

**Ghazi Estate**
**6322 Crosswinds Drive**
**Lake Barcroft, Virginia**

JAKE WORKED his way along the water's edge in the darkness and rain. His night vision goggles helped but the rain cut down some of his vision. Jake hoped that the perimeter sensors wouldn't be set up as strict near the water's edge, and he stopped regularly to check for guards. Jake hoped too that the most dedicated guards would be a little lax on a rainy night like tonight.

He moved from tree to tree, trying to blend in as much as possible. He avoided the cameras mounted because he could easily see the red LED light with the goggles.

A flash of light caught his eye. A guard about fifty yards away stepped from behind a tree and lit a cigarette. Jake moved quickly and as quietly as possible around the man. He had just passed him when there was a rustle of bushes to his right, just behind him. He froze.

A deer stood ten yards away. The animal looked directly at Jake.

The guard also heard the sound, whipped around, shined his flashlight around, and located the deer. Jake remained frozen knowing that any movement would draw the guard's attention. If the deer ran his way the guard would see him. Jake held his breath and tried not to stare at the guard. He felt that people somehow knew they were being stared at.

Miraculously the deer bolted from the light in the opposite direction of Jake. He heard the guard talking on his walkie talkie.

"Yeah...just a deer..."

Jake waited until the guard relaxed and returned to his cigarette break before he moved silently and quickly away. He could then see the mansion through the rain.

Jake moved closer to the mansion and stopped to evaluate his approach. He'd not been able to see the house from the road earlier so he would have to go in without prior recon.

The outside of the mansion was well lit as if expecting visitors, so Jake had to remove his night goggles. Besides the guards that patrolled the grounds, he could see several demons roaming the outside of the building. Jake chose the delivery entrance and moved slowly towards it in hopes that it would be the less guarded.

———

ANN WAS WATCHING out of her window. The mansion was lit up with exterior lights that had not been on before. She knew something was starting and dreaded the thought. As if on cue, the door was unlocked and her grim-faced guard motioned for her to follow. She stared at him and only moved toward the door when he grunted and motioned again. Ann took a deep breath and followed him down the hall, down the stairs, and into Ghazi's study.

Ghazi was dressed in traditional Islamic clothing. "Good evening, Miss Campbell. I'm so glad you decided to join me."

Ann glared at him silently.

Ghazi shrugged. "Have it your way then." He approached the door leading to his grotto and entered a code. The door opened and he motioned for Ann to enter, but she didn't move.

"Come, come, my dear, time is short. The world is waiting."

Ann stepped up to the door but hesitated to enter.

"This will be a night to remember," he whispered in her ear. "Now, go."

She stepped down the stairs followed by Ghazi, and the door automatically shut. Unseen by Ghazi, Ann dropped a small piece of paper at the entrance to the grotto. It was an act of desperation, and she continued down the stairs with the feeling she would never see the light of day again.

# CHAPTER THIRTY-ONE

**G Trucking**
**508 Old Tennessee Rd**
**Tysons Corner, Virginia**

AGENTS WILLIAMS and Ruiz pulled up behind the county deputy who was parked just outside the main gate of the trucking company. The building was closed, and the eight-foot chain link fence and gate were locked. They met the young deputy who waited outside his car and identified themselves as FBI agents.

"We need to get inside," said Agent Ruiz.

"No problem," said the deputy. "You have the search warrant?"

Agent Ruiz appraised the deputy and realized just how young he looked. He sighed.

"We don't have a warrant," said Agent Williams. "These are exigent circumstances. This is an emergency because we think the President's daughter is inside somewhere."

The deputy's face tightened. "I understand but without a warrant I can't go inside."

Agent Ruiz stepped up. "Young man, I understand you want to do everything proper, but this is different. As my partner said there are exigent circumstances here that will allow you to enter without a warrant."

The deputy looked confused. "I'm not sure...I'll have to call my supervisor." The deputy grabbed his radio and started calling his supervisor when they heard a helicopter turbine start up and rotors wind.

"Oh damn," said Agent Williams.

Agent Ruiz turned, ran to the car, and climbed in behind the wheel with Agent Williams on his heels. They pulled out and around the deputy who stood and watched.

"How are you going to get in?" asked Agent Williams.

"I'll knock," he said as he accelerated toward the main gate.

Agent William turned and was about to say something when he rammed the car through the gate, knocking the gate down. A piece of the gate bounced off the windshield causing spider web cracks in the windshield. They could hear the sound increase as they rounded the corner of the building and into the large parking lot. A dozen eighteen wheelers sat in the lot but the sound came from behind the parked trucks.

The pitch from the helicopter rose higher and higher. They knew they only had a few seconds before it took off, but Agent Ruiz had to negotiate around the parked semis. A pair of headlights appeared behind them and followed.

They rounded the last large truck and saw the US101 helicopter begin to lift off. They screeched to a halt and leapt out. As the helicopter lifted off the ground and turned into the night, they saw the helicopter was painted the same as Marine One.

Agent Williams drew her weapon and pointed it at the disappearing helicopter but didn't fire. She knew if she got lucky, she might hit something vital and bring it down but could kill the President's daughter if she was on board.

The approaching car squealed to a stop and two men jumped out. They recognized them as two of the Secret Service agents that had been their shadow.

"You turned around so fast back in Washington we couldn't catch up fast enough," said one of the agents.

"That looked like Marine One," said the other.

Agent Williams shook her head. "It's a copy, but we think the President's daughter is aboard."

Agent Ruiz slammed his fist down on the hood of their damaged car. "We were so close. So close!"

————

**Ghazi Estate**
**6322 Crosswinds Drive**
**Lake Barcroft, Virginia**

ANN WALKED CAREFULLY down the stone steps to the manmade cave. She entered and saw the altar with the throne lit by bright lights. On top of the altar sat the Ark of the Covenant. A large television camera sat off to one side with wires and cables running over to a large instrument panel. It appeared the stage was set. A chair sat next to the camera.

"I've made sure you have a ringside seat for the festivities," said Ghazi and pointed to the chair. "My assistant will help you get settled."

Ann turned and looked at his assistant but couldn't remember if she screamed before everything went dark.

Jake had carefully slipped up to the delivery entrance door. He was slow and careful not to attract any attention from the guards and demons. He luckily found the double doors unlocked and brought his assault rifle up to his shoulder while he slipped inside.

The room was used to unload and load goods but was unoccupied. The hair on the back of his neck stood up. Something was wrong. The outside was guarded but the inside of the house appeared to be deserted. Something was wrong. He moved cautiously through the kitchen area and into the main hallway. Mental alarms rang in his head.

He heard a slight noise and smelled sulfur. A minor demon was shuffling down the hall. Jake opened a side door and stepped into a darkened room hoping no one was inside. He took a quick look around and saw it was some sort of storage room.

The creature was dark green in color but only about five foot tall with a long snout. It had thin shoulders but wide hips. If Jake wasn't in a den of demons and terrorists, he might have laughed as it reminded him of a deformed bowling pin. When the creature passed the storage room, Jake reached out, grabbed it by the snout, and jerked it into the room. He slammed it against the wall and shoved the assault rifle against its midsection.

"You call out and you're dead," said Jake.

The creature tried to squirm away, but Jake kneed it in the stomach. It doubled over in pain.

"I don't have time for problems from you. I'm more than capable of killing you. I want to know where Ghazi is?"

The thing looked up at Jake with its yellow eyes and growled, showing its sharp teeth. Jake struck it with the butt of his rifle and slammed it against a stack of boxes. He held it down with his foot, pulled out his knife and placed it against the thing's throat. Jake poked the creature with the point just enough for it to feel it.

"Does this make you think differently? Tell me where Ghazi is, or I'll kill you and find someone else who will."

Jake could tell he got his message across as the thing's yellow eyes widened and glowed.

"But you're a human?" it said is a raspy voice.

"You're very observant. Tell me where Ghazi is."

"He's in his temple."

"Where's that?"

When the demon didn't answer Jake pushed harder with the knife.

"It's a door in his study," the thing said. "It's down the hall on your right. It needs a code. You can't get in."

"I'll just have to improvise,' said Jake. He pulled the knife back but instead of stabbing the creature he struck in the side on the head. The creature slumped down. Jake couldn't bring himself to kill it in cold blood, even if it was a demon. After finding some packing tape, he turned to the beast when it came off the ground at Jake. The hellion had been pretending to be unconscious to trick Jake. The demon swung its snout around to hit him but missed and Jake plunged the knife in the monster's chest. Wide eyed the beast crumpled to the floor. Jake cracked the door and looked out cautiously hoping no one had heard the commotion but the hallway was empty. He slipped out and worked his way down the hall towards the study.

The darkness started to fade, and Ann could see the bright lights in the grotto. She smelled the overpowering stench of decayed and burned flesh. She tried to remember what happened, looked around, and saw the creature standing to her left. Her eyes widened and she tried to scream but her mouth was taped shut.

The winged creature was a burnt orange color, thin, and at least seven feet tall. It reminded her of a huge praying mantis with a wound in its shoulder that oozed a greenish brown liquid. It looked over at her with yellow eyes and smiled.

Ann struggled to get up but was tied to the chair with ropes.

"Give up, my dear," said Ghazi's voice from behind her.

She turned and saw him flipping switches on the instrument panel.

"I'm so glad you're awake. My underling must have frightened you, but he's here to make sure nothing goes wrong. He won't bother you unless I tell him."

She looked back at the demon. It licked its lips with a bright red tongue.

Ann shivered.

Ghazi walked around to the throne and sat down. He stroked the arm of the throne and smiled. "From here I will rule the world."

He nodded to the underling who went over to the instrument panel and flipped a switch. A small television monitor came to life and Ann could see Ghazi on the screen as he sat on his throne, with the altar and ark in sight.

"My camera is programmed into a satellite that will broadcast this to the all the major networks around the world. There's a few minutes delay between signals but I'm sure they will pick it up after they hear what I have to say." He nodded to the creature who flipped several more switches with its claws and Ghazi looked directly into the camera with a smile.

"Good evening, my name is Hassan Ghazi. This broadcast is being broadcast around the world by satellite for all to hear."

Jake reached the door the demon indicated, opened it quietly and looked in. It was a study, and he scanned the room for occupants but found it empty. The room was a typical study except for a door between two bookshelves and a keypad next to it. The demon was right, it needs a code. He walked over to Ghazi's desk and looked around but found nothing.

"People of the world," Ghazi continued. "I am broadcasting from my home. After tonight a new world will begin, but with change there must be sacrifice. I call upon the people of America, England, and Israel to start the sacrifice. Far too long you have been the major force in this world that used their so-called freedom to abuse the rest of the world, but no longer. Tonight, I'm calling for their immediate surrender, and when they do so the rest of the world will follow. I'll then gladly step in and rule.

"I'm sure you're wondering how I can make this demand. At this very moment aircraft are above Washington, London, and Jerusalem. Each one is loaded with a deadly micro toxin that can be dispersed. These toxins can kill millions and will spread across the country causing disease, famine, and illness. I have devoted followers who will then sweep across the land and take charge." Ghazi leaned toward the camera. "This senseless bloodshed can be avoided if your leaders submit now."

# CHAPTER THIRTY-TWO

**Oval Office**
**The White House**
**1600 Pennsylvania Ave NW**
**Washington D.C.**

THE PRESIDENT FINISHED SIGNING a few documents and was going to call it a day when Chief of Staff Wohlman entered. From the look on his face, the President knew something was wrong.

"What is it, John?"

"Mr. President, there's something on television I think you need to see."

The President reached over, picked up his remote control, and turned on the television. The image showed Ghazi on his throne in the grotto with the ark plainly visible.

"What's this?"

"That is Hassan Ghazi, sir. He's broadcasting from his estate in Virginia. It's coming from a satellite station, and all the major networks have picked it up."

"What does the lunatic want?"

"I don't know, sir, we..."

The President held up his hand. Ghazi started explaining his reason for his broadcast and demanded their surrender. The President jumped to his feet. "What's this fool doing? Get some people out there now and stop him."

Chief of Staff Wohlman picked up a phone and began making calls. The President listened as Ghazi continued.

"Mr. President," interrupted Wohlman, "Phil Jennings said he already alerted the FBI and Homeland security. They're getting people over there ASAP."

The President nodded

Ghazi went on and explained the biochemical threat.

"John," said the President, "Call George and get him to the alternate safe location and put us in lock down."

———

**G Trucking**
**508 Old Tennessee Rd**
**Tysons Corner, Virginia**

AGENT RUIZ BRIEFED the two Secret Service agents on what they knew about the helicopter when Agent Williams' cell phone chirped. She answered and her eyes widened as she listened.

"What's wrong now?" asked Agent Ruiz.

She hung up. "That was Director Chisom. He said that madman Ghazi is on national television and wants our unconditional surrender."

"What?"

"That helicopter is loaded with biological weapons he intends to dump on the capital if we don't."

Ruiz shook his head in disgust. "And he probably has the President's daughter on board as a hostage."

"Yeah," she said in disgust. "The Director said to get to his estate now and stop him."

———

**Ghazi Estate**
**6322 Crosswinds Drive**
**Lake Barcroft, Virginia**

THE NEWS MEDIA that was already set up outside the estate because of the pharmaceutical incident was in frenzy now over the broadcast.

The two FBI agents assigned to the surveillance team were told by radio to enter the estate and stop Ghazi's broadcast. They advised the news media to move back as they drove up to the entrance. The agents identified themselves and ordered the guards to open the gate but were met by gunfire from within the estate. The news reporters and camera men ran for cover.

While a firestorm of gunfire erupted outside, Ghazi sat calmly and continued his broadcast.

"I have set up a direct line to this phone," explained Ghazi and held up a cell phone. "The U.S. President, England and Israel's Prime Ministers can call me directly.

"If you have any hopes of attacking my aircraft, I would not recommend doing so because I have certain fail safes included in my package. Aboard the aircraft over Washington is Ann Campbell, the daughter of President Campbell, and as you can see I have Israel's precious Ark of the Covenant to insure the two abroad will not be harassed. I will be waiting for your call gentlemen, but not too long." Ghazi crossed his legs and leaned back in a relaxed posture.

Upon hearing the lie about her, Ann pulled and fought against her ropes which brought an even broader smile from Ghazi.

Jake examined the door to see if there was a way to force the door open but was unable to locate even a crack or niche to gain entry. He dropped his head in frustration and his eye caught a small, crumpled piece of paper on the floor by the door. He picked it up, opened it, and found a series of numbers. Jake looked at the paper and the keypad. No, it couldn't be? He punched in the numbers and the door hissed open. Jake stepped back and raised his assault rifle in case it was a trap but saw only the stone stairs that led down.

Agents Ruiz and Williams made the turn to come in front of the

Ghazi estate and into the firefight. They pulled up among the other agents already on the scene. Several agents had already been deployed but hadn't successfully breached the estate's entrance.

They jumped from their car and used it as cover from the gunfire.

"What's the situation?" yelled Agent Ruiz to one of the other agents.

"We have ten or more hostiles inside, maybe more," yelled one of the agents from the surveillance team. "They appear to be paid hoods of Ghazi."

"We need to get in there now."

"Tell that to them," answered the agent. "The tactical unit is on the way."

Ghazi sat on his throne and drummed his fingers on the arm. "Gentlemen, I'm trying to be patient, and I know what you're doing. You're trying to determine if you can stop me before it's too late, but I assure you it's impossible. I'm sure you're planning to enter my estate to stop me, so I must warn you that I have explosives set all around the mansion." Ghazi held up a handheld remote device. "If you attempt to storm my estate, I will activate the explosives with this to bring it down upon them and your precious ark as well. It will also signal the helicopters to immediately release the micro toxins." Ghazi glared into the camera. "I'm waiting but your time's running out."

Ann sat tied and gagged as she watched Ghazi lay out his demands. She continued to struggle to free herself even though she knew it was hopeless.

Jake entered the stone stairway, the door closed automatically, and from behind him the sounds of distance gunfire erupted from outside of the mansion. He slowly descended the stairway toward the sound of voices.

———

**The Pentagon**
**1400 Defense Pentagon**
**Washington D.C.**

GENERAL SAMUEL LITTLESTONE, commander on duty of Northern Command or NORTHCOM sat at his desk when his phone rang.

"Sorry to bother you, sir," said the captain on duty in the communications and radar section. "We have an unidentified aircraft entering the ADIZ."

The Air Defense Identification Zone (ADIZ) is the area surrounding Washington D.C. and is a restricted fly zone. If an aircraft enters the area without permission a series of red and green laser lights, called the Visual Flight Signals, warns aircraft.

"Can we identify the aircraft? Perhaps it's a commercial airliner that strayed off course."

"I'll check, sir."

A moment later the captain came back on the line. "Sir, I think you should come down here. There's some maniac that said he's got a helicopter full of bio-weapons and he's going to contaminate the area."

"Notify the White House, scramble two jets, and I'm on my way." He hung up the phone and headed toward the stairs. Bio-weapons? Helicopters?

---

**The Oval Office**
**The White House**
**1600 Pennsylvania Ave NW**
**Washington D.C.**

THE STAFF or extra personnel were evacuated out of the building, and Vice President Dayton was taken to a safe alternate location. The President remained in the oval office at his desk and watched Ghazi's broadcast. Agent Meadows stood just inside the door waiting while Chief of Staff Wohman waited with the phone in his hand.

"Mr. President, it isn't safe here," he said. "We need to move you to a safe location also."

The President shook his head. "If what he says is true, there is no safe location. I'm staying here."

Wohlman nodded, spoke into the phone, and hung up. "What're you going to do, sir?"

"I will not negotiate with terrorists."

"I agree but Ghazi said your daughter is on board."

"He could be bluffing."

The phone rang and Wohlman answered. "Sir, it's the Pentagon. An unidentified aircraft has entered the ADIZ. They've scrambled to intercept."

The President nodded but didn't answer.

---

**The Pentagon**
**1400 Defense Pentagon**
**Washington D.C.**

GENERAL LITTLESTONE, the great grandson of a Sioux chief, entered the command center of the department of Homeland Security. Captain Griffin, the on-duty officer, briefed him on the television broadcasts and the location of the helicopter.

"Should we suggest an air strike on the Ghazi Estate? That would put a stop to that threat," suggested Captain Griffin.

General Littlestone shook his head. "No, we can't simply bomb a house on American soil, terrorist or not, and besides it would automatically cause them to release the toxins. We can take out the helicopter."

An airman handed Captain Griffin a message who in turn read it and frowned.

"What is it?" asked General Littlestone.

"Ghazi says the President's daughter is on board the helicopter."

General Littlestone shook his head. "Let's wait and see what the interceptors tell us. I'll be on the horn with the White House so let me know ASAP."

**Washington D.C. airspace**

AZIM WAS ENJOYING the ride as his dream of striking against the western world was about to come true. The pilot spoke over the cockpit headset.

"We have entered the ADIZ. The laser warning system has been activated."

"I understand," answered Azim. "I imagine they will try to contact us and then intercept but remain on schedule." Azim looked off to the left and then right to see the red and green lights flashing at the helicopter.

Two F-15 fighters were scrambled and airborne from Andrews Air Force Base in a matter of minutes. The lead aircraft, designated Cobra, was flown by Major Joseph Rollins. The other aircraft, Fang, was flown by his friend, Captain Ronald Cowins. Their sleek military aircraft were armed with both a 20 mm gun and AIM-9l/M sidewinder air to air missiles capable of destroying any aircraft that entered the ADIZ.

Within moments they approached the unidentified aircraft. Through the rain Major Rollins was able to visually identify the aircraft, but what he saw was not what he expected.

"Ron, do you see what I see?"

"Roger that, I see it, but I don't believe it."

"NORTHCOM, this is Cobra. We have visual contact with the unidentified aircraft, and it appears to be Marine One. Can you confirm?"

"Stand by," came the voice of one of the communications officers.

―――――――

**The Pentagon**
**1400 Defense Pentagon**
**Washington D.C.**

"GENERAL, the interceptors have tentatively identified the helicopter as Marine One," explained Captain Griffin.

"That can't be Marine One. It's sitting on the pad at Andrews but call and confirm anyway. My guess is it's a fake."

———

**Washington D.C. airspace**

THE MINUTE the two interceptor fighters appeared, the pilot became upset. "Azim, they're here. What do we do now?" he asked frantically in Arabic.

"We continue as scheduled. They're bluffing us. They will not attack us because they don't know for sure if we're the real thing or not."

———

**The Oval Office**
**The White House**
**1600 Pennsylvania Ave NW**
**Washington D.C.**

THE PRESIDENT FINISHED his phone conversation with the Prime Minister of England. They both had agreed years ago not to negotiate with terrorists, but they confirmed that agreement again just now. He waited to hear from the Prime Minister of Israel.

Janet Ruthers, the white house press secretary had quietly entered and waited until the President hung up. "Mr. President, sir, the news media has swamped us with calls. They want to know if this is some type of hoax. I need to give them some sort of response to calm them."

The President sat at his desk and rubbed his temples with his fingertips. "Janet," he said without looking up. "The part about the aircraft is real, but the part about the deadly toxins in unknown. Tell the press corps that we do not negotiate with terrorists, but we have taken emergency measures to protect the citizens of Washington."

"Mr. President," interrupted Chief of Staff Wohlman. "I'm sorry to interrupt, sir, but General Littlestone is on the line and said they have a visual on the aircraft. He says it looks like Marine One and he's going to confirm that it's not. He thinks it must be a trick."

The President nodded. "I agree with Sam. It's an obvious trick to delay us until they get close enough to the capital. What's the standard procedure now?"

"The interceptor will contact the aircraft and demand it leave restricted air space."

"And what if it doesn't?"

"We've never had one not leave."

"But what if it doesn't?"

"Procedure dictates we force it down, sir."

President Campbell felt as if he'd aged ten years in the last twenty minutes. "Follow standard procedures."

"But sir, your daughter might be on board."

The President stared at Ghazi's smiling face on television. "If Marine One is a trick, maybe having my daughter on board is too."

# CHAPTER THIRTY-THREE

**Ghazi Estate**
**6322 Crosswinds Drive**
**Lake Barcroft, Virginia**

JAKE COULD SEE light at the bottom of the stairs and peeked around the corner into the grotto. A man he assumed was Ghazi sat on a throne carved out of stone and talked into a large television camera. Jake looked at the man but noticed that something was wrong with him. It was as if Jake was watching a double exposure. The man moved and talked but overlaid was the image of a red and brown demon mimicking him. *This must be what demons look like when they disguise themselves as humans.*

Jake then noticed a young woman gagged and tied to a chair next to the camera. Due to the contour of the manmade cave, Jake couldn't see the demon standing against the wall.

Ghazi slammed his hand down on the throne's stone arm. "I'm tired of waiting. I've given you plenty of time to make your decision. You made your choice and you've brought this pestilence on yourselves. As of now I am the ruler of the known western world."

Jake wasn't sure what was going on, but he was about to end it, so he stepped out from the stairway. "I think your comedy show's over."

Ghazi looked over at Jake. "Who are you and how did you get in here?"

Ann turned her head and saw the tall man in camouflage clothes with an assault rifle. Her eyes widened and a flood of relief came over her.

"It doesn't matter how I got here but your plan is officially over," said Jake.

"Kill him," snapped Ghazi.

With a screech the tall, thin demon launched itself at the Jake who saw the demon's movement out of the corner of his eye, spun, and fired as the monster slammed into him. Jake's assault rifle was knocked away as he fired, and it slid against a far wall.

The monster took a bullet in the midsection but kept fighting. It clawed at Jake, ripping at his mesh vest and shirt. Jake shoved and pushed the creature away from him before it tore him to shreds. He grabbed his Colt 45 handgun from his shoulder holster and fired several times into the beast. It stumbled back, fell to the ground, and died.

"No," screamed Ghazi, "It's not possible."

Jake slowly got to his feet. "It's all over Ghazi."

Ghazi glared at him. "So, you do exist. There is a demon killer loose, but I'll kill you myself." Just as Jake fired Ghazi stepped off the throne which caused the round went high and hit Ghazi in the shoulder, knocking him back against the throne.

Jake pulled the trigger again, but nothing happened, the gun jammed. He grabbed the slide and tried to eject the jammed round while he kept an eye on Ghazi.

Ghazi recovered from the blow and his eyes glow a bright yellow. "Enough of this," he yelled. "You'll pay for this."

Ghazi stood and the human form faded away instantly revealing his dark red and brown fur, muscular body, and huge wings. He smiled to show off his sharp teeth.

If Jake hadn't already known what Ghazi look like he might've been shocked, but he calmly cleared the jammed round and pointed the Colt .45 at Ghazi.

———

**The Oval Office**
**The White House**
**1600 Pennsylvania Ave NW**
**Washington D.C.**

THE PRESIDENT and his staff watched while Ghazi proclaimed himself ruler. The President turned to Chief of Staff Wohlman. "Get a hold of someone on the scene there and tell them to do whatever they have to do to get in there and stop him."

Chief of Staff Wohlman grabbed the phone and dialed Director Chisom's number. The President and Press Secretary Ruthers watched the television as Ghazi suddenly turned and spoke to someone off camera. They couldn't hear Jake off camera, but they heard Ghazi when he said, "Kill him."

The camera remained on Ghazi as he watched the action out of sight of the viewers. They heard a gunshot and then shortly several more gunshots. They saw Ghazi's response when he jumped up and yelled, "So you do exist. There is a demon killer loose, but I'll kill you myself."

"Someone's in there and he's apparently on our side," said the President. "Who is it?"

"Our people haven't breached the gate yet, he's not one of ours," said Chief of Staff Wohlman. "I'll try to find out."

A second later Ghazi suddenly fell back against the stone throne with a gunshot wound to the shoulder. Their anguish and frustration turned to horror as Ghazi transformed from a human to a hideous reddish-brown monster.

"Dammit, get someone else in there…now," yelled the President.

———

**Quality Inn**
**6510 High Crest Blvd**
**Arlington, Virginia**

ELLIE AND PAM returned to the hotel and tried to busy themselves. Pam typed on her computer while Ellie watched TV.

"Oh no," said Ellie.

"What's wrong?" asked Pam.

Ellie pointed to the TV. All the channels broadcasted Ghazi's demands, so they watched as he ranted about the government's lack of response to his demands.

"That must be Ghazi. I can't believe he's doing this?" said Ellie.

"He's totally insane," said Pam.

The women watched when Ghazi turned, conversed with someone off camera, and then heard the subsequent gunshots.

"I think that might be Jake," said Ellie.

They watched Ghazi being shot and the subsequent horror of Ghazi's transformation into his true demon identity.

Ellie's eyes widened.

"Oh yeah, that has to be Jake," said Pam. "He has that effect on people."

---

**Ghazi Estate**
**6322 Crosswinds Drive**
**Lake Barcroft, Virginia**

AGENT RUIZ'S cell phone rang during the fire fight. "What?" he yelled into the phone, but then his face changed as he listened. "Yes, sir," he said and hung up.

"What idiot would call in the middle of this?" asked Agent Williams.

"It was Director Chisom and he said we need to get in there no matter what it took."

"Why?"

"You wouldn't believe me if I told you."

"Agent Best and the tactical team are on the way. Can't we wait?"

"Not according to the Director and from what he said we can't."

"What's in there?"

"Would you believe more monsters?"

Agent Williams stared at him. "You mean like the kind that attacked us?"

Agent Ruiz nodded.

"Oh great, what else could go wrong."

Agent Ruiz kept low and climbed into behind the wheel of his car.

Agent Williams opened the passenger door and crawled in the back. "You're not leaving me behind."

Agent Ruiz put on his seatbelt and jammed the car into drive. "Hold on." He spun the tires as he pulled out and ran the government car full speed at the main iron gates. The car slammed into the gates with a loud crunch of metal on metal but didn't penetrate the estate. The guards directed their gun fire on the car.

"Stay down," yelled Agent Ruiz.

The remaining agents fired to cover the two in the car as Agent Ruiz backed the car up at high speed. He slammed on the brakes and slid to a stop. He stayed slouched over to avoid incoming bullets and once again accelerated towards the gate. This time the car hit the gates, knocked one open while the other one landed on the hood of the car. He kept driving up the road toward the mansion with the iron gate on the hood. The other agents jumped in their cars and followed under the hail of gunfire.

Ghazi's body slammed into Jake as he fired but the shot missed. The blow knocked Jake back against the stairs and his head struck the solid rock. He was stunned and his vision started to get blurry.

Ghazi roared and charged at Jake again. "I'm going to rip you into pieces," he growled.

Jake shook his head to clear the cobwebs, raised both feet and kicked Ghazi in the chest sending him back across the room. Jake got to his feet quickly and realized he'd dropped his gun but couldn't find it. They stood and faced each other like gladiators in an arena. Jake could see Ghazi's wound leaking.

"It's over Ghazi. Give it up," said Jake.

Ghazi swung his big, clawed fist but Jake ducked. Jake swung up and struck Ghazi in the mid-section. Ghazi swung with the other and struck Jake on the side of his head. Jake's head spun again. Ghazi lashed out and Jake tried to dodge but was slashed across the side of the face by Ghazi's sharp claws. Jake instinctively swung with his fist and struck Ghazi in the head which staggered the demon, so Jake hit Ghazi with a round house kick that knocked Ghazi back.

Surprisingly Ghazi then laughed. "I'm impressed demon killer. We are equally matched but I'm going to win." The demon kicked out, but Jake dodged aside, and Ghazi kicked the television camera causing it to tip over.

Jake whipped his leg around, caught the back of Ghazi's legs and knocked him to the ground. Ghazi kicked out and knocked Jake back against the throne. The remote detonator fell to the ground unseen.

Ghazi swung and Jake blocked it. Ghazi stepped up and kicked him in the side, knocking Jake to the ground. He felt the stabbing pain and thought he might've broken a rib.

Ghazi laughed, strutted over, grabbed Jake with both clawed hands, and lifted him over his head. He calmly threw Jake across the grotto where he landed with a sickening thud on the throne. The force knocked the throne back several inches. Jake was stunned and had trouble breathing. His shoulder hurt from hitting the stone throne and he thought his shoulder might be dislocated

The creature strolled towards Jake with a cocky swagger. "I thought you'd be more of a challenge." Ghazi glanced at the camera on its side, leaned down and looked directly into the camera lens with his glowing yellow eyes. "Do you see? No one can stop me. It's over. I am your new ruler."

Jake lunged out of the seat and hit Ghazi with a couple of punches, one to the midsection and the other to the open wound. Ghazi staggered back in obvious pain.

---

**Quality Inn**
**6510 High Crest Blvd**
**Arlington, Virginia**

ELLIE AND PAM held hands while they watched the battle in silence. They sat side by side on the edge of the bed with their eyes glued to the television. The camera suddenly fell, and they watched the battle on a sideways angle.

They watched as Ghazi's hideous face filled the screen as he taunted the camera.

---

**Ghazi Estate**
**6322 Crosswinds Drive**
**Lake Barcroft, Virginia**

JAKE'S SHOULDER and ribs ached, but he didn't give up. Ghazi swung but Jake ducked, spun, and brought both fists down on Ghazi's back knocking the demon to the floor. Jake turned to dash for the assault rifle, but Ghazi grabbed Jake's ankle and tripped him. Ghazi pulled Jake to his feet and shoved him back against the altar. With both hands Ghazi began to choke Jake who tried to pry away Ghazi's hands.

Ghazi tilted his head back and roared with laughter.

As the world started to darken from lack of oxygen Jake saw Ghazi's throat exposed. With his last ounce of strength Jake grabbed his combat knife still attached to his calf and shoved it into Ghazi's neck.

Ghazi gasped, released Jake, and fell to the ground. Jake fell to his knees, coughed, and sucked in precious air. Ghazi tried to speak but only gurgled a putrid smelling ooze. He turned his head to one side, reached out, and activated the remote control.

Jake staggered to his feet and turned to the woman tied to the chair when suddenly the manmade cave shuttered. He looked around as the ground shook again and pieces of the ceiling fell to the ground. It didn't take but a second for Jake to realize that the device that Ghazi had activated detonated some type of explosives and they were in big trouble. Large chunks of rocks started to fall. One hit the television camera and sent electrical sparks into the air before it when blank.

Jake pulled the knife out of Ghazi and dodged falling rocks to get to the woman. He cut the ropes that held her.

She ripped off the tape across her mouth as more rocks fell all around them. "Who're you?"

"Let's get out of here first," yelled Jake over the rumble above their heads. He started for the stairs, but Ann grabbed his arm.

"What about the ark? We can't leave it here. It'll be destroyed."

Jake looked at the beautiful golden box but shook his head. "We don't have time, now c'mon." He pulled her by the arm towards the stairway when the ceiling above the stairs collapsed, blocking the exit.

"We're trapped," yelled Ann.

# CHAPTER THIRTY-FOUR

**Quality Inn**
**6510 High Crest Blvd**
**Arlington, Virginia**

THEY STAYED RIVETED on the screen as Jake battled with Ghazi. They watched as Jake stabbed and killed Ghazi. They didn't realize Ghazi had activated the explosives until the camera shook and they saw large pieces of rock falling.

"What happened? What did he do?" asked Pam.

"He set off the explosives," said Ellie.

Several more rocks fell before the screen went blank. The two women sat in silence and stared at the blank screen which then switched back to a reporter on the scene. He stood outside the estate's gate where the shooting had finally stopped.

The news switched to a news helicopter that was flying above the estate, and even in the rain they could see the explosions and watched in horror as the entire mansion imploded and collapsed in on itself in a matter of seconds.

Ellie put both hands to her mouth, afraid to say anything.

Pam put her arm around Ellie. "He got out in time. I'm sure he did."

There was a knock at the door. "Room service," said a deep voice.

———

**The Oval Office**
**The White House**
**1600 Pennsylvania Ave NW**
**Washington D.C.**

THE PRESIDENT and his staff members watched the same scene play out on their television. When the screen went blank, they saw the same news broadcast of the mansion collapsing.

"Do you think he made it out?" asked Press Secretary Ruthers.

"I doubt it," said the President. He turned to his chief of staff. "Did we find out who he was?"

Chief of Staff Wohlman shook his head. "No sir."

"Whoever he was, we owe him a great debt of thanks," said the President.

———

**Airborne above Washington D.C.**

THE AIR COMMUNICATIONS controller kept trying to contact the helicopter using the standard radio frequency, 121.5 but no one responded.

Major Rollins, Cobra, also attempted to contact the helicopter. "Attention unidentified aircraft, this is Major Rollins of the United State Air Force, you are in restricted air space, and you need to divert your route." No one responded. "If you don't respond we will be forced to bring your aircraft down, do you copy?"

Aboard the helicopter, Azim glanced at his pilot, reached in his pocket and took out the tape recorder. He held it against the microphone and pushed play.

"This is Ann Campbell, daughter of President Campbell," announced the taped voice of Ann. "Please don't shoot."

"Geesh, Joe, is that really the President's daughter?" asked Captain Cowins.

Major Rollins shook his head. "I don't know. NORTHCOM, this is Cobra, request further instructions."

Aboard the helicopter, Azim smiled. "Those fools will never fire now that they think she's on board. It's time to deliver our load and leave." Azim reached down to turn the lever, but it was gone. He looked down in a panic. "Did you remove the release handle?"

The pilot shook his head.

"Then where did it go?" Azim frantically looked around when he noticed someone in the shadows by the cabin door. A person held the release handle in one hand and a gun in another. She then stepped into the dim light of the cabin.

"Amira? What are you doing?" said the astonished Azim.

She couldn't speak but held the gun leveled at them. She pointed towards the ground with the lever handle.

"What?" asked Azim. "Don't be a fool, give me the gun."

She shook her head firmly and pointed towards the ground again.

"You want us to land?"

She nodded.

"You can't be serious. This is our chance to strike a deadly blow at all the unbelievers."

Amira glared at him and pointed to the ground with the release handle. Azim looked at the pilot who gave a sideway glance and suddenly tipped the helicopter causing Amira to lose her balance and fall against the door jamb. Azim leapt, grabbed the gun, and they struggled for the weapon.

"Amira, stop it. Give me the gun now."

Amira fought fiercely and refused to let go. Azim twisted her wrist which caused her to drop the gun that hit the metal floor and discharged. The helicopter slanted suddenly, and Azim looked back to see the pilot slumped over the controls. Amira darted back into the cabin with the release handle.

"Come back," yelled Azim. He wanted to go after her, but he had to jump into the copilot seat and grab the controls.

The two fighter pilots watched the helicopter tip and then started wobbling wildly.

"Ron, did you see that?" asked Major Rollins.

"Yep, something's going on in there."

---

**The Pentagon**
**1400 Defense Pentagon**
**Washington D.C.**

GENERAL LITTLESTONE and Captain Griffin watched the radar scope as the helicopter entered the Flight Restricted Zone (FRZ), the inner circle of the ADZ and closest to Washington. They listened to the voice communications from the two fighters.

They listened as the President's daughter's voice came across the radio.

Captain Griffin turned to the general who shook his head and picked up the direct phone line to the White House.

---

**The Oval Office**
**The White House**
**1600 Pennsylvania Ave NW**
**Washington D.C.**

THE PHONE RANG and Chief of Staff Wohlman picked it up.

"Sir, we have another problem." he said. "The two fighter interceptors reported that the helicopter has entered the FRZ."

"Tell them to take whatever action they need to," said the President.

Chief of Staff Wohlman was listening to the conversation on the phone.

"Did you hear me, John?" asked the President.

"I'm sorry, sir, but I've been told that your daughter is on the radio in the helicopter."

The President jumped up and grabbed the phone. He listened for a moment. "Play it back," he ordered. He listened again and his face went pale. "That's her," he said and handed the phone back to Wohlman. The President went over and sat on the couch.

"Sir, what are your orders?" asked Chief of Staff Wohlman.

"Can they bring it down without it crashing?"

He spoke into the phone and listened for a moment. "They said they're not sure if they can force it down with causing it to crash. They also said the helicopter suddenly tilted and is flying oddly."

The President sat and stared.

"Sir, what do you want to do?"

The President lowered his head into hands. "Tell them to take it out."

"But Mr. President…Bill…your daughter is on board."

"I know," he answered and sighed heavily. "I can't save one person and endanger thousands or even millions of lives. God forgive me. Tell them to shoot it down."

# CHAPTER THIRTY-FIVE

**Airspace over Washington D.C.**

MAJOR ROLLINS HEARD the order over his helmet earpiece but wasn't sure he heard it right. "NORTHCOM, I request confirmation on your order to destroy the aircraft?"

The air communications officer responded and advised that the order came from directly from the POTUS, the President of the United States through the Pentagon.

"But the President's daughter is on board," said Captain Cowins.

General Littlestone's voice came over the radio. "Cobra, you have your instructions directly from the POTUS, follow them."

"Yes, sir," said Major Rollins. His on-board computer locked onto the helicopter as it flew wildly through the rain. He flipped the cover up over the red button to fire the sidewinder missile. He hesitated. "I can't believe I'm going to shoot down Marine One with the President's daughter inside."

"They don't think its Marine One, Joe, but do what you think is right," said Captain Cowins.

Major Rollins waited a half a second and then pushed the button on the aircraft's control stick. With a stream of fire and a loud swoosh the AIM-91M missile rocketed out from under the wing of the F-15 and straight for the helicopter.

"Missile away," said Major Rollins.

Azim was trying to keep the helicopter in the air. He had never flown an aircraft and had no idea what he was doing. "Amira, bring the handle back, this is our last chance," he yelled.

Far back in the belly of the helicopter, Amira hid and clutched the release handle. She wasn't about to give it to him. He had no idea who Ghazi really was, and she was going to stop his plan if she could.

A flash of light caught Azim's eye and he turned as the missile rapidly approached. "Allah, protect me," he prayed as the missile slammed into the helicopter and exploded.

The two fighter pilots watched as the helicopter exploded in midair. It broke into two large flaming pieces and dropped from the sky. It crashed into a wooded section of land.

―――

**The Pentagon**
**1400 Defense Pentagon**
**Washington D.C.**

GENERAL LITTLESTONE and the staff at NORTHCOM waited quietly for the news.

"NORTHCOM, this is Cobra. The aircraft has been destroyed. It crashed but looked as if it didn't hit any buildings on the ground."

"Acknowledged," said the air communications officer. "We got lucky in that respect."

"Roger that, but we just killed the President's daughter."

General Littlestone turned and walked toward his office. "Now I have to tell the President we just shot down his daughter."

―――

**The Oval Office**

**The White House**
**1600 Pennsylvania Ave NW**
**Washington D.C.**

CHIEF OF STAFF Wohlman listened on the phone and hung up. "Mr. President, the helicopter has been destroyed. I'm sorry about Ann."

The President sat on the couch with his face in his hands. "I need for you to prepare a statement, but first I'd like to have a moment alone."

The staff members and Agent Meadows left quietly.

The President, one of the most powerful men on the earth, sat alone in his oval office and cried. He'd saved his country but lost his daughter.

———

**Ghazi Estate**
**6322 Crosswinds Drive**
**Lake Barcroft, Virginia**

THE AGENTS SPED up to the mansion and leapt from their cars as several explosions erupted around the building. They could only stand and watch as the mansion exploded and collapsed in a matter of seconds from the planted C4 explosives.

"Well, that takes care of Ghazi," said Agent Williams. "But what about the helicopter?"

Agent Ruiz grabbed his cell phone and called Director Chisom. He listened for a moment and then threw the phone onto the wet pavement. "The fighter interceptors shot the helicopter down."

"Was the President's daughter on board?"

Agent Ruiz nodded. "Hell yes she was and the order came directly from the White House."

They stood in the pouring rain, soaked to the skin, and stared at the burning rubble that was once a mansion.

"He didn't have a choice. He kept a lunatic from trying to take over the world but had to sacrifice his own daughter to do it," said Agent Ruiz.

Agent Williams slammed her fist on the top of the car. "Damned, it's our fault. If we'd been quicker, we could've stopped it."

"We did everything we could," answered Agent Ruiz sadly.

In the grotto, Jake and Ann dodged falling rocks and desperately looked for an escape.

"That was the only way out," said Ann. "He brought me down here once before."

"Even a lunatic has an escape plan," yelled Jake over the sound of falling rocks. He looked around and something caught his eye...the stone throne. He bent down and looked quickly at the base. It was off center by several inches and Jake could see what looked like an opening. "This must be it," he said to himself. He turned to Ann. "Help me push this over."

Ann ran over and together they pushed on the throne, but it didn't move. Jake's shoulder and ribs ached but he kept pushing. "Harder," he yelled.

They pushed and it slid just an inch.

Jake could see what looked like steps. "Hurry, we don't have much longer."

They pushed harder and finally the throne tilted then fell to the side and broke into pieces. Jake looked down at the dark, open hole that appeared to be some sort of tunnel.

"Where does it lead?" asked Ann.

"I don't know, but anywhere's better than here."

Jake sat on the edge and dropped down, followed by Ann. Jake fell about six feet to a landing. A set of stairs led down a small, cramped tunnel into the darkness. Jake had to bend over as they followed the stairs for about five minutes before it ended abruptly when Jake stepped into water.

"Where are we?" asked Ann.

Jake felt around on his vest and found a small florescent light stick. He broke it and illuminated the area in a greenish light. The tunnel was slightly wider, but the stairs led into a pool of water.

"What now?" asked Ann.

"My guess is the stairs lead farther down and come out by the lake."

"But why lead it into the water?"

"Demons don't require oxygen. Ghazi can walk through it without any problem. It's his way of keeping humans out."

"Do we want to try to swim out?"

Jake shook his head. "With all the rain the water level is up, so no, let's rest for a while and then we'll try."

They both sat down on the stone stairs. The rumble above had stopped indicating to Jake that the mansion had totally collapsed.

"By the way, my name's Ann."

"I'm Jake. What were you doing there anyway?"

"Ghazi kidnapped me."

He stared at her and then realized who she was. "You're the President's daughter?"

Ann smiled and nodded.

"Then they'll come searching for you down her?"

"No," said Ann sadly. "They think I'm aboard a helicopter over Washington D.C. I wish I had a phone to call someone?"

Jake remembered his cell phone and pulled it from his pocket. The face of the phone was cracked but it appeared to be working. He dialed Ellie's number but after a moment realized it wasn't connecting. "There's too much rock around us to get a good signal." He put the phone back in his pocket. He looked at Ann. "So, what was his plan?"

"Ghazi planned to dump dangerous biological toxin over three major western capital cities. It would kill everyone, and he'd take over."

Jake scratched his head. "It sounds like a typical maniac's plan. I'd heard he was going to try to take over the world, but I just didn't want to believe it."

"How did you know?"

"A demon told me."

Ann looked at him with a raised eyebrow. "So, they really were demons? He really did look like that?"

"Yeah," said Jake. "I was sent to stop him."

Ann smiled again. "And you did too but if the military didn't send you then who did?"

"An angel."

Ann stared at him with a look of puzzlement.

"I used to be in the military but now I raise cattle in Texas. It's a long story."

"I'm not going anywhere for a while. I'm all ears."

# CHAPTER THIRTY-SIX

**Quality Inn**
**6510 High Crest Blvd**
**Arlington, Virginia**

THERE WAS a knock on the door again, "Room Service."

Pam got up. "He must be at the wrong room. I'll tell him." She headed for the door when Roscoe started growling. Pam stopped and turned toward him. "What is it boy? What's wrong?"

Suddenly the door exploded inward and knocked Pam across the room and into the small hotel table which broke under her weight. Ellie jumped to her feet and stared at the door in disbelief.

A large, bulky, black, and brown colored demon stood in the doorway. His head was large and almost square with its yellow glowing eyes set in the front. Its arms were short and thick, but the body was oblong. It was covered with hair and resembled a deformed Bigfoot with black wings.

"What were you doing outside Lord Ghazi's estate?" he demanded.

Ellie backed away while Roscoe barked and growled.

"Answer me, human," he snarled.

Ellie was terrified but refused to give in. "No."

The demon swung an arm and struck Ellie across the side of the head, knocking her back against the wall where she slid down on top of Jake's gear. Roscoe leapt forward and bit the demon on the leg causing it to back away. It roared and reached down to grab Roscoe when Pam jumped onto its back.

"I'm getting really tired of monsters," she yelled as she jammed a broken piece of table leg into the creature's eye.

The monster screeched and threw Pam off, slamming her into a wall where she slid unconscious to the floor.

By then Ellie was on her feet. Her head hurt, her nose bled, and her eye was starting swell. In desperation she dodged past the demon and towards the door in hopes that she could lead it away from Pam. The demon charged after her while trying to pull the wooden stake from its eye.

Several hotel guests came out into the hallway to see what all the noise was when Ellie dashed out of the room. She turned to go down the hall when the thing caught up, grabbed her arm, but lost his footing because Roscoe was still attached to his leg, and they all fell through the door across the hall and into another room.

At seeing a woman being attacked by a deformed Bigfoot with wings with a wooden stake protruding from its eye being bitten by a wolf dog, the rest of guests quickly retreated back into their rooms.

Fortunately, the room was empty except for a guest's wheelchair which was crushed under the demon's weight. Ellie got to her feet and backed towards the door. Roscoe released his hold on the demon when they fell through the door but stood his ground and growled at the thing.

The demon climbed to its feet and jerked the stake from its eye. "Your dog can't protect you. I'm going to kill you and dine on your flesh."

From behind her back, Ellie pulled one of Jake's Colt 45s that she'd picked up when she fell on his gear. She pointed it at the demon.

The demon roared with laughter. "You can't kill me with that thing, ignorant woman."

Ellie had never used a gun before, but she was determined to stop this thing if she could. "You're right," answered Ellie as she pointed the gun at the demon's feet. "But eat this."

The creature looked down and saw a large oxygen tank attached to the crushed wheelchair. Its yellow eyes widened and before it could move, Ellie pulled the triggered as many times and as fast as she could.

The oxygen tank exploded in a huge ball of flame that knocked Ellie and Roscoe back through the doorway and into the hall. Ellie's vision went black but when she came to a moment later, she felt someone pulling her.

Pam was standing over her, trying to help her to her feet. The hallway was filled with smoke and the fire alarms were going off. "We have to get out of here," yelled Pam over the sound of the fire alarms clanging.

Guests were scrambling past them to get to the stairs. Ellie got to her feet and saw that the room with the demon was on fire. The water sprinklers immediately came on and only added to the confusion. They looked in the room and saw the demon on the floor. It had of course healed within seconds except that it was missing parts that had been blown off. The right side of its body and wings were gone, leaving only its right torso and head. It looked up at them, growled, and crawled towards them with its remaining limbs.

"Let's get out of here," yelled Pam as she shoved Ellie towards the stairs. They stumbled through the smoke to the stairs with Roscoe on her heels. He'd been shaken but not injured.

The fire department arrived as they came outside. They found refuge with the rest of the guests across the street under the awning of a closed furniture store. They watched the fire department rush in to make sure the fire was out.

"I wonder if it's still in there?" asked Pam.

"I don't know but I do know that it gets to spend eternity with only half a body."

———

**Ghazi Estate**
**6322 Crosswinds Drive**
**Lake Barcroft, Virginia**

JAKE OPENED his eyes and looked around. He'd fallen asleep and didn't realize it. The light stick had gone out and it was dark in the tunnel.

His movements awakened Ann. "I didn't know I'd fallen asleep."

"Me either." He felt around and pulled out another light stick and was about to break it when he stopped.

"What's wrong?" asked Ann.

"Look at the water."

"It's water?"

"You can see it."

The water was a lighter shade than the rest of the tunnel.

Ann sat up quickly. "You're right. There must be light coming through. What time is it?"

Jake checked his watch. "It's seven in the morning. We must've slept awhile."

Ann moved down to edge of the water and tried to look through it. "I wonder how far until it ends?"

"I guess I need to find out."

"Wait, what if they released the toxins?"

Jake shrugged. "We can't stay in here forever. There's only one way to find out."

"I'll go," said Ann firmly. "You're injured. You may not be able to go as far as I can. If I get out but can't get back in, I'll go for help."

Jake hated to admit it, but she was right. His ribs still hurt, and his shoulder was stiff.

Ann stepped into the cold water and waited a moment for her body to get accustomed to the water. She took several deep breaths, smiled, and dove under the water.

Jake set his stopwatch, sat in the dark, and waited. After two minutes he began to worry, and after three minutes he was frustrated. I should've gone, he thought. What a stupid thing to do. What was I thinking letting the President's daughter do something so dangerous? After five minutes he decided he was going after her and entered the water. He waited until his body also became accustomed to the cold water. He took a couple of deep breaths and ignored the pain in his ribs. He was about to dive when he felt the water surge around him, and Ann broke the surface. She gasped for air.

"I was getting worried about you," he said.

"I found the opening but it's a long tunnel. I didn't think I was going to make it."

Jake nodded. "You catch your breath and then we'll go together."

When she was ready, they both took in as much air as they could and dove in. They swam down into the submerged tunnel with Ann leading the way. Jake's ribs ached and his shoulder screamed in pain. Their vision was blurred so he felt along the slimy wall and swam toward the light. The farther they swam the brighter the tunnel became. Jake's lungs felt like they were going to burst and when he thought he couldn't go any farther, they exited the tunnel into the lake. With a few kicks up they broke the surface, and gulped in fresh, damp air.

"See, that wasn't so hard," said Ann with a smile.

"Piece of cake," said Jake sarcastically between gulps of air.

They swam over the bank, climbed out, and sat on the bank to recover from their swim.

"What now?" asked Ann.

Jake pulled his cell phone from his pocket and examined it. Unfortunately, it was ruined from the swim, so he slowly got to his feet. "We walk."

# CHAPTER THIRTY-SEVEN

**FBI Headquarters**
**935 Pennsylvania Avenue, NW**
**Washington, D.C.**

AFTER THE MANSION collapsed the fire department arrived and fought the huge flames while the two agents spent the entire night at the mansion tying up loose ends. Their car was not drivable and was towed away due to the damage.

They rode back to FBI headquarters with the other agents and were tired as well as soggy when they entered Agent Williams' office. Agent Sills was still there, and her eyes were swollen from crying. They knew that she and Ann had been close.

"Beth, you need to go back to the house and get some rest. You're still not completely healed," said Agent Ruiz.

"I will in a few minutes. I received a call from Agent Meadows at the White House. They examined the wreckage."

The two FBI agents didn't know what to say so they remained silent.

"They found three badly burned bodies," explained Agent Sills. "They found two males in the cockpit." She hesitated and her eyes filled up with tears. "They found a female's burned body in the rear of the helicopter. It was Ann."

Agent Ruiz put his hand on her shoulder. "I'm sorry. If I'd done more maybe she'd still be alive."

Agent Sills shook her head. "You did everything you could to get her back. I appreciate everything both of you did."

There was nothing else he could think of to say to her. She was Ann's bodyguard, so she felt the most guilt and responsibility.

———

**Quality Inn**
**6510 High Crest Blvd**
**Arlington, Virginia**

PAM AND ELLIE gathered what was left of their belongings and packed the suburban. It was somber and quiet. Ellie insisted on driving and Pam knew it would take her mind off Jake. They entered the interstate and headed west, toward home.

———

**Phil's Bait and Tackle Shop**
**1013 Creek Bend Rd**
**Lake Barcroft, Virginia**

THE RAIN STOPPED and the sun came out. Jake and Ann walked through the beautiful countryside in search of a phone. A few cars passed but they didn't try to flag one down as it would take too much explaining. They came upon a bait and tackle shop that was still closed, but there was a pay phone outside. Neither one had any change, but Jake had his wallet. He used his credit card to call Ellie's cell phone. It rang several times, but no one answered.

"That's odd," said Jake. "She always has her phone on."

"I can call someone," said Ann.

———

**FBI Headquarters**
**935 Pennsylvania Avenue, NW**
**Washington, D.C.**

AGENT SILLS CLOSED HER LAPTOP, gathered her files, and headed to the door.

"Do you need us to take you back?" asked Agent Ruiz.

"No thanks. I'm going to walk over to the deli for some breakfast, and then I'll call for a ride."

"If you need anything, call us," said Agent Williams.

Agent Sills turned to leave when her cell phone rang. She put her laptop and files down then answered it, listened for a moment, her eyes widened, and she felt lightheaded. She dropped the phone and fell against the door jamb. Agent Williams jumped up and caught her.

Agent Ruiz picked up the phone. "Hello?"

"Who's this?"

"This is Agent Ruiz with the FBI, who's this?"

"This is Ann Campbell and a friend. We need a ride."

———

**Phil's Bait and Tackle Shop**
**1013 Creek Bend Rd**
**Lake Barcroft, Virginia**

AGENTS RUIZ and Williams pulled up to the bait and tackle shop. They decided not to tell anyone else about the strange phone call until they could check it out. Agent Ruiz parked the car and Agent Williams pointed to the pay phone where the call was made, but no one was around. Fearing another ambush, they drew their weapons and approached the pay phone where it hung on the wall near the corner of the wooden frame building.

Agent Ruiz picked up the phone and checked the number. "It's the number they called from."

Agent Williams nodded and scanned the forest behind the building.

"Agent Ruiz?" said a voice from back in the brush.

"This is Agent Ruiz with the FBI. Come out with your hands up," he ordered.

A tall man in torn, damp camouflage clothing came out of the bushes with his hands in the air. "Fancy meeting you here," said Jake.

Agent Ruiz looked at him strangely. "You're the guy from the freeway? Your name's Jake?"

"Yep." Jake turned back slightly and spoke to someone behind him. "It's ok to come out. They're the good guys."

A blonde woman wearing soggy clothes stepped out from the trees. Both agents' eyes widened in disbelief. "My God, it is you," said Agent Williams.

Ann smiled.

"Can I put my hands down now?" asked Jake.

---

**The Oval Office**
**The White House**
**1600 Pennsylvania Ave NW**
**Washington D.C.**

IT'D BEEN a difficult night for the office of the Presidency. After the President gave a brief statement on national television concerning the night's events, he went to their private quarters and spent time with the First Lady.

That morning he sat in the oval office getting updates on the mansion investigation and the helicopter incident.

Chief of Staff Wohlman, FBI Director Chisom, General Littlestone, and Secretary of State Jennings sat in a semi-circle around the President's desk.

"It'll take weeks for the investigators to remove all the rubble at the mansion and locate any bodies, if they can even find what's left of them," explained FBI Director Chisom.

"I understand," said the President. "I'd like to identify the man that stopped Ghazi."

Director Chisom nodded. "We will, sir. Also, the NTSB's and our investigators are at the other scene...the helicopter crash." He hesitated. "The bodies were taken to the medical examiner's office."

"I was briefed on that earlier," said the President sadly. "As soon as they're done and give us the official word, the First Lady will be flying Ann's body back to Colorado for the funeral."

"How's the First Lady doing?" asked General Littlestone.

"She's doing well considering I ordered her daughter's death."

"There's nothing you could've done different, sir, you made the only possible decision."

The President nodded. "I know it and she does too, but it'll take time."

CIA Director Heppell quietly entered during their discussion. "I do have some good news, Mr. President. I received a teletype from Interpol. They were able to stop the two helicopters before they reached their destinations. The micro toxins were removed by their Haz Mat teams."

"Thank God for that," said the President. "Now, if I can only fight off the scavengers that are circling the White House. They've called for an immediate congressional hearing even before we're through with the full investigation with Senator Wilson leading the witch hunt. He's blaming me for everything and demanding that impeachment proceedings begin."

"He can't be serious," said Secretary of State Jennings.

"He's accusing Ghazi and me of conspiring to take over the world. He's pointing his finger directly at the White House."

"That's ludicrous, sir," grumbled Director Chisom. "Everyone knows you had nothing to do with it."

"But we have to be able to prove it. Ghazi's dead, the mansion's destroyed, and the people in the helicopter were killed. Not many witnesses to help our defense."

"Your daughter died in that helicopter," said Chief of Staff Wohlman. "That alone should prove your innocence?"

"Wilson's saying that she was part of the conspiracy, and that the kidnapping was a hoax." The President shook his head. "Gentlemen, we have our work cut out to prove that..."

Suddenly there was a disturbance coming from outside the oval office. Voices were raised and the door came open. The President's secretary was yelling at them not to go in, but Agent Meadows followed by Agent Sills stormed into the oval office.

"What's going on?' demanded Chief of Staff Wohlman.

Agent Meadows spoke up. "Mr. President, I'm sorry for the interruption but something's come up you need to know."

"It had better be for a good reason," warned Secretary of State Jennings. "This is highly improper."

Agent Sills stepped forward and with a smile held out her cell phone. "Mr. President, your daughter wants to talk to you."

# CHAPTER THIRTY-EIGHT

**Interstate 95**
**Southern Virginia**

ELLIE AND PAM were well on their way down I-95 when Ellie noticed red and blue lights behind her. She slowed to allow the oncoming Virginia State trooper to pass but the vehicle remained behind the suburban.

"What's going on?" asked Pam when she noticed Ellie slowing down.

"There's a state trooper behind us?"

"Were you speeding?"

Ellie rolled her eyes. "No, I wasn't speeding. I don't know why he's stopping me."

She pulled over and stopped. A moment later a young Virginia State trooper approached the suburban.

"Good morning, I'm trooper Harris with the Virginia Highway Patrol. May I please see your driver's license?"

Ellie pulled her driver's license and handed it to the trooper. "Is there a problem, officer?" she asked.

The trooper looked at her driver's license. "Please remain here, and I'll be right back." Without giving a reason for the traffic stop, he turned and walked back to his car.

After waiting for over fifteen minutes, the two women were getting anxious. Ellie stepped out of the suburban at the same time the trooper approached. "Officer, is everything ok? Is there a problem?" asked Ellie.

The trooper was polite but professional. "I've been informed to hold you here for a few more minutes."

"By whom?"

"I'm not at liberty to say. Please be patient and wait in your car."

Ellie climbed back into the suburban. "He said we have to wait a few more minutes."

Pam raised both eyebrows and looked back at the trooper. "Why?"

"He wouldn't say," said Ellie with a shrug.

Ten minutes later two black Chevrolet Suburbans pulled up. The windows were dark tinted while red and blue lights flashed from behind their front grills. Two men in suits stepped out of the first suburban and spoke with the trooper. Ellie and Pam watched as the trooper handed Ellie's driver's license to one of the men, a middle-aged man wearing a dark grey suit. He approached them. "Are you Ellie Thompson?"

"Yes, I am," but before she could ask what was going on, he turned to Pam.

"Are you Pamela Martin?"

"Yes," replied Pam, wide eyed.

"I'm Agent Edwards with the United States Secret Service. Please come with me."

The two women looked at each other and silently climbed out of their vehicle.

"What's this all about?" asked Ellie.

"We have orders to escort you back to Washington," said Agent Edwards.

Ellie stopped in her tracks. "Why? We haven't done anything."

The agent forced a slight smile. "All will be explained later. Please come with us."

"What about our Suburban? What's going to happen to it?"

The agent looked at the primer gray and blue suburban with its plastic covered windows, and obvious dents, claw marks and scratches. He raised an eyebrow. "Your…uh…vehicle will be taken care of, now please follow me."

"What about Roscoe?"

"Roscoe?"

Ellie opened the side door and Roscoe leaped out of the suburban. He stood next to Ellie and growled at the Secret Service Agent.

"The dog cannot come."

"Then we don't go," snapped Ellie, and folded her arms across her chest in defiance.

The agent frowned. "We can take you in handcuffs if we have to."

"Try it."

The agent stared at the two women. The dark-haired woman had a black eye and a swollen lip. The blonde woman's left cheek and jaw were bruised. Roscoe growled and bared his teeth.

The other agent approached, and they spoke in whispers.

"Wait here," said the agent.

"We'll be right here," replied Ellie sarcastically.

The two agents walked back to their suburban and began talking on a cell phone.

"Are you crazy?" whispered Pam. "That's the Secret Service."

"I don't care who they are. I'm in no mood to be pushed around. We're not leaving without Roscoe." She reached down and scratched him behind the ear.

The agent returned. "The wolf…dog…animal can come."

They followed the two agents to the suburban and climbed into the back seat. The two agents rode in the front seat, and they drove in silence for several minutes.

"We are in like, so much trouble," whispered Pam. "I told you we were going to get in trouble after the run in with the FBI."

"Shush," whispered Ellie.

"My Christmas cards will have a return address of cell block 9. I look bad in black and white prison stripes."

Ellie just rolled her eyes. "Where are we going?" she asked the two agents.

The agent in the passenger seat turned back to her. "All will be explained," he said stoically.

"Geesh, don't these guys have a bigger vocabulary?" said Pam sarcastically.

They rode for another twenty minutes in silence. Ellie stroked Roscoe's fur as they looked out of the vehicle's windows. She started thinking about Jake and wanted to cry, but she knew she had to be strong until they got out of this newest situation, whatever it was. They took the downtown exit and drove straight up 15th Street and passed Constitution Avenue.

"I've never been to D.C.," said Pam. "I just hope I get to leave."

They came into view of the White House and stopped at one of the large steel barricades erected after September 11th.

Pam looked out the window at the White House.

"Why are they stopping outside the White House?" asked Pam.

Ellie shrugged. "I don't know. Maybe they need to check on something first."

After the driver spoke to the officer that approached them, another officer walked around the vehicle with a mirror mounted on a small wheel. He scanned around the underside of the vehicle for anything unwanted. The officer gave a nod, and the four-foot steel wall was lowered and allowed the vehicles to drive onto the grounds of the White House. Pam and Ellie watched wide eyed as they drove up the drive, past the well-manicured lawn and around to the west wing of the White House.

"Oh, we are in so much trouble," said Pam to herself.

"We don't know that," said Ellie.

Pam shook her head. "When the Secret Service stops you and brings you to the White House against your will, it means you're in deep trouble."

They stopped and two more Secret Service agents approached and opened their door. "Please step out and follow us."

Pam and Ellie climbed out and followed one of the men while the other followed behind them. They entered the lobby on the north side of the west wing of the White House. They followed the agent to the right and into a hallway. Ellie held Roscoe by his leash as they walked down a long-carpeted hallway, past several offices with titles such as Assistant to Chief of Staff, Assistant to the President, Deputy Chief of Staff, and Vice President. Neither woman spoke as they turned left and continued down the hall. Roscoe's ears perked up and he lurched forward out of Ellie's grasp.

"Roscoe, no, come back," she said but it was too late. Roscoe trotted down the hall and turned left into a room with the lead agent running after him. As they approached the room Roscoe darted into, the door name plate said *The Roosevelt Room*. A windowless room that had been used in the 1800's as the President's office but was now a conference room. The group stopped at the door and looked in. The first thing Ellie saw was Roscoe licking the face of a man seated in a chair. The man wore black and gray camouflage clothes with a blanket around his shoulders. She knew in an instant and ran into the room as the man stood up. Ellie stood on his tip toes, wrapped her arms around his neck, and kissed him hard. She then kissed him several more times while tears ran down her cheeks. "Jake, oh, Jake, you're alive," she said.

Jake smiled. "I'm ok, but I was worried about you."

Pam stood speechless for once.

Ellie realized that there were other people in the room. She looked around and saw several men in suits. A young woman with a blanket wrapped around her stood next to an older woman. Ellie blushed as she wiped away the tears.

Jake spoke to the group of people. "I'd like ya'll to meet Ellie Thompson, pastor of Shady Oak Community Church, and her friend Pamela Martin." Jake motioned toward the man and woman. "Ellie and Pam, I'd like you to meet President Campbell, the First Lady, and their daughter Ann."

Ellie was embarrassed. "Mr. President, I'm so honored to meet you, sir. I'm so sorry for my sudden behavior but I thought Jake was dead."

The President and First Lady stepped forward and shook her hand. "There's no need to apologize," said the First Lady. "I thought my daughter, Ann, was dead. When I saw her earlier there was some considerable crying and hugging."

The President turned to Pam. "You must be the newspaper woman I've heard all about."

Pam blushed and shook the President's hand. "I'm the editor of the Shady Oak Gazette, sir, and I hope what Jake told you wasn't exaggerated."

The President laughed. "He said you were a great friend and a big help." He stepped back and put his arm around his daughter and wife. "You three did a great service to your country and to the world. From what I've been told by Mr. Taft, you've also been busy. There's no way to thank you enough."

The trio smiled and thanked the President for his praise.

"My staff has arranged for you to stay in a nearby hotel," said the First Lady. "I insist that you come for a small reception here at the White House tonight." With that said the First family left the room.

"What happened to you? I tried to call you," asked Jake.

"Our phones were ruined by the water from the fire sprinkler system," explained Ellie.

"The sprinkler system? And what about your eye?"

"I went three rounds with a demon."

"And since you're here and he isn't, you won?"

"Let's just say it was a tie. He sort of went to pieces."

Jake, Ellie, and Pam were taken to the Marriott hotel, a guest of the U.S. Government but guarded by the FBI as future material witnesses.

After showers and some fresh clothes, they were escorted back to the White House while Roscoe took a well needed rest on the huge bed in Jake's room.

They again marveled at the White House as they arrived and escorted to the *Roosevelt Room* again where a full buffet of food waited.

Pam and Ellie were introduced to Agent Ruiz and Williams as well as Agent Sills, Chief of Staff John Wohlman, Secretary of State

Phil Jennings, General Littelstone, FBI Director Chisom, and several more.

A few minutes later the President, First Lady, and Ann entered. The President then addressed the small crowd. "I am forever grateful to each of you for everything that you did to get my daughter back and for saving millions of lives. I wish I could call this a celebration but I'm afraid it's not. Certain members of Congress are demanding an immediate inquiry into all of this. They want my head on a platter."

"We'll support you in every way we can," said Chief of Staff Wohlman.

Jake nodded in agreement. "Whatever we can do to help, we will."

"Thank you. You've done more than anyone could've asked for. Your testimony will go a long way in helping clear this mess up. Ann was given a portable disk drive by someone at the mansion that has information on it about the conspirators, but I'm afraid it might not be enough."

The kitchen staff began uncovering the buffet.

"But for now, let's enjoy this evening. I can't remember the last time I ate. I'm starved. Let's eat."

The oddly matched group filled their plates and ate while making small talk. Jake stood and talked to The First Lady, Trish Campbell, and Ann.

"So, what are your plans now?" he asked Ann.

"After all this gets cleared up, I'm headed back to Colorado to finish school. I'll have to wait until Beth's healthy though. It wouldn't be the same without her." Ann looked across the room at the Secret Service agent who was talking to other staff member. She saw Ann looking, smiled, and waved.

"And what are your plans, Mr. Taft?" asked the First Lady.

"I'm not sure. I have my ranch in Texas, but I'm not sure. Right now, I'm taking one step at a time."

Director Chisom joined their group. "Was the kidnapper who gave you the thumb drive a woman with no tongue?" he asked Ann.

Ann nodded. "Her name is Amira. The thumb drive was slipped

in a napkin with my food one morning. She's the only one that could've done it. She made a call to the FBI and got caught. Ghazi cut her tongue out for it."

Director Chisom nodded. "We believe her body was the one found on the crashed helicopter. She was found in the back section still clutching the release handle to the toxins. After what you've told us, we think she might've been trying to stop them from releasing the toxins."

"Poor Amira," said Ann. "She truly believed in her cause, but she was fooled by terrorist and apparently demons."

Meanwhile Ellie and Pam were talking to the President and Chief of Staff Wohlman.

"Have they found anything at the Ghazi's mansion that could help you?" asked Pam.

"They're still sifting through the rubble but I'm afraid it will take months to get it sorted out and the inquiry will be over by then," answered the President.

"Why the big rush?" asked Pam.

"I don't know but I suspect there's more to this story than even we know."

"It's a shame Israel's Ark of the Covenant was destroyed," said Ellie. "It would've been great to have it returned to them."

The President nodded. "I agree, but I'm afraid it's pulverized under tons of rock. I spoke with the Prime Minister and assured him if we found anything left, we'd retuned it to him."

"Where is the Vice President?" asked Pam.

"In times of crisis, we sent the Vice President off to a secure location in case something happens. Vice President Dayton will be returning in a few days."

Agent Ruiz and Williams came over to Jake, Ann, and the First Lady.

"I wanted to say thank you for saving my skin back on the freeway," said Agent Ruiz.

"You're welcome," said Jake. "I'm sorry we weren't able to stay around but we were on a tight schedule."

"So those really were demons?" asked Agent Williams.

Jake nodded. "Yes, they're real."

"I never would've believed it until I saw it, but I definitely saw it," said Agent Ruiz

"And I have the proof," said Agent Williams pointing to the healing claw marks on her face.

# CHAPTER THIRTY-NINE

**Senate Office Building**
**226 Dirksen**
**Washington, D.C.**

THE CHERRY BLOSSOM trees around Washington D.C. were in full bloom. It was three weeks after the foiled bio-weapon attack on Washington D.C. and the news media was having a hay day throwing speculation about aliens, mutants from secret CIA experiments, and of course, demons.

The capital buzzed about the start of the hearings conducted by a select committee in the Senate, the House Judiciary Committee, and chaired by Senator Amos Wilson.

Jake, Ellie, and Pam were kept out of the press and the spotlight, for fear of more attacks, human or otherwise until the hearings. A black Chevrolet suburban rolled up in front of the Marriott hotel and quietly drove the trio to the Dirksen Senate office building for the hearings. They entered a side door to avoid the mob of media staged in front. Ellie and Pam were dressed in professional attire and Jake reluctantly purchased a suit and new Stetson.

Upon entering the building, they were met by Agent Ruiz and Williams.

"Good to see you again," said Agent Ruiz as he shook hands with each one.

Agent Williams hugged Ellie and Pam but shook Jake's hand. They all looked better than the last time she saw them. Most of their scratches and bruises had healed.

Jake smiled. "I just wish I was glad to be here. I hate anything to do with this."

Ellie slipped her arm around Jake's elbow. "What Jake means is he's glad to help but he hates the circus around it."

Agent Ruiz nodded. "I know what you mean. Senator Wilson is out for blood. Agent Williams and I already testified, and he raked us over the coals pretty badly."

"He made us look incompetent," snapped Agent Williams.

"I don't like that man," said Pam with a frown.

"You did a great job considering what you were up against," said Jake. "I'm sure a lot of information didn't come out."

"You're right about that, I just hope it all comes out in the wash," said Agent Williams.

"It will," said Ellie. "We just have to have faith."

They followed the two FBI agents into the large room and took their assigned seats on the front row. Several chairs were left reserved on the front row next to them. The hearings had taken a recess after they finished with a testimony from several agents concerning the incident at the gate of the Ghazi estate.

It was now time for Ellie to testify, and one of the officials called her name. She glanced at Jake and smiled. He could tell she was scared as she stepped up to the table from where she would testify, raised her right hand, and was administered her oath to tell the truth. She sat alone at the table and was aware of the media and television cameras all around. She felt like a guppy in a shark tank.

Senator Wilson looked down at her from his position as Chairman. "Please state your name and occupation."

"Ellie Thompson, pastor of the Shady Oak Community Church, Shady Oak, Texas."

"Pastor Thompson," asked Senator Billings of Oklahoma. "Are you aware that you have the right to have an attorney during these proceedings?"

Senator Wilson looked at him and frowned.

"I am aware of that, sir, but I declined one."

"Very well then, shall we proceed?' said Senator Wilson with a wicked grin. "Miss Thompson, what part did you play in this incident?"

Ellie told her story starting with her initial meeting with Jake to her unusual trip to the White House. When she was finished, there was a dead silence throughout the packed room.

"Thank you for your story, Pastor Thompson," said Senator Miles of New Hampshire. "I do have a few questions to ask however..."

"Do you expect us to believe this line of lies?" blurted out Senator Wilson.

Senator Miles frowned.

"None of this was a lie," answered Ellie.

"Do you expect us to believe that an angel came down and told you to go kill demons and save the world?"

"As I explained," she said as calmly as she could. "The angel Malachy did not appear to me, but to Mr. Taft." She felt her anger growing and her face was getting hot. She took a deep breath and tried to relax.

"Yes, Mr. Taft, of course. Is it true that you were there when Mr. Taft stormed into the Martech laboratory headquarters in Atlanta so he could harass the now deceased president of Martech labs?"

"Mr. Taft wanted to warn him about the possible attack on his life and those of his employees."

"And then you went to the Farnswarth estate later?"

"Yes." Ellie could see where this line of questions was heading and dreaded it.

"And you were there when Mr. Taft killed Dr. Farnswarth and his wife?"

"No," she glared. "The demons killed them. We arrived afterward."

"You killed the so-called demons but then left the scene instead of waiting on the police?"

"Mr. Taft killed the demons and we needed to get to Jackson to stop more bloodshed."

"And you went from there to New Orleans where you learned about Mr. Ghazi's plan to take over the world?"

"Yes."

"And you learned this from a demon in charge of an old mansion?"

"Yes."

"Do you have any physical proof of this?"

Ellie sat and glared at him. "No."

"Then you drove to Virginia and dropped off Mr. Taft at the Ghazi estate so he could attack Mr. Ghazi?"

"I dropped Mr. Taft off so that he could stop Mr. Ghazi."

"But you had no idea what Mr. Ghazi was planning, did you?"

"As I said we knew he was planning on taking over the world and it had something to do with Martech labs."

"So, you and Mr. Taft made plans for him to trespass on the Ghazi estate and either attack or kill Mr. Ghazi based on what a mysterious demon told you?"

"Didn't you see what he said and did on television? Isn't that proof enough?" snapped Ellie.

Senator Wilson smiled a wicked smile. "But without the camera or other evidence, you can't prove that transmission was even real. How do we know you and Mr. Taft didn't stage that?"

"That's ridiculous."

"Pastor Thompson," said Senator Miles softly. "We want to believe your story but without some sort of physical evidence it's hard. Do you have any?"

"No."

Senator Miles nodded sadly. Senator Wilson grinned.

Ellie was dismissed and Jake's name was called. He passed Ellie and she looked distraught, so he smiled and winked. He went forward, raised his right hand, and swore to tell the truth.

"Please state your name and occupation," said Senator Wilson.

"My name is Jacob Travis Taft. I'm a cattle rancher from Texas."

"Please inform us about your part in this crime?"

"Mr. Chairman," interrupted Senator Miles. "There has not been a decision that a crime has been committed. This is simply a fact-finding hearing. Please let the record show this."

Senator Wilson frowned but nodded.

"Mr. Taft, as with Pastor Thompson, you have the right to an attorney," explained Senator Miles.

"He doesn't need an attorney, he's guilty," blurted out Senator Wilson.

"Mr. Chairman, you're out of order," snapped Senator Billings.

"Thank you, Senator, but I don't need an attorney," said Jake.

"Then tell us about what happened during your cri...I mean, your encounter?" asked Senator Wilson.

Jake very carefully gave a detailed account of his experience with Malachy and the subsequent events. As with Ellie's testimony, when he was finished the room was quiet.

Senator Wilson shook his head. "Mr. Taft, how do you expect us to believe this incredible story?"

"I don't."

"What?"

"I don't expect you to believe it. I didn't do this for you to believe or for you to approve. I did it because it was the right thing to do."

"Mr. Taft," said Senator Billings. "We're here to gather all the information so we can to determine what happened and who is responsible. We need proof of your statements."

Jake nodded. "I understand, but as you already know we have little physical proof."

"Are you aware you could be looking at very serious charges and possible prison time?" asked Senator Billings.

"I understand but my story remains the same."

Senator Wilson spoke up. "So, you claim to have killed demons along the way but have no proof of it?"

"We tried to stay low key and out of the mainstream," explained Jake.

"But there were no reports of monsters found or killed, so how did you do these acts without someone noticing?" asked Senator Miles.

"Most of the incidents were perceived as something else. One dead creature was perceived as a high school prank while another was thought to be a bear attack. These creatures have a much higher metabolism, and they decompose at an incredible rate which leaves very little evidence once they're dead."

"How convenient," said Senator Wilson sarcastically. "And what about the Farnswarths, did a bear or high school prank explain the violent deaths they experienced?"

Jake gritted his teeth. "No."

Senator Wilson grinned. "And did a bear, animal or high school prank explain what happened to Mr. Ghazi?"

"No, I went there to see what he was planning and to stop him if I could."

Senator Wilson shook his head. "Were you in the military?"

"Yes," answered Jake suspiciously.

"My records show that you were in a unit that specialized in covert operations that often meant killing people."

Jake frowned. "I served my country honorably."

"Isn't it true that the President recruited you to assassinate Ghazi because it was the president that had plans on taking over the country and announcing himself as a new king?'

"No."

"Isn't it true that the President Campbell and Hassan Ghazi were conspiring to turn the country into their own personal kingdom and rule as kings?"

"No."

"Senator Wilson," said Senator Miles. "This line of questioning is out of line. There's no proof to this line of questions. If you have no more questions other than this, I suggest we dismiss the witness."

"Very well, Mr. Taft, you are dismissed until further questioning is needed by the appropriate authorities."

Jake glared at Senator Wilson and nodded. He got up and went back to his seat.

After a fifteen-minute recess they all took their seats. A few minutes later the door came open and several Secret Service agents came in followed by Ann Campbell and Agent Sills. They sat on the front row and then President Campbell entered with several more Secret Service agents. The entire room stood as the President walked to the front table followed by his personal attorney.

Agent Meadows took the remaining seat on the front row next to Agent Ruiz, and the crowd resumed their seats. The President raised his hand and took the oath to tell the truth.

"State your name and occupation for the record please," said Senator Wilson.

"I am William S. Campbell, President of the United States of America."

"Mr. President," broke in Senator Miles. "We appreciate your willingness to testify in public, but I urge you to reconsider. We can conduct this in privacy."

Senator Wilson glared at her.

The President smiled. "Thank you, Senator Miles, but I feel it's necessary to do this in public. I want the world to see the outcome. I have my attorney, James Belton, here next to me if I need any advice. Please continue."

"Mr. President, will you explain to us your part in this incident?" asked Senator Wilson.

The President slowly and articulately explained when he was notified about his daughter's kidnapping and the subsequent events. After several minutes of testimony, he finished his testimony with a final statement. "I want to publicly thank Mr. Jacob Taft, Miss Ellie Thompson, and Miss Pamela Martin for their unselfish acts that led to the prevention of the terrorist attacks on our nation. I also want to commend FBI Agents Oscar Ruiz and Stephanie Williams for their unending work in bringing my daughter back safely."

The crowd gave a round of applause.

When the applause died down, Senator Wilson began his questions. "That was an admirable explanation but not quite complete."

"How so?" asked the President.

"Isn't it true that you knew Hassan Ghazi well and had several meetings with him?"

"No, I've never met the man."

"Isn't it true that you and Ghazi conspired to take over the United States with threats of biological weapons?"

The President's face turned red in anger. "That's preposterous. I never even knew who he was until he kidnapped my daughter."

"As for your daughter, was she really kidnapped? It was convenient that she wasn't in the helicopter when it was destroyed. It sounds like our defenses over Washington stopped you before you could succeed."

The President waited a moment before speaking. "Senator Wilson, that's a lie. You have no proof of any of those allegations."

"But you have no proof to show otherwise," said Senator Wilson with a smile. "I am going to call for immediate impeachment proceedings to begin."

Jake sat with his Stetson in his lap. He leaned over and whispered something to Agent Ruiz whose eyes widened. He nodded back to Jake and slid something under Jake's hat. Agent Ruiz then whispered something to Agent Meadows who showed no emotion but simply nodded. A second later Agent Meadows quickly spoke into his lapel mic.

The President turned and spoke to his attorney. The attorney opened his briefcase and removed several items. He laid several files on the table and held a small device the size of a cigarette lighter.

"Mr. Chairman, I do have proof."

Senator Wilson glared at the President. "That's not possible."

The President smiled and held up the device. "This is a portable disk drive, commonly called a thumb drive. It was smuggled to my daughter by one of the kidnappers that figured out Ghazi's plan and tried to help stop it."

"That's not possible," snapped Senator Wilson. "This is another fabrication."

"Senator, you're out of order," said Senator Billings. He turned to the President. "What does it contain, sir?"

"It is a very detailed account of Ghazi's activities and his business dealings. It has copies of his financial records and voice copies of his phone calls."

Senator Wilson jumped to his feet. "This is wrong. This is obviously another attempt to cover up the conspiracy."

"Senator, sit down," ordered Senator Billings.

The President continued. "These files show how Hassan Ghazi and a United States Senator worked together to plan and execute this terrorist attack."

"Do these files identify this senator's name?" asked Senator Billings.

"Yes."

"Who is it?" asked Senator Miles.

"In his own voice, these tapes identify Senator Wilson as the one."

"That's a lie. It's all lies," yelled Senator Wilson.

"All of this can be confirmed through various agencies and records. As we speak, Deputy Director Ross is executing a search warrant at the Senator's office and residence. I would imagine at the end of the investigation an indictment will be forth coming."

"Traitors, they're all traitors," screamed Senator Wilson. "Don't you all see this? It's all a big conspiracy. There's no such thing as demons or monsters."

The room had grown silent again. The crowd, media, and members of the congressional hearing watched as Senator Wilson ranted like a mad man. He stood up and pointed his finger at the President. "It's over, Campbell, I'll see to it right...."

"Now," yelled Jake.

Agent Ruiz along with Agent Meadows dove forward and forced the President to the floor. Jake stood up and kicked the table forward as if to block something. He pulled Agent Ruiz's semi-auto handgun out from under his Stetson hat and fired it directly ahead, in the direction of Senator Wilson. People scattered and Senator Wilson ducked down below the table. The sound was deafening in the room as camera shutters clicked and television cameras took it all in.

Senator Miles suddenly screamed and pointed at the floor between Senator Wilson and the President. On the floor, dead, was a large grotesque blob of a creature. It was greenish purple and huge black leathery wings. It had thin hair like tentacles protruded from its body that led back over the table and wrapped around Senator Wilson's waist. It had a single gunshot between its yellow eyes. The Senator screeched and tried to remove the tentacles, but the more he tried the more he entangled himself. The cameras clicked and captured the creature and the Senator's attempt to escape its tentacles.

"Senator," said Jake. "There's your proof. That's what we call a demon and I think it's been your constant companion for many years. I watched it manipulate you and then leap to attack the President. If anyone wants to examine it, you'd better hurry because it decomposes rapidly."

The President was helped up from the floor. The remaining Secret Service agents swarmed around him. He turned to his daughter Ann, who Agent Sills had pushed behind some chairs. She stood and smiled.

"It's over," he said.

She smiled back and hugged him hard. She put her arm in his and they walked out to the thunder of applause and camera shutters clicking.

After the Presidential family and Secret Service agents left the building, Agent Ruiz and Williams approached Senator Wilson. Some of his aides were trying to untangle him. The room began to smell badly of sulfur and decomposing flesh.

"Senator Wilson," said Agent Ruiz. "When you get loose from this thing, you need to come with us. We have a lot to talk about."

Jake turned to Ellie and Pam.

"I think we're done here."

"Let's go home," said Ellie with a smile.

Jake smiled, put on his brand-new Stetson and walked out arm in arm with Ellie.

# CHAPTER FORTY

**The Marriott Hotel**
**919 Eight Street**
**Washington D.C.**

JAKE, Ellie, and Pam were escorted back to the hotel about eight in the evening and stood outside their rooms with their FBI agent assigned to guard them.

"Do we still need a guard now that Senator Wilson has been exposed?" asked Ellie.

"Our orders are to be here until you leave Washington," explained the young FBI agent.

"It must be boring babysitting us for this long," said Pam.

The agent smiled. "We rotate every couple of hours so it's not too bad."

Pam said goodnight and went into the room. Jake and Ellie felt awkward standing by her door with an FBI agent nearby.

She grinned and kissed Jake on the cheek. "Goodnight." She slipped in and closed the door.

Jake opened his door and turned to the FBI agent. "If you need anything just knock."

"I'll be fine, thanks."

Jake went in and found Roscoe asleep on the bed. He began getting ready for bed while whistling a country tune.

Pam was stretched out on the couch when Ellie entered.

"Are you going to bed now?" asked Ellie.

"I need to sign on and check my email first. I'm just glad this is over. The President offered me a one-on-one interview."

"That's great. Maybe you should write a book."

"Hey, that's a good idea."

Ellie walked over and gazed out of the window at the Washington D.C. skyline. "What a beautiful view, but I'll be glad to get home."

"Yes, and this is a fabulous hotel," answered Pam while typing on her laptop. "Except for the ugly gargoyles they have on each corner of the roof."

Ellie laughed. "There are no gargoyles on this hotel, silly."

"Yes, there are. I saw them when we came in."

Ellie's smile faded and she slowly backed away from the window. "Pam…I think…we need to get out of this room."

Jake was just starting his shower when he heard a crash followed by a scream. "What the…?" He stepped out of the bathroom and heard gun shots. He threw his door open and ran into the hallway. Ellie and Pam's door was open, and the FBI agent was gone. More shots sounded from their room, and he dashed into the room. Pam was behind the FBI agent who pointed his gun toward the window. The glass was shattered and covered the carpet while the curtains were blowing in the wind.

"What happened?" yelled Jake.

The FBI agent was pale. "Something came through the window. I shot it but it didn't stop."

Pam stared wide eyed. "Jake, it took Ellie."

"What?" snapped Jake as he looked around the room for Ellie.

"One of them came in the window and took her."

———

**FBI Headquarters**
**935 Pennsylvania Avenue, NW**
**Washington, D.C.**

AFTER A LONG DAY of testifying and subsequent interview with the Senator, Agent Williams dropped Agent Ruiz off at the FBI building to pick up his bag from his locker before heading back to Sleepy Hollow. He'd just reached the lobby when his cell phone rang. He answered, listened for a minute, and dashed back out to the car. He jerked the car door open as Agent Williams hung up her cell phone.

"I just heard too," she said.

"Will this nightmare ever end?"

———

**The Marriott Hotel**
**919 Eight Street**
**Washington D.C.**

AGENTS RUIZ and Williams exited the elevator and found the hallway full of police and hotel security. Agent Ruiz found Jake, Pam, and the young FBI agent.

"What happened?"

"One of those things came in through the window and took Miss Thompson," explained Agent Paulson.

"It went straight for Ellie before anyone could do anything," Pam added.

Agent Ruiz nodded and turned to Jake who looked furious. "I'm sorry, Jake, any idea why?"

"No, but they left a message. One of your crime scene techs has it."

They went into the hotel room where several agents took photos and collected the shell casings and pieces of the shattered window. One agent handed Agent Ruiz a plastic bag with a piece of paper inside. Agent Ruiz read the note. "Is this for real?"

Jake nodded, "Apparently so."

Agent Williams read the note. "They want you and Miss Martin to come to the bank of the Anacostia River at 10 p.m. where it enters the Potomac alone or they'll kill Miss Thompson?"

"No way," said Agent Ruiz. "You'd be playing right into their hands."

"They want us all together," said Jake.

"Exactly and that's why you're not going," said Agent Ruiz.

"We don't have a choice."

# CHAPTER FORTY-ONE

**Anacostia River**
**Washington, D.C.**

AFTER GATHERING a few things Jake requested, they arrived ten minutes early and waited in the dark, damp night for almost thirty minutes before a four-foot-tall black demon came out of the darkness.

"You're late," grumbled Jake.

The yellow eyed creature stared at them for a moment. It had a curved head and sharp beak-like face. Its arms were thin, but its claws were large. "We wanted to make sure you were alone. Do you have weapons?"

"No."

The demon stepped forward and checked Jake for weapons or communication devices. It turned to Pam. It cackled and its black tongue snaked out while drool dripped from the side of its snout. Pam stepped back in fear and trembled causing another cackle from the demon.

"You need to be afraid," it said.

"Are you done?" said Jake sarcastically.

It glared at Jake, but left Pam unmolested. "Follow me."

"Where is she?"

"The woman is in good health and will remain so as long as you do as I say."

They reluctantly followed the creature down and along the bank of the river. The Anacostia River is a small river that flows into the Potomac River in downtown Washington D.C. Unfortunately, over the years of rain runoff the water's become badly polluted due to overflow from sewage, oil, sediment, and other unwanted toxins.

They came to one of the seventeen large rainwater overflow discharge tunnels and entered. The water mixed with trash and sewage was ankle deep as they trudged into the darkness. They followed the bird-like demon deeper into the maze of sewage tunnels, and the farther in they went the worse the stench became. It led them further on and switched into different tunnels. Jake found it more and more difficult to keep track of which tunnel they turned or which direction they went.

They finally stopped at an opening in the tunnel. It appeared to be a section of an old drainage tunnel that had been bricked up in the past but had been opened, by the demons most likely. Jake glanced back down the tunnel and quietly stepped in. Again, they followed the demon for several more minutes and crisscrossed many old tunnels that led off into the darkness. This area was a bit drier, but the stench of sewage was overtaken by the smell of sulfur and ash.

Several minutes after the trio entered the old tunnel, a dark form appeared at the entrance. The form bent down on one knee, looked at a small handheld device and shined a small flashlight down the tunnel. The form then entered the tunnel cautiously.

As the trio rounded a curve, they saw the end of the tunnel section. The closer they approached the worse the smell of sulfur became. At the end of the tunnel the demon stepped out, but the two humans stopped. Jake looked around and his heart sank.

The dome shaped room was a large junction where several of the tunnels intersected. The walls were covered with algae and slime with a single raised cement section in the middle. Scattered around the junction were bones of all shapes and sizes, including human. In the center stood Ellie surrounded by hundreds of demons. She appeared to be fine except for a few minor scratches and bruises.

"Welcome," said a deep, croaky voice.

Jake looked over and a dark blue demon stepped forward. The thing appeared to be a smaller form of Ghazi. One of Ghazi's underlings thought Jake. He ignored the creature and turned to Ellie. "Are you ok?"

Ellie managed a slight smile. "Yes, I'm fine but you shouldn't have come." She looked at Pam and raised an eyebrow. "Pam?"

Jake winked at her.

"I am so pleased you were able to come," said the demon sarcastically. "As you can see, the woman is virtually unharmed, for now."

Jake's eyes narrowed as he stared at the creature. "What do you want?"

The demon smiled. "Why, we just wanted to meet you." It turned to the crowd of demons, "Didn't we?"

The room roared with hoots, clicks, grunts, and growls. The demon held up his clawed hand and the roar died down.

"I wanted to meet the now infamous demon killer and the newspaper woman. I thought we might be in for some trouble after you killed Lord Ghazi and exposed the senator," continued the demon. "But I had a brilliant idea." The demon raised a single talon in the air as if he was a professor lecturing to a class. "If I caught and slaughtered the demon killer, perhaps his majesty Lucifer would promote me. I could become lord of this region."

The room came alive again with clicks and grunts. Jake glanced around at the hundreds of demons that packed the room. They were all shapes, sizes, and colors. The sound of talons scraping on rock, and wings brushing against wings made the scene surreal. Jake's quickly devised plan for rescue looked dim.

He suddenly stepped up and put his arm around Ellie. She looked up and tried to smile.

"Isn't that sweet?" said the demon. "Two little love birds spending their last moments together." His remark brought more hoots, grunts, and clicks from the ugly crowd.

Agent Ruiz squatted in the tunnel just out of sight with his gun drawn. He knew it would have no effect on the demons, but it made him feel better. He'd followed Jake with the use of a tiny GPS device in Jake's pocket. Even from his limited standpoint he could see more demons than they'd estimated. He shook his head in disgust as he thought about all these things running around above ground everyday invisible to us. He hoped Jake's plan worked or they were all dead meat.

"Now," said the blue demon. "The question is how do we do this?" He waved his arms and addressed the crowd of demons. "Do we kill him quick or slow?"

The crowd erupted with laughs and shouts of "SLOW".

Jake hoped that Agent Ruiz had everything in place, or the rescue was over before it started. He looked over at Pam and nodded slightly.

The blonde woman wasn't Pam but was in fact Agent Williams. She and Pam were both blonde, similar in height and shape, so Director Chisom only went along with the plan if Agent Williams took Pam's place. They hoped that none of the demons would know or care what Pam actually looked like and so far the ruse had worked.

"Do you have a name?" asked Jake.

"I am Kateb. I was Ghazi assistant until you killed him. Why?"

"I just like to know who I'm going to kill."

Kateb looked confused but then roared with laughter. The room filled with more laughter. "You're a jokester, demon killer."

"It's no joke," said Jake with a smile.

Kateb's smile faded. "This is growing tiresome."

Jake stepped slightly away from Ellie. "I agree. It's growing very tiresome."

Since Agent Williams act of being terrified at the demon earlier had worked and she wasn't searched she jerked a 9mm semi-auto handgun from a hidden pouch and tossed it to Jake.

Kateb saw the exchange and before he could react, Jake shot the dark blue demon through the chest. Jake turned and shot several more demons that stood in the way of the tunnel. The shots threw the entire place into chaos which gave them the few seconds they needed.

"Run, and stay to the left," yelled Jake as he shot another demon.

Agent Williams and Ellie darted into the tunnel as Jake backed up to the entrance and fired several more times, then turned and ran after the two women.

With their newest leader dead, it took a few moments for the demons to regroup before several ran after the retreating trio. A mob soon gathered and began to pursue them. The trio rounded a curve and found Agent Ruiz waiting.

"Hurry, this way," he said.

"Give me the remote," said Jake. "It won't work unless I do it."

Agent Ruiz handed a small remote-control device to Jake as they all fled down the tunnel.

"Stay left," reminded Agent Ruiz.

Several demons made the curve and Jake shot them, using up the remaining bullets in his gun. "Run," he yelled down the passageway.

The group fled down the tunnel and passed several rectangular objects set up on the right side of the tunnel.

The group couldn't make good time in the tunnel due to the dim light and the ankle-deep sewage. The sound of grunts, clicks, and talons scraping on cement came closer as the demons began to over-take them.

"They're almost here," yelled Jake. "Stop and take cover."

They could hear the distant sounds of their pursuers when Jake flipped a switch on the handheld device. The group hunched over as best they could in the sewage filled tunnel as several explosions erupted. The ground shook, a shock wave reverberated down the tunnel, and the group was struck by dirt, small rocks and debris. After a few seconds the sound and dust died down.

Jake looked around. "Is everyone ok?"

The other three raised their heads and nodded.

"I think we killed some of them and blocked the tunnel with the anti-personnel mines," said Jake.

"Then let's get out of here," said Agent Williams.

The group ran down the tunnel for several hundred yards and

came to another junction of tunnels. Agent Ruiz held up his hand to stop the group and shined his flashlight around.

"Which way?" Jake asked.

"I don't know. They all look the same," said Agent Ruiz.

The group turned and ran down the tunnel toward what they hoped was an exit. After several minutes of crossing tunnels, Jake knew they'd gotten badly off course. They stopped to catch their breath.

"We don't know which way to go do we?" asked Agent Williams. "We could be circling back to their nest."

Agent Ruiz shined his light up one of the tunnels. "Let's go a little farther up this tunnel. It's doesn't seem to be filled with sewage as much as the rest."

The group followed the tunnel to where the large passage ended, and a smaller tunnel led off to the left.

"I feel cool air," said Agent Williams.

They each crawled into the smaller tunnel which they followed for about a hundred feet before it turned upwards.

Agent Ruiz was in the lead. "I can see a grate above me," he yelled back down the tunnel. "There's a metal ladder attached to the wall." He climbed up to the grate and pushed it up and over. The fresh, damp air felt good. He climbed out and looked around. "You're not going to believe this until you see it," he yelled back into the tunnel.

The other three climbed out of the access tunnel and into the night air. They looked around to get their bearings and looked up at the building they stood next to.

"Isn't this the Jefferson Memorial?' asked Ellie.

"Yep," said Jake.

The group made their way around to the front of the monument. The building was lit up and a small crowd still mingled around despite the late hour.

"I'll make a call and get us back to the command post," said Agent Ruiz.

"We must have gotten way off course," said Agent Williams. "The mobile command post is across the river."

"I'll tell them to send a taxi," said Agent Ruiz with a smile. As he reached for his cell phone, he glanced at Jake who wasn't smiling. "What's wrong?"

Jake looked back toward the rear of the monument.

"What is it?" asked Ellie.

"I hear scratching and sounds of wings flapping," said Jake with a frown. "It's coming this way." He looked around at the people still milling around the building and his eyes widened. "They're coming for us and with all these people here. We have to clear the area."

They all knew what could happen so Agent Ruiz put his phone away, and together they began flashing their badges and yelling at the small crowd to leave. Several people obeyed and headed toward the paths leading away but others just stared at the dirt covered, smelly, agents.

A national park ranger stationed at the monument walked up. "What are you yelling for? Are you two crazy?"

"I'm an FBI agent and there's an emergency, so clear the area," yelled Agent Ruiz.

"Are those badges real?" asked a man standing with his family. "You don't look or smell like the FBI."

"Clear the area," yelled Agent Williams. "That's an order."

"What's that sound?" asked an elderly man.

Several people turned toward the sound as several demons suddenly appeared, flying in low.

"What are those things?' screamed a young woman.

Her male companion grabbed her arm. "I don't know but I'm not staying to find out. Run."

"Give me your gun, mine's empty," yelled Jake to Agent Ruiz.

Agent Ruiz handed his gun to Jake and dodged quickly out of the way of a diving demon.

One of the demons landed on a man and knocked him to the ground. Another grabbed a woman and threw her against one of the interior walls of the monument. It leapt on top of her as Jake shot it through the back of the head and splattered demon brain matter against the monument's wall.

Jake turned and shot the demon on top of the man, but it was too late, the man was dead.

People screamed and ran in all directions as demons landed along the steps. Jake shot as many demons as he could but more flew in. We're sitting ducks, thought Jake. "We need a place to hold up."

"We can hide on the lower level," said the frightened park ranger.

"Get them downstairs then," yelled Jake as he shot another demon.

Ellie, the park ranger, and the two FBI agents herded people into the door that led downstairs.

A green demon landed on the back of a short, stocky woman and knocked her down. It hissed, raised its claws when Agent Williams kicked it in the side of head. The blow knocked the demon off the woman and stunned it which allowed Agent Williams time to grab the woman and help her to her feet. They both ran towards the stairs with the demon in pursuit until Jake shot it.

In the lower level the clerk in the gift store was in the process of closing the store when a flood of people rushed down the stairs.

"We're about to close," she said.

Several of the people ran screaming past but one stopped to explain. "There are monsters upstairs, monsters."

The park ranger approached. "Keep it open. Find someplace to hide these people, especially the children."

"Monsters?" asked the clerk.

"Just do it," yelled the park ranger.

Jake backed down the stairs, shooting demons as he went. The demon mob became more cautious about rushing down the stairs and getting killed. One occasionally tried to rush down and was immediately shot by Jake.

Most of the visitors and children took refuge in a storage room. The park ranger used a key and locked off the elevator.

Agent Ruiz dug out his cell phone again and dialed the command post. He briefed the communications agent and hung up. "They're on their way."

# CHAPTER FORTY-TWO

**FBI Mobile Command Post**
**Washington D.C.**

THE MOBILE COMMAND post was parked on a side street near the river. It was a converted mobile home that contained communication devices and extra equipment. Deputy Director Ross and several agents waited impatiently for word from the rescuers. Pam sat off to the side and watched out the window.

Deputy Director Ross paced up and down the length of the converted motor coach. "Any word?"

The agent assigned to communications shook his head.

"I knew I shouldn't have let them go in without a wire."

"They would've found it and made things worse, sir."

Deputy Director Ross frowned and nodded. "I know you're right. I'm just worried."

The phone rang and startled everyone. Several agents gathered around as the communications agent picked it up. He listened and turned to the deputy director.

"It's FBI headquarters. They say there's a report of shots fired at the Jefferson Memorial."

Deputy Director Ross glanced out one of the windows. "That's across the river. Are the capital police on the way?"

The agent nodded.

"Good, let them handle it."

The agent turned back and conversed on the phone but spoke up again. "Sir, this is strange. People are reporting that smelly people impersonating the FBI are shooting at giant bats over there."

Deputy Director Ross raised an eyebrow. "What? Giant bats at the Jefferson Monument?"

Pam stepped up. "Deputy Director, I can assure you that if there's screaming, running, shooting, and giant bats it's got to be Jake."

The deputy director looked at her expecting a punch line to a joke, but she looked dead serious. He thought for a moment. "Very well, let's close this thing up and head over there. I just hope you're right."

"I am. I just hope we're not too late."

---

**The Jefferson Monument**
**Washington, D.C.**

JAKE RELOADED the 9mm handgun with the last magazine. The demons were getting bolder and sending two at a time now and Jake was getting worried.

Suddenly three men and a woman came out of the gift shop carrying scissors and box cutters.

"What are you doing? Go back inside the gift shop," ordered Agent Ruiz.

One man spoke up. "This is our city, our country, and our monument. We aren't going to give it up to a group of monsters without a fight."

Before Agent Ruiz could respond they heard sirens approaching.

"Thank goodness, the police are here," said the woman.

Ellie shook her head. "They may not be any help." She pointed at Jake. "He's the only one can kill these creatures."

They listened as the sirens died, followed by gunshots, and screams of terror. There was a sudden rush of bodies as several demons rushed down the stairs. Jake fired several times and cut down a few but a small demon got by and flew into the group behind him. The thing landed on the park ranger and hissed as it tried to claw at the ranger's throat. Agents Ruiz and Williams kicked and hit the creature until it fell off. The park ranger scrambled back as the others stabbed and cut the demon in a vain attempt to kill it. The demon screamed and lashed out as they stabbed it only to watch as the wounds immediately heal up.

Jake was busy as he killed another demon and watched the body count of demons pile up. The room filled quickly with the smell of decaying flesh and sulfur.

He quickly turned and shot the screaming demon that had gotten past him, but the move almost cost him as a demon reached out, grabbed Jake by the shoulder, and sunk its sharp talons in. Jake felt the stabbing pain, spun, and shot the thing through the eye. It released its grip on Jake and fell back as demon gore splattered on the stairway wall. Jake gritted his teeth as more demons poured down the stairs. He pointed his weapon only to see the slide all the way back and empty.

The mobile command post came rumbled down the drive on its way to the monument when the communications Agent turned to Deputy Director Ross. "Sir, Agent Ruiz is on the phone. They're hold up on the bottom level of the monument and being attacked by the demon creatures."

Deputy Director Ross simply nodded.

" Sir, there's been another problem at the monument."

"What now?"

"The capital police just arrived and were attacked by the same large creatures. The first two officers were killed before they backed off. Their weapons had no effect on the things."

Deputy Director shook his head. "Tell any agents approaching to do so with caution. We don't want to lose any more people."

JAKE DROPPED the empty gun and snatched up a spiral knife dropped by one of the demons. As more demons attacked, Jake cut one down only to be replaced by two more. He slashed and stabbed while demons attacked Jake with claws, swords, and knives. The bodies piled up as Jake tried to use the dead bodies as a wall to keep the others out. The creatures screamed, clicked, hissed, and growled as they leapt at Jake, only to be added to the death count, but eventually the mass of demons forced Jake backwards down the stairs.

The park ranger heard a scratching sound by the elevator. "They're coming down the elevator shaft."

"Get into the gift store and lock the door," yelled Agent Ruiz.

No one moved. "We're standing with you."

"You can't stop these things," said Ellie.

"Then we'll die trying."

Agent Ruiz pointed toward the elevator. "Then keep them from coming in through the elevator.

The small group gathered around the elevator doors. Each knew they had little chance of stopping them but were determined to try. The elevator doors slowly cracked open, and they saw demon talons prying the door open. The humans pushed on the doors and tried to keep them closed but the door came open several inches and arms reached out. They tried to grab the humans inside who in turn stabbed at the beasts with their scissors and box cutters. The park ranger grabbed a fire extinguisher off the wall and fired it into the elevator which temporarily fended off the creatures.

As Jake fought back the ever-increasing number of demons they heard a strange sound. It was a low, deep, sound blown through a horn of some type. The sound apparently had an effect on the demons because they stopped their forward attack, fled up the stairs, and disappeared. Jake slumped against the wall, bloodied, cut, and tired. They again heard the deep bellow of a horn.

The elevator doors closed and the sounds of the demons in the elevator shaft stopped.

Ellie stepped over to Jake and grabbed his arm. "Are you ok?"

Jake nodded. He was too tired to answer.

Agent Ruiz approached the stairs. "Are they gone?"

"I hope so?" said Ellie.

They waited and listened but heard nothing. The small group of defenders gathered around. Jake motioned for the rest to stay behind and took a few steps up.

"Jacob?" said a familiar voice.

Jake glanced up the stairs and saw Malachy standing on the stairs. His white tunic was torn, and he was scratched from head to toe. Jake smiled. "I'm glad to see you, my friend."

Malachy nodded. "I'm glad to see you're alive. Shortly after Ghazi's down fall Satan launched legion after legion to prevent us from helping. It looks like we broke through just in time."

"But that was almost three weeks ago," said Jake.

Malachy nodded.

"Your timing was great," said Ellie.

The group watched in awe as more angels came down the stairs.

"Are these?" asked a wide-eyed park ranger.

"Yes, they are," said Ellie with a big smile.

"Jacob, we need to finish cleaning out this nest of vipers, so we'll take it from here," explained Malachy.

Jake held out his hand over the huge pile of dead demons. "Be careful."

Malachy's huge hand engulfed Jake's. "Go with God."

Malachy and the other angels turned and disappeared up the stairs. Jake turned to the group. "Let's get out of here."

"I'll go tell the others it's safe to come out," said the park ranger as he headed in the gift store.

Instead of climbing over the huge pile of rapidly decaying demons, they all took the elevator up to the ground level and welcomed the fresh night air as they exited the elevator.

The FBI mobile command post parked just down the street from the perimeter that had been quickly set up by the capital police. The FBI agents leapt out and ran towards the monument as Deputy Director Ross met with the Capital police supervisor.

"The creatures dispersed just moments ago," said the Capital police supervisor. "We don't know why. One minute there were hundreds of flying creatures and then they simply fled."

Pam stood by the mobile command post and watched as people began exiting the elevators. "Look, they're coming out."

The groups of people walked down the stairs and were met by police and EMS personnel who wrapped them in blankets and then escorted them to waiting emergency vehicles. Pam ran up the steps leading into the famous building where she found Jake and Ellie standing near the statue of Thomas Jefferson. Jake was ragged, bloodied, and Ellie was scratched and bruised, but both were alive. She ran and hugged them both.

"I was getting worried about you two," she said as she wiped tears from her eyes.

"It looked bad for a while until the cavalry arrived," explained Ellie.

"Huh?"

"An army of angels came to our rescue."

Pam smiled and nodded

"But what was that sound we heard, some sort of horn?" asked Jake.

Ellie smiled. "If I'm right I'd say it was a Shofar, a ram's horn made into a horn like a bugle."

She looked at Jake who was staring at one of the inscriptions engraved in the monument. Pam and Ellie looked up and read, *I have sworn upon the altar of God eternal hostility against every form of tyranny...*

# EPILOGUE

## J Double T Ranch
## Sutton County, Texas

TWO RIDERS SAT at the crest of the hill overlooking Jake's ranch. One wore a Stetson and the other wore a baseball cap with the Presidential seal.

"Your ranch is beautiful, Jake."

"Thank you, Mr. President."

The President smiled. "Out here I'm just Bill."

"Yes sir, but I'm surprised Agent Meadows didn't come out here with us."

"He said if I wasn't safe with you, I wasn't safe anywhere."

Jake laughed.

The President tilted the baseball cap back on his head. "So, what're your plans?"

"I'll keep working my ranch," answered Jake. "Agent Ruiz, now Deputy Director Ruiz, and Agent Williams are part of a new task force designed to counter demonic or supernatural terrorism here and abroad. He's asked me to give some assistance. Beyond that I'll see what happens."

The President nodded. "After all this and the incident at the Jefferson Monument there was little opposition when I recommended creating that task force."

"What about you? What're your plans?" asked Jake.

"In a day or so we're headed back to Washington. Senator Wilson's trial starts in a week, and I have to start my plans for re-election."

"You have my vote."

"Thank you," said the President with a laugh. "In the meantime, I'm going to enjoy myself." With that he spurred his horse and galloped down the hill toward the ranch house with Jake close behind.

They rode past a large Pecan tree near the top of the hill and under the tree sat a small head stone marking a grave. The name on the stone simply said, "Mobak".

A small group on the porch of the ranch house watched as the two riders galloped toward them. While Agent Meadows watched through binoculars, one woman sat in a rocking chair, another woman leaned against a post, and Roscoe slept in the shade.

"He's going to break his neck if he's not careful," said Agent Meadows.

Ann Campbell laughed. "You're too protective. Dad was raised on a ranch in Utah."

Agent Sills sat in the rocking chair and frowned. "After everything that's happened, we're all just a little overprotective."

Ellie and the First Lady came out on the porch. "Are they back from their romp around the ranch?" asked the First Lady.

Ann nodded and pointed to the two riders. "Just like two kids on a vacation, but they've earned it."

Ellie put her arm around Ann's shoulders. "We all have, now come inside before dinner gets cold. The two ranch hands can eat when they get here."

They all giggled and laughed as they went inside. Roscoe opened one eye, snorted, and went back to sleep. Unseen to most of the guests, Ned sat in the rocking chair next to Roscoe, smoked his pipe and smiled.

After dinner Jake led Ellie down to the barn. "I have something I want to show you." He pointed to something covered with a tarp next to the bales of hay. "Close your eyes," he said.

Ellie closed her eyes while Jake pulled the tarp away.

"You can look now."

She opened her eyes, stared wide eyed, and couldn't' believe what she saw. On the soft hay in the corner of the barn sat the Ark of the Covenant.

"Is it real?"

Jake nodded. "I have a friend that's good at finding things we thought were gone."

"Malachy?"

Jake nodded. "He removed it right before the ceiling collapsed."

Ellie raised an eyebrow. "So, if he was there, why didn't he help you with Ghazi?"

"I don't think he arrived until after Ghazi was dead and we were gone into the tunnel," said Jake with a shrug. "That's when the fallen started their attack that delayed Malachy for several weeks. Besides, from what I've learned angels intervene at certain times and not at others. That's a mystery we humans may never understand."

Ellie walked over to the ark and examined it. "It's beautiful. What're you going to do with it?"

Jake put his arm around her. "I'll give it to the President tomorrow. He can present it to the Israeli Prime Minister. It should boost his foreign relations, and chances for re-election."

Jake reached into his pocket, removed a small box, and suddenly knelt on one knee. Ellie looked at him in surprise as he opened the small box and revealed a particularly special diamond ring. "Ellie Thompson, would you give me the honor of marrying me? I don't know where all this will lead me, but will you take that walk with me?"

Tears filled her eyes. She nodded, "Yes."

Jake stood and slipped the ring onto her finger. She kissed him and they held each other while looking at the ark.

"Who else in the world has a wedding gift like this?" said Ellie.

They both laughed.

In the dark a large golden brass colored figure sat on the front porch steps. He scratched Roscoe's ear. "It's only begun, Roscoe, it's only begun."

# A LOOK AT DEMON HUNTER BOOK TWO: THE DEMON STRAIN

**The demons have a new plot—one that involves bringing Hitler back from the dead.**

Jacob "Jake" Taft has battled more than his fair share of demons and is deserving of a break. Sadly, a new horde of demons—more insidious than the last—have targeted him and his friends.

This time, it's going to take more than just Jake and the FBI to stop the explosive plans of Degen and his host of science experiments that would terrify Frankenstein himself. So, reinforcements are called in—and only the most qualified agents from Russia and Germany pass the test.

But when the battle is moved to Berlin, and plans to start the Fourth Reich are revealed, will the entire team survive?

**Join Jake, Ellie, Pam, and a whole host of action-packed characters as they fight demon hordes and a mutant demon created from the bones of a most sinister man—Adolf Hitler.**

Scroll up and click "Read for Free" or "Buy now with 1-click" to join ex-covert ops Army Major Jake Taft and his team of civilians as they battle what they can't see, but do believe in. Are you brave enough to join the Demon Hunter team?

*AVAILABLE NOW ON AMAZON*

# ABOUT THE AUTHOR

**Kerry Adcock** is a graduate of Angelo State University with a Bachelor of Arts degree. After serving in the U.S. Air Force, he then spent 37 years in law enforcement working in patrol, and as a detective in the Special Victims Section as well as in the Homicide unit.

He has lectured and taught classes on sexual assault and sex offenders to the police academy as well as local and national women's groups. He's received awards such as the Police Medal of Valor and Detective of the Year. He is currently retired and lives in Arlington, Texas.

Kerry is an accomplished artist as well, focusing primarily on painting acrylic on canvas.